Jennifer L. Armentrout lives in West Virginia. All the rumors you've heard about her state aren't true. Well, mostly. When she's not hard at work writing, she spends her time reading, working out, watching zombie movies, and pretending to write. She shares her home with her husband, his K-9 partner named Diesel, and her hyper Jack Russell Loki. Her dreams of becoming an author started in algebra class, where she spent her time writing short stories . . . therefore explaining her dismal grades in math. Jennifer writes Adult and Young Adult Urban Fantasy and Romance.

Find out more at www.jenniferarmentrout.com

JENNIFER L. ARMENTROUT

Unchained

Nephilim Rising

HODDER

Unchained first published in the United States of America in ebook in 2013
by Entangled Publishing, LLC

This paperback edition first published in Great Britain in 2015
by Hodder & Stoughton
An Hachette UK company

1

Paperback ISBN 978 1 473 61593 9
eBook ISBN 978 1 444 79933 0

Typeset by Hewer Text UK Ltd, Edinburgh
Printed and bound by Clays ltd, St Ives plc

Hodder & Stoughton policy is to use papers that are natural, renewable
and recyclable products and made from wood grown in sustainable forests.
The logging and manufacturing processes are expected to conform
to the environmental regulations of the country of origin.

Hodder & Stoughton Ltd
Carmelite House
50 Victoria Embankment
London
EC4Y 0DZ

www.hodder.co.uk

CHAPTER ONE

The rhythmic tap of Lily Marks's combat boots echoed off the steel roof of the Nancy Hanks Center, sending pigeons scattering into the dark sky. No one could hear her far above the corner of Twelfth and Pennsylvania Avenue.

Lily estimated the distance between the clock tower and observation deck to be about a hundred feet. Her emerald eyes narrowed on the tower as she clutched the bag close to her chest. Her plaid skirt swished around her thighs as she whirled, then leaped over the gap, grabbing the tower window's ledge. After hoisting herself up, she sat on the edge, legs dangling in the air. Tucking a strand of auburn hair behind her ear, she glanced furtively over her shoulder.

No one had followed her.

She ripped into the bag to retrieve her prize. As she sank her teeth into the burger, she immediately moaned at the taste of perfectly cooked, greasy mystery meat. In this world, where she spent most of her time knocking the crap out of stupid creatures that thought they could take her on, it was the little things that made her happy. Give her some artery-clogging burgers, and she was in heaven. Pathetic as it was, she needed moments like this.

1

She flicked a fry into her mouth and then froze. The feeling snaking down her spine was undeniable. He came so close, so fast, that she knew it was him.

"Damn it," she muttered. Solitude and the privilege to eat her food in peace couldn't even be gained sitting on a damn clock tower.

Ignoring him would be a pointless endeavor. The tingling sensation grew as Lily peered down onto the observation deck and, like every time before, the mere sight of him stole her ability to form an intelligent thought. He had a name she couldn't begin to pronounce or spell, so she'd always known him as Julian.

And when he wasn't around, she simply knew him as the pain in her ass.

"Hello, my Lily."

She closed her eyes. Damn his voice to Hell and back. The sound, the deep timbre of the way he'd said her name, crawled all the way to the pit of her stomach, where it smoldered.

She pried one eye open.

Julian's lips formed a predatory smile. A full bottom lip and a thinner one on top curved in a way that was downright sinful. Those lips whispered promised pleasures, and they also carried an intensely real threat.

She needed to remember that.

Her wry gaze flickered over his face, and she bit back a sigh. She knew he was bad. Oh, he was so bad that almost all of her kind feared him. That knowledge did nothing to dampen her appreciation of his beauty. Male or female—both were in awe of him.

After all, Julian had been an angel.

Tonight, he wore black trousers and a buttoned-down white shirt. He must have grown bored with the buttons, though. Only half of them were done, and hard, pale flesh peeked through.

She found an ounce of common sense along with her voice. "What do you want?"

His smile widened. "Isn't that a loaded question?"

She rolled her eyes, taking a bite of her burger. "I'm on lunch break. So if you expect me to chase you off, you're mistaken."

He inched closer, the soft breeze tugging at his shoulder-length blond hair. "What kind of Nephilim doesn't chase a fallen angel?"

"A hungry one," she muttered.

"Perhaps I've grown on you."

She thought about that for a moment. He'd been her shadow for nearly eight years. Sometimes she looked forward to their interactions. They were usually amusing if nothing else. "No."

"I don't believe you," he said softly.

His voice did funny things to her stomach, and she shifted uncomfortably. Her eyes met his brilliant blue gaze. "Don't you have something better to do?"

He tipped his head to the side, chuckling. "After all this time, are you still afraid of me, my Lily?"

What the hell was up with this "my Lily" crap? She hated it when he called her that. It was like she belonged to him in some way. That was a big, fat no. Lily belonged to no one. Okay, that wasn't true, either.

She belonged to the Sanctuary.

"Are you?" he prodded when she didn't answer.

The skin puckered between her brows. He could kill her with a single blow, but he had never seriously injured her. Not even once when she had managed to shove her blade between his ribs. He had simply knocked her away like a fly and continued about his business.

She remembered that night like it was yesterday. It was the second time she'd seen him. At seventeen, she'd been out hunting alone for the first time and was cornered by a deadhead while three more had snuck up behind her. She'd taken care of the one with no problem, but the others had been wound up. One wrong move and Lily had been cornered. They'd circled her like vultures and, just when she thought she was about to bite the big one, Julian had swooped in from out of nowhere, disposing of the gruesome threesome.

Lily had stabbed him for it.

The second time he'd saved her life was something she refused to think about. Like ever. "No. I'm not afraid of you," she said finally.

He flashed a set of perfect white teeth. "You lie."

"You're annoying." She took another bite and briefly considered dumping the fries on his head.

"How can you eat that crap?" he asked.

"It's not crap. It's delicious, and you're interrupting."

"I only care about the state of your arteries."

Total bullshit and she knew it. "I seriously doubt that's what's going to kill me."

"I worry about you."

Her fingers dug into the sesame bun as she flat-out disregarded that statement. "Why are you always following me?"

"I have to."

"Why?" The better question was how he was able to follow her in the first place. Nephilim like her were protected by a celestial shield that prevented the Fallen and their stupid, little minions—a cheesy nickname others of her kind had called Nephilim who'd been corrupted—from sensing their whereabouts.

He flashed her a wicked smile as the hue of his eyes deepened.

"How can you find me?" Since he appeared to be in a chatty mood and wasn't going anywhere, she asked something she'd always wondered. "Is my heavenly mojo not working or something?"

"Your celestial shield is fine." He tipped his head back, exposing his neck. A stupid move considering how vulnerable that made him, but then again, Lily knew he wasn't afraid of her at all. "I will always know where you are."

A shiver tiptoed down her spine. "That's . . . that's kind of creepy. Care to explain?"

"Care to come down here, my Lily?"

"Stop calling me that!"

His laugh was overtly masculine, dark. "I think you like it when I do."

Her mouth dropped open as she stared in disbelief. Her temper, which she never really had a good grasp on, rose to the occasion. Shoving her half-eaten burger into the bag, she placed it on the ledge and then jumped from the clock tower. Landing in a nimble crouch a few feet from the fallen angel, she popped up, releasing the blades from the silver bracelets around her slim wrists. The polished bracelets weren't just for looks.

His smile spread. "You're incredibly sexy when you're angry."

Something akin to pleasure shimmied over her skin, and that just pissed her off. There was a good chance she was angrier with herself than him, but at least she could act like a Nephilim was supposed to when confronted with their most dangerous of all enemies.

"I'm so done with you tonight. I have things to do. Like deadheads to hunt, minions to kill, and an order of fries with my name on it." She stopped in front of him, craning her neck to look him squarely in the eye. Being that he was well over six and a half feet, this wasn't easy to do for someone who barely stood five foot three . . . in heels. "Now get going or else."

"Or what?" He reached out, running the tip of his finger over the sharpened edge of her blade. The way he caressed it elicited another shiver from her. "What will you do?"

She smiled sweetly. A second later, she spun around and slammed her booted heel into his midsection. He grunted but did little else, which really ticked her off. She swung at him.

Julian caught her hand and whirled her around, drawing her against his chest and pinning one arm between her heaving breasts. "You can do better than that, my Lily."

Her first thought after he'd subdued her so quickly was, wow. The second was, holy shit, I'm dead. She drew in a ragged breath, fully aware of how her body fitted against his hard slabs of muscles and the . . . other thing that seemed equally proportioned to his large body. He smelled decadent, like deep, rich male spice. Liquid heat pooled low in her belly, which was wrong on so many different levels it wasn't even funny.

And worse yet, behind the tempting heat building inside her was raw fear. Not good. Fear wasn't something Lily was accustomed to, but Anna hadn't known fear, either. And wasn't she doing the same thing Anna had done? Allowed one of the Fallen to get too close, to get under her skin? Her heart picked up as ice drenched her veins. Look at what happened to Anna.

Anna was dead—slaughtered like an animal.

Heart racing, she gripped Julian's arm as she shoved her elbow into his chest with all her strength. Startled, he let go. Not wasting any time, she darted away and whirled around, raising her— What the hell? Where were her blades? She shook her wrists, releasing them from the silver cuffs once more. "Don't ever do that again."

"I can smell your fear," he said softly.

"You smelled my revulsion." She stepped back. "Never my fear. I'm not afraid of anything, especially not you."

7

"You're a terrible liar." He prowled forward, stopping when she moved into an offensive crouch. His hands clenched at his sides. "Do you know what else scents this air? Your arousal."

Her cheeks burned. Thank God it was night or she would have to stab him again. "You're insane. There's no way I'd ever think—"

He *tsked* softly, and then he was in front of her, moving faster than even she could. "You want to test that out?"

"No." She tried not to breathe. His scent was purely intoxicating. Taking another small step, she wondered how in the world she kept ending up in situations like this. Of all the Nephilim in the world, why was she the one stuck with a Fallen who liked to play with his food before he devoured it?

He lifted his chin, and his nostrils flared. A smug smile graced his lips. "Ah, yes, you're afraid and you're . . . aroused. I can practically taste it on my tongue."

Heat flared somewhere it shouldn't. "That's disgusting."

His smile turned indulgent as he leaned forward. "You know what?"

Lily inhaled. The smell of him swamped her senses. Julian usually stayed at arm's distance unless he was feeling particularly froggy. Guess tonight was going to be one of those nights. "What?"

"Twice tonight you've disengaged your blades."

Her gaze dropped. Goddamn it, he was right.

Unconsciously, she had released them again. She really needed to stab him.

"And you want to know what else?" His words stirred the tendrils of hair that had escaped her messy twist.

Awareness coursed down her neck, and her nipples tightened. Oh crap, she needed to get away. Right now. No ifs, ands, or buts. Their encounters were always relatively brief, and Lily knew better than to hang around. Twisting to flee, she gasped.

Julian stood in front of her, so close that the tips of his Italian leather shoes brushed her boots. At least he had good taste in shoes. "I know what you're really afraid of. You're attracted to me, though you loathe the very idea of it."

Angels had no sense of decency or the ability to be humble. Apparently the Fallen were no exception. She fixed a smirk upon her face. "Not likely."

His burning gaze slipped downward. "Then why are your nipples as hard as pebbles, my Lily?"

She flushed all the way to where her toes curled inside her boots. At a loss for words, she simply stared. *Run, Lily,* the sane part of her whispered. *Run right now and never look back. You'll end up like Anna.*

Julian then did the strangest thing. He reached behind her, untying her hair. A mass of auburn waves fell around her shoulders and tumbled down her back. Pleased with his work, he threaded one hand deep into her tresses. "You blush like a virgin."

As impossible as it seemed, she was sure her face turned even redder.

His eyes widened. Lily couldn't think of a time when she'd seen him surprised. Well, when she stabbed him. That had surprised him. But now he gaped like he'd found a diamond he hadn't expected in a pile of rocks.

"You are a virgin," he whispered somewhat unsteadily.

"No, I'm not." Clenched hands shaking and body burning, she tried to step away, but his grip tightened. "And it's none of your business."

His grip relaxed, fingers finding their way through the mass of her hair to run the sensitive skin of her scalp. "There is no shame in that."

"I'm not ashamed!" She knocked at his hand. "Stop touching my hair."

His lips parted. "How is it possible that you're a virgin? I've seen you with guys . . . Nephilim. You like to go to that club downtown. This is a curious development."

Sweet Jesus, did he follow her everywhere? Her sex life was something she was never going to discuss with him. She punched him in the stomach, but he didn't even flinch. "I swear to God, if you don't let me go . . ."

Unfazed, he shook his head. A sandy lock fell across his forehead as his hand circled the nape of her neck. "What does a Fallen do with a virgin? Dear God, there are so many options."

"Would you stop saying that!" Her heart raced, and the skin under his hands tingled in a way it shouldn't.

"And let go of me." There was no way to break his grip without breaking her neck. Warning bells were going off everywhere in her. "What has gotten into you?"

He didn't respond. Instead, he let his free hand roam down her arm.

She jerked. "Don't."

"Don't what?" he whispered darkly. "I'm not hurting you. I'm not trying to persuade you or possess you, am I?"

He wasn't. Julian wasn't deploying any of the mind tricks the Fallen were notorious for. Nope, the warming in her was all her own. It was why this was so wrong, so stupid. What was happening was going to get her in trouble, one way or another. If any other Nephilim spotted them, she would be in a world of hurt. Standing here and not killing him was breaking an entire set of rules, let alone allowing him to touch her.

Julian had to know that.

He caressed the back of her neck. His fingers went to work soothing the tight muscles in a way that surprised her. She never had her neck rubbed before, and she really had been missing out. It felt so, so good.

Her neck arched into his hand without her realizing it, and her insides turned to molten lava. The warming in her stomach spread lower, her body relaxing and tensing at the same time.

"Those men—those boys—you've allowed to touch you? You've never allowed them more than this?" His hand trailed over the tips of her fingers and then across her concave stomach. She jerked again, bringing them

11

closer. Too close. She couldn't breathe. Her senses were alive, snapping heat through her veins. His hand dropped to the front of her skirt, right above her sex. He growled deep in his throat.

Part of her that was still operating at a rational level fired off countless reasons why this was one of the stupidest things she'd ever allowed. Besides the obvious fact that he was a Fallen, there was her duty to kill him. That was what she had been trained for. The Fallen were evil, devoid of any type of moral code. He could snap her neck right now. She was exposed to him, completely vulnerable. That's what the Fallen did. They lured their victims in and left them for dead.

Julian's hand drifted to the hem of her skirt while his other arm snaked around her waist. "I can bring you more pleasure than any of them."

Her insides tightened. "No."

He turned her around, moving her easily. "Let me give you this."

Oh God, this wasn't good. This was insane, and his warm breath against her cheek was driving her crazy. "No."

Julian pressed her backward, slipping a hand up her leg. "Let me in."

She bit her lip against the enticing pleasure of his hand creeping up her thigh, skimming over a pink, handprint-sized scar. His gentle touch there should have served as a painful reminder of what happened when one of the Fallen got too close. Instead a whimper escaped her, and he pressed against her harder. His breath trailed over the curve of her jaw and then down the slope of her neck. This was insane, dangerous ... and deliciously wicked.

He lifted his head, his lips hovering over hers. "Such a pretty little Lily."

Her ears perked, and icy knots formed in her belly. A keening howl reverberated inside her skull. There was no mistaking that sound. Julian heard it, too. The air around them changed in an instant, but the sexual charge still thrummed through her blood. Craning her neck to the right, she pinpointed the exact location.

Several blocks over, in the part of town where tourists wouldn't dare venture, she knew a freshly misled soul just crammed itself deep into the body of an unsuspecting human. Damn deadheads. She hated them as much as she hated fallen angels.

"Let me go," she ordered.

Julian focused on her again. Lust hardened his eyes into brilliant blue chips. "Stay with me a little longer."

If she stayed a second more, she was going to regret it. Big-time. Not to mention the mayhem that was about to take place once the soul latched its tentacles into a very alive body and got settled. It was sure to be epic. And she only had minutes before the once perfectly humane human went on a nut-jump killing spree.

She released her blade and pressed the wickedly sharp edge against the underside of his chin. "Let. Me. Go."

For a second, she didn't think he was going to, and there was a part—a teeny, tiny part of her body—that throbbed at the prospect.

"Why?" he asked.

His question gave her pause. Why? He was a Fallen—that's why. Then again, Julian had always acted oddly when compared to other Fallen. The howl of a dead-head came again, causing a sharp pain to shoot through her temples.

He released her, taking a step back. "Busy little Nephilim. You better get going . . . before I change my mind."

Her breath caught, but before she could respond or even flip him off, he disappeared. Just like that. With a disgusted sigh, she turned toward the Seventh District. Someone was about to get their unholy ass kicked.

CHAPTER TWO

"All available units, we have a ten-one-oh-three, possible ten-one-oh-three-M at Ritchie's Liquors in the Seventh District."

Sighing wearily, Officer Michael Cons radioed in. "This is unit seven-fifty. Please be advised I'm near that location."

He waited for the endless crackle to clear. "Ten-four unit seven-fifty," said the muffled voice. "Caller states he heard someone behind his business screaming prayers. He went outside but didn't find anything. He'd like an officer to check out the area."

Michael's eyebrows rose. Great—just perfect. This night couldn't get any better. "Ten-four."

As soon as he put the microphone down his cell rang. He slid it out of the sun visor, not even checking to see who was calling. "What?"

"Sounds like you got yourself a crazy or a drunk, rookie."

He flipped on the lights and turned the cruiser around. "My kind of luck, Cole. I've already had three drunk-and-disorderly calls, two domestics, and a woman claiming her cat had tapped her phones."

Laughter sounded. "What?"

15

"I'm not fucking kidding you." He glanced at the street signs. "The lady wanted the Pentagon Police since it was an issue of national security."

"Man, tough night."

"Yeah, it's been one of those nights."

Michael wasn't joking, either. His partner, Rodriquez, called off the shift, claiming swine flu or mad cow disease—whatever. The damn calls had been coming in nonstop, and the nutcases were out in force. This was one of those nights when he seriously wished he'd stayed at his desk job, one that had been far away from the crazy public.

He squinted at the bright neon lights of Ritchie's Liquors as he parked the cruiser. "I've gotta go check this shit out."

"Sure man," responded Cole. "Have fun with your praying drunk."

"Screw you." Michael shoved the cell back into the visor and unclipped the duty flashlight as he radioed in. "Ten-ninety-seven."

Michael didn't bother going into the liquor store. He skirted around the dilapidated building, entering the mouth of the narrow alley. Immediately the smell of rotting food and urine filled his nostrils. There went his appetite.

He moved the light over the numerous black garbage bags. "Hello? This is Officer Cons. Anybody here?"

The only sounds were the thugs from across the street and the passing cars behind him. Wishing he could somehow not breathe in the rank smell, he ventured deeper into the darkness and peered into one of the Dumpsters.

His hand dropped to his gun as his sensitive ears picked up a noise to his left. "This is the police. Show yourself now!"

Under the yellow glare of the light, the boxes wobbled before scattering across the dirty gravel. Several rats scurried out from the mess. He grimaced. Damn, he hated rats.

Slowly a bright orange shirt appeared, then dirtied blue jeans. Michael stepped back as the form staggered to its feet. The gray-tinted curls and the slack, wrinkled face of an old man came into view. His eyes held that glazed-over appearance drunks favored.

Michael relaxed. "Sir, this is the police. Are you doing okay?"

The old man glanced down at his shirt and let out a choked laugh. He ran his hands over the Washington Nats emblem. Part of Michael pitied the old man for various reasons.

"Sir"—he tried again—"how much have you had to drink tonight?"

After examining his own clothing, the old guy finally looked up at him. "Drink?" he asked, his voice gravelly with age.

Michael nodded as he placed the flashlight under his arm and took a step forward. "Sir, do you have any family I could call? Someone who could come get you?"

The old man eyed him strangely and then smiled. Flashing a row of yellowish teeth, he launched at him.

Unprepared for the sudden attack, Michael stumbled backward. Before he could recover, the old man was on him. Using shocking strength, the elderly male wrapped one bony hand around his throat and tossed him several feet.

Michael slammed into the brick wall and slid down. A brief surge of panic shot through him as he recalled the hours of training meant to prepare him for all the random shit one came into contact with on the street, but this . . . this was different. He struggled to his feet just as the old man backhanded him against the wall, cracking his head in the process. Dazed, he tasted blood on his lip.

The man bent down, a greasy lock of gray hair falling across his face. He picked Michael back up by the throat, dangling him several feet off the ground. "Officers of the peace are always my favorite to kill or turn."

Gasping for air, Michael pried on the old man's bony fingers. The pint-size grandfather held him, all six feet and then some, suspended in air. No amount of training at the academy could have prepared him for this. To be honest, he'd never been this scared shitless before. Not even when, at the age of six, he found his mother dead from self-inflicted slits to her wrists.

The man brought Michael's head close to his and laughed. His heart slammed painfully against his ribs as the man brought his head close and laughed, the raw sewage and sulfur stench of his breath engulfed him. Week-old vomit or rotten meat smelled better than this.

Then he saw his eyes. A black, frothy liquid seeped from the corners and spread over the whites of his eyes, covering the dull blue irises. Terror turned Michael's flesh cold. He knew he was going to die. Here, in a rat-infested alley in Anacostia, murdered by a deranged nursing-home patient. He reached for his gun, but it was too late. Just as he took what he knew would be his last breath, he heard something land softly behind the old man. Without warning, the grip on his throat was released.

Michael crumpled to the dirty alley, clutching his bruised throat. Even in his shocked state, he registered the silver dagger that pierced through the man's chest, right through the heart. A wound like that should have been a bloody mess, but there was no blood. Not even a trickle.

The dagger retracted quickly, and the man slumped to the ground in a lifeless heap. Only a whisper of air reminded him he was not alone. Climbing to his feet, he leveled his gun at his would-be rescuer.

A young woman stood in front of him. She was a tiny thing, with snapping, angry green eyes and a head full of auburn waves that fell past her breasts.

"I just saved your ass, and you're going to shoot me?"

For a moment he did nothing, and then he sputtered, "What the hell just happened?"

The woman glanced down at the body and then slowly back at him. "What does it look like?"

Michael shook his head as he reached for his hand-cuffs. "All right, you're under arrest. Drop your weapon now, and put your hands up!"

19

The feisty little redhead snickered, holding up her hands. "What weapon?"

His gaze darted over her hands. They were empty. The only thing he noticed was two wide silver cuffs adorning both wrists. "Where's the knife?" he demanded through clenched teeth. "The knife you used to kill the man!"

She dropped her hands to her hips. "You mean the man who was choking the life out of you?"

"Show me the weapon now." He reached for his shoulder radio, needing to call this in. A would-be murderer and a murderer. There was going to be a crap-ton of paperwork to do tonight.

She simply scowled at him. "You know, I really don't have time for this."

His gun lowered a fraction of an inch. "What?"

That was all she needed. She moved lightning quick. Before he could squeeze off a round, she knocked the gun out of his hand with her forearm and punched him right in the jaw.

His head snapped back, but not before he caught the startled look on her face, and as he slipped into oblivion he heard her shout, "Crap!"

Lily stared down at the young officer, astonished and more than a little disturbed. Nervously wiping her hand across the front of her white tank, she stepped back. The minute her hand had connected with his flesh, she had known.

Damn it all to Hell. And she'd bet her rosy left butt

cheek from the way he froze in front of the deadhead, he had no clue what he was. Cursing again, she pulled out her beat-up cell from her back pocket and dialed Luke.

He answered on the second ring. "What up?"

"We've got an epic problem in Anacostia. I need you and Remy now. You better call Nathaniel, too. This is going to involve the police."

"Aw man, Lily. What the hell did you do now?"

Lily rolled her eyes, clicking the phone shut without answering. She nudged the cop with the tip of her boot. Yep, he was out cold and not coming around anytime soon. Squatting, she studied his lax face.

"Crap. Crap. Crap," she hissed.

It wasn't like she'd known when she punched him. She wouldn't have if she did. On second thought, she probably would've still clocked him. But she may have softened the blow a little if she'd realized he was one of her kind.

A Nephilim.

CHAPTER THREE

"You knocked him out cold, Lily. Damn."

She spared a wondrous smile for Luke. "He was going to shoot me."

He frowned, glancing back at the softly snoring man sprawled across the bed tucked away in the Sanctuary. "I thought he was going to arrest you."

"That was after he was going to shoot me," she corrected.

His handsome face soured as he turned back to her. "I don't think I like him."

Ah, there was that dangerous undertone. Luke saw her as the little sister he probably never wanted. Hell, she grew up idolizing him while he spent time showing her the ropes. She still idolized him even when it was widely known that her skill surpassed his. Still, whenever anything seriously threatened her—which wasn't often—his boyish charm and easy nature would disappear. Luke could be downright murderous when provoked, especially after Anna.

Wincing at the thought of the beautiful Nephilim Luke had most definitely loved, she patted his heavily muscled arm. "Nah, I don't think he would have seriously shot me."

That did nothing to erase the scowl. "Better wake up soon."

Lily glanced back at the officer, reading his name tag. Officer M. Con? "I bet his first name is Michael."

He snorted. "That's what we call irony if so."

The Archangel Michael, the patron saint of police officers, was probably rolling his eyes somewhere up there or having a chuckle. Or he was sharpening his righteous blade and taking aim at this young man's neck. Archangels didn't look too kindly on the Nephilim, although they fought on the same side of the big guy upstairs. Well, most of the time.

"He's still out?"

They looked up as Remy entered the room with a broad smile spread across the deep chocolate hue of his face. His ropy dreads were tucked back. He cuffed Lily on the shoulder. "Damn, girl, always something."

She shrugged dainty shoulders, glancing back at the officer. He'd been out since the moment he'd hit the ground. He hadn't even made a sound as Remy and Luke carried him back to the Sanctuary. Her gaze flickered over her unblemished knuckles. *Damn, I'm good*.

He had to be young. Maybe late twenties. Kind of hot, too. All of the male Nephilim were attractive. They got good looks courtesy of their fathers.

This one had dark auburn hair and it was cropped short, a style favored by most police officers. At rest, his face held the youthful, innocent quality that alone proved he had no idea what he was. All Nephilim had a hardness about them, even her. The curve of his jaw was strong, and his cheeks chiseled. Thick lashes fanned those cheeks. He had the face of an angel.

Remy folded his arms across his broad chest as he inspected their newly acquired Nephilim. "Damn, can't say I'm not surprised you knocked out another police officer."

She winced.

Luke stood beside Remy. Immediately, she shifted to the other side of the bed. She hated when they towered over her. The boys' height was a characteristic of their kind that Lily had missed out on. All male Nephilim were well over six feet and counting, practically giants, while she was small enough to be thrown on their backs like a backpack.

"Do you really think he's Nephilim?" Luke directed toward Remy.

Lily sighed. "Touch him and find out."

"How could a Nephilim make it this long and not know what he is?" Luke asked. "Better yet, not get swayed by the Fallen?"

"How would I know? Go ahead and touch him," she urged. "You'll know." Both Luke and Remy appeared doubtful. "Just touch him and get it over with."

Remy sneered. "God, not when you say it like that."

Lily flipped him off.

Muttering under his breath, Luke leaned over the man and slowly placed his hand against the guy's forehead. Luke shot back as if jolted—a fine zap of electricity that fired when coming into contact with another Nephilim. "Damn it."

She rocked back on her heels, grinning. "I told you he's Nephilim."

Remy shook his head in wonder. "Wow, he is one lucky SOB, then, that you knocked his lights out."

Her smile grew to ridiculous proportions. She loved to be complimented. It was so few and far between these—

"Lillian Marks! Get your ass in here right now!"

Lily jumped, eyes widening. Two floors separating them and Nathaniel was that loud. Luke snickered, and she shot him a dirty look. "Thanks," she muttered.

Remy at least had the decency to give her warning. "Nathaniel is pissed. You have no idea how many favors he had to call in tonight."

Her shoulders slumped as she moved around the bed slowly. Luke patted her on top of the head when she passed. She swung at him, but he darted out of the way, laughing. "I hate you both."

Remy shuffled closer to the bed as she headed to the door. "Do you know how hard it will be to train him at this age?"

She stopped in the doorway. It would be damn near impossible. They couldn't train him. It was too late. The best thing they could do is put him back in the cruiser and wish for the best. Cruel, but there was no way Officer Prettypants could do his job and live through the night.

But it was not her problem.

Lily walked down the dimly lit corridor of level five, a housing unit five floors underground the Sanctuary office building. Buried so deep under the third tallest building in DC, no one made it to this level uninvited. Taking the elevator, she descended to level seven where Nathaniel kept his real office and living quarters.

Nathaniel sat behind a large oval desk finished in a cherry stain that was polished to the point she could see her reflection in it. Lily was well familiar with that. She spent a lot of time staring at her own face in his desk as she was lectured over the latest stunt she'd pulled—or Julian, especially over him. He'd become quite the main theme of her most recent lectures.

She stumbled. She never stumbled. Unless it was about her not-so-angelic stalker Julian, and when it was, everything went to Hell.

Nathaniel set his phone down quietly, motioning her into his office. "Sit."

It was like she was thirteen again, and she sat awkwardly, folding her hands in her lap like some misbehaving child. She was a full-grown woman who could take down an entire room of minions without breaking a single nail, but none of that mattered when she sat in front of Nathaniel.

He had this look when he was upset with her. It usually started with him absently brushing back his brown hair, then tucking the longer strands behind his ears. His lips would turn down, and he would pierce her with those pale blue eyes. Then fine lines would form around them, marring his otherwise youthful face.

She had no idea how old he was. No one she knew did.

He had to be at least several hundred years old,

though he looked about thirty. The same as he had the night he'd pulled her, shrieking and crying, away from her mother's corpse. She had been five.

"Lily."

She squirmed. "Nathaniel."

"First off, what the hell are you wearing?"

Surprised, she glanced down at herself. She was wearing the same thing she'd had on earlier. "Huh?"

"You're out hunting in a skirt that barely covers your ass," he remarked.

She bristled even though her cheeks flamed. "Excuse me, fashion police, I didn't realize I needed your permission on what I could wear."

He sighed wearily. "I'm only looking out for you."

"I don't need anyone looking out for me."

"That may be, but we've got a mess here." He leaned back in his chair, pinching the bridge of his nose. "Lily, you know things are heating up. The Fallen are corrupting more and more of the Nephilim. We are losing an increasing number of souls to them, and that means countless innocent people."

Boy did she know. The Fallen were snatching up the young Nephilim before the Sanctuary could get them safely tucked away. Once the Fallen had them, they were lost. Corrupt as the angels that had fathered them. Those Nephilim turned minion and became the very thing their kind was supposed to hunt.

"The last thing we need is to be exposed."

Lily shifted, the leather creaking under her slight weight. "I know."

"Do you even know how many favors I had to call in? Danyal put his neck on the line so no one would question why that young man didn't come off his shift."

She fidgeted in the seat. Danyal had enmeshed himself deep within the police department just in case they needed someone in times like these. But favors were always few and hard to cover up.

"I taught you to strike and get the hell out. It's as simple as that."

Her lips pursed. That had been the plan, but her temper had gotten the best of her.

"You need to be more careful," he said quietly.

What he hadn't said hung in the air between them. She knew he was remembering Anna and what had happened to her. Damn it, she missed her friend fiercely. Anna and Lily had had a tight relationship. She'd been older than Lily, accepting the Contract decades ago. But Anna had first lost her heart and then her head to one of the Fallen.

Foolish, beautiful Anna.

There were so few female Nephilim. Most children were born male, but every few decades a female half-breed would surface. Besides Michelle, who'd been reassigned to New York, Anna had been the only other female hunter in the DC section.

The pain of her loss still reverberated through the halls of the Sanctuary, and no two people were more affected by it than Nathaniel and Luke. They had seen her death as their own personal failure. Lily knew

Nathaniel took full blame, believing he hadn't trained her well enough. Part of her knew Luke agreed with him. The last six weeks had been tough, and the tension between the two males had only grown.

Nathaniel unfolded his arms, letting out a world-weary sigh. "The good thing about this is that we got him instead of the Fallen. I have no idea how he made it this long, but he'll have the right training now and be able to step fully into his destiny."

"What?" She shot from the chair.

"Lily," he warned.

"We can't train him. He's too old."

Nathaniel frowned. "He looked about thirty."

"Yes! Thirty years of absolutely no knowledge of the Nephilim or the Fallen!"

He raised a brow. "You're younger than him."

She sputtered. "I've had years of training, and I've accepted the Contract. We cannot train him with everything that is going on!"

"We'll find a way." He stopped, glancing up. "Better yet, you'll find a way."

She was about two seconds from grabbing her hair and pulling. "You're kidding."

He smiled. "No."

"You can't do this to me. I can't train anyone. You know I don't have any patience. I'm better as a hunter."

"Lily, you're great as a hunter. You're one of the best. Hell, you are probably the best," he admitted. "But this is an order I'm giving you."

Her hands fell uselessly to her sides. He rarely

ordered her to do anything. She knew there was no point in arguing.

"Don't sulk." He stood and headed around the desk.

She noticed then that his clothes were wrinkled. Guilt gnawed at her insides. Here she was, adding to his enormous pile of things to worry over. "You haven't slept have you?"

He paused, looking down at himself. "Is it that obvious?"

She nodded. Frankly, she'd seen him worse, but there was a weariness that clung to his skin. "It's bad, isn't it?" she whispered.

He leaned against the desk, stretching his long legs, appearing to choose his words wisely. "I'm afraid someone is betraying us."

She gaped. Okay, she knew it was bad. She just hadn't expected it to be that bad. "What do you mean?"

He pushed away from the desk and went to the large cabinet that took up the entire side of the wall. She followed his movements. Curious, she waited quietly.

"Someone is feeding the Fallen a list of every Nephilim we are aware of. I also think the same person is actively seeking ones we have yet to re-locate." He ran his hand over the wood. "With this knowledge, they will quickly outnumber us by the hundreds. It's sheer numbers. They take more souls and infect more humans."

And there were so many souls nowadays. Those who perished unexpectedly were vulnerable to persuasion.

Those poor souls clung to any hope of life, even the false hope minions provided them.

They invaded the bodies of the living, truly believing it was a second chance at life. But once their soul mingled with the host, things went downhill fast. The human became a deadhead—the human souls withering away for them both.

"With the Fallen operating behind the scenes, where we can't reach them, we're left cleaning up their mess time after time."

She looked up. "Do you know who it is?"

He faced her. "That's what's been keeping me up at night."

She inclined her head. "Do the Powers That Be know?" That's what she called the angels and whoever else ran this show.

"They haven't talked to me in a long time."

That gave her pause. Nathaniel was the Nephilim's only connection to the Powers That Be who called the shots from their lofty position. She always imagined them perched on a cloud full of morals and pomp, stringing their golden harps while staring at their beautiful reflections.

Lily didn't like angels, especially their politics.

They viewed her kind as an abomination that had, unfortunately, become necessary. If they were ever successful in eradicating the Fallen and their legions, the Nephilim would be next on their heavenly hit list.

"Well crap," she muttered.

Nathaniel chuckled. "Exactly. Don't mention any

31

of what I've shared with you about my suspicions. Only the circle is aware of the issue. I want it to stay that way."

The circle consisted of the oldest and most skilled Nephilim in each chapter of the Sanctuary. They were in charge of various things such as disciplinary issues, the most secretive of missions, and the occasional social event that required their participation.

In the DC chapter, it was Nathaniel and Luke, Remy, and about nine other Nephilim. Then there was Lily. She was by far the youngest, but the most skilled. She had a habit of reminding them of that.

"Of course," she agreed.

"Just keep your ear to the ground for me and report anything that seems odd. Now get back to the cop and make sure you brief him on what he is. You will meet resistance, but try to have patience."

She arched an eyebrow but didn't respond.

"Use Remy and Luke for all you need. I trust them. You can also reach out to Rafe." He flashed a weak smile. "Keep Michael out of the school. I don't want the young ones to freak him out. You know how they can be."

Lily smiled at that. The school housed young Nephilim anywhere from five to eighteen. The teen-agers were by far the worst, and the youngest ones just hadn't developed a self-censor system yet. She kind of liked them for that.

Nathaniel smiled fondly at the auburn head that didn't even reach his chest. "Lily?"

"Yes?"

"Be nice. And, God, please don't kill him."

"No promises."

She left the room and made her way back to level five, deciding she'd gotten off light this time. Her ass had been chewed off far worse than that in the past. Pulling from a seemingly endless supply of energy, she bounded up the stairs.

Cory Roberts hurried across the manicured lawn, breathing a sigh of relief when he spotted the senator's limousine in its designated spot. It was past midnight, and all he wanted was to be home in bed with his wife.

Tomorrow would be jam-packed with meetings, tedious conference calls, a baby or two to be kissed on the cheek, and the senator's latest scandal to be dealt with.

He juggled the stack of folders in one arm, barely retaining his limp grasp on his coffee. This was why he was losing sleep. Caffeine at midnight and another dose at the crack of dawn was a wretched combination for his heart.

Middle-aged and already balding, with high blood pressure and a sinking suspicion he was developing an ulcer, Cory had had a shitty day. The wire-frame glasses slipped down his nose. This latest affair would surely be the senator's undoing. There was no way they could cover this up, and the senator's bitch of a wife was already booking the early-morning talk shows.

The senator couldn't keep his dick in his pants, and

that dick was going to get them all in the unemployment line. Without this job, Cory would lose everything: the money, the illusion of power, the house his wife loved, and even his wife.

He would give his soul for this whole mess to disappear.

The driver stepped forward, opening the door. Cory spared him a tight smile and slid in. Clutching the folders and coffee to his chest, he glanced across the seat, expecting the senator or, at the very least, his whore of a secretary.

The coffee slipped from his fingers.

Cory loved his wife of ten years—had always loved women. He never questioned his sexuality until that moment. It shattered his world.

The man was painstakingly beautiful. Darkly exquisite in a way that bordered on the odd. His face was perfect, and the blue of his eyes promised bliss. Cory reacted to him in a way only his wife had been able to provoke from him. He struggled for air, unable to escape the man's scent and the faint smell of sulfur.

The man's full lips curved into a slight smile, as if he knew his effect. His brilliant gaze flickered over the spilled coffee, then back to Cory. "Hello, Mr. Roberts."

At the sound of the stranger's voice, Cory's head splintered with pain. He wanted to sob and he wanted to run, but he couldn't move.

"You may call me Asmodeus, and I'm here to do you a favor."

Cory started to respond, but his heart seized. Files

toppled to the floor as he clutched his chest, wide-eyed and wheezing. He stared up at the man, inherently knowing he had brought this sudden pain on.

Asmodeus's smile grew. "I can make the senator's scandal go away. You can keep your job, the fancy house on the hill . . . and your wife."

Cory gasped as the air in his lungs expelled painfully. "What . . . are you?"

He waved a dismissive hand. "All you have to do is return the favor to me. There's someone that . . . I need."

CHAPTER FOUR

Michael felt as if he'd been hit over the head by an NFL linebacker and then walked through the Mojave Desert. He had never been so thirsty in his life.

"Oh, I think he's waking up."

He flinched. Those words were exceptionally loud. He had no idea why his head hurt. Finally the fog that had settled over his memories started to clear. There'd been a disturbance call in an alley and an old man. Michael remembered that.

"I guess I don't know my own strength."

And he remembered that voice and who it belonged to. His eyes snapped open. He was looking into a pair of startling green eyes. He stared dumbly at the girl perched on a chair beside his bed, wearing this little half smile.

The richness of her auburn-colored hair flattered the pinkish tone of her flawless skin, causing her eyes to shine like emerald jewels. Her rosy lips were lush. Lips that would've normally had his cock jumping out of his pants, but something about her turned his insides ice cold.

The girl wiggled her fingers. "Hello."

He tore his gaze from her, realizing they weren't

alone. Two hulking males stood at the foot of his bed. By the intricate tattoos covering the arms and hands of the lighter-skinned one, he knew they weren't fellow police officers.

Which would mean? He reached for his gun but came up empty. He jerked up, wincing, and grappled for the small microphone that connected to the radio system. But that was gone, too.

"I'd be careful," she said. "You shouldn't move too quickly."

He turned back to her, stunned this tiny thing had knocked him out. Anger flared, tightening the muscles in his gut and, beyond that, a sense of weariness. "Where is my duty belt?"

Her smile never faltered. "We took it. None of us wanted to get shot. The doctor here hates pulling things out of us."

"Where's my gun?"

"Now, boy"—the lighter-skinned one took a menacing step forward—"you watch your tone."

Michael's gaze swiveled to him. "Who are you?"

His lips twisted into a sneer. "I'm the one who'll put you in your coffin if you talk to me like that again."

Michael swung his legs off the bed and stood. To hell with the thumping in his head and jaw, and forget the fact that he swayed on his feet. "Is that so?"

The girl sighed. "Boys."

Neither of them listened. The fair-skinned one cocked his head to the side. "If you weren't already knocked out once today, you'd be on the ground."

Then the girl was in front of him, firmly planting herself between them. They towered over her, but there wasn't an ounce of fear in her eyes. "We don't have time for the pissing contest about to take place," she said sweetly. "So let's all take a breather before I kick the crap out of both of you."

Amused by the pint-size terror, he glanced down. The humor fled when he saw a blade at his throat. The little bitch . . . But part of him still wanted to laugh.

"You going to behave?" she asked.

Drawing in a deep breath, he stepped back. "All right, I want to know where I am."

The blade disappeared into the bracelet. "How about we introduce ourselves first? My name is Lily." Pausing, she gestured at the angry one. "This is Luke. And this is Remy."

Instinct told him he'd get nowhere with an attitude, so he pushed his temper as far down as he could and tried to remain calm. "My name is Officer Michael Cons, and you guys are in a lot of trouble."

Luke snorted. "That's doubtful."

"Michael?" Lily murmured. "Go figure. Anyway, you're at the Sanctuary."

"The security firm in Federal Triangle?" he asked, praying he had misheard. If so, he was far out of his district. When she nodded, he lost his cool. "Where in the hell is my cruiser? And why do you have me here?"

Luke took a step forward, but Lily arched a single brow at him. "Your cruiser is back at the station in the Seventh District. You've been clocked out, and, actually, you've requested some leave due to personal issues." She smiled demurely and added, "Courtesy of us."

He shook his head faintly. He didn't know whether to be angry or laugh. This was utter bullshit and had to be some bizarre hallucination.

"I can see you're a bit shocked. It may help if we explain things to you." The one named Remy stepped forward with a friendly smile.

"You may want to sit down," Lily advised.

"I'm fine standing."

She shrugged. "Luke, can you grab something to drink?"

"Whatever. You're just trying to get me out of the room. You know he's going to lose it."

She turned her bright eyes on Luke. "Please?"

The permanent scowl on Luke's face started to soften, surprising Michael.

"What do you want?" Luke sighed.

"A milkshake," she requested with an excitement that he was envious of.

"You've got to be kidding me." Luke shook his head. "I'll have to make one or go buy you one, Lily. Come on."

She pouted. "A milkshake."

Remy laughed. "You might as well go ahead and get her one." He paused. "And get me one while you're at it."

Luke cursed, but he pivoted swiftly and left the room.

Lily turned back to Michael, folding her arms. "Do you remember anything from the alley?"

"Besides you punching an officer?" he replied.

She smiled evenly. "I mean the old man. Do you remember anything about him?"

He remembered the old man's brute strength. And his foul breath and some other weird stuff he accounted to the knock he took on his skull. "The one you murdered?"

"The one who was about to rip out your throat and make pretty pictures on the wall with your blood?" She threw back at him. "Yeah, that one."

He bit down on the inside of his cheek. Something was entirely wrong with these people. His cruiser was somewhere, his gun missing, and the whole department was probably searching for him since he hadn't responded to any of their calls. They would have found the dead man by now.

"He was going to kill you, Michael. That's what their kind does," she went on. "I intervened because that is what we do."

Seriously? He gave a low whistle, not sure where to start with that load of crazy. "Okay. Why would he want to do that?"

She glanced at Remy, who shrugged. "A minion—which is one of our kind who's been corrupted by a fallen angel—persuaded a soul to invade the man's body. The soul possessed him."

When she didn't laugh or admit she was joking, he started to get worried. "Excuse me?"

"There is no easy way to tell you, and I really don't have the patience to ease you into this."

"This is the part where you might want to sit down," Remy advised.

He ignored him, focusing on her. "Look, I don't know what game you guys are playing, but I think it's best you let me go."

"We can't," she said.

The hairs on his neck rose. He quickly surveyed the room, noting only one exit. "So let me get this straight. You're holding me against my will?"

The green flecks in her eyes flared as she stepped forward. "Whatever. That's not important." She placed her hands on her hips. "Michael, if you leave the safety of the Sanctuary, every Fallen, minion, and human possessed will be gunning for your ass."

He gaped at her. She was absolutely crazy. Further gone than the woman who thought her cat was tapping her phone lines. What did he do to deserve a night like this? Damn, he was a good person.

After graduating with top honors from college and spending several years as an accountant for a law firm in Sterling, the need to do something more with his life had overcome him. Like an idiot, he applied for the Metropolitan Police Department the second he'd learned they were hiring. Six months ago he had graduated from the academy.

And this is what he got for it, for fuck's sake.

"I'm out of here." Michael pushed past her. He heard Remy chuckle deeply, and then he was off his feet. Somehow, little Lily had picked him up and pinned him down on the bed.

Staring into the greenest eyes framed with the thickest lashes he'd ever seen, he admitted he would've been generally pleased with the unexpected turn of events. But once again, he felt as if someone blew cold air down his spine. And he knew a normal woman of her size couldn't do that.

Oh, hell no. Something wasn't right. He'd been brought down by a woman with superhuman strength. Man, he'd seriously underestimated the situation.

Right now, he really missed the crazy cat lady.

CHAPTER FIVE

"What happened to having patience?" Remy asked, clearly amused.

"Patience is overrated." Lily glared down at her captive. "Now you're going to listen to me. I'm going to let you up, but you will sit quietly and hear us out."

Michael stared up at her. The blue of his eyes had deepened. At first she didn't think he was going to answer her, but he finally nodded.

"I mean it," she warned. "Next time you try to bolt, I'm going to let Remy take care of you. And he will make it hurt. Do you understand me?"

He tensed. "Okay."

She smiled broadly. "Good." Pushing off him, she landed nimbly on her feet. The shock on his face pleased her. She watched as he sat up awkwardly.

He let out a deep breath as he glanced up, pinning her with his eyes. "Are you going to tell me what is going on?"

Remy pulled out a chair from along the wall and sat. "Do you know Danyal Archer? I believe he's a sergeant in your district."

Recognition flickered across his face. "Detective Archer?"

Remy smiled as he pulled a dread loose, twisting it around his long fingers. "Danyal is a very good friend of ours. When Lily realized the . . . error she had made, we called Danyal and explained to him what had happened. He took care of everything. As far as your department knows, you had a family emergency and had to leave. No one will question him."

She jumped in. "We took your belt and radio because we couldn't risk you ruining all of Danyal's hard work. He stuck his neck out there and, buddy, our necks are tremendously valuable."

Michael rubbed the underside of his jaw absently. "Why would Detective Archer help you?"

"Because he's one of us," she said softly. He opened his mouth, but she cut him off. "I'm going to start from the beginning. All I ask is that you don't interrupt and you silently pray Luke returns with a milkshake quickly, because they make me happy. And you want to keep me happy."

His expression soured.

"And you keep an open mind," Remy threw in. "You have to already know that we aren't your average Joes."

Michael snorted. "I don't know what to think. Some old man almost killed me. This one seems to be able to throw around men three times her size. Man, tell me whatever you want."

Lily almost laughed. She tried to remember what it was like when she had learned the truth about what she was, but she had been so young and scared.

Nathaniel could've told her anything, and she would've believed him. Pushing those darker memories to the back of her mind, she cleared her throat. "Have you ever heard of fallen angels?"

His brows flew up. "Other than you mentioning it a few minutes ago, you're going to have to refresh my memory, thank you."

Instead of being the general bully that she was, Lily sat in a chair and pushed at her tangled mess of hair. "Angels used to walk among man, serving as sources of enlightenment and faith. Only God's most trusted angels were sent to Earth—one-third of all the angels in Heaven. He had faith they would not disobey him.

"The angels who were sent to Earth became entranced with humans," she continued. "Maybe it was the humans' fragile nature or the fact they had souls, and that alone made them passionate in a way angels could never be. In the end, it didn't really matter. The angels took women as their lovers and, after doing so, they fell. They became the Fallen."

"Wait a second," Michael interrupted. "You are talking angels screwing women?"

She nodded. "And they had children called Nephilim. As you can imagine, this enraged God. He did everything under His control to stop the spread of the half-human and half-angel children. He sent more angels to snatch them away from their mothers, burned down entire villages, and even flooded the earth. The Fallen were resilient though. He could never stop them, and soon that became the least of His worries."

"See, God no longer spoke to them, and this angered the Fallen," Remy said, leaning forward. "The angels see God as their father, and to the ones that fell, God had abandoned them. Their hatred festered, turning them against the humans they once treasured. Once they fell, they lost all compassion for man. Instead of helping them, the Fallen began to find ways to harm them, therefore harming God in the process."

Michael looked doubtful. "How did they harm people?"

Lily tried to determine where Michael was in all of this. Currently, he stared at them, dazed, a mixture of befuddlement and morbid fascination on his face. But the next phase of information was where things would get a little hairy.

Thankfully Remy always knew when to put his two cents in and help out. There was a certain ease about him that people, Nephilim or not, responded to. "You see, angels and Nephilim have a very unique ability. When people die, their souls should ascend to Heaven or, in some cases, go to Hell." He broke off with a half smile. "However, there are some souls that are vulnerable. They don't know where to go and, in most cases, they refuse to let go of life. Angels are expected to guide them to where they are supposed to be. It's a trait the Fallen retained after their fall and passed on to the Nephilim."

Michael's eyebrows raised a fraction with each word that came out of Remy's mouth. He glanced at Lily, and she smiled sympathetically. It was about to get so much worse. Learning about angels was one thing.

Learning what souls could do to relatively normal people was another story. Getting told he wasn't really human was going to be the icing on the cake, but she was going to leave that part for later.

Remy explained swiftly and with such an earnestness that the biggest cynic had to believe him. He described how the Fallen had learned they could persuade the souls into human bodies, and the devastating consequences of such an act. By doing this, the Fallen had made two strikes with one blow. Not only did they damage the soul that had recently passed, but they also destroyed the soul and the body of the one possessed.

"Everything changed then," she said quietly. "It was no longer an issue of their disobedience or bedroom activities. Who cared if they were producing children? They were destroying innocent souls, and when they realized their children could also sense these souls, they saw their revenge against God."

Michael let out a low whistle. "You guys realize how crazy this sounds, right?"

She laughed. It was about to sound even crazier. "The Fallen are very angry with God and extremely jealous of humans. It's a nasty mix of raw emotions."

"Okay," he said slowly. "You're telling me there are evil angels running around and half-breed children? Why should I care? Why should you?"

Lily wondered if he was slow. Why couldn't he put two and two together and make this easy for her? "Because I'm Nephilim and so are Luke and Remy."

His lips parted as if he wanted to laugh. "If you're Nephilim, aren't you just as bad as those angels?"

She was about to answer, but fortunately spied what Luke carried into the room. She jumped from her seat, racing over to him. "Thank you. I owe you, Luke. I really do." She grabbed one of the frosted glasses.

Luke rolled his eyes, handing the other one to Remy. "So how is the cop handling everything?"

Clutching the glass in her hands, she sank into the chair. She glanced up. Michael was watching her. "Want some?"

He blinked. "No. No thanks."

She grinned. "We were just about to tell Michael the difference between us and the Fallen."

Luke propped himself against the wall. "Well, that's easy. They're basically out to destroy humanity. We're here to stop them. It's plain and simple. We kill the Fallen and those who work with them—no questions asked."

Sucking on her straw, she glared at Luke. Yeah, that didn't help. She took a huge gulp of the cold, thick liquid and swallowed. "There are good and bad Nephilim. Obviously"—she tipped the glass to her chest—"we're good. All of us at the Sanctuary—and there are many of us—are good. We operate like a checks-and-balances system."

Michael leaned back, running his hands down his face as he stared at her. The expression he wore told her that he was bordering on running again, and she couldn't afford that. Not with Luke here. He would do far worse than pin him down. She glanced at her nearly empty glass with a frown. She should have asked for two.

"Since we can feel the souls that are vulnerable, we should get to them first. There are some of our kind that deal only with finding those souls and helping them cross over. The people who can talk to the dead?" She paused, letting that part sink in. "They are Nephilim, and their job is to help those souls, but we aren't always fast enough."

Michael nodded like he understood. "What happens if you don't?"

"It's what happened to the poor man in the alley. Once a soul enters a human, it's too late. The soul is corrupted and becomes evil. We call them deadheads. I know—not very creative or classy, but that's what we know them as. When it happens, the human has to be killed."

He gave a short laugh, closing his eyes. "This has been one hell of a night. So you guys run around killing people that you believe are possessed by evil souls?"

"It's not what we believe," Remy corrected. "It's what we know. We can sense the souls before they enter a body—and once they do. It feels like death: cold and final. You know it when it happens. There's no mistaking it."

Michael turned back to Lily. "So you killed that man because he had a bad soul in him? Why didn't you just . . . exorcise the soul?"

Luke laughed. "This isn't television, buddy. You

49

can't remove a soul once it gets into a body. Like she said, the soul turns evil the moment it climbs down the throat of the unlucky sap who happened to be within distance of it. You should know what would've happened if it climbed down yours."

There was a good chance she would throw her glass at Luke's head. With willpower she didn't realize she had, she put the glass on the floor and folded her hands. "Look at it this way, Michael. The soul infects the host. Just like a cold or a virus does, but this kind of infection is permanent. They no longer remember who they are. They don't care about pesky things like morals or compassion. They turn into killing machines, and it becomes our job to take care of them. We have been trained to . . . dispose of them."

Michael shook his head. "You guys are freaking insane."

So much for hoping he would sop up information like a wet sponge and then ask where he could sign up for the job. She knew it was well past midnight, and she had no idea how long Michael had been on his shift before she'd run into him. She figured he only had a few more hours in him before he shut down, and whether he liked it or not, she planned to use them.

"I just have a couple more things to tell you. Then we have something we want to show you." She ignored the sense of confusion Remy and Luke shot her way. "It's really important you know what is out there. There are people like us who are bad. They were Nephilim once, but the Fallen corrupted them. What they've become now is what we call a minion. Yep, once again, we suck at names, but there is a legion of them."

Michael started to stand, but he sat back down. A sort of lopsided smile formed, but his face paled several shades. "I was hoping I had misheard you earlier when you said minion."

"Sorry, but you didn't. The minions are constantly out there searching for souls and . . . for Nephilim like us."

"They want to kill us," Luke added nonchalantly. "And so do the Fallen."

Michael's weary gaze shifted to Luke. "I don't see how that is my problem."

"Well . . ." Lily began with a tight smile. "It kind of is your problem. Remember how I warned you that every minion and Fallen would be out looking for you?" He nodded. "Well, once the soul enters a human body, whatever it sees or feels is communicated back to the minion that persuaded it and then back to the Fallen that corrupted it. It's kind of like a fucked-up instant-messaging system."

Michael's brows slanted together. "So?"

She took a deep breath, exhaling slowly. "The Fallen and the Nephilim can sense one another. So can the souls. It's an internal warning system. Kind of comes in handy, too, but that's beside the point."

"Just spit it out, Lily," Luke grumbled from his corner.

She glared at him. "It's because you're like us, Michael. Your father was one of the Fallen, and that makes you one of us."

"Bullshit," he whispered.

"And since the soul knew what you are, that means the minion does, too . . . and the Fallen as well. They know you're untrained, virtually helpless to them. They'll come for you. First, they're going to try to coerce you to join them."

"Go all dark side and all." Remy grinned.

"And if you don't?" she continued. "They will kill you."

Michael handled that little part surprisingly well. He stared at them and then laughed so hard she thought he'd hurt himself.

"We're not joking," she said, meeting and holding his gaze. "At all."

He started to stand but didn't make it very far. "This . . . this is crazy."

He pretty much didn't say a lot of anything after that. He was already shutting down, and there was so much he didn't know about. She still hadn't even touched on the fact that the Fallen were behind half of the dirty politicians in this city.

She stood and stretched. They had a couple of hours before the sun rose and the minions crawled back into whatever dank, dark place they could find. Well, they probably lived in some sweet penthouses, but whatever. "I know it's getting late, but there's something we need to show you. I think it will help."

"I don't think anything will help me understand," he responded drily.

She flashed him a smile. "No, this will. At the very worst, you'll definitely know we aren't crazy." Then she laughed when she saw the pissy look of disbelief on his face. "I'm not going to kill another old man if that's what you're thinking."

Remy pushed away from the wall. "Are we going down to the old St. Mary's Reform School?"

She nodded, earning a wide grin from Luke. She turned back to Michael. "I'll make you a promise. If you come along with us, and we don't prove that everything we've told you is true, then we'll leave you alone, and you'll never see us again."

His brows lowered in doubt.

She offered him her pinkie. "I pinkie swear."

Michael shook his head, standing. "I can go home and never have to worry about angels or . . . whatever again?"

She almost felt bad for doing this to him. "I promise."

He took a long breath before agreeing. She pivoted, passing Luke on the way out. "Be nice."

An overtly innocent look appeared on his face. "Of course."

"Where is she going?" Michael immediately demanded.

Luke turned to him, his grin cold. "You'll see soon enough."

Rolling her eyes, she headed out the door. Damn,

she hoped Luke didn't kill him before she wrangled up a minion . . . or two.

Michael followed the two men through the streets of DC in a surreal daze. After he'd stripped off his navy-blue uniform shirt and vest, he felt strangely naked in his Under Armor shirt. He didn't even know why he'd agreed. Maybe it was because underneath the disbelief, confusion, and even a little bit of fear, he was curious. And besides knocking him out earlier, none of them had tried to seriously injure him, and he knew they could.

The only thought that propelled him through the fog was the knowledge that he could leave this all behind him soon. Chalk it up to a night full of lunatics; wake up tomorrow to happily go about his business as if none of this had ever happened.

They turned off the sidewalk, heading across a street bridge. He wished they'd given him his gun back. Shit, he could be recognized even out of uniform. Streets around here were not kind. "Where are we going?"

Remy glanced at him. "You know the old reform school near Congress Heights?"

He did. Everyone knew where Congress Heights was. It had been one of the most neglected neighborhoods in DC, and only recently had urban developers moved in. With the increased police presence and general cleanup effort, it had improved, but it still wasn't great.

The three of them turned onto Clay Street, and

looming ahead was the once-prestigious reform school that had long since been forgotten. He frowned as Remy grabbed the chain-link fence and, with a simple twist of his wrist, snapped the lock.

His stomach went cold. *What the hell have I gotten myself into?* He may not believe in angels and all that crap, but there was no doubt there was something drastically different about these people. Maybe they were the product of some covert government experiment gone awry. More believable than the Nephilim bullshit, but still pretty terrifying.

The lawn hadn't been tended in years, and grass had grown to his knees. Bushes and weeds choked the old circular driveway, and sticker bushes latched onto his pants.

"Are we going in there?" he wondered out loud.

Remy passed him a grin before disappearing around the side of the building. Michael turned to Luke, folding his arms. "What are we doing?"

"Remy is going to find us a way in. One that isn't too obvious."

"Why would we want to go in there?"

The smirk on Luke's face deepened. "You ask a lot of stupid questions, you know that?"

His anger flared. He wanted nothing more than to punch the cocky grin off his face, and although the man was a good deal bigger than him, Michael figured he could take him. Or at least do some damage in the process.

Luke motioned him to follow around the side of the

run-down brick building. "Come on, Remy," he muttered, "we don't have much time."

Much time until what? God, did he even want to know?

One of the boards covering a lower window splintered apart, startling him. Remy stuck his head out, reminding him of a deranged Jack Nicholson. "Come on in."

He halted. Every cell in his body warned him not to go in there. Besides the fact that he was pretty sure the floors had to be rotten to the point that it wouldn't be safe, he also inherently knew he wouldn't like where any of this was heading.

Luke stepped to move behind him. He held out his arm. "In."

Michael gritted his teeth. Seeing no way out of this, he threw a dirty look over his shoulder and climbed through the window as carefully as possible. Once inside, he could barely detect his surroundings.

Luke jumped through the window and landed on his feet beside him. *How can such a large guy be so quiet?*

"They are near." Remy headed toward the door. "Follow me."

Michael did his best to keep up with him through the maze of broken desks and toppled chairs. Wherever moonlight was able to filter through, he saw gang graffiti painted on the walls and floors.

They left the room in silence, entering the hallway. He was careful to track Remy's sure footsteps. Sections of the floor had rotted away, but somehow the guys avoided them without even looking. Maybe they were ninjas.

He almost laughed but doubted either man would appreciate that.

They went upstairs and, tired of the silence, he demanded to know what the plan was. Luke threw him a cynical smile, but Remy was a little more informative. "Something you need to see that will bring things into perspective."

He hesitated at the top of the stairs. "There isn't anything you can show me that will bring any perspective to this night."

Luke chuckled but didn't respond as they made their way down the hallway. At the end, Remy pushed open double doors covered with faded red paint and rust.

Half expecting something to jump out in front of him, Michael was a little disappointed when he realized they were above an empty gymnasium. He turned to Remy. "Is there a game I'm unaware of?"

Remy tipped back his head, laughing. "A game of sorts."

Rolling his eyes, he turned back to the cracked floor below them. The bleachers had been removed, and only one basketball pole remained. The net was missing and the backboard hung at an odd angle. He felt the men go still beside him.

Luke tapped him on his arm. "Be quiet."

He wanted to break that goddamned finger, but footsteps echoed across the floor and something . . . something fluttered in his stomach. It was the kind of feeling he got when he was about to make an arrest but stronger—much stronger. Nervous excitement mingled with apprehension crawled out of his stomach and traveled up his spine in a shudder. He leaned to peer over the railing, but Luke threw his arm out.

"Move back," he hissed.

From his new vantage point he could still see the area below but was hidden in the shadows that crept over the walls and ceiling.

Someone entered from the court-level doors on the opposite side of the gymnasium, stopping in the middle of the court, beneath a shaft of moonlight streaming through a broken window. It was a boy. Young. Probably not even in his midtwenties by the looks of it. His black hair was spiked, and he wore heavy eyeliner that accented unusually pale eyes. Michael could make out a band on the boy's black shirt, but the logo had faded.

His palms grew sweaty. "Who is that?" he whispered.

Luke glanced at him sternly. "He was once a Nephilim," he responded in a hushed voice, "but he's not warm and fuzzy anymore. He's a minion."

The boy raised his head, sniffing the air. Michael's eyes widened as the kid reached into a pocket of his black cargo pants, withdrawing a nasty-looking knife. The kind he imagined was used to gut a deer.

"What is he doing?"

Luke exhaled slowly. "He's looking for Lily. He senses us, but he thinks it's her."

Michael was caught off guard by the little spitfire's

sudden appearance across from them. Perched on the edge of the balcony railing, she had her arms at her sides, her head bent down.

"Just watch," Luke whispered.

He did, transfixed by Lily's wild beauty. She crouched there with an ease that was uncommon. With her hair pulled up in a messy bun and a rather pleased smile on her face, she appeared casually bored, as if she were about to go grocery shopping or something. Then, under his watchful stare, she stood gracefully and jumped to the floor below.

A surge of protectiveness flared from deep within him. Lily was a girl—and they were supposed to just stand there? Fuck that. Every instinct in him demanded he do something.

Luke and Remy must've sensed his sudden shock because they moved to block him. But he pushed, and he pushed hard. Both men fell to the side, and he easily closed the distance between them and the railing. He leaned over, yelling her name. "Lily!"

The boy's head jerked up, his mouth open. He let out a scream that sliced through Michael's insides. The howl traveled all the way to his soul, leaving it cold. The boy's mouth hung wide, distorting until it became a gaping hole of darkness that nearly swallowed his entire face.

The sound kept coming, screeching until it turned into a keening that filled the entire gymnasium. "Nephilim!" he screamed.

Heart thundering, Michael stumbled back from the

railing. He couldn't have imagined that. Not in his wildest dreams. There was no way he could take that sight back or forget it.

That thing on the floor with Lily was not human.

Holy fuck, everything they'd said was true.

CHAPTER SIX

Lily was exceptionally proud of herself. She'd tracked the minion clear across DC, and then practically threw herself at him. Once he'd gained sight of her, the chase was on, and she had led him right where she had wanted.

But then she jumped, landing on the balls of her feet, and everything went to hell the moment Michael called out her name. The emo minion let out his battle cry, whirling on her. She caught sight of the sharp blade poised high in the air. There were several feet between them, but the young minion scaled the distance with a single leap.

Minions were stupid, but they were strong.

She shook her wrists and the silver, icicle-shaped daggers released from the cuffs she wore. Inches from her, the minion came down with the knife clenched in one fist. Raising an arm aimed straight at his chest, she laughed. Only a blow to the heart from silver inscribed and honed in holy water would kill one of their own.

Nephilim had designed those blades. Minions would simply use anything to cut into the Nephilim until nothing was left or rip them limb from limb. It could be a bloody mess if caught unprepared, but she rarely missed. This time would prove no different.

Her blade made contact with the minion's chest, sinking through the soft flesh and bone with a quickness that required little effort.

The minion's transparent eyes widened. "Shit."

"Sorry. You picked the wrong side, buddy," she whispered, pulling out the blade. By the time the blades retracted into the cuffs, the minion trembled once, and then his skin started to flake off. Her shoulders slumped as apathy filled her. The young Nephilim had a choice. Like humans, they all had free will, and this one chose to turn minion. Within seconds, not much more than a fine layer of dust remained.

She glanced up and found her new targets. "Really?" she yelled, throwing up her arms. "You couldn't keep him quiet for a few more seconds?"

Luke had the decency to cringe. "Sorry. He's stronger than he looks."

Disgusted with them, she shook her head. With a running start, she launched herself onto the balcony, landing on the railing in front of Michael.

His face paled. "Christ."

She rolled her eyes and dropped in front of him. "That's what we needed to show you."

Michael was rubbing a spot over his heart as if it bothered him.

"You okay, man?" asked Remy.

Luke snorted. "I think he's officially checked out."

She smacked Luke on his arm. "Michael, are you here with us?"

He still didn't answer. Hoping the fresh air would

rouse him, they led him back through the abandoned school and into the night.

Once outside, Michael bent over and rested his hands on his knees, gulping the air as if he was starving for oxygen. Luke scowled before drifting off toward the front of the building, but Remy and Lily remained by Michael's side, giving him as much time as he needed to come to grips with what he had just witnessed.

Lily tried to remember the first time she had seen a Nephilim who had gone bad. She'd been around ten, and Nathaniel and Luke had captured a lone female who had turned minion. In an attempt to somehow bring her back, they'd locked her in one of the cells at the Sanctuary. It was the first time she heard the horrific screams. She had been so frightened, and the sounds had been so horrible, that she had hurled. She'd spent the night latched onto Luke with a death grip, too afraid to sleep alone.

Perverted beyond saving, the minion eventually had to be put down. As terrified as Lily had been, it had been hard for her to understand that.

Michael slowly stood, scrubbing the back of his hand over his mouth. "What was that?"

"What they told you he was," she answered gently. "A minion."

He turned to her. "All that shit . . . is true?"

She smiled. "Every bit of it, and the part I told you about your father—especially that part."

His eyes bored into her as he spoke. "I don't . . .

know what to say. I've never believed in that stuff, but I know what I saw was real."

"As real as a minion-horde attack," she quipped.

"Fuck," he said.

Remy stepped forward, clapping the man on the shoulder. "How about we call it a night?"

He agreed weakly, and the bewilderment settled back on his face. "I want to go home."

She turned to Remy wearily, and he nodded. Michael needed to go back to the Sanctuary where he would be safe. Now a minion plus a possessed human had spotted him. He had to already be the topic of discussion among the Fallen.

Remy whispered something to him she couldn't hear. She trusted Remy with Michael. Of all of them, he was the most understanding and the least impatient. That brought her back to Luke and the conversation she needed to have with him.

She took one last look at the young cop and felt an odd stirring inside of her. Was it sympathy? Possibly even understanding? Pity? Pity got people killed. She pushed whatever it was back down, leaving to find Luke.

He was outside by the gate. She watched him quietly for a moment. His usually expressive lips formed a hard line. He ran a hand through his short, brown waves, cursing softly. Luke had changed since Anna's death. Became harder and colder. She never really knew what their relationship had been, but she assumed it was more than a friendship. It made her death so much harder for him.

She stepped to his side, tapping his arm. "Hey."

He glanced down at her, a wry smile forming on his face. "How is our newest recruit?"

Shrugging, she stared across the empty street. "He's doing as expected."

"Great," he muttered.

She turned back to him. "I don't like this, either. I think it's foolish to try to train him now, but what can we do? They'll get him one way or another if we don't."

He frowned but didn't say anything.

She reached out, lightly wrapping her hand around his. "An order is an order. This is what Nathaniel wants. At least if he's trained, he can protect himself."

"I don't give a shit what Nathaniel wants."

She sighed. "Then care about what I want. I can't do this alone. You know I'm terrible with the newbie Nephilim. I end up breaking them, and I need your help with this. Please, Luke. Be nice for me."

He stared down at their intertwined hands. With a sigh that said he knew she was wrapping him around her little pinkie, he consented. "All right . . . I'll try."

Finally, something was going right today.

"But if he talks smack to me again, I can't promise anything."

"Okay. That's a deal," she agreed. Deciding to test out his new attitude, she asked for her first favor. "Can you make sure Remy gets him back to the Sanctuary? I'm beat." She started to pull away, but Luke tightened his grip on her hand.

"Why don't you stay at the Sanctuary?"

She rolled her shoulders. "I want to go to my place."

"Nathaniel doesn't like that you stay there," he countered. "He doesn't even like the idea of you having your own place."

But it was her place, her little piece of the world, and she didn't have to share it with anyone. It was she who remodeled the studio apartment, carving it into something uniquely hers. The small garden on the balcony she painstakingly worked on whenever she had time was her personal treasure. It was where she went to be at peace, and where she escaped to when she needed to be normal.

There she could blend in. Leave her apartment through the door, walk down the stairs and out into the ordinary world where angels just existed in the bible and on paintings. Outside her place, there were movie theaters, restaurants, and cafés. The busy hustle warmed her in a way the Sanctuary never could.

She wouldn't give it up for anything. Not for Luke, not for Nathaniel.

"I thought you didn't give a shit what Nathaniel wants," she reminded him.

His lips curved into a genuine smile. "When it comes to you I do."

And Anna, but she wasn't ignorant enough to mention that. "Luke, I'm not going to cave."

Jaw tensing, he let her hand slip free. "Be careful."

She stood on the tips of her toes, and he leaned down. She placed a chaste kiss on his cheek and murmured, "As always."

"I mean it."

"You know you're my favorite. Right?"

He blew out a breath. "Whatever. Go."

Grinning, she pivoted and took off. A lot of the Nephilim preferred more normal modes of traveling, like taking the subway, but she favored the more solitary route to get to where she was going, which was not home like Luke expected. Instead, she went in the opposite direction. Hunting the minion and her subsequent kill had her blood all fired up. And okay, the run-in with Julian also had her wound up. She was antsy. There was no way she'd be going home like the good little Nephilim Nathaniel and Luke expected of her.

She darted between two apartment buildings. Making sure no one was watching, she crouched and pushed off the ground. She made it onto the fire escape on the seventh floor. From there, she easily jumped to the other building. Hopscotching across the old steel staircases, she reached the roof quickly.

Leaping from one shadowed rooftop to the next, she exhaled deeply. She loved the rush of air, the uncertainty of the fall, and the way the night reached down to her. As close to flying as possible, she was at her best. This is what a full-blooded angel must feel— weightless and free.

Here, Lily didn't think about Anna. In the air, she didn't worry about Nathaniel or Luke. As she flew over the buildings, she didn't think of Michael and how hard it would be for him. It was just her.

Hopping rooftops like the people on the ground hopped trains, it took her fifteen minutes to scamper down the fire escape next to the club frequented by humans and Nephilim alike. Straightening her skirt, she rounded the squat, two-story brick building and gave the bouncer at Deuces Wild a saucy grin.

Bruno—probably not his real name—parted the rope, letting her dip past the very pissed-off patrons waiting in line.

The heavy beat of techno music infiltrated her blood immediately, adding to the agitation pooling inside her. People converged before an S-shaped stage, dancing together in something that loosely resembled a fully clothed orgy. On the stage, scantily clad club girls danced, though the ones dancing in the cages hanging from the vaulted ceilings fascinated her the most. How did those girls dance like that in six-inch platform heels?

Heading straight to the bar, she grabbed the first empty seat. Sammy, the bartender, came to her spot. Even in the dim lighting he recognized her immediately. She really needed to get a life. Or a hobby.

"The usual?" he asked, flipping a white towel over his shoulder with a heavily tattooed hand. Hell, every exposed piece of flesh—including his face—was tattooed.

"Yep. Rough night." She propped her elbows on the bar as Sammy gave her a dubious grin, which looked funny considering there was a dragon on his cheek.

"Can't be that bad, hon."

"It's always that bad." It was the same conversation they exchanged whenever she came here. Sammy never asked what made her nights so bad. He probably thought she was a prostitute, for all she knew. Funny, but she doubted the truth would faze him.

She people-watched until Sammy returned. Mostly college-age kids filled the club, getting wasted, hoping to get screwed in one form or another. So was she . . . in a way. As her gaze flitted over them, she wondered how many would actually make it home tonight. And how many she'd be facing in the near future, shoving a blade into their chest. Shit. Now she was depressing herself.

"Here you go," Sammy announced.

She whirled in her seat, clasping her hands together. "You're the best, you know that?"

He slid the single-serving carton of Ben & Jerry's and the Diet Coke toward her. Pitfall of being a Nephilim: no amount of alcohol in this world could get her drunk. A plant, when cooked and stewed correctly, could do the trick, but it was highly addictive. Nathaniel would have her ass if he caught her with Angel's Triumphant . . . again.

Sammy ran a hand over his bald head as his gaze slid behind her. "One of your boys just arrived. Try not to destroy the laundry room this time."

A fierce flush crossed her cheeks as she pried open the lid and dug in, waiting for the familiar sensation of another Nephilim to trickle down her spine. One of her boys really meant one person. Gabe. And they hadn't destroyed the laundry room last time. Not really.

The chunky-chocolate goodness was almost gone by

the time Gabe decided to acknowledge her, which was fine. If she was here, and he was here, it only meant one thing.

Gabe stopped behind the occupied bar chair beside her. It took one glower from him, and the drunk dude nearly fell out of the seat. Gabe slid into it, completely unrepentant, his full lips curving into a wicked, knowing smile. He was a twin, hot damn. Tall and with a crop of curly brown hair, muscular, and wildly mischievous, he was way more laid back than his silent and moody brother, Damon. He was also one of the few trusted to be in the circle, along with his brother.

"Hey," she said, dropping her spoon into the empty carton. She faced him, letting her knee push into his. "What's up?"

"Nothing." He leaned in, his knee slowly pushing her legs apart until his leather-clad thigh pressed against her bare one. "I expected you'd be here after the night you had."

She sighed. It figured all the Nephilim would know about her and the cop. It was like there was some kind of secret-squirrel message board she was unaware of. "If I'd known what he was, I wouldn't have knocked him out."

"Yes, you would've." He grinned. "I ran into Remy. He said you guys showed him the . . . nightlife. Heard it wasn't pretty."

"He freaked." She sipped her Coke, loving the way it fizzed on her tongue. "But what can you expect? The

70

guy had no clue what he was. He's going to be prime pickings."

"Can't believe Nate's going to try to train him." His large hand dropped to her knee, and his thumb slipped where the skin creased, smoothing back and forth idly. "It's going to be a waste of time."

"A waste of my time," she corrected. "I have to train him."

She got the momentary satisfaction of seeing his normally bored expression fade to surprise. "You're shitting me," he said.

"Afraid not."

"You're so going to break him." He laughed.

"Or kill him accidentally, but we'll see." She placed her hand over his, sliding his hand up her thigh. Taking one last sip of her Coke, she stood, threading her fingers through his calloused ones.

Gabe bent his head to her ear, voice low and already thick. "Going fast tonight?"

Her insides tightened, and liquid heat replaced some of the agitation. She leaned into him, pressing her body against his. "You have a problem with that?"

"It's the last thing in this world I'd have a problem with, love."

"Good." Turning, she led him around the bar. Sammy rolled his eyes and went back to cleaning glasses.

They didn't talk as Lily led him toward the back of the bar and through the door clearly marked Employees Only. But when she stopped to let her eyes adjust to the darkness of the narrow corridor, she felt him against her back, rigid and thick. Nope. Gabe sure didn't mind going fast.

Finding the laundry room took very little time. Getting down to business once the door shut behind them was even quicker. A second after she pulled on the metal string dangling in the middle of the room, throwing the room into complete darkness, his arms came around her waist, lifting her up onto the tips of her boots.

His hands then traveled northward, cresting over her breasts, finding the nipples covered by cloth and satin. She arched against his hands, biting back a moan as his thumbs slid under her tank top and teased the satin-covered peaks. She never made a sound. Never.

Gabe growled low in his throat, grinding his pelvis against her. The rush of heat flooding her core had her rocking back against him. One hand left her breast, slipping down the curve of her stomach and flare of her hip. His hand slid under her skirt, skimming over her thighs. When his fingers brushed her already damp panties, he growled again.

Just like Julian had predicted on the rooftop, the fragile barrier of clothing remained. Gabe palmed her covered sex, rubbing his thumb over her clit until she squirmed against his hand.

Desperation rose in her so sharply she almost cried out. The desire—the need to lose herself in nothing but sensation, even for just a few moments—took over.

Then, without any warning, the image of Julian flashed behind her closed lids. What the hell? She didn't want him in her head while she was doing this. She focused on Gabe's handsome face, and when that failed, she pictured other men. But once her mind provided the image of Julian, the forbidden fantasy took root.

It was him moving behind her, holding her in his strong arms, his fingers teasing her mercilessly. Heart racing, she gripped Gabe's arms as the intense pressure began to build in her core.

Gabe pulled back, turning her and grasping her hips. He lifted her onto the edge of the washer, parting her thighs with his hands and legs. They were positioned like two lovers would be, fully ready to take part in each other's flesh. But there were rules, boundaries between them that would never be crossed. No kissing. No penetration of any kind. Gabe never pushed it, never talked about it. And he never complained when it was done. Or talked about what they did. She knew he believed Luke would chop off his balls if he even suspected him of messing with her. So their private shenanigans worked for them.

After all this time—and damn Julian for somehow figuring it out—she was still a virgin. Barely. As messed up as it sounded, it was the only thing that was truly hers. The only thing she could give someone that didn't belong to the Sanctuary and wasn't controlled by her Contract.

She kept her eyes closed, her treacherous mind holding the image of Julian in front of her. No matter how many times she pushed him from her thoughts, he came right back with a vengeance. Damn him.

But oh—oh, my—the fantasy was driving her to new heights. Her skin was on fire as she reached down, unzipped his fly, and pulled him out. His free hand slammed into the washer, denting it as she wrapped her hand around his cock.

Sammy was going to be pissed.

"Damn," Gabe groaned, thrusting into her palm as she worked him ruthlessly. "Really bad night, huh?"

"You have no idea." She buried her head in his neck as she scooted closer, bringing their bodies so close he had to shift to keep his hand between her legs.

She wrapped a leg around his hips as the tension built deep inside her. The tip of his cock nestled just below his hand. Their bodies rocked together, but still apart. His cock was swelling in her hand, and she knew he probably wanted to bury himself deep inside her—but he wouldn't. And then the tension was spiraling, breaking apart and shattering. She threw her head back, biting down on her lips until she tasted blood. Bliss washed over her. In those moments, as lightning zinged through her veins, she was free of the chains she wore. Her brain clicked off. It was just her body and the delicious feeling of her inner muscles spasming.

Gabe's hoarse shout came, and he jerked back a little, spilling warm liquid over her thigh. His cock jumped in her hand as his body spasmed. They stayed like that for a few moments, breathing heavily and riding out the weak aftershocks. Then he groped blindly for the pile of clean white towels, cleaned her up, and then himself.

When he was done, he pressed his lips to the spot just below her ear. "Have more bad nights, love."

All of her clever responses dried up and vanished. He was gone before she opened her eyes. Normally that wouldn't have bothered her. They were two consenting adults, and they hadn't even had sex. But as she sat on the edge of the washer and the pounding in her heart slowed, she felt a yearning for . . . something more than this.

This was what she was outside of the Sanctuary, driven to impersonal hookups in a dark—she sniffed daintily—funny-smelling laundry room with co-workers. Sure, there was fondness between them, but this wasn't about love or even lust.

It was just two people working off stress and getting off.

Loneliness, the kind she'd never been familiar with, settled in her chest. *This is my life*, she realized dumbly. This was what she sacrificed for a higher calling. Hell, maybe she should've read the fine print in her Contract.

CHAPTER SEVEN

Nathaniel glanced up from the enormous Book of Names. It was far too early for him to be up, and even more so for Luke. But it seemed like Luke was sleeping as little as he was. He slipped his hand over the Book, closing it.

The Book of Names was exactly what it sounded like. It contained all the names of those fostered by the Fallen from creation to today. When a Nephilim was created, the name and location would appear. A mark would emerge by their name once their mother passed. It was then when they went for the child. Never would he take a youngling from the arms of their mother. Not even Nathaniel knew how the Book worked or who was behind the knowledge. He was simply the reader, and only a trusted few were sent to retrieve the children. He hoped one day he could entrust Luke with such a duty.

"Where's Lily?" Nathaniel asked.

Luke pushed away from the door. "At her place."

Nathaniel's eyes closed briefly. The girl would be the death of him. From the moment he'd brought the screaming child home, she had hooked herself around his heart.

"I tried to get her to stay at the Sanctuary, but you know how she is."

Nathaniel stood, fishing a golden key from his pocket. He approached the large cabinet, unlocking the lower half. "Is that one still following her?"

"Yes." Luke's hands balled into fists. "I don't know what he's about. He's fast, so questioning him is nearly impossible."

He placed the timeless Book in its place. The key went back into his pocket. He faced Luke. "Don't go after him."

Luke scowled. "So we should let him do what he wants with Lily? Is that what you are suggesting?"

"Lily is not Anna. You know that."

Luke went still. His eyes turned glacial. There was a full minute before he spoke. "Don't speak to me about Anna."

His eyes locked with the younger Nephilim. A wealth of regret swelled in him. "Luke, I—"

"I don't like where any of this is heading with Lily," he cut him off. "This is how it started with Anna."

"I don't like his obsession with her any more than you do," he responded quietly. "But Julian has never attempted to hurt her."

"You've got to be kidding me," Luke spat out. "That's what the Fallen did to Anna. He followed her, protected her, and gained her trust, only to spin that trust back on her. You can't trust him!"

Nathaniel's brows rose. "Do you think that I do? I

trust Lily. That is what matters. She would never be so foolish to entertain anything with him."

What had happened to Anna hung between the two and had created a gulf that would always remain. Nathaniel knew Luke blamed him for allowing Anna to have too much freedom. Just like Lily. But there were things he could never share about Julian. That fallen angel was the least of his worries at the moment.

Nathaniel went back to his desk. The distant laughter of children and the stern teacher hushing their excitement brought a faint smile to his face. "I am sure you're not here about Lily."

Luke nodded stiffly. "Micah spotted Asmodeus last night. He was with a senator's aide."

"Jesus." Nathaniel rubbed the bridge of his nose. Asmodeus was one of the first angels to fall, and by far one of the most dangerous. If there was a hierarchy among the Fallen, then Asmodeus would serve beside Lucifer. Growing concerned of what was unfolding, he prodded Luke to continue.

"The aide works for the senator who's been in the papers over screwing a secretary or something. This morning, the story broke that the secretary had been lying, trying to get money out of the senator, and admitted to falsely accusing him. How convenient, huh?"

"Great." He was starting to get a headache just thinking about what kind of deal had been made to make it go away that quickly. "So, I'm assuming Asmodeus must've had a hand in that."

"Exactly, but why would Asmodeus be making

deals? You'd think that's below him, but he must want something if he's the one whispering in the senator's ear."

Unease shifted through Nathaniel's gut. The Fallen congregated in and around the nation's capital for obvious reasons. There were so many power players in DC to sink their claws into, and the Sanctuary typically ran interference, guarding politicians as best they could. But they couldn't be everywhere. Some slipped through their fingers and ended up in the Fallen's hands. It was a constant battle.

But for Asmodeus to be personally involved? "Something's not adding up here. Who'd you say spotted him?"

"Micah. He's been keeping an eye on the senator and his aide," Luke advised.

He stroked his chin absently. "Make sure Micah is careful. He's not to approach Asmodeus for any reason."

"I would like to handle this." Luke stepped forward, shoulders stiffening. "Micah is far too young to be handling something as serious as Asmodeus. With your . . . permission I would like to take over detail on Asmodeus."

Luke had a point, Nathaniel admitted. Micah was far too young to handle the oldest of the Fallen. "Yes, that will be fine."

With a curt nod, Luke headed toward the door but stopped. A muscle popped along his jaw. "You know, if Asmodeus is here, that also means Baal is back."

As if Nathaniel didn't already know that. His hand curled around the edge of the desk. The wood creaked. "Make sure Lily goes nowhere near him."

"I don't think she'd be that stupid again." Luke ran a hand through his hair. "You don't think he'd go after her?"

Something akin to fear clenched his heart, bringing him back to the night he'd truly believed he had lost Lily. "Have Micah keep an eye on her, but don't go into detail about why. You know how she is when it comes to Baal. That may lessen the blow of removing him from Asmodeus."

Relief washed over Luke's face before he left this time. Nathaniel remained in front of his desk, lost in thought. The reappearance of Asmodeus didn't bode well, especially with his recent suspicions that one of his own was betraying the Sanctuary. He could only hope it didn't involve Asmodeus.

Cory stared listlessly at the beige walls of his study. His wife had stressed for weeks on the color scheme before finally settling on the earthy tone. All the paint chips he had been forced to stare at had driven him crazy. They all had looked the same to him, and only to stave off a fight with his wife, he had picked one blindly. Cory ended up hating the color. Now it seemed pointless.

The file lay open on his desk. A picture of a male in his late twenties was clipped to a basic information sheet: name, date of birth, and occupation. Like

Asmodeus hadn't already known that information. It had been the address Asmodeus needed. The fucking angel had been blocked from finding the guy's location for whatever screwed-up celestial reason.

He'd done this to find out where a fucking cop lived.

Cory wiped a hand over his sweaty brow as he stared down at the small pistol he kept in his desk in case there were intruders.

He choked on his dry laughter. He may have fooled his wife, but he would've never had the courage to shoot someone. The idea of taking someone's life had once sickened him.

Letting out a broken sob, he palmed the small gun. Religion had never appealed to him before, but after what he had done . . . what he had agreed to . . . All so he could keep a job he hated, a power he didn't really have, and a wife twenty years younger than him.

"I've fucked up," he whispered to the empty room.

Cory had, and he knew it. He had done as the thing had asked. Then this . . . urge filled him, riding him hard. He couldn't shake it nor could he push the endless chant from his thoughts. *Do it. End it. End it all. Do it.* From the moment he left that thing in his limo it had begun. There were no other options, no other end result.

He had given up his soul for what?

Numbness came over Cory; a sense of resignation filled his heart and mind. He gazed down at the gun in his trembling hands and then at the picture of his wife and their young daughter. Without looking away, he put the gun to his temple and pulled the trigger.

Michael shifted the bag of groceries to his other arm as he stepped off the elevator. He barely remembered getting up, showering, and heading out to the corner store. A surreal haze had settled over him last night, and it hadn't lifted.

It was just a messed-up dream—all of it.

Yeah, he'd keep telling himself that until he believed it. Because whenever he closed his eyes, he saw the boy's face distorting and heard that horrible scream.

He still had no clue what he was going to do. Over an hour ago, he was supposed to meet the asshole named Luke at the Sanctuary. It wasn't like he'd been given an option. Just told to show up. Screw that.

Heading down the hall toward his apartment, he fished out his keys. A sudden tingling at the base of his spine drew him to the alert. His gaze fell to the door. The shiver increased, and all the hairs on his body rose. Drawing his off-duty gun, he nudged the door.

It inched open.

Shit. Releasing the safety, he drew in a deep breath and entered.

What he saw was like a punch in the gut and winning the lottery rolled into one. There was a beautiful woman in his apartment. Score. That beautiful woman wasn't human. Fail.

Sitting on his counter, as if she belonged there, Lily unfurled one leather-encased leg. A brief smile appeared, and then she was off the counter and in front of him before he could blink. Before the second blink, she had him disarmed.

Jesus H. Christ, this woman was a pain in his ass.

"They didn't teach you that at the academy, did they?" she taunted, turning the barrel of the gun on him.

He held onto his bag of groceries even though he wanted to throttle her. He had never been disarmed before, and his heart raced at the fact that she now pointed his gun straight at his forehead. He gritted his teeth. "What are you doing in here?"

She cocked her head to the side, smiling sweetly. "We had a date tonight, didn't we? At around eight? That was an hour and a half ago. I don't like to wait."

He ignored that. "How did you get in?"

"I picked your lock."

"That's breaking and entering."

She smirked. "I don't care."

"I could have you arrested in a second," he threatened in a low voice.

Her lips twitched again. "I'd like to see you try."

He stared at her silently. From the way her green eyes blazed and the fact that her arm did not waver, he knew she was not bluffing. "I don't like a gun pointed in my face."

"Neither do I, and you keep pointing it at me." Her gaze dropped to the bag he was holding. Glancing down, he removed a loaf of bakery bread, spaghetti noodles, and sauce. Then she flipped the gun, offering it to him handle first. "We've gotten off on a bad start, haven't we?"

He looked at her warily. Wearing a tank top and tight leather pants that hugged her legs and ass, she appeared every bit the badass he knew she could be. Funny, she was the kind of girl that usually had him going wild. But all he felt was . . . reluctant amusement.

He took the gun from her, sliding it back into the concealed holster. "You didn't have to come here."

She watched him continue to unload the bag. "You didn't come to us. We had no other choice."

"There's always a choice," he said.

"The problem with that ideology is that you're thinking on the human level of things." She paused, pursing her full lips. "You accept what I am, but you don't accept what you are."

"I'm nothing like you."

Sighing, she placed her elbows on the counter. "You know, your story is no different than any of ours."

He set the jar of sauce in front of her hands and studied her closely. The mass of hair had parted, falling forward and baring her shoulders to him. Inked in deep black, two wings sprouted from the base of her spine. From what he could see of the intricate tattoo, each wing spread to the edge of her shoulder and then swept downward to disappear under the band of her top.

A sudden urge to reach out and run his fingers over the fine lines etched into her skin was almost too hard to ignore. He clenched his fists, then picked up the spaghetti. "I doubt our stories are the same."

She supported her chin with her folded hands. "Let me take a guess. Your mother committed suicide. You've never met your father. Blah . . . blah . . . blah."

He froze, feeling the skin between his brows puckering. "Don't go there."

"Listen, Michael. We've all been there. My mother and Luke's mother?" she said softly. "All of our mothers died by their own hand, and none of us have ever had the misfortune of meeting our fathers."

He slammed the container of spaghetti down. The edges of the box split, spewing uncooked noodles across the counter. "My family is not something I will ever discuss with you."

She leaned back, staring at the noodles. "I know this is hard for you. I know every rational bone in your body is telling me to screw off, but there has to be some part in you that knows what you are. You sensed I was in here, didn't you? You knew."

"Not a single part of me believes I'm a damn half-breed whatever! Okay?" He swiped the noodles off the counter, and they bounced off the tile. "I'm never going to believe that."

"You just don't want to believe it, but you know it's true. Do you want to know why your mother killed herself? It's the same reason for all of our mothers! Loving an angel—a Fallen angel—drives you insane. It may only take days, or it may take years, but the end is always the same!"

He came around the counter, hands balled into fists. "Get the hell out of my apartment!"

She didn't move. "Michael, you have to listen to me!"

He stepped up to her. Damn, he was a good foot taller and probably had a hundred pounds on her, but the little thing held her ground. She had balls. He'd give her that. "Get out—" He stopped, going cold for no reason, feeling off-balance. It was the way he had felt before opening the door to his apartment, but worse. Worse than when he saw that boy and heard him scream.

"Shit." Lily's eyes narrowed into thin slits as she reached into her back pocket, yanking out her cell. "Luke? Where are you? I have at least three minions and, I don't know, two or three deadheads. Yeah, gotcha." She snapped the phone shut, brushing past him. "Do the stairs in the hallway lead to the rooftop?"

He had already drawn his gun. "Yes. Why?"

Lily glanced at the gun. "I hope that has the kind of caliber that leaves a big hole."

His insides tightened, and he swallowed. There was . . . something coming. Goddamn it all, he could feel it. The sensation slithered through him, leaving behind tendrils of dread. But the gun was a reassuring weight in his hand. "Why?"

"Because that gun isn't going to do shit for what's coming. We need to get out of here and now."

CHAPTER EIGHT

Color Lily surprised when Michael didn't question her. She could feel him at her back when she went to the door. "Damn it. They've found you out, buddy." She glanced over her shoulder at him. "I warned you. So did Remy and Luke. But we didn't think it would happen so soon, because they hadn't found you before."

"If they are after anyone, it's you," he said. "You brought this bad shit on me."

"Ha!" She grasped the doorknob. "I thought cops had to be smart. You, my dear, are as dumb as a deadhead."

He tried pushing past her, but she blocked him easily. "Let me check the hallway."

"Really?" she drawled slowly. "You want to try that one out and see what happens? Get back. Watch and learn, Mikey."

Sparks practically flared from his eyes. "Don't call me that."

Flipping him off, she yanked open the door. On the other side of the threshold stood a minion dressed in a business suit. He would have looked rather normal if it wasn't for the dead eyes and twisted mouth.

Michael raised his gun, but she was faster. The

daggers came out of her silver cuffs as she shoved one deep into the minion's chest. He jerked back before he fell to the floor. He didn't even get a chance to make a sound. That's how she liked them, silent and dead.

"One down," she counted airily, "two to go!" She stepped over the already dissolving body. "Maybe I underestimated the deadhead count. There's more than three."

Michael came up beside her. "I'm getting this weird feeling you may be enjoying this."

Shrugging, she edged around the hallway. "What can I say? It's the little things."

His eyes rolled. "How many do you think there are?"

"Maybe five." The light in the hallway flickered and then went out. She bit back a bored sigh. They always had to be dramatic, flaunting their evil bag of parlor tricks as if it would actually scare her.

"What the hell?" he muttered behind her.

"Don't pay attention to that. Stairwell anywhere nearby?"

He gestured across from her. "Why not go downstairs?"

"You would think that." She sighed. "All right, Mikey Mike, things are about to get a tad bit messy."

"What?" He stopped behind her.

"Whatever you do"—she reached the stairwell—"please do not shoot me accidentally."

He snorted. "I have better aim than that, thank you very much."

"I hope so." She opened the door and stepped into

the stairway. Thankfully, the lights were still on there. Although she could see fine in the dark, she wasn't sure where Michael was with that, and she didn't want him fumbling with the gun in the dark.

They weren't in the stairwell for five seconds before the door busted open a floor below. She glanced down. "How many floors is this?"

"Ten."

"And we are on what floor?"

"Five," he responded a little impatiently.

Damn it, she hated running up stairs. "Mikey, get behind me." When he gave her a me-man-you-woman expression, she physically pushed him up a step. It was just in time, because what sounded like a herd of elephants rounded the level below them. She leaned over, peering down.

Goody gumdrops, we're about to have a party.

Two possessed humans—deadheads—sprang around the corner, clamoring over one another. The younger one looked about twenty-five and was drooling. She grimaced. The other was fresh and frighteningly fast. Behind them was a minion calling the shots, and she knew there were at least two more deadheads and another minion somewhere.

A voice rang out, echoing through the brick stairwell. "Kill the female. Do not kill the male."

Lily tipped her head back at the startled man behind her. "And I'm the one bringing you the bad shit?"

His eyes were wide in disbelief.

"Shoot them in the head. It will slow them down."

She turned back to the deadheads. "Don't worry about their bodies. I'll take care of them before anyone has a chance to call the police."

The fresh one crested the landing, wearing gym shorts and Nike shoes. Apparently they had gotten her on an evening run. An iPod was still hooked to her arm, creating the illusion she was still human. It was all rather disturbing. Once she got a sight of Lily, she laughed hysterically. "Kill the female," she sang. "Kill the female."

Lily arched a brow at her. That one definitely did not have a singing career in her future. Or breathing. She leaned back just as a gun went off in her ear. She flinched as the bullet zinged past her face, smacking into the woman's chest. Sweet baby Jesus! She patted her cheek to make sure he didn't graze her.

The runner glanced down at her top. There was a hole in her shirt a few inches off from her heart. "Kill the female."

"The head, Michael!" she yelled. "I said the head!"

He gaped. "Holy shit."

Exactly. She leaned back, planting her foot right in the face of the woman. The deadhead stumbled backward, crashing into the slower one. A middle-aged man who had the appearance of a professor lifted his head, roaring a string of guttural words.

"Get up the steps, Michael." She went down a step, kicking the runner again. This time the deadhead fell back against the wall with an enraged scream. "And don't shoot again, okay? Just put the damn gun away!"

With that, she hopped down next to the professor and slammed the dagger into his chest. He toppled over the railing and, as he fell, his skin began to flake off.

The woman struggled to her feet, and Lily whirled to face her. Instead of listening, Michael was now on the landing beside her.

Apparently, he'd decided bullets weren't effective. He pistol-whipped the deadhead. Her head snapped to the side with a sickening crunch. Even with her neck broken, she managed to turn back to Michael and laugh.

"Screw this," he whispered as he fired the gun at point-blank range in her forehead. She fell backward and slid to the floor, twitching and screeching.

Lily sidestepped the runner's flailing legs, bringing the dagger down. Such a shame. The girl had been pretty.

"Stab them in the chest with this type of silver etched with holy symbols and they are done for. Anyplace else is just going to hurt like crazy and piss them off," she informed him coolly. "Those bullets are pretty damn useless."

Michael stared at her. "Are you trying to teach me?"

She pushed him up the steps. "Get."

"Nephilim," called the minion from the landing below, "wanna play?"

Taking a deep breath, Lily turned and smiled. Like the one from the previous night, this minion was young, but the similarities ended there. Instead of black hair, his hair was dyed ice blond, and he didn't bare any of the gothic trappings. He looked rather preppy in his pressed polo and designer jeans, smiling up at her.

She positioned herself in front of Michael, hoping he didn't bum-rush past her like an idiot. "William, how have you been? Grow back that finger?"

The grin slipped from the minion's face. "Why don't you come down here and find out?"

She pretended to consider his request. Most minions were all fight and no brains, but William retained his cognitive thinking skills, and he had a couple of scores to settle with her. One of them involved the four-fingered left hand.

Edging Michael back, she sensed another was coming up behind William. Stuck in a cramped landing wasn't the ideal place to take care of business. "So who's holding your leash, Willy?"

"You'll find out soon enough."

Not convinced, she rolled her eyes. It was more likely for her to kiss William's rosy butt cheek before one of the Fallen actually involved themselves in a fight. Her gaze darted toward the newest arrival. Practically a carbon copy of William, the other minion stepped in front of him. Ah, the pawn. Before her were the brains and then the brawn. The pawn rushed the steps.

Behind her, Michael shifted and raised his gun. Distracted, she called out a warning to him. "Don't do that!"

She realized a second too late that he didn't know any better. Trained to fire a gun when his life was threatened, it had to be hard for him to overcome the logic behind it. He squeezed off a round and bull's-eye! The bullet struck the one on the steps right between the eyes.

She cringed inwardly, crouching. This wasn't going to be pretty.

And she was right.

The minion roared to life, charging the steps two at time.

She launched herself at him, managing to block his attempt to rush past her. They crashed into each other, slipping down a step or two in a tangle of leather and pressed khaki. When the minion reared back, she twisted out of his grasp. The light from the bulb above caught the glint of silver in his hand. It wasn't that he had a blade that jolted her into action. All of the minions had some sort of weapon. It was the intricate writing scrolled on the length of the blade that made her take notice. It was just like hers, which meant it could kill her.

Not having time to consider where they might have gotten their grubby hands on a Nephilim blade, she sank hers deep into the minion's flesh. His weight fell against her. "Ugh," she grunted.

Michael came down the steps two at time, plucking the minion off her. By the time he heaved the creature over the railing, the face had already begun to disintegrate.

She passed him a thankful smile. "Two down . . ."

Michael's lips twitched. "One more to go."

She snatched up the blade the minion had held and turned back to William. Three more deadheads surrounded him. And they were all brand spanking new to the world of possession. How many human lives were wasted tonight?

"Kill her," William ordered coldly.

All three lifted their heads, stares fixed on Lily. Normally, she would have happily gone after all three and William, but there was Michael. The deadheads were surely a decoy to get to him. They would keep her busy enough so William could go for him. Michael's aim had drastically improved, but William was strong and smart. She didn't believe Michael was ready for that.

"It's your lucky day," she announced. Not giving either one enough time to figure out what she was doing. She pivoted and grabbed Michael's hand. "Come on!" Pulling him behind her, she raced up the stairs.

"We're running?" He sounded shocked.

"I can't let them get you. That's Willy boy's plan." She rounded the eighth level. "They've got a hard on for you, boy."

"Why are they coming after me?"

She passed him a dubious look over her shoulder. "You seriously have to ask that—really?" She rounded another level with Michael on her heels. She let go of his hand, grabbing the railing. "You're an adult Nephilim who has no knowledge of what he is. They will either use you or kill you."

He shifted and was at her side. "It can't be true."

Irritated by him and the fact she was running up the

stairs, which had to be her own personal Hell, she fought the urge to backhand some sense into him. They rounded the last landing, and she reached for the door.

Sickness crept over her. The tremor that ran through her was different than the tingling the minions gave off. She faltered at the door to the rooftop. "Michael?"

"Yes?" He was right beside her, eyes narrowing as he studied her face. "What is it?"

She backed away from the door. *Where in the hell is Luke?* She needed to get Michael out of here. Now. There was no more time. On the other side of the door was death, and below them were William and his crew.

They had been trapped, and she had run right into it.

She cursed under her breath, looking around wildly. The only way out of this was going through William and his minions.

"What is it, Lily?" Michael asked as he kept his gun cocked and ready. He took a step closer to her. "Lily?"

She turned to him with wide eyes. "If I tell you to run, Michael, you run. Don't ask why, and . . . please listen to me."

"Bullshit." The tips of his cheekbones flushed. "I'm not leaving you."

She grabbed his free hand once again, dragging him back down the steps, hearing the sounds of a scuffle and William cursing. Then the unmistakable fleshy smack of a body hitting the ground and then another.

"Lily, you up?" Luke called out from four floors below.

Relieved, she opened her mouth to respond but was

cut off. Turning, she felt her heart drop as the door above them swung open. At once, she twisted and leaped in front of Michael, forcing him behind her. "Michael, please listen to me."

A cold laugh echoed around them, etching its way down her spine. She shuddered once. The smell of sulfur filled the cramped stairwell. Her step faltered a bit as she clenched the railing tightly.

She paled as he came into view, her heart sinking. Rage and fear swirled inside her, making her dizzy. His name came to her lips, blistering them. "Baal . . ."

CHAPTER NINE

There was a wild, instinctive part of Michael that realized whatever was coming down the stairs was far worse than what waited below.

Lily whirled around in front of him, her face washed of color and eyes wide. "Run!"

He wasn't used to taking orders from just anyone, but the fear in Lily's voice propelled him forward. He'd only known her for twenty-four hours, and during that time he'd seen her do things without so much as a grimace that would have made a seasoned officer cringe in horror. Now, she was scared—visibly so. Although he knew this, curiosity was far stronger than any ounce of common sense. As Lily dragged him down the stairs, he hesitated.

And looked over his shoulder.

A man dressed all in black stood above them. It wasn't the impeccable line of his designer suit or the trendy cut of his black hair that gave Michael pause. The man called Baal was absolutely stunning. Inherently, he knew this thing was an angel. No mere mortal could have such a perfect visage or eyes such a brilliant, unnatural blue.

His sudden lack of movement must've thrown Lily

off-balance because he felt her stumble over the next step. Whipping around, he saw her arms flail as she tried to catch herself. "Shit!" He reached for her, but it was too late.

Her fall was thankfully short-lived, but her temple cracked off the handrail. She slid down the cement wall, seemingly stunned.

"Lily!" he roared. He felt the stare on his back like hot coals. "Shit—Lily!"

Climbing to her feet, she swayed a little. "I'm . . . fine."

Baal laughed. "The great Lily taken down a step or two? I think I may have seen this before."

Michael wrapped his arm around her waist, holding her steady. "Come on."

She pressed the palm of her hand against her temple, wincing. "Go, Michael. What are you doing? Go now!"

"My little Lily pad," Baal murmured, slowly advancing down the stairs. His smile never reached his eyes. "How is that leg of yours?"

She lifted her head. "Doing just great."

"Really?" he asked. Baal slid one hand idly down the railing. The yellow paint cracked and bubbled under his touch. Tendrils of smoke wafted into the air. "I do believe I left my mark behind."

She swallowed as she lowered her hand and turned to Michael. "Don't let him touch you, whatever you do."

Holy shit. He couldn't stop staring at the paint.

Baal simpered. "Don't go and ruin all my surprises." His gaze slowly drifted over them.

Lily backed up, and Michael edged along with her. Her arm quivered against him, and he thought it was fear, but the firm set of her lips told him different. A heat wave of rage radiated from the tiny thing.

"You do realize if you run I will catch you," Baal sneered. "We did have so much fun before. I so loved hearing your screams."

Footsteps pounded up the stairwell. Luke's head came into view. "Sorry, I got hung up on . . . Oh shit."

Baal spared Luke a glance, his full lips twisting. "I bore of this already."

Suddenly, Lily shifted and pushed Michael toward Luke. A silent message passed between the two, and Luke grabbed his arm.

"Damn it all to Hell, Lily!" yelled Luke over his shoulder as he dragged Michael down. "Fall back! Fall back!"

"What the fuck?" Michael tried to pull from Luke's grasp. He wanted to get Lily between them. It wasn't right she was bringing up the rear with that . . . that thing behind them. "Get Lily out of here! Don't worry about me!"

She pushed on his back. "You're an idiot!"

Michael continued to protest, but the smell of sulfur increased, and his eyes burned. Gagging, he felt her push on his back harder. He stumbled but regained his footing. Then, over the pounding of his heart, he heard her gasp.

And then, she started screaming. The kind of screams he'd heard on calls involving shootings and stabbings. Whirling around, his heart stopped.

Lily was on her knees. The fallen angel—Baal—had her by the forearm. Sadistic pleasure washed over Baal's face. Burned flesh overcame the smell of sulfur.

Swearing vehemently, Luke pushed him out of the way. "Lily!"

"On your knees?" said Baal with a chuckle. "Once again, I find this all so terribly familiar. And a bit cliché."

He saw Lily lean forward and place one hand on the floor just before a flash of light went up through the stairwell, blinding him. A second later, the light cleared. The impact had sent Baal several feet up the stairs, and Lily had her forehead pressed to the floor, her arm cradled to her chest.

He started forward but came up short. Someone had already reached her side. It wasn't Luke.

It was a man with shoulder-length blond hair, tall as a mountain and built like a brick house. His features rivaled those of Baal in terms of the inhuman level of beauty, but they were obscured as he swooped down and picked up her crumpled form with surprising gentleness. He placed Lily on her feet and gave her a slight push. "Go. I will give you enough time to escape. Go." Then the stranger turned to Baal with a sardonic grin. "Old friend, we meet again."

Baal stumbled to his feet, his hands curling into fists. "This is getting repetitive, Julian. Have you forgotten what you are? Who you serve?"

The man laughed as he shot up the stairs, grasping Baal around the throat. "I serve no one."

The entire building shook as the two creatures slammed each other into the wall of the stairwell. Plaster and dust rained so heavily that it looked like snow.

Luke grabbed Lily's uninjured arm. "Let's get the hell out of here before they bring the building down on us."

Her head bobbed weakly, and she looked over her shoulder once more before Luke pulled her the rest of the way. Michael hated that as injured as she was, they were herding him to safety.

Once outside, they slowed as people began spilling out of the apartment building, concerned and curious. Police sirens could be heard in the distance.

A little boy latched onto his mom's hand and kept pointing upward. "Ma, look up. Ma!"

Michael followed the boy's chubby finger, spotting the Fallen called Julian and Baal on the rooftop before they disappeared back into the night sky. Damn, that would be hard to cover up.

They pushed through the throng of people. He kept a wary eye on Lily. She hadn't spoken since Baal had touched her. A fine sheen of sweat covered her drawn face, and her lips were pressed together tightly.

Luke guided them to where Remy waited across the street in a Cayenne. Michael climbed in the front seat without arguing, turning to where Luke had forced Lily into the backseat.

"Let me see your arm," Luke demanded.

She pulled away from him. "It's not . . . not that bad."

"Bullshit." He reached out, prying her arm from her body. He stared down at the blistered skin shaped like a handprint. Luke exhaled slowly. "Get us back to the Sanctuary. Now, Remy."

"What happened in there?" Remy asked as he pulled away before the squad of police cars and fire trucks arrived. "What the hell, guys?"

Michael ignored him. "Are you okay?"

"Does it look like she's okay?" demanded Luke, eyes burning.

"The next time I tell you to run"—a shudder racked her body—"please listen to me."

Michael stared at her face contorted with pain. His gaze dropped to her arm, and he swallowed thickly. Her skin literally bubbled. "I'm sorry. I was . . ." He was what? Transfixed? He'd never seen an angel before, but that wasn't a good excuse.

She shifted in the seat, her brow creasing. "Just listen to us. Okay? When we tell you to run, we aren't kidding around. There's a very good reason for it." She paused, prying one eye open. "What happened to William and his goons?"

Luke pulled his stare from her. "I killed him and the deadheads."

Her other eye snapped open. "Really?" she asked in a tiny voice. "No shit?"

He nodded.

Lily giggled halfheartedly. "Ah damn, that's good news. Wish I could've . . . seen the jerk's face when you pinned him. Good job, Luke."

Remy rolled his eyes. "Is anyone going to tell me what happened?"

"We will," Luke spoke up. "Just get us to the Sanctuary first."

Lily turned her face to Luke, who leaned over and whispered something Michael couldn't hear. She pulled away from the seat, scowling as Luke slid an arm around her back, carefully pulling her to him. He held her arm immobile, and eventually her eyes closed.

Part of him wanted to climb back in the seat and apologize again. It had been his fault she'd gotten hurt. If he hadn't stopped, they would've made it outside.

He faced forward, staring blindly at the crowded streets. She could've died in there, and for what? He rested the side of his head against the window, closing his eyes. Shit. He couldn't deny that those things had been after him. They'd even been willing to kill Lily to get to him. Acid burned through his stomach.

He was definitely one of them . . . or something.

As soon as they arrived at the Sanctuary, Lily was handed off to an extraordinarily tall man that Luke had called Nathaniel. He had met them in a large and surprisingly normal reception area. Michael sensed this Nathaniel seemed to be the leader around here. With one glimpse at her arm, he had sworn furiously and then disappeared with her down a corridor. He had wanted to follow them, but Luke steered him in the opposite direction.

Seated at a desk in the middle of the large oval room was a pretty blonde. She smiled as they made their way past her. Scrawled in large letters across the back wall and in what suspiciously looked like pure gold was the word Sanctuary.

Luke leaned over, tweaking the sleeve of the receptionist's blouse. "Working late, Sandy?"

She smiled. "It's always a late night around here."

They left her behind as they went through a set of double doors. Just inside, two armed guards were posted. All of this was new to him. When he left the night before, they had done so through an intricate tunnel system under the Sanctuary.

"Damn, you guys have more security than Fort Knox," he muttered.

Remy snorted. "There's a reason for that."

The guards tipped their heads at the men. The one on the left with a name tag that read Number 1 stepped forward, entering a code into the small computer interface. The steel doors shuddered before swinging open. They stepped into a room that held two elevators. He looked at Luke, who grinned.

"Want to get something to eat?" Luke offered.

He glanced back, but the doors had closed. "Sure."

Luke herded them into the elevator that Michael quickly realized led to the floors aboveground. They stopped on the second floor. Remy rubbed his stomach. "I hope the cafeteria is still open."

"There's a cafeteria in here?" Michael asked.

Remy nodded as he followed behind Luke. "The second floor has a fully operational kitchen and cafeteria." He gestured at a set of glass doors. "There's the gym, and if you go back down to the main level, you'll find a pool and a daycare center for the employees who have children. Upstairs is the security firm."

Michael's brows furrowed. "There really is a security firm?"

Luke chuckled as he nudged open the cafeteria doors. "Yes. Several of the floors are a dedicated call center. Above that are the cubicle farms that house analysts, and then our executive offices take up the top two floors. All human-operated and supervised by Nephilim."

"Do they know what you are?"

"Yes."

His eyes narrowed on Luke. "You can trust them with that?"

Remy glanced over his shoulder. "Yes. If they told anyone about us, no one would believe them anyway."

"And we'd kill them," Luke added nonchalantly.

He stumbled. "Are you serious?"

"No." Remy shot Luke a dirty look. "We wouldn't. We can't kill humans who aren't possessed—no matter what. The act alone would turn us minionic."

Good to know.

Luke stared down at several slices of pizza that had been warming in a tin container under a heat lamp. "And he means no matter what. We can't even kill them if they're trying to kill us." He picked up three slices and dropped them onto his plate. "Sucks ass if you ask me, but no one ever does."

Michael mulled that over as he picked up a white plate and dropped two slices on it. He wasn't letting himself think too much. He felt frayed at the edges.

"Is Lily going to be okay?" he asked.

Remy grabbed three sodas out of the cooler and brought them over to the table Luke had sat at. "I'd think so, but then again I have no clue what happened."

Luke swallowed a huge bite of pizza. "She'll be okay. Nathaniel will get her fixed up. We have some of the best doctors here. Those who are suited for the type of injuries we show up with."

He sat across from them. "What was that back there?"

Remy popped open his soda. "Yes. Do tell."

"Baal," said Luke with a mouth full of pizza.

Remy gave a low whistle. "Oh man."

"He talked as if he knew Lily," Michael said.

Luke stiffened. "When Lily was fresh, she made the mistake of going after Baal when she spotted him with a police commissioner he was corrupting. No—don't ask who. I'm not telling." He pushed away his plate, the last slice of pizza untouched. "You never take on a Fallen alone, and especially not Baal."

He really wanted to know who the commissioner was, but the closed expression on Luke's face said he wouldn't get an answer from him. "Why would she do that?"

Remy shrugged. "Because she's Lily, and believe it or not, what you see today is a toned-down version of what she used to be." He shook his head, sending dreads into his oval-shaped face. "She was really young when she went after Baal. At seventeen, our Nephilim are ready to fight. She learned the hard way."

"Seventeen?" He couldn't believe it. "You guys let kids go out and fight?"

"Our seventeen-year-old Nephilim can kick your ass clear across town." Luke fiddled with his soda. "Age has nothing to do with fighting the Fallen. She knew better, but . . . shit, she's Lily."

"How old is she now?"

Remy's lips curved. "Lily's twenty-six. She accepted the Contract at twenty-two."

Shit, that girl barely looked twenty-two. "Contract?" When neither man answered, he sighed. What knowledge they had shared about Lily's previous run-in with Baal was vague, and he was sure they were leaving out details for her sake. "The burn on her arm was from him touching her?"

"Eat something, and I'll tell you everything." When Michael complied, Luke leaned back in his seat and folded his arms over his chest. "Baal is one of the most evil bastards you will ever meet. He's been on Earth since the days of Adam and Eve. His touch, if he wills it, can burn anything."

Remy gestured at him with his pizza slice. "Rumor has it that when other angels began to fall, Baal burned and ripped the wings from their backs."

107

Michael had trouble swallowing the food. "What was he doing there?"

"Apparently he was bored," stated Luke. "Or he was coming after you. It's very odd. The Fallen don't make a habit of getting their hands dirty."

He, too, pushed away his plate. He had no real appetite. Not after everything that had happened. "Was the other one a . . . good angel?"

Remy slowly turned to Luke, his expression expectant. "And who would that be?"

"Julian," muttered Luke.

Remy dropped the slice he was holding. "No shit? You're serious?"

Luke's face puckered. "Would I joke about something like that?"

"So who is Julian? What's the big deal?" Michael asked. "He saved our ass back there."

"Julian is one of the Fallen," Luke said. "He fell hundreds of years ago, if not more. He isn't one of the good guys."

"That makes no sense. You had said the Fallen were evil. Then why would he help us?"

"He wasn't helping us." Luke wrapped his fingers around the empty can of soda. "Julian doesn't give two shits about us. He was helping Lily."

That didn't clear up anything for him.

Remy eyed Luke warily. "He's like the friendly neighborhood angelic stalker."

"What?" he spit out.

Remy leaned back and added, "Julian is complicated.

He's helped Lily out a couple of times. The last time Baal got his hands on her, Julian was the one who got her out."

Luke squashed the soda can and stared at Michael. "Julian cannot be trusted. Yes, his stalking habits come in handy from time to time, but you cannot trust him. If he got hold of any one of us, he wouldn't think twice about ending our lives."

Michael slid his half-full soda away from Luke. He wasn't hungry, but he was thirsty. "Does Lily trust him?"

Remy glanced away, but Luke exploded. "No! Lily is not that stupid."

Michael's eyes narrowed on Remy, who raised a brow, passing him a warning look not to continue with the Julian business. "You know you can't go back to your apartment," said Remy in a matter-of-fact way. "They know where you live."

He closed his eyes, rubbing his forehead. He could keep denying what was obvious, or he could face the truth. Neither option was going to be easy.

"When it's safe, we'll send a team to retrieve your personal belongings," continued Remy. "It is not safe for you to go there. It may never be."

His world shifted, the weight of it nearly oppressive. "You really believe I am . . . Nephilim? That my father was a fallen angel?"

Luke observed him. "Yes."

He leaned back, exhausted. "So my life is over now?" Wasn't like he had much of a life anyway. He'd only had his mother, but when she died, that was the last of his family. Though he wasn't close to anyone in particular, still, it had been his life.

Cocking his head to the side, Luke smiled. It was a real smile. The first Michael had ever seen on his face. "No. Your life begins now."

Baal stormed through his penthouse, laying waste to three minions that had stepped forward to service him. Their screams didn't assuage his anger. Nothing would. That bitch had gotten away from him again because of Julian. Baal wanted nothing more than to spread that little bitch's thighs and burn her from the inside out while Julian watched.

He threw open the French doors to his bedroom and paused.

A young boy stood by his bed, his hands folded neatly. In a tailor-made suit to fit a child of his size, he looked like he was attending Sunday mass. It amused Asmodeus to dress him so. Children possessed by a misled soul decayed at a slower rate. Sometimes it took years for it to happen. Asmodeus soon hoped to have more like the boy, but ones who would never show the signs of possession.

"Baal," the boy spoke with a soft accent, "I've brought you a present."

That he did. Sprawled across black satin was a young woman with deep brown hair and curvy legs that peeked out from the edge of her pencil skirt. Her white blouse had been ripped down the middle, and her ample breasts spilled through the cloth.

Asmodeus's little prodigy always knew how to please people. Baal approached the bed, staring down at the lovely thing. "Is she alive?"

"Of course," he answered. "Do you wish for anything else?"

"No."

The young boy bowed before quietly shutting the doors behind him. Baal turned back to the unconscious woman. He leaned over her, running his hand through her hair. She stirred, and a breathless whimper escaped her parted lips.

"Wake," he ordered softly. He watched as her lashes fluttered against her cheeks and then, much to his delight, striking green eyes met his. Ah, he would need to give special thanks to his boy. He had done well.

The young woman's eyes widened as she took in Baal. He knew what she saw. His beauty choked her terror, made her forget how she got there.

"What is your name?"

She wetted her lips. "Alicia."

Baal smiled fully. "Come to me, Alicia."

She climbed to her knees before him, flushed and eager. Her chest rose and fell rapidly. Baal reached out and ran the tips of his fingers along her face.

"Remove your blouse."

She complied with a small shudder. His gaze slipped to the rosy peaks. The tips hardened under his stare. Maybe this would soften his foul mood? He would try at least.

"Enjoying yourself?" Asmodeus asked.

111

He didn't look away from the woman at the sound of his voice. "I am about to."

"Why did you involve yourself this evening?"

Baal lowered his hand to one of the fleshy mounds and squeezed. The woman moaned a sound of pain mixed with pleasure. "I sensed William's intent to take the new Nephilim. I would have had him if it wasn't for Julian. The Nephilim would've been my gift to you."

Asmodeus stepped from the darkened corner of the room. "Julian is not the problem."

"I want to kill him," announced Baal as he idly flicked the young woman's nipple. He hardened at the sound of her soft cry.

"In time, but he is of no concern to me at this moment." Asmodeus stepped closer to the bed.

The woman glanced at him anxiously. Baal could easily read her feelings. She was shocked, turned on by the two beautiful men. He knew she considered bedding them both, and then she looked into Asmodeus's eyes. She shrank back, showing real fear for the first time.

Baal caught her by the chin, tipping her head up, forcing her back to arch. He relished the rapid beat of her pulse and the pungent smell of her uncertainty. "What do you want with the cop? I don't understand what is so important about him." He glanced at Asmodeus. "He's just another Nephilim."

Asmodeus drifted away, smirking. "He is very important to me. I don't expect you to understand."

"And the senator?" he asked.

"The aide served his purpose, but he is of no more

use. To anything." Asmodeus laughed, and the woman shuddered at the cold sound. "I will be meeting with the senator soon."

Baal's grip tightened on her chin; his skin flared. The woman shrieked, but he held on as the smell of burned flesh wafted through the air. "Be quiet, Alicia."

"I shall leave you to your . . . pleasures." He paused at the door. "I do have one request, Baal."

Baal lifted his mouth from where her pulse beat frantically. "Yes?"

"If you go after the female Nephilim one more time, you will wish I had simply removed your head from your body."

A second later, Asmodeus was gone. The female Nephilim may be off-limits now, but that did nothing to ease the desire to rip the little whore to pieces. Closing his eyes, he swore under his breath and pictured Lily before him, which wasn't hard given the resemblance. Wordlessly, he moved his head down her throat and lower. The young woman's whimpers turned into terrified screams.

Baal smiled.

CHAPTER TEN

Lily snuck out of the Sanctuary through one of the numerous tunnels, then rode the metro home the following morning. Nathaniel was going to be pissed when he discovered her missing without so much as a note, but he would know where she'd gone, and he wouldn't follow.

Not after last night.

She unlocked her door and stepped into her apartment with a shaky sigh. Nathaniel's shock at seeing her arm last night kept gnawing at her. He'd known immediately that Baal had come for Michael, which made no sense. Sure, Michael was an untrained Nephilim, one who could be easily swayed, but why the hell would Baal care? While the doctors had tended to her arm, Nathaniel had questioned her until she'd fallen asleep. Whatever she said to him was useless. She had no clue as to why one of the original Fallen would be interested in the cop.

She dropped her keys on the counter, going straight to the fridge and pulling out a bottle of OJ. Gulping the juice down in one long swallow, she ran the back of her hand over her mouth.

The memory of Baal's touch was too fresh. It had

taken her months to get back into the swing of things after the first time he laid the smackdown on her. And it had taken years for the nightmares to go away. His brutality back then had left her unsure if she could do her duty.

She shuddered, trying to shake off the horror. She didn't have the luxury now to let it affect her.

Anger and desperation welled up, and in one quick turn, she threw the empty bottle across the room. It made a less-than-satisfying thud.

She was an utter mess after having slept in her clothes. Her shirt was wrinkled beyond recognition, and the knees of her leather pants were scuffed. Leaving the kitchen and the minor mess she just created, she went into the dark bedroom.

Normally the first thing she'd do when home was throw open the curtains and let in the sunshine. Her rooms at the Sanctuary were several levels underground, where no light could penetrate. It had been one of the reasons she'd picked an apartment that afforded so many sources of natural light.

But today she left the heavy curtains in place. In total darkness, she stripped and went into the adjoining bathroom, where she drew a scalding bath. She sat on the edge of the garden tub while steam filled the air. Her gaze fell to her thigh. The irregular pink flesh seemed as noticeable today as it had the first time she'd seen it.

The doctors had kept her leg wrapped for days, and at that time, it hadn't been her biggest concern.

Baal had done a number on her. He'd broken two of her ribs, cracked three more, and fractured her arm. He had also dislocated her jaw and splintered her left eye socket. But it could have been much worse—she knew that.

Her insides tightened as nausea swept through her.

The horrific things Baal had whispered to her as he pinned her down on the dirty floor, prying her legs apart, leaving his mark behind as she cried, would haunt her forever. If Julian hadn't shown up . . .

She swallowed the sudden thickening in her throat. Somehow Julian had healed the worst of her injuries after fighting off Baal, exposing the fact that he had retained some of his angelic powers from the days before he fell. The doctors had questioned how she had healed so quickly, but for reasons unbeknownst to her, she had kept his ability a secret.

She'd been lucky this time around.

Lily turned off the water and then sank down, letting out a sigh of bliss as her rigid muscles relaxed. Keeping her bandaged arm above water, she slipped her head under, wishing the simple action could wash away her mind, too.

The silence was welcoming. The last two days had been the longest ever, and the week had only begun.

Running out of air, she broke the surface and opened her eyes, steamy water streaming down her face.

Two extraordinarily bright blue eyes locked onto hers. For a second, her brain didn't recognize what was happening, and all she could do was stare.

Julian sat on the edge of the tub, staring back at her. There was a mischievous quirk to his lips that faded when his gaze dropped to her rosy peaks.

Snapping out of the shock, she shrieked and jerked up. Water sloshed over the rim and Julian's leg as she covered her breasts and curled up her legs. "What in God's name are you doing in here?"

He tipped his head to the side. "I wanted to see you."

Her heart was throwing itself against her ribs. "In my bathroom? How the hell did you even get in here?"

"I wanted to be here, so I'm here." His gaze dropped to her hands—and the skin she couldn't cover. She flushed. "It's really quite easy."

"How is it that easy?" Her jaw hurt from how tightly she clenched her teeth.

His lips twitched. "You want to see?"

Not really. "Yes."

There was a certain playful quality to how he leaned back, catching her wide-eyed gaze and holding it. He winked, and then he was simply gone.

Her mouth dropped open as she twisted around frantically. He was nowhere in her bathroom. Unless he was hiding in her cabinet, and that seemed unlikely. This perhaps explained how quickly he moved, because he wasn't really moving. He was disappearing.

"Julian?" she whispered.

The air shimmered by the tub, so faintly she almost didn't notice it, and then he was sitting on the edge once more. "Yes."

117

She jerked back, knocking her shoulder against the tub. "Well, that . . . that comes in handy. Can all of you do that?"

"We can only go to a place we know. I can't pop in just anywhere."

She gaped. "How do you know where I live?"

That was a very good question, because she was always careful when she went to her apartment, taking different routes each time and glancing over her shoulder in paranoia. Then again, this morning she'd been too drained to pay attention. But she would've sensed a minion or a Fallen if one had been nearby.

"I've always known where you live." He reached out, brushing a wet strand of hair off her shoulder.

She flinched. "Don't."

His eyes narrowed on hers.

"How many more know where I live?" Tears sprang to her eyes. If the Fallen knew where she was and could pop in anytime, she'd have to give up the only place that was truly hers.

The hard line of his jaw softened. "They don't know about this place. You have nothing to fear."

A little bit of relief coursed through her. She believed him. So far, as odd as it was, he hadn't ever lied to her. But she was still naked, and Julian was staring at her hands so intently she wondered if he had X-ray vision. Her nipples hardened against her hands. She looked away.

Julian sighed. "I'll wait for you to finish."

And then he was gone . . . again. Lily slipped back

under the water and squeezed her eyes shut, mind racing. What was he doing here? And how long had he been watching her? Instead of disgust, her body went in the opposite direction, getting warm at the idea.

She broke the surface. "Crap."

This wasn't good.

Climbing out of the tub, she quickly dried off and grabbed the silk robe hanging on the back of the door. She could still sense that he was here. She snatched the bracelets off the vanity and slapped them on before she opened the door. Her gaze went to the bed, and she breathed a sigh of relief. At least he wasn't there.

Julian stood in front of the reinforced glass doors that led out to the balcony, his back to her. He wore a plain white T-shirt stretched over broad shoulders and a pair of dark slacks that hung low on his narrow hips.

He turned, his intense eyes drifting from her face to the tips of her toes. "That was quick."

"You kind of killed the idea of relaxing."

"I'm sorry."

She knew she needed to tell him to leave, then go crawl into her bed and pretend he'd never popped into her bathroom and gotten a look at her goods. But that was what she should do, not what she wanted. Curiosity was getting the best of her, which was dangerous and stupid. "What are you doing here, Julian?"

He stared at her as if she should know. Well, she didn't, and so she waited for his explanation. "I wanted to make sure you were okay."

119

That wasn't the response she expected. She stepped back, her fingers tightening around her robe until her knuckles turned white. "Of course I'm okay."

"Baal hurt you again," he stated, his voice hard.

She pulled her eyes from him, staring over his shoulder. The scuff mark left behind from her earlier temper tantrum became a sole point of interest to her. "Thank you . . . for coming when you did."

He was silent for a moment. "I remember the first time you thanked me. It had been months later. You waited for me, didn't you? You knew I'd come."

She lowered her gaze to her carpet. She had waited for him on the damn clock building after Baal's attack.

"You thanked me and then ran off as if the very devil was on your heels."

"You saved my life." She lifted her eyes, meeting his. "I had to thank you. But it wasn't like I could hang around. Everyone was keeping an eye on me after . . . what happened." And they would probably do the same now. Great.

"I know," he said. "But I didn't come here for you to thank me."

Biting her lower lip, she decided she wasn't going to touch that statement with a ten-foot pole.

Julian tipped his head to the side, inhaling deeply. "You're wondering why I saved you." The way his eyes drifted shut and his lips curved into a small smile made her quiver in all the wrong—right—places. "If anyone is to kill you, it will be me."

She arched a brow. That wasn't the first time he'd

said that. "That makes no sense. You've had plenty of opportunities to kill me. Why haven't you?"

He shrugged his broad shoulders. The small smile played across his face until two deep dimples appeared. "Do you want me to?"

That didn't deserve a response. Instead her eyes dropped to his lips, and she flushed. She remembered picturing Julian when she'd been with Gabe. This was getting outright stupid.

"How is your arm?"

She blinked. "Um, it will be okay, and it doesn't even hurt now." That was a lie, but he didn't need to know that.

Silence stretched between them, and she couldn't help but notice how he seemed to take up all the oxygen in the room.

"Why do you do this?" he asked finally.

She frowned as he jumped topics. "Do what?"

"This life?" he clarified. "Doesn't it grow tiresome? Always hunting with no real end in sight? Knowing the Fallen will always be one step ahead simply because they outnumber the Nephilim?"

"Well, when you put it that way," she drawled slowly. "I don't really have a choice. I was born to this."

He stared at her curiously. "You always have a choice."

Strange, but Michael had said the same thing. "I may have had a choice, but I don't any longer. I signed the Contract. Can't get out of it now."

Turning serious, he nodded. "Now you have forever, and it's just you and your duty."

"Oh the joy." She stepped around him, checking the locks on the door. They were thrown. Wow! He seriously did just blink into her apartment. When she turned around, the air hitched in her throat. The level of intensity in which he observed her made her nervous, really nervous—and hot. "You should leave."

"It must be a lonely existence for you," he said as if he hadn't heard.

Her fingers curled around the edge of her robe. Of course her life was freaking lonely. The closest intimate contact she had recently took place in a bar's laundry room. And she wouldn't be surprised if Julian knew that.

"What about you?" she threw the question back at him as she walked toward the kitchen. "I'm sure you have lots of people to occupy your time."

"Not anymore," he whispered.

She stiffened. She felt him behind her and, immediately, her body came alive. Answering some sort of call she didn't understand, her nipples tightened against the smooth silk and heat pooled between her legs. "Why is that?" she whispered.

Julian gently brushed the mass of wet hair over her shoulder as he leaned forward. His breath stirred the small hairs at the nape of her neck, sending fine shivers through her. "Things changed for me."

She darted away from the door, putting some space between them. But that space lasted a second, because when she blinked, he was behind her again. Every cell in her body warred. Fight him, stand still. Tell him to leave, or not say anything at all.

He lowered his head so that his lips brushed the exposed skin of her neck. "It was never a why, you know. More like a when . . ."

"Oh." It wasn't one of the most intelligent responses, but it was the best she had at the moment.

Julian trailed his lips over her skin lightly. "Eight years ago to be exact."

The significance of the date did not pass Lily. Some inane part of her wanted to hear him say it. "What happened eight years ago?"

He chuckled as his hands settled on her shoulders. "You," he said as he brought his hands down to her elbows in one smooth caress. "You happened."

"I didn't do anything." *Ah, this is dangerous and stupid.* But she couldn't seem to stop herself. She tipped her head back against his hard chest. Just a little longer, and then she'd kick him out. Just a few more minutes with this magnificent thing behind her, and the glorious heat he created in her. Then she would let it go. She had to, because this was idiotic. Because this was how it all started with Anna.

"You didn't?" His hands followed the curve of her arms, resting where she tightly held the edges of her robe.

"Other than stabbing you?" She started to pull away, but he held her in place. "No."

The deep rumble of Julian's laugh vibrated down

the length of her, and a small sigh escaped her lips. "That wasn't what I had in mind." His fingers closed over hers. "Ah, Lily, you drive me to do insane things."

She drove him to do insane things? What was she doing? Allowing him to be this close and to forget all the ways this could go bad. Like everything had gone bad for Anna. Ice drenched her veins, and she tensed. This was wrong.

Julian squeezed her hands gently. "It's okay," he whispered just below her ear. "I'm not going to hurt you. If you tell me to stop, I will."

Her mouth opened to tell him to stop, but his thumbs brushed against the swell of her breasts and the words left her. Heat pulsed through her body, melting the ice.

"I will stop, Lily. I won't do anything you don't want me to do," he continued, pressing his lips against her pulse. "Just don't shut me out in fear. Don't let fear control you. That's all I'll ask from you today."

Her heart tripled its beat, and her fingers loosened their hold on the soft material. "I can't do this."

"How do you know?" He gently pulled her hands away from the material, bringing them to her sides. The loose robe immediately gaped.

Air hitched in her throat. Every cell in her body waited as he brought his hands back to her shoulders. She needed to pull away, but she remained there, filled with a wanton curiosity that excited her in a way she'd never been before.

"Do you want me to stop?" he asked.

The words formed on her lips, but they went no further. Her body and mind were fighting. Hormones were definitely winning at this point.

Julian brushed the silk over her slight shoulders and down her arms. The cool air whispered against her bare skin, and when she should've been fighting him, she was instead thrilled. He ran a finger over the outline of her tattoo. "I knew you would be beautiful with wings."

The same could be said about him if he still had his. Then the thought flew out of her mind when she felt his tongue tracing the same line his finger had. Sweet Jesus, every muscle in her body locked up. "Julian, I . . . this . . ."

"Do you want me to stop?" When she didn't answer, he hauled her back so that she was flush with him. "You and I share this ache. Fight it all you want, but it is the truth."

There was no denying that. The ache was driving her crazy.

"Let me take the edge off all that loneliness." He lifted her chin, his thumb tracing idle circles over the delicate expanse of her neck. "So beautiful," he murmured as his other hand roamed across her quivering stomach. "No one will know. No Nephilim. No Fallen. It is just you and me."

Her eyes fluttered shut, and when his hand drifted up her stomach and stopped just under one round globe, she almost cried out.

"Tell me to stop." His voice was thick. "And damn it all to Hell, I will."

Her lips parted, but she didn't speak.

Julian growled low in his throat and then brought his mouth down on hers.

CHAPTER ELEVEN

It had been years since she had kissed anyone. She'd been a teenager, before Baal and before she accepted the Contract. She'd forgotten how much pleasure a kiss could bring, but she never remembered being kissed like this before.

Julian claimed her lips as if he were laying stake to her soul. The possibility that he had already done so should have served as a dire warning, but she was far too immersed in the feelings Julian was working out of her. His lips were demanding, and when he tugged on her lower lip with his teeth, she yielded to him. The kiss deepened, and his tongue slid over hers. She let out a little breathless moan against his hot mouth. The taste of him, his smell . . . all of him invaded her, burning her. She was so hot, so wet.

His lips began to leisurely explore hers as his hand finally, finally smoothed over her breast. He touched her like he'd been starving to do so. His deft fingers plucked at her nipple, causing her to do something she'd never done before.

She moaned into his mouth.

His chest rumbled against her back as he left her mouth. "I will not force you. Even though every cell in my body demands that I take you now. You have a choice, Lily."

What choice was he giving her when his fingers moved to her other breast, drifting over her pebbled nipple? The liquid fire in her was too potent to be ignored. But she was gasping for air, knowing she'd already gone too far.

But there was still a choice. Even as worked up as she was, she could regain control of herself, but it was more than the physical. She was so incredibly lonely and he . . . he had saved her twice now. And his touch, there was nothing like it. Her response ran deeper than trying to ease some of the loneliness, but she wasn't ready to delve too deeply into that.

"I want to give you pleasure," he said, smoothing his thumb over her bottom lip as his other one did the same to her nipple. The combination was maddening. "That is all, Lily. This will be nothing more."

"It won't?" Doubt colored her words.

"Oh, I want to do more. Much, much more. I want to sink deep inside you. I want to fill you while you scream my name."

Her body shuddered.

"All you have to do is tell me no." His hand left the tip of her breast, dropping to where the robe was still knotted. "No?"

She bit down on her lip. Her breast ached from the loss of contact.

He quickly unraveled the haphazard tie she had made, and the robe completely parted. "So beautiful," he whispered again.

Her eyes opened into thin slits as his fingers made their way to the soft mound between her legs. She held her breath. A finger skimmed over her damp lips, barely touching her, but she jerked against his hand. No one—no one had touched her without some sort of barrier between her flesh and theirs. And without thinking about it, she parted her thighs, giving him more access.

He gently explored her heated flesh. She was quickly losing herself to him, breathing like she'd run five flights of stairs. When his thumb pressed against the little bundle of nerves, she whimpered.

"Stop?" he asked.

When she said nothing, he increased the pressure until her hips began moving, rocking against his hand. A fierce heat surfaced, overshadowing anything she had felt before. Building and building till she feared it would consume her.

Julian lazily ran a slender finger over her wet slit. The tension coiled inside her as she pressed into his hand, wildly seeking whatever it was he would offer.

"Look at me, Lily," he ordered roughly. "Tell me what you want."

A ragged breath escaped her parted lips, and her eyes met his.

He pressed against her, his cock thick and hard against the small of her back. "Tell me to stop."

Everything seemed to come down to this moment. Her hips were still thrusting against his hand, twisting until sharp spikes of pleasure shot through her.

Jennifer L. Armentrout

"What will it be?" He pressed his lips to the bruise on her temple. "Do you want me to stop?"

"No," she gasped.

He made a triumphant sound and scooped her up in his arms. His movements blurred, and then he was placing her on the bed. Julian removed the robe from where it had been trapped around her arms and laid siege to her lips. He kissed her until her fingers sunk into his hair, pulling.

Groaning with pleasure, he lifted his mouth and trailed his lips down her neck. She wanted—no, needed—to feel his skin against her. With trembling fingers, she grabbed hold of his shirt and lifted. Wordlessly, he paused and raised his arms. She tossed the shirt aside. Each hard plane and ripple of his chest begged to be touched.

And she did, running her hands over him. Damn, he was utterly magnificent. His skin was like silk stretched over steel. Every part of him was hard and smooth.

Then his lips settled over her nipple, sucking long and hard. "Julian," she begged in a heated whisper.

Answering her plea, he pressed his hand against her, slipping one finger into her wetness. Her back arched off the bed as she ground her hips against his hand. The feeling of him—his finger inside her—had her thrashing.

He slipped in two fingers, and the fire in her core flared. His name was like a sinful prayer on her lips, urging him on. Julian's mouth glided from one breast to the next and then back to her lips. She felt the thick length of him against her and sparks flew. Her fingers dug into his skin as he pressed his entire body against her.

The tension building in her expanded, her hand dropped to the band of his pants. More, she wanted more. "Please," she pleaded. "Please, Julian."

"Don't," he grunted against her lips as he slowly pumped his fingers.

Ignoring this, she jerked the fragile material. Buttons snapped, scattering across the dark room. She yanked the material over his hips, and his cock sprang forward. Figures. He would go commando. And damn, he was huge. She wrapped her hand around him, and he jerked as if he had been burned.

He groaned, arching into her hand. "What you do to me. Ah, Lily, don't."

She didn't listen. She ran her hand down him, marveling at the length and width. His breath was coming out in short, little gasps, and she was awed at what her touch could do. Soon, he was pushing into her hand as he carefully thrust his fingers into her.

He pressed his thumb against her clit. "Come for me, Lily," he ordered.

The coil within her started to spin madly. Her grip on him tightened. "I want to feel you inside me. Please."

Julian groaned, swirling his thumb over her clit. She felt him swell in her hand. The whirling force inside her spiraled out of control, and the first wave of pure bliss crashed over her. She cried out, tensing against his hand. Spasms racked her body, and her toes curled. With wide eyes, she saw Julian stiffen and felt his cock jump in her tight grasp. Then he, too, joined her in release, their hearts racing as their bodies spent themselves.

The force of her orgasm left her speechless, and as her heart slowly returned to normal, Julian gently removed his fingers. He gave a shaky sort of laugh, pressing his lips to her damp forehead. "That's not what I had in mind," he said gruffly.

Lily realized her hand was still wrapped around him, and he was already hardening under her touch. She pulled her hand away, flushing. "Sorry," she whispered. "I guess I got carried away."

He eased himself beside her and gently cupped her cheek. "No. Don't apologize." He leaned down and kissed her softly. "Sweet Lily, you surprise me."

Her hand fell idly to his chest. She was warm and fuzzy all over, and her bones felt like they had melted somewhere along with her sanity. "Do I?"

He nodded, sliding one arm under her, and nestled her against him.

Falling quiet, she tried to reconcile everything she knew about the Fallen with what she knew about Julian. What they had just done—what they had shared—had been true bliss. How could someone so evil be so patient, so gentle? And bring her such pleasure.

Unease crept over her. For the first time since she knew what she was, she doubted what she knew. All

Fallen were evil. They lacked compassion and were totally immoral—that's what she had been taught. But she couldn't bring herself to think of Julian that way.

He leaned over, placing a kiss against her cheek. "What are you thinking?"

She tipped her head back, looking at him. There was no way around it. "Why did you fall?"

His stare didn't waver. "Why do you think I did?"

She shrugged. "Sleeping with young maidens?" *Please don't say you killed an entire family of four because you felt like it,* she begged silently.

He was silent for a moment, and then he leaned down and kissed the pulse at the nape of her neck. "You would think that, wouldn't you?" He lifted his head, staring down at her. "It was a long time ago, Lily. I had been foolish and very prideful."

She bit her lip. That wasn't much of an answer. She pushed. "You didn't kill an innocent person or something?"

His gaze sharpened and his brows rose. "What does that Nathaniel teach you? No. I did not kill anyone . . . who was innocent."

Lily held his gaze for a moment. "Okay," she whispered. "I believe you." It made her a fool, considering that wasn't much of an explanation, but she did.

He lightly grasped her chin, bringing her lips to his. When he was done, he pulled her into his arms. "I better not see you at Deuces Wild again," he said gruffly, pressing her cheek to his bare chest.

Sated and strangely happier than she had felt in

years, she smiled sleepily as his heart thundered under her cheek.

Michael's head was going to explode.

He was full of knowledge—and it was way too much. He had spent the bulk of the day cloistered away with Luke, and now Remy. It was like being in school again. Except what he was learning was far more bizarre and interesting than anything college could have taught him.

From what he had gathered from Lily that first night he had learned of the Fallen and what he learned today, he decided they were screwed.

It was sheer statistics.

Luke had explained that only so many Nephilim were born a year. The now-infamous Nathaniel—who he'd yet to hold a conversation with personally—would receive the name somehow. He'd called bullshit on that, which had earned him a sharp look from his impromptu teacher. Out of those Nephilim born, only about fifty percent actually survived the first year. Apparently his kind were needy babies.

From that fifty percent, the Nephilim saved only twenty percent. The Fallen got to the rest.

Once again, sheer statistics.

So yeah, they were screwed.

He wondered why he was still sitting there instead of packing up everything he owned and leaving town. He was on the losing side, but he didn't leave. And honestly, wouldn't it all eventually catch up with him anyway? Thinking back to reasons why he'd left his comfy job and joined the police force, he began to understand a part of him that had lain dormant. This whole time he had been searching for something missing in his life. The elusive purpose people always talked about. He thought being a police officer would seal up the hole in him. But it had only been a step in the right direction.

A step that had led him to Lily—and the truth about himself.

He explored the Sanctuary, lost in his own thoughts. He learned the security-firm portion of the Sanctuary was one of the best. It offered protection to some of the world's richest people and provided software security for the top companies in the world. He saw more than one supercompany listed on documents carried by one human or another. Fucking unreal.

Over the course of the day, he realized he was able to pick out the other Nephilim who mingled among the human workforce. A strange tingling sensation appeared before a Nephilim stepped off the elevator in front of him or walked past the door.

After wandering the upper levels, he went underground. Without asking who he was, the guards stepped aside, allowing him access to the real Sanctuary. Underground, his senses were firing left and right. There were Nephilim everywhere. Aboveground, the humans at least smiled at him, but the Nephilim didn't look his way as they passed. Even more strange was the fact that he had not seen one single female Nephilim.

The first level was laid out like a school. It had several occupied classrooms. He heard muted laughter and a young female voice hushing the students, and his curiosity got the best of him. He peered into the room.

It was like any normal kindergarten class, with a dozen children scurrying about the room carrying construction paper and crayons. A slender teacher stood at the head of the classroom, a patient smile fixed across her pretty face. It was then he noticed a little girl Nephilim with paint staining her chubby hands. So now he knew of two female Nephilim. The teacher he wasn't sure about.

Moving past that room, he glanced into a couple more. There were students of all ages, and some seemed near graduation age. This level had its own cafeteria, playground, and what he guessed was a basketball court by the sounds echoing from behind closed doors. The second and third floors were housing levels for the students, and one looked like a giant Toys R Us store. He quickly backed out of there. Sighing, he moved onto the fourth level, and it was like finding Heaven.

The amount of weapons stored there would have made the militia's mouth water. Michael slowly made his way down the hallway. Each room was the size of a gymnasium and had a theme. In one room, guns of all sizes lined the walls. All of them had cryptic writing engraved into their handles or on their barrels. Some were models he had never seen before.

Another room was littered with explosives and detonating devices. Michael didn't like the looks of it and found another room housing razor-sharp knives and swords ranging from samurai to the small daggers Lily carried. All were polished and, like the guns, had strange images carved into them. He wanted to touch them—all of them—but the sound of sparring drew his attention.

At the end of the hallway, he found several large training rooms. Inside one, he immediately recognized Remy sparring with a younger Nephilim. He clearly outskilled the deeply tanned teenager, but he was patient as the boy fumbled over his feet or dropped his sword.

In another corner, several older Nephilim were teaching Brazilian jujitsu to a rapt audience. Farther back, men were grappling. At first glance, Michael thought they were really fighting because of the intensity in the way they went after one another and the hard falls some were taking. He was surprised when a brown-haired Nephilim stood up and laughed as he used the back of his hand to wipe blood off his split lip.

The swarthy-skinned Nephilim grinned. "Your twin fights better than you."

"Whatever." The other man laughed again. "I'm better than him on all other levels. Ones that count outside the training room."

Both men grinned, falling back into defensive stances.

Michael backed away, heading for the next level before he could be spotted. On the fifth floor were additional housing quarters, each one under lock and key. The key to his was securely in his pocket.

Knowing there was only one more level to

investigate, he was curious when he found guards posted at the sixth level. Apparently he didn't have clearance for that floor and was turned away. He returned to the seventh level, where his room was, and decided to poke around there. He knew it held chambers meant for housing, a library, and a large computer lab.

Drifting through the library, he scanned the stacks. Several of the books were in languages he couldn't read. There were many bibles of various ages and versions. On the bottom shelf, way in the back, he found some volumes of mythology. One in particular caught his eye.

"The Book of Enoch," he said, and crouched down. "You've got to be kidding."

Sliding out the ancient book, he cracked the spine. A plume of dust hit the air. He thumbed through some of the aged pages. "And they became pregnant, and they bore great giants, whose height was three thousand ells: Who consumed all the acquisitions of men. And when men could no longer sustain them, the giants turned against them and devoured mankind. They began to sin against birds, and beasts, and reptiles, and fish, and to devour one another's flesh, and drink the blood." Whoa. Michael shook his head, but he was morbidly fascinated by it all.

Just as he read a verse about God, Uriel, and Noah—as in Noah's Ark—someone cleared his throat behind him. He looked up, finding Nathaniel standing between the two stacks.

"I see you've discovered the library," Nathaniel said.

He nodded. "I haven't heard of half of these books. And this?" He waved the dusty volume around. "Crazy."

Nathaniel smiled. "No, you wouldn't have."

"Of course not . . ." He glanced around the room. "So you're Nathaniel?"

"I'm sorry I haven't had a chance to introduce myself. I've been extremely busy and was hoping Luke would keep you occupied."

"He has been, but I guess he thought I needed a break."

Nathaniel smiled. "Sensory overload, I take it?"

He laughed, but it sounded rough. "You have no idea." He watched Nathaniel slowly come to a halt before him and was struck by how tall he was. Michael was by no means short, but standing next to Nathaniel he felt like an ant. An old accent he couldn't place clung to the man's words. Maybe Mediterranean by the look of his naturally tanned skin and the russet color of his hair. "How is Lily?"

"She's fine. No need to worry about her. She is a very strong girl."

Michael could think of numerous words to describe her. Not one of them was the word girl. "You run this place?"

One fine brow arched. "As much as I can. Although I find it runs me more often than not."

Michael was growing more uncomfortable by the moment. The man's stare made him feel as if Nathaniel could see into his very soul and flip through all his secrets. Not that he had any secrets that rivaled what the Sanctuary held. He shifted, folding his arms over his chest.

Nathaniel cocked his head to the side. "May I ask you a question?" When Michael nodded, he continued. "All these years you have slipped past us and the Fallen unnoticed. It's a very curious situation. Have you ever sensed one of us before?"

"I don't think so," he answered truthfully. "If I had, I would have ignored it or chalked it up to some bad food. Now, I can't explain it. I can . . . feel them . . . the other Nephilim."

"I'm assuming that side of you has lain dormant. However, I've been advised that you have worked closely with Danyal. I'm at a loss to explain how he did not sense what you are and vice versa."

"Well, wasn't my name in that book? I guess someone dropped the ball." Looking back, Michael would've been grateful if Nathaniel's crew had found him. Living here would have been a lot easier than being shuffled from one foster home to another.

A strange shadow flickered over Nathaniel's face. "That's the mystery, Michael. Your name never appeared in the Book."

He wasn't sure how to take that. The idea that there was a book where names of Nephilim would randomly appear seemed preposterous to him. Then again, all of this would have struck him that way a week ago.

Nathaniel tilted his head as if he heard something. "I

do believe Remy is calling for you. You have a lot to learn ahead." He paused and smiled slightly. "Your training will be intense. But I have faith in you. You will struggle like all Nephilim do at the beginning, but you'll pull through. You see, Michael, you're very special."

"Special?" he repeated, not sure if it was an insult or not. But Nathaniel had already left him alone. Sighing, he glanced down at the book. It was probably the lamest reading material he could've ever found, but he tucked it under his arm and left the library.

CHAPTER TWELVE

Lily checked out her reflection in the window of the Sanctuary. Smoothing down the wild waves, she studied her expression. She looked normal, not like she had spent the night having mind-blowing orgasms. It wasn't like "I fooled around with Julian" was stamped across her face. God, she hoped not—she'd be mortified. Okay, not mortified. Strangely, she wasn't ashamed by what she did. She knew she should be but couldn't find an ounce of regret in her.

Maybe orgasms wiped out common sense.

If that was the case, then she had none left considering how many she'd had over the last twelve hours. She was surprised the muscles in her legs still worked. After falling asleep in Julian's arms, she had been awakened by a deep kiss directed at a very private place. She had protested at first, but he had coaxed her through it.

A rush of heated memories forced her eyes closed. She had things she needed to do, but the way his tongue had teased her . . . and he had done it over and over. Never once did he enter her, not even when she had begged. Damn, she had begged, too. A lot. She had only pulled herself out of his arms an hour ago. She wasn't surprised when she found him gone after

142

her quick shower, but the single red rose that had been left on her counter had startled her. Even more shocking was her reaction to it. She'd immediately grabbed an unused vase and filled it with water, placing the rose near a window. The stupid smile spread across her face again.

Sighing, she rushed through the reception hall and greeted Sandy. "Hey, girl."

"How is your arm?"

Lily glanced down at the bandage. "Ah, it's doing great."

Sandy smiled, murmuring her relief. After asking Sandy about her latest boyfriend, she left the reception hall and waited for the underground elevator, not paying attention to the tingle that shifted down her spine. At the Sanctuary, you learned to ignore that feeling since the place was teeming with Nephilim.

Once in the elevator, her nerves made her fidget. She pressed the button for level five, exhaling loudly. Nathaniel wasn't going to be happy with her disappearing all day, especially since she kind of dumped Michael on Luke. Trying to forget about that, she wondered how his first day at the Sanctuary had been. Hopefully, he believed them now.

If not, she was going to drop-kick him in the face.

The elevator came to a stop, and the heavy doors slid open to reveal Luke. Lily gave a little yelp of surprise and stepped back. "Jeez, Luke."

"Where have you been all day?" he demanded.

"Aw, did you miss me?"

He snickered. "Nathaniel isn't too pleased with you."

Her shoulders slumped. "Like that's anything new."

He made a face as he stepped into the small elevator with her. "You're coming with me."

She crossed her arms. "Where am I going?"

He pushed the button for the bottom level that led to the subway systems, studying her closely. "We're going to Michael's to retrieve some of his personal crap. Micah will be meeting us there." He stopped, squinting. "You look different. Did you do something with your hair?"

Eyes wide, she self-consciously ran a hand over the loose hair. "No."

He shrugged. "There's something I want to talk to you about."

She bit back a sigh of relief, happy with the change of subject. "What?"

Luke placed a finger to his lips. She rolled her eyes but remained silent as the elevator doors opened once more. They quickly made their way down the corridor where two guards waited. The door was unlocked, and they stepped into the dimly lit tunnel.

"So what have you been doing that was so important you weren't here to help us with your cop?"

Her eyes narrowed dangerously. "First off, he's not my cop. I just punched him. That's all I lay claim to. Secondly, it's really not any of your freaking business."

Luke stopped, turning so suddenly that Lily crashed into him. He placed his hands on her shoulders and dipped his head, peering down at her. "I just don't want to see you do anything stupid."

She opened her mouth to bite off a scathing remark but stopped. What she had done was stupid, and she had a sinking suspicion Luke somehow knew she didn't go home and rest all day in bed. Feeling exposed and a little bit like a liar, a burn crawled up her chest as her temper flared. "Luke."

"I don't want you to get hurt."

She let out an exasperated sound. "Everyone keeps saying that, like I'm two. Damn it! I'm stronger than half of the Nephilim here, and I can take care of myself. I'm not that little girl, anymore. You and Nathaniel both need to remember that."

"We worry about you! You run off half-cocked. Do you remember what happened the last time you disappeared all day?"

She flinched at the reminder of her first run-in with Baal. "Luke, don't go there. I went back to my place. I needed some time alone."

"You needed some time to yourself? Did you think about anyone else? Do you want to know what I thought today?" He didn't give her a chance to respond. "That day eight years ago when the son of a bitch Julian brought you back to us. I kept seeing you lying there, lifeless. And every other night you run off, telling no one where you're going? I fear I'm going to see you like that again. Half-cocked, Lily. It's what you are." He broke off, taking an unsteady breath. "I can't lose you, too."

Her shoulders slumped as her anger evaporated, and her heart ached. No. She hadn't thought of any of that this morning. It didn't once cross her mind as she lay in Julian's arms. Guilt gnawed at her stomach. "I'm sorry," she whispered. "You won't lose me. I'm not her, Luke."

"Say you won't do anything stupid, Lily." His eyes closed briefly, hands dropping to his sides. "I want you to promise me that."

She heard the strife in his tone, the discord evident all over his handsome face. Knowing she was lying— because she couldn't take back what she'd done—Lily promised him. Then she stood on the tips of her toes, wrapping her arms around him. Inhaling his familiar scent, she rested her head against his chest. "What would I do without you?" she murmured into the cotton shirt he wore.

He relaxed, holding her close. "I don't know. Either you'd be running amok through the streets of DC or you'd have Nathaniel eating out of your little hand."

She pulled back, smiling. "I don't see anything wrong with either of those."

"Yeah, you already have Nathaniel eating out of your hand. The damn man is getting too old to fall for your games." He lightly cuffed her chin. "You trust me, right?"

That was an odd and incredibly stupid question. "With my life," she affirmed fiercely. "What's that about?"

He walked to the exit that led to the subway. She

stared at his back for a moment, puzzled. Why would he ask that? Glancing around, she hurried after him. "Luke?"

"I know Nathaniel has shared his fear with you," he said quietly.

She cringed. "Did he tell you?"

He nodded, looking up the empty tunnel that could only be accessed by the Sanctuary. "That's why I didn't want to talk about this in the Sanctuary. If Nathaniel is correct, it could be anyone."

Lily wrapped her arms against the sudden chill of the dark, damp tunnel, wishing she had worn something more than a pair of 5.11 Tactical pants and a thin shirt. "Do you have any idea who it could be?" She followed him down another tunnel. She hated using the tunnel systems. Sure, they were useful and connected to just about every subway platform in the city, but they reminded her of one long cell. Never one to like closed and confined places, she found it difficult to get enough air in her lungs.

"No," he said. "Who knows if we ever will?" Luke stopped, entering in a pass code on the thick, round door. "Micah has discovered something potentially big." The door swung open smoothly, and he peered through to make sure the platform was empty. "He spotted a major player with a senator's aide a few days ago—a Senator Sharpe."

She followed him through and shut the door behind her. Once in the open area of the subway, she breathed a little better. "Who did he see?"

"Asmodeus," he answered quietly.

Lily nearly tripped over her feet. "What?" Baal was back and now this? Christ.

Luke surveyed the empty platform. "The aide is now recently deceased due to a self-inflicted gunshot wound."

"Of course," she muttered. "Do you think whoever is sending the Fallen names is actually working with Asmodeus?" When he nodded, she cursed again. "Oh God, that is not good." She wanted nothing more than to beat the living crap out of whoever that was. "Why would someone do this? Everyone is like family here."

He stared down the tracks, a far-off look in his pale eyes. "Someone who hates the Sanctuary," he said quietly. "Maybe someone who hates Nate."

"Hates Nate?" she questioned.

Luke shrugged. "He's the boss. Could be a vendetta against him, someone who wants to cause as much destruction as possible."

None of those were a good enough reason for her. The Nephilim were already sorely outnumbered by the Fallen and minions. To lose any more to the Fallen would hurt them severely. "We need to find out who this person is, because God only knows what Asmodeus is doing with those young Nephilim . . . or if it has anything to do with the senator."

Her gaze followed Luke's, and the bright lights of the approaching train cast them both in an eerie yellowish glow. As the train slowed, she felt a sudden flicker of unease. She stepped closer, wrapping her arm around Luke. "I don't want to believe that one of us would shack up with Asmodeus."

He glanced down at her. "Me, neither, but we need to make it a priority—you and I."

The train came to a stop in front of her. As the door creaked open, she wrinkled her nose against the smell of body odor and disinfectant. She looked up at Luke, half of his face shadowed. The unease grew. "Like old times?" she whispered.

"Like old times."

It didn't take them long to make it to Michael's apartment. Lily balked at the door to the stairwell. The idea of getting cornered in there again twisted her stomach. With a disgruntled glance at her bandaged arm, she pushed Luke toward the elevator.

"What? You have post-traumatic stress now?" he joked.

Like old times apparently meant making fun of her.

Luke relented when she threatened to push him down the elevator shaft and took a hefty swing at his head.

He fished out a key from his pocket.

Lily raised her brows. "Does Michael know you have that?"

He shrugged, slipping inside. "No."

She rolled her eyes, following him and then closing the door behind her. They stood in the dark, empty apartment. Having been too pissed off the last time she'd been in here, she really hadn't looked at anything.

Now she roamed over to his coffee table and picked up a small picture frame. "I have no idea what he would want. Do you?"

Luke headed straight to the small kitchen, throwing open cabinets until he found a box of garbage bags. "Just grab clothes and anything you think is personal." He handed her several bags, shuffling past to a tiny matchbox-sized bathroom.

How would she know? She flipped over the picture, staring down at it. A pretty young blonde smiled at the camera, her arms wrapped around a small boy who grinned impishly up at her. The little thing was Michael, but that wasn't what caught her eye. It was the woman she assumed was his mother. The photo had captured the woman's happiness in a way that struck her. She couldn't help but compare her few memories of her own mother to this picture. Her mom had never been happy. A depressed, bitter, angry shell of a woman was who her mother had been.

Lifting the picture, she noticed a small crucifix around both Michael's neck and the woman's. "I feel wrong going through his stuff," she called to Luke as she slid the frame into one of the larger pockets of her pants.

He snorted from the bathroom. "Really, I would've never thought that would bother you." He was quiet for a moment. "Did you know Michael's name never came up in the Book of Names?"

Shocked, she paused halfway between Michael's bedroom and the living room. "What?"

"Yeah." He came out of the bathroom. "Wonder what that means?"

She gaped at him. "Did Nathaniel tell you this?"

He nodded. "He didn't want anyone to know. I guess he's worried about how the other Nephilim would take that little piece of knowledge. So don't go running back to Nathaniel demanding answers."

Stung, she did want to run back to Nathaniel and demand why he hadn't told her.

Obviously he didn't trust her with the information, and she wanted to know why. Did he think she was the rat? *He wouldn't. He knows me.*

Luke glided into the kitchen with a bag full of personal items. Her gaze dropped to her empty bag and she sighed. He popped open the fridge, pulling out a bottle of beer.

Shaking her head, she watched him unscrew the cap. She had no idea why Luke insisted on drinking beer. It was rather pointless.

She strode off to Michael's bedroom to gather up as much clothing as possible. Not sure what he preferred, she started throwing everything she could get her hands on into the garbage bag. Opening one drawer, she wondered how one man could have so many pairs of socks that didn't match.

Turning on a bedside lamp, she spied a little crystal dish that had been shoved to the back of the table. Inside the dish were two crucifixes. Lily scooped up the necklaces and slipped them into her pocket with the frame.

Seeing a small shoe box on top of the dresser, she dropped the bag of Michael's possessions and stepped over to it. She quickly slid off the lid, rifling through the documents. Inside were a couple more pictures of his mom and him, a few newspaper clippings announcing his graduation, and several personal-identification documents. One of the pictures caught her eye. She pulled it out, holding it gently between her fingers. His mother was a beautiful woman; her smile simply radiated. Lily couldn't help but think this woman didn't look like someone mourning the loss of a fallen angel.

No. She'd appeared happy to be alive and with her son. Not someone intending to take her own life as a way to escape the painful wound that a Fallen always left in his wake.

CHAPTER THIRTEEN

Lily trailed behind Luke and Micah, only half listening to their argument. They had been at it since the moment they had climbed into the Escalade. All she gathered was that Micah was upset about Luke pulling him off an assignment. He had been hunting longer than Lily but nowhere near the amount of time Luke had been at it. She recognized how dangerous Asmodeus was, and why Luke was better suited, but she also understood how butt-sore Micah was. She was feeling quite the same way after learning about Michael and the Book of Names. It never felt good to be doubted . . . or left out.

Clutching the little shoe box in her hands, she let out a weary sigh. I came back here for this? She wished she knew where they had stashed Michael so she didn't have to listen to the bitchfest that would never end. The ride had been bad enough, but the awkwardness in the elevator was something she never wanted to repeat.

They stopped on level seven, which surprised her. Only Nathaniel and the circle had rooms on this level. Michael was just superspecial since he was "thou shall not be named" in the Book.

153

Micah hauled the bag of goods she had packed to his shoulder. He was tall, like all male Nephilim were, with red hair and a pale complexion. There was even a splattering of freckles over his nose. He was probably one of the few men who could rock red hair well, and he also had the temper to match it.

"This is bullshit, man. If you guys think I can't handle the Fallen, then why in the hell do you allow me to hunt alone?" he said, turning to her. "Lily, you haven't said a thing. Did you know about this?"

There went staying out of the argument. She focused on the tall redhead, forcing a casual shrug. "Not really."

"Don't bring her into this." Luke shifted the bag he had gathered from Michael's apartment. "An order is an order. So deal with it."

Ah, Luke had such a way with people. Micah straightened, coming to his full height. "Excuse me?" he uttered dangerously.

There was no doubt they would come to blows if given the opportunity. "Micah, I'm not allowed to approach Baal or Asmodeus, either," she said, stepping between the two. "It's nothing personal. Chill out, okay?"

Micah glanced at the bandage around her arm. "I can understand why you aren't allowed. You've been tagged twice, Lily. He's gunning for your ass. Not to mention you can't go anywhere without the freak, Julian, showing up."

Stopping midstep, she stared up at him. Her very

fingers itched to dig into him. "Do you want to rethink what you just said, buddy?"

Luke stepped away, looking rather amused with the sudden turn of events. A few Nephilim who were on their way out to hunt skirted around them with curious glances.

Micah sighed. "Lily, I didn't mean anything by that."

She cocked her head to the side. "Do you want to know how I got tagged? I fought him. Which is more than I can say you have ever done, and that *freak*? I trust him to save my ass more than I trust you."

"Lily," Luke warned, immediately at her side.

She turned to him, ready to lay into him, too, when she realized what she had done. She'd defended Julian in front of not just two Nephilim but two of Nathaniel's most trusted. Defending a Fallen was a rather unseemly thing.

And it went over like a ton of bricks. Micah pressed his lips together, taking a step back. His lip curled in disgust as he turned and headed for Michael's room without another word.

She squeezed her eyes shut, heart pounding. *Shit!* That was just perfect. She shrugged off Luke's hand and started after Micah.

Luke swore, picking up the bags. "Lily," he hissed under his breath. "You promised me earlier."

She swung toward him. "I did. Just drop it, okay? Please?"

He stared at her hard and then grunted his disapproval.

They caught up with Micah, and as the trio slowed, she could hear the sounds of childish giggles mingled with the deep rumble of Michael's voice.

"Do you really get to shoot the bad guys?" asked one of the younger Nephilim.

"I try not to," Michael responded.

"But they are bad, and bad things deserve to die," stated another child.

Lily cringed at that statement, but Michael laughed softly. "Not all bad things deserve to die. Sometimes bad people are just confused and need someone to talk to or help them. I would try that before I would . . ."

"Kill 'em!" squealed a child.

Oh boy. Lily stepped around the two louts who suddenly had put away their differences in mutual amusement. "All right, runts, what are you doing down here?"

Michael and two very small heads turned toward her. A little dark-haired boy named Julio, in his Scooby pajamas no less, jumped to his feet and rushed at her. "Lily! Lily!"

She shifted the shoe box under her arm and braced herself. "Julio, what are you doing out of bed?"

The little boy wrapped his tiny arms around her legs and held on. "Donnie said there was a cop here, and I didn't believe him and . . . and he made me."

"Na-uh, I didn't!" The other child shot to his feet, planting his little fists on his hips.

She raised a brow at Donovan. He was about a year older than Julio, therefore the unofficial ringleader. "I doubt anyone can make you do something you don't want to do," she said to Julio as she pried his arms off her legs. "Isn't that so?"

He stared at her quizzically. "No. No one can make me do what I don't want to."

She patted the top of his head. "That's good to hear, but you two really need to be in bed. It is far too late, and you don't want grumpy old Nathaniel to catch you. Do you?"

Luke snorted somewhere behind her, but little Julio's eyebrows flew straight up and his eyes widened. "No. No." He glanced back at a pale Donovan. "We should go back to our rooms."

Donovan nodded, rushing to Lily's side. She knelt down, leaning her head forward. "Kiss?"

Both boys placed a wet kiss on each side of her face before rushing from the room. She heard Donovan squeal as one of the men made a playful grab for him. Lily stood, wiping the back of her hand over her cheek. "Yuck."

"That was mean," Luke said as he shuffled past her.

She giggled. "They're so scared of Nathaniel," she explained to Michael. "I really shouldn't use it against them, but it works."

Micah pushed past her, dropping Michael's stuff in the middle of the room. He didn't even acknowledge the man seated on the bed. He spared Lily a scathing look before leaving the room.

Luke shook his head as he laid his bags down. "Get some rest, Michael. You've got a long day ahead of you tomorrow." Then to Lily and much lower, "You've really done it now."

She watched Luke leave, hoping he managed to stop Micah before he went to Nathaniel. That was one lecture she'd like to avoid tonight.

"What is up with that?" Michael asked as he poked around in the bags.

She grimaced. "You don't want to know."

He ran a hand through his cropped hair. "You're good with kids."

"So are you."

"Foster care," he offered. "I spent a lot of time with children."

She sat on the edge of the bed, resting the shoe box in her lap. "It was a long time before I was around kids. When I came here, there were only a few kids, and I was one of them. Only in the last couple of years have we been able to offer a school and keep them here. I guess I think of them as mine. We can't reproduce, or at least none have been able to. So they're the closest things to children I'll ever have." She laughed self-consciously. "And I'm rambling. Sorry."

He sat beside her, brows furrowed. "I didn't know that."

She met his stare. He looked . . . sad for her. She tore her gaze away, uncomfortable. Did he want children? Well, she'd just busted his bubble. "Anyway, we brought back some of your stuff."

"I see that." He rubbed his hands down the front of his jean-clad thighs. "So do I have to stay here forever?"

"Just until you are better prepared for what's out there." She tucked a strand of hair behind her ear. "Most Nephilim do stay, though. They like it. Everything is provided for them, and it's safe. It's not really that bad."

"Do you stay here?"

"Most of the time," she answered, staring down at the box.

"And the rest of the time?" he prodded.

"I have my own place away from here." She tapped her fingers along the lid. "Sometimes I like to get away from everyone."

"I can understand that. I've only been here twenty-four hours, and I already feel claustrophobic." He gestured toward the box in her hands. "Mine?"

"Oh!" She handed it to him. "I thought you may want your personal stuff. We . . . um . . . grabbed what we thought you could use until you decide if you want to stay here or not."

He seemed surprised by that. "I really do have a choice?"

She grinned. Did he think they were the mob? "You have a choice. If you want to leave once you're trained, you can. It's on you." She paused. "Though I think you should pick a different apartment."

His brows rose. "I've figured that. You know, I was normal up until . . ."

"You met me?" She laughed softly. "Trust me, you were far from normal. I just happened along." She watched as he opened the box and poked around.

He put the lid back on the box. "Thank you for getting my stuff."

"Ah, don't thank me. I felt like a snoop having to go through your things."

He set the box on the floor. "This has been one hell of a day. I used to think my first day on the job would be the strangest day of my life, but I really had no idea." He rubbed a hand over his chest, shaking his head slightly. "I guess I don't have to worry about days on the force anymore, huh?"

"Why?"

His expression became dubious. "Not like I get to go back to work after this. Hopefully, the Sanctuary pays well."

"The Sanctuary pays extremely well, but you still get to keep your day job if you want." She waited while a slow smile crept across his face. For some reason, she smiled, too. "You just need to come up with a good reason why you had a family emergency when your four weeks are over."

"Great," he joked. "That should be easy. Maybe I should tell them I had a psychotic break with reality."

She chuckled. "Yeah, I don't know if that would be such a great idea."

"Well, after all the crap I learned today about your . . . my kind? Anyway, the Nephilim and the angel stuff? I feel like I need to see a head doctor."

"What did Luke talk to you about?"

He folded his arms across his chest and stared up at

the ceiling, recounting all that he had learned while Lily listened attentively to what Luke had divulged. It was all the basics, nothing too spectacular. By the time Michael had finished, his shoulders had slumped forward and he rubbed under his eyes wearily.

Lily stood and offered him a genuine smile. "Get some rest. Tomorrow we'll start training. It's going to be a long couple of weeks for you." It would be for her, too. Just because she was training Michael didn't mean she didn't have to hunt. She would be burning the candle at both ends.

He nodded, seemingly lost in his thoughts. She made it to the door before she remembered the frame in her pocket and the necklaces. "Oh, I almost forgot." She pulled out the photo along with the two small crucifixes. "I figured you may want these."

He took the picture and necklaces, his throat working. "This was my favorite picture. I was four," he murmured.

Lily placed one hand on the door. She couldn't read his expression, but he sounded sad. "Your mom looked really happy."

He glanced up. "She was. She was always happy." He set the picture on his nightstand, next to a tattered book. "I guess that's why I never understood . . ." He trailed off.

"Why she would take her own life?" she said softly.

"Yeah, I guess we never know people."

She focused on the picture. The woman in the photo smiled happily at them. Once again, she was struck by the difference between her mom and his. Lily paused in deep thought and, after a moment, excused herself.

Hurrying from the room, she waited until she stepped out of the elevator before digging out her cell. The phone rang twice. "Hey, Lily, good to see you're still alive. What's up?"

She frowned. "Danyal, can you do me a favor?"

He sighed loudly. "I'm afraid to ask after the last one."

"No, it's nothing like that. I wanted to see if you could pull an autopsy for me and tell me what you think?"

"You got a suspicious death?"

"I'm not sure," she admitted. "It's on a Sharon Cons. I believe she may have died in Hillsboro, Virginia."

"Wait. Is this Michael's mother?"

"Yeah." She unlocked the heavy steel door and stepped out onto the rooftop. "Can you look into it for me?"

There was a pause before he answered. "Sure. I'll let you know in a little while."

"Thanks." Lily slipped the cell back into her pocket and headed toward the edge of the rooftop. She couldn't shake the feeling that something wasn't right. As far as she knew, all of their mothers had been miserable and broken women, but the pictures of Michael's mother proved differently. There was more to it. She was certain.

The resonance of a soul slipping into the body of a human caught Lily's attention. She closed her eyes, slowing her breathing. Alert, she zeroed in on the possessed's location in the teeming city. Turning gracefully on her heel, she took flight over the rooftops. Another night, another innocent human lost.

She really needed to up her pay grade.

CHAPTER FOURTEEN

"Rafe, meet your new friend Michael," Lily said, stifling a yawn with one small hand. "Michael, say hello to Rafe. He'll be kicking your ass for the foreseeable future."

Rafe chuckled, extending his hand. "It's nice to meet you. Don't listen to Lily. There will be mutual ass kicking."

Michael shook the man's hand, shooting Lily a sour look. Did she get any sleep last night? She'd appeared in his room at the crack of dawn, dressed in sweats and a tank top with a strong cup of coffee in hand. She looked better prepared for bed than training.

When he first laid eyes on the tall Spaniard, all he could think was this man had to be dangerous. Well over six feet tall and built like a pro wrestler, he was certain Rafe was the kind of man that didn't leave many adversaries standing. *Oh, this is going to be fun.*

Lily floated away from the mats, plopping down in the corner. Casting a sideways glance at her, he saw her sitting cross-legged with her chin resting on a hand. Her cup of coffee sat in front of her, virtually untouched.

"So you're a police officer, right? That should mean you've got some basic fighting skills."

He wondered what Rafe considered basic fighting skills. What he saw Lily do wasn't anything in the scope of what he was taught at the police academy.

Rafe folded his large arms over his chest. "The training is going to be difficult, and there will be times you'll want to give up. I'll push you to your breaking point. Only then will your real training begin."

Michael rolled his eyes. He couldn't help it. He heard this before. "Yeah, I know. Knock me down to build me back up. Been there, done that."

Lily snickered from the sidelines. He frowned over at her. She picked up the coffee and took a drink. Her eyes danced over the rim of the cup. He had the distinct feeling she was laughing at him.

"Whatever you've learned at the police academy is nothing compared to what we are going to teach you," Rafe continued as if he hadn't heard him. "You will learn several different fighting techniques. Grappling, mixed martial arts, jujitsu—to name a few. You will also learn how to fight with blades."

"Oh, really?" he asked with raised brows.

Rafe grinned. He grabbed two blades from a low bench that held several sharp instruments. "You will need to master this." He motioned to Lily.

She pushed herself off the mat. "It's a little early for this, Rafe."

He snorted. "Let's show him how it's done, and then you can go sit down, look pretty, or whatever it is you're doing over there."

The blades slipped from her cuffs. Lily smirked. "Ass . . ."

Michael was fascinated by those things. The cuffs around her slender wrists were only three inches wide and yet the blades were at least six inches long. He stepped forward, curious. "How do those work?"

Lily glanced down. "Huh? Oh this. Remy is the resident weapons expert. He's a genius actually. The things he can come up with." She lifted her wrist so he could get a closer view of the blade. She pointed out several fine breaks in the steel. "I don't know the mechanics of it, but the blade simply collapses within itself when it's not in use. See." She flicked her wrist, and the blade sank down, disappearing into the cuffs. Then she moved her hand again, and the blade shot out, quickly opening one layer after the other. "Comes in pretty handy, don't you think? The silver is reinforced with Inconel—a type of metal used in aerospace. It's super strong and does the job."

"I imagine," he responded drily.

"You ready?" Rafe called, growing impatient.

She sighed. "Sure. Let's do this."

Michael backed off.

Rafe launched himself at Lily with a set of deadly looking daggers. She moved with him, blocking each slice of his hand with her forearm. On and on they danced in a mixture of martial arts and knife play. He saw how deadly this form of fighting was. They took turns missing blocks so he could see the kill shot or at least what should have been a kill shot. Moving fast, the knife would either hit the throat or the chest.

Lily dropped and spun around, knocking Rafe's feet out from underneath him. She brought her blade to Rafe's exposed chest. "No matter what, you have to stay on your feet," she explained. "Minions are trained the same way we are. Once they get you down, you're done for. You die."

Rafe knocked her arm away. "Thanks, Lily," he muttered.

She spared him a cheeky grin and stood up. "Blades are the deadliest weapon against our kind. For the most part, the minions don't have the type of blades we do, but they are just as skilled with a knife." She retracted the daggers and brushed off her knees. "Minions love to slice and dice."

"Why can't I just shoot them?" he asked, only half-serious.

"Because your bullets won't stop minions, and they'll barely make a difference on possessed humans," announced Remy from behind them.

Michael whirled around. He hadn't heard the man come in. Did they all move like ghosts? It was creepy and a little annoying.

"Unless you have my bullets," continued Remy. "Then you will do some major damage."

That got Michael's attention. *Screw knife fighting. Give me a gun.* Now this was something he could get into. "What kind of bullets?"

Rafe handed the blades over to Remy, who held them up. "Notice the engravings. They're holy symbols."

Michael had seen the markings on Lily's blades but

hadn't had a flipping clue what they were. Remy ran a finger over the first symbol. "This is the Chi-Rho. It is the earliest cruciform symbol." It looked an elongated P with an X drawn through the middle. He then slid his finger over more scratches in the silver. "This is a holy symbol against possession."

Upon closer inspection, Michael saw it looked like an X with a diamond on the top.

Remy slid his finger over another design—two crosses upside down and crossed.

Michael frowned. "Isn't that Satanic?"

"No," Remy replied. "It's a symbol of death. These are two Latin crosses that represent death in battle."

He didn't understand how pictures were of any significance. "What's the last one? It looks like an arrow or the middle of a peace sign."

"Another death symbol."

I see a trend here. "Kind of depressing," he muttered.

"These different symbols are all very powerful," explained Remy. "You can even say magical in the sense that they pack a punch if created correctly. Any silver reinforced with Inconel, then marked with these symbols in water that is blessed and fire that is pure, will deliver a death blow. It's a bit harder to get all these markings on a bullet, but it's doable. These symbols are also deadly to us . . . keep that in mind. We get stabbed anywhere with these, the silver will eat into us. It won't heal like a normal stab wound. You get hit with these blades, you'll need to get the hell out of Dodge fast. And you're going to be in for some pain."

Michael slid a glance at Lily. There was a bored look about her as she stared at the wall. "So if I load a gun with those kinds of bullets, it will kill a minion or a Fallen?"

"Shoot a minion in the heart or a deadhead in the head, you will take them out," answered Rafe. "But a Fallen will not go down with just a bullet, no matter how powerful it is. That is why you cannot solely rely on a gun. Eventually you will face a Fallen, and no gun or amount of special bullets will save your ass."

Remy snickered. "If you use a semiautomatic assault rifle and shoot them enough in the head, I'm sure that will do the trick."

Lily winced. "Ew . . ."

"Yeah, good luck getting a Fallen to stand still and let you shoot them multiple times. That is likely to happen," added Rafe.

Remy continued to smile good-naturedly. "You gotta shoot fast, my brother."

"The Fallen aren't just going to stand there and let you shoot them," Lily elaborated. "Their reflexes are quicker than ours. By the time it takes you to pull out your gun they've already snapped your neck. They're extremely fast and strong. It takes nothing for them to rip your head off your shoulders."

Oh shit.

"Anyway, back to the important training." Rafe brushed past Remy.

Lily went back to her spot on the mat. "Their

strength isn't the only thing you have to worry about. Some of them have retained their angelic powers. Remember Baal?"

He nodded. How could he forget? Not like he saw a guy burn metal and skin with a single touch every day.

She held up her arm and quickly removed the white gauze. The skin of her upper arm was soft and smooth, but as his gaze fell upon her forearm he tried not to show any reaction. He seriously hoped he didn't.

The skin was a bright cherry red, and it stretched around her forearm. It looked like a birthmark now instead of the blistering burn he'd last seen. She flipped over her arm, and he could clearly make out the impression of fingers. "Jesus."

"Baal obviously has an affinity for fire. His touch can burn anything. I imagine he brought down entire cities in his heyday." She shrugged. "Hurts like a bitch, I'll tell you that much."

He swallowed and looked away. It didn't seem right she was fighting a creature who could do something like that to her. "Can all of them do that?"

"No," she said. "Only the oldest ones seem to have retained some of their powers. We know a few can bring death with a single touch, while others can still heal." She saw the expression on his face. "You don't want to know how we found out who did what."

"Is there anything else I should know about these things?" he asked.

"All of them have the ability to influence humans. It's a compulsion even we can feel. We aren't as susceptible to it though." She picked up her coffee, staring down at it. "All it takes is a whisper or a single word from them. The compulsion is that powerful. I guess angels used to use their ability as sources of inspiration. Not so much anymore."

His first response was to dismiss what she had just told him, but then he remembered the stuff he had seen. Each time he heard something crazier than the last, it became a little easier to accept. Slowly but surely, he was becoming immersed in this world.

He wasn't sure if that was a good or bad thing.

Michael didn't have much time to dwell on that. Rafe called him over and began his training with a hellish warm-up that included burpees, suicide springs, and a ridiculous amount of squats.

Then he got his ass handed to him on a silver platter.

Not once and not twice, but over a dozen or so times—and all before lunch. Rafe had started off with grappling, and Michael felt like he had been blindsided into a street brawl. Between the painful takedowns and throws, he didn't even want to know what Rafe had planned for him after lunch.

Unfortunately, he found out all too quickly. He learned how to correctly do a clinch hold and set up for a takedown or throw. Lily helped, if laughing every time Rafe twisted out of Michael's clinch could be considered helping. Then came the submission holds. Oh boy, they were fucking great. Getting choked wasn't something Michael looked forward to, especially when he had an arm the size of a tree trunk pinned against his throat.

By the time the first day of training was over, Michael wondered what he'd agreed to. Every bone in his body hurt, every muscle ached, and he was pretty sure he suffered a mild concussion or two. Then he got up the next day and started it all over.

Again and again, his body and stamina were pushed to the limits. From grappling to jujitsu, Michael had the crap beat out of him day after day. There was improvement, but nothing he could really be proud of.

Other Nephilim helped during the first week of his training. They weren't any easier on him. Then there was Luke, who usually showed up to give Lily a hard time, but he would eventually turn his attention to Michael. That was when the real pain began.

At the end of each day, he spent time with Remy in the weapons room. He liked it in there. Not because he wasn't getting the snot kicked out of him, but because Remy really was a genius when it came to weapons. Michael was in awe of him.

Lily stayed with him throughout the training but never engaged him in battle. When she helped Rafe go through techniques, she usually gained the upper hand. She was a fierce little thing.

He wasn't sure if it was the hits he took to his noggin, but each day he thought Lily grew to respect him a little more. Her taunting lessened, and her general coolness toward him shifted to a warmer tolerance. He just hoped this training wasn't in vain, and that the first time he faced a minion, he didn't end up being sliced and diced, as Lily put it.

The graying senator tipped the glass of chardonnay, the cool liquid swirling in the crystal flute. He bore the look of power and prestige, a natural-born leader with unlimited potential. Inside, he was quaking.

The filet mignon sat untouched on his plate, the chair across from him empty.

Senator Robert Sharpe hated to wait. His lack of self-control was what got him in this situation in the first place. He came from a blue-blood family, raised in the world of politics and groomed to be more than just a senator. His father—God, rest his soul—would roll over in his grave if he knew that his son's chances at the presidency could have been lost the moment he slipped his dick into his pretty redheaded secretary.

When Cory had brought the oddly beautiful man to him, it had only taken one touch from the fallen angel, and Sharpe had learned everything about the Fallen and the Nephilim. Everything except what was going to be expected of him.

Sharpe felt the air stir around him, his attention turned back to the chair across from him. The devil had arrived.

Dressed in a suit just as expensive as the one the senator wore, the man exuded supremacy and malevolence. Still, the man before him was as beautiful as he was cold. Sharpe pushed down the ugly tendril of fear with a sip of wine. "You've cost me an aide."

Asmodeus smiled. "I could cost you much more than that."

Senator Sharpe set the wineglass down, his hand trembling slightly. Truer words had never been spoken. "So . . . my problem has been taken care of?"

He waved his hand. "It is as if it never happened."

The senator breathed a sigh of relief, but the reprieve quickly vanished when he realized the thing across from him wanted something in return, and he was yet to know what he could do for a . . . fallen angel. "What is the price?" he asked, never one to beat around the bush.

Asmodeus leaned back in the chair, smiling in that cold way. "My request is fairly simple, and I'm confident you will be successful. I don't think you want to end up like poor Cory."

He swallowed heavily at the reminder. It left a sour taste in his mouth, but he would never end up like Cory. He was stronger, smarter than his aide. "No. I won't be like him."

"Good. It warms my heart to hear you say that." Asmodeus leaned forward, resting his elbows on the table. "I've recently acquired a large stretch of land in Hillsboro, nestled deep in the wine country. The previous owner vacated the property unexpectedly."

He didn't want to know what happened to the previous owner.

Asmodeus snapped his fingers, and a man stepped out of the shadows, carrying a rolled parchment. "I wish to build a compound on my land." Asmodeus unrolled the parchment, revealing building plans for an enormous structure. "I do not need any funding, but I do need a public face for it."

The senator began to sweat under his costly suit. "I don't see how I could be of assistance. My time is full . . ."

"Your time is my time now." Asmodeus idly plucked a piece of lint off his shoulder. "Cory's demise was just five words whispered to him. Did you know that? I imagine you didn't." The senator didn't respond. "Construction will begin within the next week or so. You will tell the press and all your little politician friends that you are building a school for underprivileged youths."

Sharpe loosened the collar around his throat. "And what will I tell them when they question why there are no children in this school?"

"What a silly worry." He grasped the man's hand. The contact was enough to send the senator into a near panic, considering what happened the last time he was touched by the fallen angel. Other than the hot-and-cold feeling, nothing else occurred. "Indeed there will be children. Many of them. And all of them are special."

Then Asmodeus was gone, moving too fast for the senator to follow. He was left alone in the restaurant, alone with the deal he had made. What was a fallen angel planning with children? Special children? Nausea rolled through him. *What have I done?*

But it was too late for second guesses or redemption. One scandal too many had put the senator in the position to lose his seat and his reputation. Out of desperation, he had thought he had made a deal with an angel—and instead, he had sold his soul to the devil.

After spending the week watching Rafe and numerous Nephilim wipe the floor with Michael's face, Lily was starting to feel kind of bad for the dude. She really believed he deserved a break, at least over the weekend.

Man, he was a trooper though. It had been a long time since she had seen someone take a beating like he had and get back up. She was hesitant to say it, but he was going to make one kick-ass hunter once effectively trained.

Being with Michael during training killed two birds with one stone. Many of the Nephilim were interested in him, and most of them floated through the training room at some point. Some lingered longer than others, and those were the ones Lily showed interest in.

She knew there was a traitor among them intent on betraying the Sanctuary. That Nephilim would have to be interested in Michael, especially since he was feeding the Fallen names of those who appeared in the Book, and Michael's name never appeared. She bet that threw the asswipe into a shit storm.

But none of the Nephilim screamed traitor. Maybe she just didn't want to see it in someone she knew.

Growing restless, she left the training room to plead her case for Michael's minivacation. Granted, it was also for her. She could really use a day or two off. Between spending the day with Michael and going on hunts with Luke—who seemed to be stuck to her like glue nowadays—she needed to disappear to her apartment for a few days.

She descended the stairs to level seven. As she neared Nathaniel's office, the tingle of Nephilim nearby slowed her. She couldn't explain it, but it was a different feeling. Not the one she usually got from Nathaniel. Lily took off, covering the small distance in two steps. If she sensed the other Nephilim, that meant she was sensed, too.

The door to Nathaniel's office was ajar, but it swung open so fast that Lily stepped back. Her eyes widened at the Nephilim who stepped out of the empty office. "What are you doing in Nathaniel's office, Micah?"

CHAPTER FIFTEEN

Lily's fingers itched to release her blades. Her dislike of Micah ever since she returned from Michael's apartment was no secret. The feeling was mutual, but she never expected to find him snooping around Nathaniel's obviously empty office.

His pale eyes narrowed upon her. "I was waiting for Nate."

She shifted, blocking him. "Alone in his office?"

"Yeah, what's the big deal?"

"Nothing at all," she said. "Do you want me to leave him a message or anything?"

"No." He tried to step around her. "Do you mind?"

"Sorry!" she chirped innocently. "Don't let me keep you, Micah."

His reddish-blond brows furrowed at her. With a faint shake of his head, he left level seven under her watchful eye. Had she just caught him with his hands in the proverbial cookie jar? She tipped open the door to Nate's office and stepped inside. Nothing seemed out of place, but there was no telling how long he had been in there uninterrupted.

Closing the door behind her, she observed the room she'd been in over a thousand times. She stepped forward, her lips pressed together. Yeah, she totally recognized the hypocrisy of her busting Micah for snooping around Nathaniel's office and then doing just that herself. *However, I'm different*, she reasoned. *I'm Lily.*

Going to his desk and sliding open the drawer where he kept the keys to the cabinet, she swiped the one that unlocked the personnel files. It took only seconds for her to grab Michael's file and a few others. She quickly made a copy of each, put them back, and locked up.

She thought she'd make a great spy one day.

Taking the stack of copied files she'd swiped, she went back to her room. After reading through Michael's, she didn't know if she should laugh or feel sorry for him. His life had been painstakingly boring. With the exception of his mom's suicide, nothing remotely exciting had happened in his life—not that his mom killing herself was exciting.

She frowned. She needed to be less callous. Think a little more before she allowed certain thoughts to process into coherent sentences. If she had a soul—and who knew—she was dooming herself to Hell with some of the whoppers that came across her thoughts.

There was nothing remarkable about him other than the fact that he wasn't in the Book of Names. She set his file aside, grabbing Micah's next.

He'd never really done anything to her, but the thought of him soured her stomach.

Maybe it was how he styled his hair in the trendy

messy style. Yeah, the way one styled their hair was a valid reason for not trusting them.

He had to have been up to something in Nathaniel's office, and she doubted it was something good. She thumbed through his papers, finding numerous write-ups for failure to obey orders. Well, damn, Lily would have a stack of those suckers. She flipped over that page, finding something that made her eyebrows raise. Another Nephilim complained Micah displayed excessive and brutal force while carrying out his duty.

Their job was pretty excessive and brutal. They killed things. Couldn't get any more brutal than that. But to be considered excessive and brutal in their line of work, you had to do some real damage. It usually involved torture of some sort. The Powers That Be really frowned on stuff like that. So did Nathaniel.

Minions and the Fallen were evil, but they were still living and breathing creatures that had been in God's grace at one point. Their job was to dispose of them mercifully, which meant as quickly and cleanly as possible. Sometimes that wasn't always possible, especially with the Fallen. They were messy. Lord, were they ever. However, torture was never in the equation. It was just wrong.

This revelation left a bitter taste in her mouth. She flipped through some more pages. The only other unusual thing was a note about excessive time off. Lily found that odd. They got time off, just like humans did from their jobs, but even more. Nephilim had a more stressful work environment than those in cubicle farms.

She supposed if he were sneaking off to meet up with the Fallen he'd need some time off to do that. Closing Micah's file, she picked up Rafe's. Okay, she really didn't suspect Rafe. Other than the fact that he had the sex appeal of a fallen angel, and probably the conquests to match, he was a pretty good Nephilim. A go-to kind of guy with a ready smile and even readier helping hand. The kind of helping hand that perked up her walk when she needed a friendly pat on her ass. She had been on the receiving end of quite a few. There was nothing in his file that caught her eye.

Rubbing her hand over her face, she reached for another stack of papers. The twins: Damon and Gabe. The only reason she grabbed their stuff was because they had access to all the young Nephilim. More often than not, they were sent to retrieve them when their names received a mark. That alone warranted suspicion.

But she knew Gabe pretty well—obviously. She'd seen more parts of him than any of the others. And he was way too easygoing to be caught up in such treachery. That left his twin. Identical to the point that even she could barely tell the two apart, Damon and Gabe were pretty much hot stuff. Whenever the two were together, they communicated silently with each other. It wasn't a proven thing, but she totally believed it. She had seen them one too many times look at each other silently, then act in the exact same manner.

Damon was far too serious. Out of any Nephilim she knew, he was the most reserved, which was kind of funny considering Gabe was the total opposite. Hell, she hadn't been to Deuces Wild in days, and she had a feeling she wouldn't go back for a while. That was something she didn't want to examine too closely.

There was nothing in their files, either.

She stood, gathering the papers together and sliding them into her desk drawer. She dug out her cell phone and dialed Luke. Of course, she wasn't going to tell him what she had done. She just wanted to see if he'd answer. If so, she knew she had a hunting buddy for the evening.

He didn't answer.

Grinning, she slipped her phone back into the pocket of her skirt and headed out of the Sanctuary. It was a quarter past midnight, the streets of the city still full of people. Lily kept to the sidewalks, listening and watching.

She rounded a corner and heard the eerie whining of a soul slipping into a live body. *Come out, come out, wherever you are!* It didn't take long to zero in on the poor sap. Off in Rock Creek Park. *What the hell?* Since when did souls go into the wilderness? They were more of an urban issue.

Damn it, she needed to pick up her pace. Maybe she could swing by the zoo afterward. She loved to drop in at night and check out the animals.

Hitting the back alleys so she could truly reach the type of speed that would give humans a startle or two, she sped toward the park. It was less than ten miles, but it was a heavily populated ten miles of major DC thoroughfare, and eventually she could no longer hide in the shadows.

Slowing down to what could be considered a normal speed, she tugged at her skirt and wished she had worn something that could at least be passable as jogging clothing. The little skirt she had on probably made her look more like a prostitute running from her pimp than anything else.

Lily jogged up the ramp to Beach Drive. Once inside the nearly two-thousand-acre national park, she was surrounded by nature smack-dab in the middle of DC. It was like being in a different world. Sticking to the thick tree line, she let her senses carry her through. She rounded a bend and spotted the deadhead.

Damn. It was a park ranger. She liked park rangers and their hats. This one was missing his hat. He was young, and she kind of felt bad about having to kill him. She winced as he stumbled out onto the bike path, lifting his face to the sky. His mouth hung open at an odd angle. It was a silent scream. The kind of scream before they really started screaming and annoying the crap out of her.

She started forward but halted, watching, stunned, as three more deadheads scrambled out onto the path to stand beside the park ranger. One looked homeless, another was a jogger, and the third was . . . really gross.

It was once a person. Though, she couldn't be sure. The hair had fallen out, the skin had turned brown, crusted over in decay, and the ears had sharpened to points. This one was not fresh. Oh no, it had been riding out the human body until it turned into what people would call a monster. Actually, it reminded Lily of primitive drawings humans did of minions. They had no clue minions were actually rather attractive. What they had drawn was a deadhead past its expiration date.

They were a whole different type of problem. At some point, the body hardened, and the evil in them became darker. They were fierce—almost as bad as a minion.

And, God, did they smell horrible.

She rolled her eyes. Of course, it had to be her to hear the call. She shouldn't be so bitchy about it, but these kinds of deadheads sucked. Starting forward once more, she didn't make it very far. Cocking her head to the side, she felt a shiver go down her spine.

Before she could say Mississippi, the head of the jogger snapped to the side. She went down like a bag of rocks, twitching and moaning. Then the park ranger flew up in the air and, after several hard bounces, fell in a heap to the left of the path. He made a sickening crunch when he landed. He twitched, too.

Julian appeared in front of the deadhead, wrinkling his nose. "You want to handle this one?"

She stepped out of the bushes, ignoring the sudden warm feeling that coursed through her. This was so not the time for that. "Oh no, you're doing so well. Go ahead. Don't let me stop your fun."

The deadhead tipped back its head and wailed. The

sound, a cross between a coyote and a bobcat, was enough to make Lily's ears bleed. Julian regarded it with annoyance. "Oh shut up." He twisted the head right off the thing.

"Holy smokes." Lily plunged her blade into the jogger's heart. The twitching stopped. "That was . . . wow."

Julian glanced down at his hands in disgust. "I'll be right back."

Lily made her way over to the park ranger. Goodness, he was young. His name tag said Officer Joel Curry. "Sorry, Joel," she whispered.

The deadhead that was once Joel looked up at her through blank brown eyes. She sank the blade into his chest.

By the time Julian had returned, all the bodies had faded. She noticed wet spots on his black trousers. Apparently he was disgusted enough to wash his hands. He stood a few feet down the path, stunning in the pale light of the moon. Tonight he wore a very expensive-looking suit. The shirt underneath was unbuttoned, exposing his perfectly chiseled stomach. She sighed.

"I missed you, Lily." His voice dropped low and sensual.

Oh, it curled deep inside her. Reminded her of what had passed between them in her apartment a week ago, but she needed to play this cool. "I doubt that. I'm sure you had a bevy of women to occupy your time."

He smiled and stepped forward. "You know that's not true."

She stepped back, deciding to change the topic. "You know, I had that handled. You didn't have to butt in."

He shrugged. "They were going to take up too much of your time. Now, I have you to myself."

For the past week she had done her best not to think about him, not to lie in her tiny bed at the Sanctuary and remember what his lips felt like against her mouth, against her flesh. She had made a promise to Luke. "Julian, we can't."

He came to her side. "We can't do what?" He reached down, catching her hair around his finger.

His heat swamped her, and when he drew the strand of hair out in front of her, she stared at his fingers. That wasn't a good idea. She snatched her hair back. "Why aren't you off doing . . . Fallen . . . stuff?"

"Fallen stuff?" he repeated with a chuckle. "What silly notions you have."

She made a face and started walking toward the entrance. "I have a lot of hunting to do," she told him. "It's early."

He fell into step beside her. "Then I'll come with you."

Lily stopped. "You can't come with me."

"Why not?"

"You can't help me hunt, Julian. I appreciate it, but no. You can't."

He frowned. It didn't take away from his beauty at all. "Then we are at a standstill."

Crossing her arms, she stared up at him. "How so?" she demanded.

"I wish to spend time with you," he explained quite seriously. "If you cannot hunt with me, then I fear I cannot allow you to hunt."

"Julian . . ."

"I like your skirt, by the way. What is it the humans say? Easy access or something?" he said with a flirtatious wink. "Anyway, I have nothing to do other than torment you."

Flushing, she glanced down at the black pleats. She liked it, too. "Um thanks. I think." She cleared her throat. "Seriously, Julian, I've got work to do."

He smiled rather angelically, which was totally wrong. "I said I would work with you. I find your fighting incredibly sexy. Alluring really—the way you move?" He trailed off. The angelic look faded into something akin to sinful. "I'm fixated. Show me your nightlife, baby."

Fighting a stupid grin, she knew she shouldn't be enjoying any of this. There was stuff to do—things to kill. Things like him. Yet, here she was, bantering back and forth with him. And she was having fun. Stupid Lily . . . and stupid hormones . . .

She was so doomed.

Lily sighed. She had to hunt, but no matter where she was in the city she would hear a minion if one got frisky, and there were other Nephilim out there. So what if she spent some time in the park with Julian? She bit down on her lip. *I'm selfish, totally selfish.*

"All right," she agreed. "But if I hear a minion, I have to go, and you can't follow me. No questions asked. That is the only deal I am making."

"No deal."

Her eyes narrowed upon him. "What?"

"Give me your hand. We shall do this like normal people."

She looked at him curiously. "Do what exactly?"

"A date," he said. "A walk in the park is considered a date by human standards. It's a rather lame date, but it's not like I can take you out to dinner without having the entire Sanctuary descending on us."

"A date?" she repeated dumbly.

"Yes."

"Haven't we kind of skipped right past that?" she asked.

Julian bent down, brushing his lips over hers. "We can skip right to that again, but I am trying to be a gentleman."

What was funnier? The idea of going on a date with him or him trying to be a gentleman, she couldn't tell. "We don't date. Our two kinds? No way, buddy." She gave him her hand anyway. "Here, if this will make you happy."

Julian smiled widely. He grasped her hand in his warm one. "We don't date? There goes my movie idea."

"Ha-ha." Lily let him steer her back toward the mouth of the park. She observed her hand wrapped in his. "This is by far the weirdest thing I have ever done."

"Really?" he inquired. "I find that hard to believe."

She thought for a moment. "Yeah, it is. Man, if any of them catch me right now I am so dead."

Julian led her off the beaten trail, into the woods. "Do you care so much about what they think?"

"No," she immediately answered. "Yes. I mean, what this is? I don't even know what this is, but it's not allowed. They'd think the . . . worst."

His eyes sparkled in amusement. "And what would that be?"

Her lips pursed. "That we are . . . you know, doing it." Julian tipped his head back and laughed deeply. She scowled at him. "It's not funny."

"But we aren't doing it." He stopped under a large oak tree and pulled her against him.

The air caught in her lungs, and where her traitorous body brushed his, she came alive. "What are we doing?" she whispered.

"I really don't know."

His response seemed truthful, and she didn't pull away when he bent his lips to hers. Nor did she stop him when the whisper of a kiss turned into something more. He parted her lips, deepening the kiss.

Julian's hands slipped under the hem of her skirt, teasing and daring. He lifted his mouth just an inch. "Do you know how badly I've missed you this week?"

Her fingers curled against his chest as she stared up at him.

A small lifting of his lips softened his harsh beauty. "That Nephilim has been everywhere you've been. I don't like it."

189

She slid her hand along the collar of his shirt. "Luke worries about me."

He brushed his cheek against hers. "It's the only reason I tolerate his presence."

She opened her mouth to respond, but he took advantage of the moment, delving his tongue deep into her mouth. When he broke the kiss and stepped back to capture just her hand again, Lily frowned.

He flashed a knowing grin and started walking. "Ask me anything."

"Um," she said, running a shaky hand through her hair. "Okay . . . what do you do in your spare time?"

"Besides follow you?"

Well, he got points for honesty. "Yeah, besides follow me."

"Well, I don't sleep all day in my lair if that is what you think." He led her around a small creek fed by the Potomac. "I actually own a couple of businesses in Maryland and a few in the city—clubs and bars."

That was not what she expected. The shock must have been transparent, because Julian laughed. "I'm easily bored, especially after centuries. It's not uncommon for us to acquire certain things. You'd be surprised."

Lily really needed to share that with the circle. "What kind of clubs?"

"The kind you'd get into," he said with a grin. "The clubs are all the rage among the rich Georgetown students and yuppies looking for a good time."

"So is this an illegal thing or a way to . . . reach more

humans?" Meaning corrupt more humans through exploiting their vices. It was something the Fallen were very good at.

Julian glanced down at her questioning face. "At times, yes. For the most part, it's just a trendy club people go to when they want to enjoy themselves. I don't prey on everyone who walks through the doors of my establishments. Though some of my clubs are private. Places for people who'll pay good money to relax and not be seen."

Politicians and celebrities? It appeared Julian was ever the opportunist.

"You?" he prodded after a moment.

"I don't really do anything exciting," she said drily. "No secretive businesses or intrigue." She paused. "I did go to American University."

"College grad?" he asked. "Hot."

Lily laughed softly. "I didn't graduate. The job kind of got in the way."

He seemed to digest that tidbit of information. "Your job is everything. It's all you have."

When it was put that way it sounded sort of depressing. But she loved her job. Hell, it was more than a job. It was a duty to a higher calling. She was lucky to have such an important role in life.

It sounded like a pep talk even to her.

When she didn't answer, Julian peppered her with questions and eventually drew more information out of her. There really wasn't much for her to tell him. Other than being a Nephilim, she lived a boring life.

He didn't seem to think so. Not by the rapt attention he was paying her.

A few minutes passed and the beauty of the park settled around them. That was when Lily came up with the most inappropriate question she could ask. "How many Nephilim have you fathered?"

"Children?" He tilted his head to the side, and a lock of hair fell across his broad cheek. "None."

CHAPTER SIXTEEN

Lily busted out laughing. "Whatever. You tell me to ask you anything and then you lie."

The skin between Julian's brows puckered. "I'm not lying."

Her smile faded. Either he had an awesome poker face or he was telling the truth. But there was no way he had not fathered a Nephilim. It was just . . . what they did. Like over and over again. But he stared at her with this serious and somewhat offended expression on his face.

"You can't be serious," hissed Lily.

"Why would I lie about that?"

They had stopped walking. Underneath an old stone bridge that was no longer in use, she withdrew her hand from his. "Not a single Nephilim?"

He sighed. "If I had known you would've been disappointed by that, I would've lied to you."

"No." She bit her lip. "I'm not disappointed. I'm just surprised. I mean, what Fallen doesn't produce a Nephilim? We're like your first 'in your face' to God."

Julian actually laughed. "I guess I'm a very poor Fallen."

"Wow," she murmured. He was full of surprises,

and this latest one was rather telling. She had thought his inexplicable fondness for her and flippant manner of destroying the creatures his kind created was strange, but this was beyond that. "Are there others like you?"

He reached down, unfolding her arms. "I imagine there are some who've grown tired of this path we have chosen. Who have carved out a different life, leaving what made them fall behind."

That didn't sit well with Lily. All the years of training and education on the Fallen started to unravel. The lines between them were always an issue of black and white. Yet Julian was proof that wasn't always the truth. And there could be more like him? Out there? Fallen but not completely evil? And her kind was killing them?

She needed to get away, to think. All of this confused her.

Julian rubbed his hands over her arms. "It bothers you, doesn't it?"

"What does?"

He smiled slightly. "Knowing everything you've been taught isn't always the right thing. That no amount of training could prepare you for the knowledge that there are a lot of gray areas."

Damn, he was good. It didn't mean she would admit to it, no matter how right he was. "Why aren't you like them?"

A dark look flickered across his face as he stared up at the sky. "Who says I'm not?"

Okay then. Deciding it was well past time for her to

get back into the city and hunt, she pulled herself away. "Julian, I have to get back—"

Her words were cut off by the sheer intensity in the way he claimed her lips with his. Sliding his arms around her waist, he lifted her against him. Damn, it was so incredibly hot when he did that.

He raised his head. "I know. Just give me a few minutes."

"A few minutes?" she murmured, dazed by his passion. She had a few minutes. A few minutes wouldn't hurt anything.

Then he started kissing her again. *I guess no answer is a yes answer.* Who the hell was she kidding? She liked when he kissed her like the very taste of her was enough for him to live on. Julian was so wrong yet so right for her.

He turned and pressed her against the rough stone blocks. Not the most comfortable position, but there was something about the cold bricks at her back and the warmth of Julian at her front. Fire and ice—that was what he was.

One arm tightened around her as he slipped a hand under the hem of her skirt. Up and up it went until his fingers skimmed the curve of her buttocks. She moaned into his mouth, the need his touch brought on was sudden and powerful, but when he slipped his fingers under her panties, her eyes flew open.

"Julian!" she hissed. "Someone will freaking see us!" She wasn't a prude, but she didn't feel like giving the homeless people and the park rangers a free show.

He chuckled deeply, pressing her further against the wall. "No one will see us." He worked his fingers back to where they had been.

"Julian!" It started off as an order to let her go, but ended in a moan as he slipped one finger over her wet cleft. Lily jerked against his hand as he lowered his mouth to hers. His kisses were intoxicating. Timing the thrusts of his tongue with the gentle plunge of his finger, her protests evaporated. *Screw the moral outrage.*

When his thumb pressed against the little bundle of nerves, she rocked against his hand. He was relentless, and it didn't take long. Not when he shifted and brought his knee between her thighs. The pressure between the thick cord of muscles and his hand brought her over the edge. His mouth swallowed the sounds of her orgasm.

Shaken and breathless, it took quite a few minutes for her to come to her senses. When Julian eased her back to her feet, she felt his arousal. She shifted, pressing against him.

His head dipped to her neck. "You little minx."

Her fingers sifted through his soft hair. "I want to do that for you."

He groaned. "Keep talking like that and you will."

It may have made her a really bad person, but his words turned her on nonetheless. Her hand snaked between them, cupping him through his pants. "I wouldn't mind."

He lifted his head, pinning her with a feral look. It

nearly knocked the air from her lungs. She was snared in his molten gaze. The liquid fire that ran through her body was too potent to be ignored. Her sex swelled with anticipation. She'd do anything he asked—anything he demanded.

Something darkly possessive flickered over his features, sharpening them. "Then do it."

Breathless, she watched him unbutton his pants and pull out his manhood. He was thick, fully engorged, and her heart leaped into her throat.

"Touch me," he ordered roughly.

A wicked thrill went through her as she reached for him.

"No." He stopped her. "Not like that." He cupped her cheek, leaning down to place his mouth over hers. The kiss was deep, intense. He sucked her tongue into his mouth expertly. "Like that," he said, voice gruff and leaving no room for disobedience. "Suck me."

A sharp swirl of tingles sped over her. Would she do this, out here where anyone could see them? Wicked excitement filled her. Legs wobbly, she dropped to her knees in front of his towering frame. A deep groan of triumph radiated from him as she wrapped her hand around the base. He jerked in her hand as she ran her fingers to the tip, running her thumb over the liquid beading there.

She inhaled his musky scent as she took him in her mouth, scraping her teeth all the way to his root. He groaned, balling his hand in her hair as he flexed his hips. Working him hard and fast, she was amazed by

197

how he trembled before her, fascinated by how he swelled inside her mouth, ready to explode. Then he was thrusting so deeply, his movements becoming more erratic as her mouth drew him in deeper.

He made a hoarse noise and tried to pull back, but she held on, unwilling to let him go. She raked her nails over his ass, and that did it. His release came, and he growled her name as his hand clenched the back of her head. The grip was almost painful, but something primitive rose in her, reveling in the feeling of him spasming endlessly. When he finally broke her hold, he staggered a bit.

Still on her knees, she darted her tongue over her lower lip.

Staring down at her, his blue eyes blazed. "Sweet Jesus," he said. Then he reached down, grasped her shoulders, and hauled her to her feet. He pressed her back against the wall, kissing her with such ferocity that his teeth cut into her lower lip.

She tasted a bit of blood as she grasped his head, kissing him back with just as much hunger. Julian lifted her again, wrapping her legs around his hips. She felt him, already hard and thick again, pressing against the center of her damp panties. Locking her ankles together, she ground her pelvis against his. Small whimpers escaped between kisses. He could take her right here, and she wouldn't stop him. She was so close to begging. She wanted him, wanted him so badly she ached in ways that went beyond the physical.

Her back hit the wall again, and she felt his hand go

under her skirt, slipping under the band on her panties. Her blood boiled. She wanted him to rip off her panties and rip into— She stiffened, eyes popping open and going wide.

Julian pulled back, his eyes swirling with lust. "Lily . . ."

There was no mistaking the feeling sliding down her spine. A human had just been possessed, and it was somewhere close. "You've got to be kidding me."

He stared at her like he thought the same thing.

Flushed, hot, and ready to strip off her clothes and jump him, she closed her eyes. "I'm sorry. Really, I am. I have . . . I have to go." Oh dear God, she didn't want to go.

Pulling from what was probably centuries of restraint—which she was completely lacking—he disentangled her legs from his hips and set her down gently. "I understand." His voice was rough, husky. "I made you a promise. Go."

Adjusting her skirt and shirt, she had no idea what to say now. So she settled on the lame, "See you around?"

"Lily," he called out. "Be careful. Please."

She threw a cocky grin over her shoulder. "Now, I think you're beginning to like me, Julian. Don't worry, I'm always careful." Then she raced off toward the front of the park.

Hoping the run would somehow clear her heated thoughts to the point she could successfully fight, she pushed hard and fast. The soul was somewhere on the road leading to the park. It didn't take her long. Besides the fact she felt like she ran in one giant circle, she was feeling good. Okay, she was feeling pretty damn fine. Even after she dealt with the deadhead, she hadn't lost the afterglow.

Damn, she actually felt alive. Her skin tingled, blood buzzed.

Her good mood lingered after the ensuing cat-and-mouse game began between her and the minion she had glimpsed near the Verizon Center. She chased the coward through DC and back. She'd give the little bastard one thing: he sure could run like a minion.

Halfway through the chase, Luke called and wanted to chat, even after she explained she was kind of busy. Then she had to explain exactly why she was busy. He proceeded to laugh. Apparently, chasing a runt of a minion around the city was hilarious if it wasn't his ass doing the running.

She finally hung up on him.

Once she cornered the minion, it only took her thirty seconds to dispatch him. Vanquishing deadheads bothered her more than minions did. The poor body that the soul had crept down into didn't have a choice. Their life had been stolen. The minion, on the other hand, made the choice to go to the dark side. Lily couldn't work up any pity when it came to minions.

Would she take pity on a Fallen who'd blended in with humans? Her lips pursed. She couldn't answer that question, and that troubled her. She picked up her pace.

Freaking starving, she was happily surprised when Luke appeared with two bags of fast food. She nearly threw herself at him. "Oh my God, I love you."

He chuckled. "I figured you earned it after all that running."

She fell into step beside him, eagerly prying open the bag. All her happiness faded, and her voice became shrill. "You got me a Happy Meal?" Simply unacceptable. This girl had an appetite, and a Happy Meal wasn't going to cut it.

He hooted with laughter. Several people stopped to look at them, and she wanted to punch him. He opened his bag for her. "Hey, I got you a Big Mac, too."

Lily narrowed her eyes at him. "Food is not a joking matter. How many times do I have to tell you that?" She snatched the carton from him. "I love you, Mr. Big Mac. I'd marry you if you'd promise me an endless supply. Do you think I'd get an endless supply if I dated Ronald McDonald? The clown makeup scares the shit out of me, but it would be worth it."

"Maybe if you gave him head."

Her cheeks flushed, but she forced those other thoughts away. She tipped her head to the side, staring at the wonderful creation. "Doable."

Luke made at face at her. "You're bizarre."

"But you love me," she reminded him around a mouthful of burger. Lily attacked her food with the same ferocity she displayed in her battles. And apparently other things. She ate the Big Mac, the cheeseburger, and the fries within three minutes. It wasn't her best time, but given the fact she was walking, it was pretty good.

"How many kills tonight?" Luke asked as he grabbed her empty bag and rolled it into a ball. He tossed it on the ground, along with his.

"Luke!" She bent down, picking up the discarded bags.

"What?" he asked innocently.

She pinned him with look that said he knew better, then tossed the bags into a nearby trash bin. She decided she could count the one Julian had ripped the head off. Luke wouldn't know the difference. "Six."

"I got eight, slacker."

Lily pushed him out into the busy road. He narrowly missed getting hit by a taxi. The driver blew its horn at him, and he flipped him off.

"I had to chase one through seven districts. That should account for two more at least." She knew she was whining, but oh well.

He pushed her in front of some street thug. Something in the way she smiled at the teenager warned him not to have a problem with it. "The night is still young. Maybe you can catch up to me, but probably not," Luke taunted.

"Douche," she muttered.

"Tool," he tossed back. "All right, check you later."

"Hey, hold on a second," she called out. "I found Micah in Nathaniel's office. I think he was snooping."

Luke frowned. "Why would he be doing that?"

She gave him a duh look. "Someone is betraying us."

"So you think it's him?" Luke's frown deepened. "Shit, Lily. I don't know. Micah is good a guy."

"Whoever is betraying us is a damn good actor, right? If not, they would have slipped up."

He stepped back as a young woman walked between them. She was a tall, pretty brunette. In her tight jeans and colorful blouse, she was a head turner. Luke did a double take. "Damn."

The girl turned, flashing a smile at him. Of course she would. Lily rolled her eyes. Most women would pay good money to get that kind of attention from him. With his chiseled features and broad body, he turned a few heads himself.

"Um, pay attention to the important thing at hand," she reminded him drily.

Luke tore his gaze from the brunette. "What?"

She sighed. "Someone is betraying us, blah blah blah."

"I'll mention it to Nate and see what he thinks." Luke glanced behind him. "Good catch, by the way. I'm kind of proud of you." He lightly chucked her on the chin with one meaty fist. "I gotta go. Be careful."

"Peace out, home skillet."

He rolled his eyes at her and disappeared down an alley. She headed toward the Washington Nationals stadium. She was sure to run into some deadheads, minions, or general bad folk on the way.

By the end of the night she'd gotten three more. Luke got four and the girl. He felt like sharing that, and in great detail. He was such a douche. As she headed back to the Sanctuary, her cell rang. She fished the thing out. It was Danyal. Sighing, she answered, "Yep?"

"I got that info for you."

"Oh great." She perked up. "Lay it on me."

"Whatever suspicion you had, you're on to something," Danyal told her. "I don't see how the coroner missed this. She had several cuts on her fingers and hands. There was also bilateral bruising around the wrists that occurred before death."

"Self-defense wounds," she stated as she dropped from the roof of the General Accounting building onto its lower ledge.

"Either the coroner was an idiot or he was paid off," he said. "I don't think Michael's mom killed herself. I've never seen a suicide with that many hesitation marks, especially ones on the fingers."

Unease formed little balls of ice in her belly. "So she didn't kill herself?"

"Hold on." He radioed in a command. "Sorry. No. My professional instincts tell me no."

"Damn." That was really weird.

"What made you check into this?"

"I saw some pictures of his mom," she admitted. "You know how all our moms were, right?"

There was a silence. Then he answered, "Coldhearted and soulless."

"Exactly," she responded. "Except in every single picture of his mom, she was smiling. I mean, really smiling. I don't know. It just struck me as odd."

"I really don't know what this could mean. If

Michael's mom was murdered, then were the Fallen behind it?"

Lily wished she could ask Danyal about Michael not showing up in the Book, but she wasn't supposed to know that. "And why would they kill his mom?" she finished for him.

"You should bring this to Nate. You never know. It could be a coincidence, or it could mean something."

Lily nodded and then frowned at herself. *Not like he can see you nod, idiot.* "Yeah, I will." She pushed on the lobby doors. "Thanks, Danyal. Be safe out there."

"Same to you," he responded.

Once inside, she went in search of Nathaniel but wasn't able to find him. She headed back to her room, digging out the file on Michael again. Scanning through it a second time, she still didn't find anything that stood out to her.

Sitting down on the bed, she tried to piece together the connection between Michael's mother's death and the fact that his name never showed in the Book. Luke would probably tell her there was no connection at all, but she couldn't shake the feeling there was, and she was missing it somehow.

CHAPTER SEVENTEEN

Nathaniel stared down at the Contract on his desk. "Interesting," he murmured.

Is that all he would say to finding out Micah was snooping around his office? Disappointed, Lily's shoulders slumped. "I figured you'd be more intrigued with the news."

He arched a brow at her. "Intrigued is not a word I would use, Lily. Disappointed and angry are better-suited words. I have known Micah for decades. To suspect someone like him is not something I can take lightly."

She tucked a leg under her. "It has to be someone in the circle," she pointed out. "Those are the only ones who know where the Book is."

Nathaniel tapped his fingers. "I will talk with him. See what information I can get. I'll admit I hope your suspicions are incorrect."

"If they are, then it only means it's someone else you trust. No matter what happens, it isn't going to be pretty." She bit her lip, rubbing her palms over her knees. "Is that Michael's Contract?"

"Yes. Have you mentioned it to him yet?"

She laughed. "No. I figured I'd leave that to you."

Nathaniel leaned back, placing his hands behind his head. "I've sent Luke to retrieve him. I think it would be good if you could hang out here for just a few more minutes."

She didn't like the sound of that. "Why?"

His lips curved into a smile. "Lily, you grew up knowing about the Contract. You accepted it. Hell, you worked toward it. It's not the same with Michael. It's going to come as a shock."

"Oh yeah, good point," she murmured absently. She hadn't really paid much thought to the idea of the Contract being offered to Michael. Now that she did, she kind of wished she had somehow escaped this meeting. She couldn't imagine him not freaking out once he heard the terms. "It's pretty heavy stuff. Are you really going to offer it to him now?"

"No, but I think he should have a good idea of what it is."

She wanted to laugh, but Michael arrived with Luke trailing behind him. Nathaniel motioned for Michael to sit. Luke could have pulled up a chair, but he chose to hover behind her.

She inspected Michael. He was dressed in the customary sweats and shirt. Poor guy looked like he could use some sleep. But although a little ragged around the edges, he was still something to look at. Especially with his hair grown out a bit. He wasn't tatted up, and his masculine beauty seemed much more refined than the wilder look the other male Nephilim favored.

Lost in her own thoughts, she realized she had missed a good part of the conversation—and all of them were staring at her.

"What?" she asked.

Luke leaned over the back of her chair, grinning. "Nate asked if you had any input on the rookie's training."

"Oh! Um," she fumbled as she turned to Nathaniel. "He's doing really well, picking up the jujitsu and grappling training faster than I thought he would. He does need to improve on his knife fighting, but that's expected. Also, his blocking could improve." She stopped, sparing Michael a smile. "He has the determination and stamina of a Nephilim. He will make a good fighter."

Michael looked like he'd fall out of his chair.

"Good," Nate answered. "Luke?"

"He still needs improvement," he said bluntly.

She tipped her head back. "You spend what—an hour or so a day with him? How can you even answer that?"

Luke cocked a brow. "Nate asked for my opinion."

Ignoring him, she looked at Michael. His brows had knitted together. "So, how do you think you are doing?" she asked.

"I'm doing damn good. Take into consideration that a week or so ago I would've thought you all were on crack," he retorted. "Not to mention my training consists of me getting my ass handed to me on a regular basis, and I am still standing."

208

Nathaniel had remained quiet up until that point. "That may be, but in reality, out on the streets your ass won't be handed to you if you fail. You will die."

A red flush traveled over Michael's features, and his lips thinned. "I know I can improve." He leaned forward, meeting Nathaniel's gaze with his own level one. "Lily is right. I need better blocking. I need to not end up on my back every five seconds, but I can get this done. I can do this."

At the moment, Lily was sort of proud of him. Like a mother who just saw her child do something right.

"I don't believe you can do this," Nathaniel said. "I believe you can master this."

Michael once again looked startled. "Thank you."

He continued. "I know you are curious about the Contract and what it entails. I think at this point in your training, it's a good idea to discuss what it is."

"What? Are you for real?" Luke exploded. The chair Lily sat in rocked forward.

She pushed his arm off the back of her chair. "Jesus," she muttered crossly. "Not necessary."

Luke stood straight, crossing his thick arms. "Nate, he's only been training for little over a week. He didn't even know he was Nephilim until recently. There's a lot for him to learn, to experience before he can accept the Contract. He's nowhere near ready for such a commitment and responsibility!"

Nathaniel regarded him calmly. "Is there anything else you wish to add?"

"Oh, give me a few seconds, and I'm sure I can come

up with a dozen or more reasons why he shouldn't be offered the Contract."

Michael shot to his feet. "Is this a conversation you'd rather have without me here? I have this feeling it doesn't matter if I'm here or not."

"I happen to agree," Luke responded, forever the smart-ass.

Michael whirled on him. "Man, what the fuck is your problem?"

Lily sighed wearily. This wasn't going as planned. "Michael, sit down. Luke, shut up." It was a sad day for Nephilim around the world when she played mediator. "If you guys want to pull out your dicks and see whose is bigger, can you go ahead and do it so we can move on?"

The men looked at her like she had sprouted two heads, but Michael did sit down at least. Luke seemed like he was going to do as she asked, which she seriously hoped he didn't. That was something she didn't want to see. Ever. "Luke?"

He stared at her for a moment. "Whatever. Go ahead."

"Thank you for your permission," Nathaniel said evenly. There was a glint in his eyes that warned Luke against any other outbursts. "Michael, once your training is complete, you will be paired up with hunters. Nephilim like Lily and Luke."

She hoped he didn't pair Michael with Luke anytime soon. One of them wouldn't make it back.

"What is this Contract exactly?" Michael asked.

She slid a curious glance at Nathaniel. How was he

going to explain this? Eternal life and all that jargon wasn't going to be easy.

"The Contract is an agreement between you and the Sanctuary. It entails your duty to the Sanctuary, and what's expected of you as a hunter. Hunters do not guide souls. You're the hand that moves against evil. You'll agree to stand against the Fallen, the Nephilim that have turned minion, and the disposal of humans who have become possessed by souls. You agree to protect your fellow Nephilim—even if it means with your life." He paused long enough to take a breath. "You will be rewarded greatly; monetarily on Earth and spiritually in Heaven. You shall want for nothing. There is no limit to what you are paid."

That was the God's honest truth.

Lily didn't know how much she had in her bank account. She stopped counting about two years ago. She could buy and sell half of the DC elites. Money was never an issue.

"There would be no need for you to keep your job as a police officer unless you want to. Danyal is the example. He has successfully done both jobs for years, and he has proven to be an invaluable asset."

There was no hesitation. "So where do I sign up?" he asked.

He has no idea. Nathaniel had left out some very important details. "Michael, it's not your kind of lifetime agreement—like twenty years till retirement and you get to spend your golden years playing golf down in Florida."

211

He looked at her blandly. "Gee, really?"

"You won't get the golden years. Once you sign the Contract, you will not age. It's forever." She stopped with a slight frown. "Or till you die. Whatever. But it's not just a job. It's a duty you will always have to uphold." Something she was desperately in need of being reminded of. "Your life will become your duty. It is everything."

Michael stared at her, clearly unsure that he had heard her correctly. "Not age?" he repeated dumbly.

She nodded. "The Nephilim who accept the Contract do so knowing they could walk Earth for eternity, fighting the Fallen and their creations." She tipped her head at Nathaniel. "God knows how old he is. Luke is well over eighty."

Michael's eyes widened. "Shit . . ."

"What Lily is trying to say is the Contract is not something you can take lightly," Nathaniel advised. "It is until death in most cases—and that death could be eons from now. Very rarely do we ever revoke the Contract once it is made. If you accept this, Michael, you will have a very long life ahead of you."

Michael paled by several degrees. He sat back in his chair, blinking rapidly. "Wow."

It didn't pass by Nathaniel. "I think that is enough for now. You can have the rest of the afternoon and evening off. Take some time and relax. I don't expect an answer from you anytime soon." Nathaniel paused, meeting Michael's wide-eyed stare. "Frankly, not until you've made your first kill will I even consider your answer. This is the kind of life you have to experience before you can decide it is what you want."

"And if I don't?"

Lily glanced down at the floor. She had never asked that question. Signing the Contract had been all she ever wanted. When she was younger, she idolized the ones who accepted the Contract, leaving every night to hunt the Fallen and their creations. To her, they were like superheroes, and she wanted to be one of them. Now, hearing Michael ask a question she never considered, she was curious as to how Nathaniel would answer.

"There are many Nephilim who don't accept the Contract and are an asset to the Sanctuary. Most are guides to souls, while others have assumed positions within the Sanctuary's more public sectors. We even have a few Nephilim politicians. They age like any other person would."

"So they don't hunt?" he asked, confused.

"Yes, but it is not often," Lily answered softly. "It's very dangerous for them. See, when you take the Contract you are gifted with certain things. Not just the fountain-of-youth stuff. You will be healthier, resistant to most injuries, be able to jump and run faster than you ever believed possible. You will be stronger in battle, quicker in your attacks. The Contract makes you a better hunter. Without it, you are just a human going up against creatures that aren't."

"Why would anyone choose to hunt and not take the Contract? That doesn't make any sense."

The clock on the wall ticked ten times before anyone answered. Surprisingly it was Luke who did. "That's why most do it, but if they have their heart set on hunting while remaining as human as they possibly can, then so be it."

Michael shook his head. "I don't get it."

"It's like this." Lily leaned forward, placing her hand on his arm. "The ones who want to remain as human as possible want more out of the life than this . . . duty. Some want to marry, want to grow old. Guiding souls is as important as hunting, and it affords you with a chance to have more of a personal life."

"So, if I accept this Contract, then I don't have a life?"

"You have a different life," she said. "When you don't age, it kind of raises a lot of questions. Eventually you will have to quit the police department. Not to mention, you don't meet the greatest people when you're hunting. The stuff we hunt are kind of like cockroaches—they only come out at night, and so do we. Those who don't accept the Contract tend to meet others and live out their lives blissfully in love." The last part was a tad bit sarcastic, even for her.

He looked at Lily, his eyes piercing. "You didn't want that? Someone you could love and live your years with? Have a life with?"

She removed her hand as if she'd been burned. His question caught her off guard, bringing the image of Julian to mind. She looked away, uncomfortable by the intensity in his eyes and the image of Julian she

214

couldn't push away as much as she tried. "It's just not what I chose."

A week ago, Michael didn't believe in immortality. Shit, he hadn't believed in fallen angels and Nephilim, either. And if he was honest with himself, he probably didn't believe in angels at all.

It was hard for him to wrap his head around the idea of living forever—or at least living until something killed him. And it seemed things were always trying to kill the Nephilim.

What kind of life could he have if he signed the Contract?

He shuffled from his bed to the small dresser and picked up the jar Rafe had given him a few days earlier. Unscrewing the lid, he tilted his head back as the smell of peppermint nearly knocked him over. Supposedly the salve was good for aching muscles and bruises. The goopy balm was cold and caused him to flinch, but the icy burn went to work at easing the sore muscles in his sides immediately.

He tried distracting himself from the meeting he'd just had, but nothing in this room could keep his attention long enough. If he had a soft woman under him, that would be a different story. Then he could forget everything.

A knock on the door pulled him out of his thoughts. "Yeah?" he yelled.

The door opened, revealing a smiling Remy. His thick dreads were tied back, but one fell forward, bouncing off his cheek as he strode into the room. "Just wanted to check in and see how you were doing."

Sitting down on the edge of the bed, Michael snorted. "Dealing, I guess."

The easy smile didn't falter. "Heard you learned about the Contract."

"Damn. Word travels fast here."

Remy leaned against the wall, folding his arms. "That it does. The Contract is some heavy shit. Not an easy call."

"If you're wondering if I'm going to sign it, I really don't know. I mean, the increase in strength and the crazy shit I've seen some of you do seems cool, but the whole living forever part? I don't know."

Remy laughed. "That's the funny thing about mortals. Most think they'd jump at a chance to live forever, but when presented with the option, it's not as great as it seems."

"Did you sign the Contract?" Michael asked, curious.

"Yep, some fifty years ago." He flashed another broad smile. "I'm aging well."

"Damn." Michael blinked. The man didn't look a day beyond thirty, and that was pushing it. "And Luke's really close to eighty?"

"Yep. There are some who signed the Contract hundreds of years ago." Remy tipped his head to the side. "This freaking you out?"

In a way, yes, but out of everything else he'd learned, he figured this was the least crazy. Maybe. "What about Lily?"

"She signed the Contract when she was twenty-two or twenty-three. So around three or four years ago. She's the baby of the group. Well, except for you if you take the Contract. Then you'll be the baby."

Michael ignored the last statement. "So that's why some of the guys around here are protective of her."

Remy laughed. "Lily can take care of herself. It's not her age that has them running around like idiots."

"Julian?" Michael said, remembering his first day here. "See, man, I don't get that. He's a fallen angel. Why would he want to protect Lily?"

"Who knows?" Remy stretched. "It's been like that ever since she started hunting. Probably wouldn't be so bad if it wasn't for Anna."

"Anna?"

Remy glanced at the open door before he continued. "Anna was one of us. A really damn good hunter and one the sweetest gals you'd ever meet. You'd have liked her." The ever-present smile faded from his face. "She was nothing like Lily. Don't get me wrong, Lily is . . . well, Lily. But Anna was always smiling, and she was the type of girl you'd want to take home to momma, you know what I mean?"

Michael nodded. He couldn't picture taking Lily to a nice restaurant, let alone home to meet his mom, if she'd still been alive.

"Anyway, she got too close to a Fallen. No one really knew about it until Luke caught Anna with the fallen angel. Nate forbid her from continuing to see him, but she didn't listen. Anna could see the good in

217

anything. She felt sorry for the minions, the dead-heads." He shook his head. "The fallen angel eventually killed her. And it was pretty bad. Luke found her shortly after. Killed the bastard responsible, but it tore him up pretty badly. All of us, actually."

"Jesus. Why would Lily trust Julian after all that?"

Remy didn't immediately answer. "I don't know that she does. Lily . . . tolerates him, but I don't know if it's any more than that."

"Luke seems to hate Julian."

"Well, that's because of Anna. Luke had a thing for that girl. And I think he's worried he'll lose Lily the same way. She's like a sister to him, so he gets all ass-sore when he thinks something, or someone, is threatening her."

Michael's lip twitched.

"You know, the strangest thing about Julian is that I don't think he's touched a Nephilim since he started following Lily," Remy continued. "Luke has crossed his path. So have I. He won't fight us. And I know he isn't scared of us."

Michael leaned to the side, trying to ease his muscles. "Maybe he's different?"

"Don't let anyone else hear you say that," Remy advised softly. "Things are pretty black-and-white around here. The Fallen are evil, no questions asked."

Being on the force was like that. You broke the law or you didn't. There was no in-between, but in this world there seemed to be a lot of gray area. And Michael wasn't ready to side one way or the other. "Is that what you think?"

Remy smiled. "Between you, me, and God, I really don't know. The fine line is hard to walk. And I personally believe not every two things in this world are the same. Look how we started compared to what we are today."

"What do you mean?"

"Ah, sorry. I keep forgetting you don't know the history of us." Remy tucked the loose dread back. "The short version is the very first Nephilim to ever walk this Earth weren't the nicest folks to be around—not all of them, but most. And they were way different than us. First-generation Nephilim carried some of the angelic power from their fathers, since they didn't fall until the actual act of . . . conception."

"Wait. What?" Michael rubbed his temples. He was getting a headache. Again.

"The angels fell after having sex. Who knows if that was the reason they fell in the first place. No one really knows. Anyway, their children—the very first Nephilim—had gifts. Whatever their angelic father had. Remember how Baal could burn with his touch? Well, others could inspire or torment. Some could rain brimstone and fire. Any Nephilim produced after an angel fell were just regular Nephilim. Anyway, the first Nephilim abused their power and gifts. They weren't good."

"The flood," Michael murmured, and noted the Book of Enoch.

"Exactly." Remy shrugged. "So, you see. We weren't good when we first came around. So who's to say some

219

of the Fallen haven't changed. No one knows. But most believe it's too much of a risk to take."

"Are any of the original Nephilim left?"

A small smile appeared on Remy's lips. "Very few. Some even believe firstborn Nephilim still pop up every once in a while."

"Shit. No way. Like today, running around with angelic superpowers?"

Remy laughed. "Yep. It's a rumor, but hell, anything is possible."

"And are these Nephilim bad?"

"We're born with free will, bud. None of us are born bad or good." He paused, glancing up at the ceiling. "But can you imagine what would happen if the Fallen got hold of a firstborn Nephilim and corrupted him? With him having angelic-like power, we'd be screwed."

CHAPTER EIGHTEEN

Lily ditched Luke somewhere between Georgia and New Hampshire avenues. It was surprisingly easier than she thought it would be. She pointed out a group of college girls leaving a bar and then "lover boy" had to go do his thing.

Guys—Nephilim or not—were so damn predictable.

The night was almost over, but she wasn't tired. A lot was floating around her head, thoughts she wasn't very comfortable with. Something about Michael's question had latched onto her and wouldn't let go.

Just because she signed the Contract didn't mean she couldn't have a personal life. The guys were a perfect example of that. They dated—using the word "dating" very loosely—they had lives. Being contracted didn't mean you couldn't have sex or form bonds with humans. It just made things complicated. She could marry if she found a Nephilim she wanted, but she never cared about that before.

There were times when she spied upon the humans and other Nephilim that had settled down to normal lives. She saw the moments couples snuck when they thought no one was watching—the long looks of yearning they would share, the whispered promises and secret smiles. Those stolen moments would sometimes ignite an ache deep inside her.

Loneliness mixed with the desire to be close, really close to someone. It was more than a longing for the physical. Could it be she wanted to share her life with someone?

This—all of this—needed to be squashed. She'd made her decision a long time ago, and there was nothing that could be done now to change it. Even thinking about it was wrong. She was a hunter. That didn't leave room for a nice little husband she could whisper sweet nothings to. It would make her weak. She would falter, and ultimately fail at her duty.

And love made people do stupid things. Having a life didn't mean love had to be in it. Love and life—they weren't codependent.

She came to a halt on top of the Hilton, staring down at the busy Connecticut Avenue intersection. I have a life. I do. I have friends and I have . . . Julian. Wrong. Wrong. Wrong.

So many things wrong with that. She didn't have Julian—she couldn't have Julian. It wasn't like he was another Nephilim or even a human—a human would have been better choice.

A rabid opossum would have been a smarter choice.

Pushing away from the ledge, she marched across the rooftop. What the hell was wrong with her? What was it about Julian that was worth risking everything for? As soon as that thought finished, the familiar feeling shifted over her, and she was reminded quite plainly of one of the reasons why she was risking everything.

Julian came out of the shadows, moving much like a ghost. One minute she was alone, contemplating the laundry list of things she was doing wrong, and the next second she was in Julian's arms, adding to her list.

He didn't say anything to her. Nope. He laid claim to her instead. Pulled against his hard chest, she was seized by his demanding kiss. And damn, did she like it. The way he devoured her, how her body melted against his perfectly, and the ache he brought to life deep within her.

He broke away, but his hands lingered on her waist. "You taste like Heaven. I would know."

She rolled her eyes, doing her best to stop her grin. "You've waited all day to use that one, right?"

"Maybe," he murmured, unfazed. He brushed his lips over the tip of her nose. "What were you thinking about?"

Her forehead wrinkled. "When do you mean?" A few moments ago she was thinking about how delicious he felt against her, but she wasn't going to admit that.

"Before you felt my presence."

She placed her hands against his chest, not sure if she was keeping him at bay or steadying herself. "You've been following me again?"

"Of course," he answered, unabashed. He probably saw nothing wrong with it.

She stepped out of his reach. Tonight he wore a simple white shirt that stretched over his muscles and a pair of denim jeans. Even dressed this casual, he looked magnificent. She had changed into a pair of plain olive-green fatigues and a lightweight tank. Next to him, she felt painfully boring. "You know that's considered stalking and is illegal is most states."

"Killing humans, possessed or not, is illegal in all states," he pointed out casually. "You don't see me splitting hairs."

Lily frowned. Well, he had a good point. "I was just thinking."

Julian cocked his head to the side; the deep blue of his eyes seemed unnaturally bright. "Are you upset?"

She ran a hand through her hair, looking away. "Why do you think that?"

He came forward. With the tips of his fingers, he guided her head back. "I could sense the tension in your body."

That was rather unsettling to hear. "And you sensing just means you're very observant, right?"

He simply smiled. "So what bothers you?" His hand slipped around, circling her neck. The way his fingers moved across the taut muscles was absolutely divine. She relaxed into the soothing movement, and her eyes drifted shut. She really needed to visit a masseuse or get Julian to do this more often.

"You like that, don't you?" he asked, his voice barely a whisper.

"Mmm," she murmured.

He placed a soft kiss against her forehead. "Tell me what troubles you."

"It's just something I was asked today." God, I'm as easy as a nut to crack. "Why I had chosen the life of a hunter and not a life where I could have some sort of normalcy."

"And that bothered you?"

As long as he continued with those magic fingers, she'd answer any of his questions. Was it sad? Yes, but totally true. "Yes. It made me feel like a freak. Like I should've been a guide or simply walked away. That there is something wrong with me for not going after the husband and the white-picket-fence bullshit."

His fingers stilled. "Is that what you want?"

The magic was broken just like that. She opened her eyes and met his extraordinarily intense ones. "No." She forced a laugh. "It's not for me." She slipped away from him.

He clearly looked like he didn't believe her. "Lily."

She barked out a short laugh. "I'm not that type of girl, Julian. I've never been."

"What is that type of girl? Isn't that what everyone wants underneath it all? Why wouldn't you want more than the Sanctuary?"

"What more could I have?" She laughed at her own question. "Besides the fact I'll outlive everything in this city if I don't get snuffed out anytime soon, I have so much money I should be ashamed. I love my job. How many humans can say that?"

"How many humans want to live forever only

having their job?" he countered evenly. "And is it really a job? Is it not your duty—an obligation?"

"It's an obligation to a higher purpose!"

"I hate when you call it a higher purpose." His lips curled. "Your higher purpose is killing indiscriminately, Lily. You're told something is evil and not to question that, believing it all has a divine objective."

Her muscles tensed, replacing the wonderfully relaxed feeling he had created only moments before. "First off, I don't kill indiscriminately. Secondly, the things we are told are evil are, in fact, evil!"

"By your reasoning, that would make me evil. So where is your duty? Where is your higher purpose?" he countered.

She sputtered. "Oh, this is stupid. You're not . . . like them. Okay? Happy I said it?" She threw up her hands. "But it doesn't change that the vast majority of your kind are evil. You can't deny that."

Julian laughed harshly. "How convenient, as I am the only Fallen you've taken enough time to actually speak to before you shove a blade into my heart."

"If I remember it correctly, I did shove a blade into you. Unfortunately, I experienced a rare act of bad aim," she retorted, reveling in the red-hot anger.

His spine stiffened as the blue of his eyes heated. "You are a puppet of the Sanctuary. And you don't even realize it."

"A puppet—are you kidding me?" She leaned forward. "I don't corrupt people! I don't kill innocents!"

"Neither do I!" he roared.

If anything, Julian's anger should have been a warning, but she was so beyond the point of caring. All the wild emotions he incited the night she had found Michael came to the surface. It was dizzying, heady, and powerful. This was, after all, his fault. It had nothing to do with the fact that anything he said could possibly be true. Not at all. "So what, you don't do it now, but you did. Yet you judge me for being loyal to my duty—to the Sanctuary?"

"I'm not judging you, Lily." He stepped toward her. "All I am saying is maybe there is more to the world than being a Nephilim and doing everything the Sanctuary tells you to do."

"Uh, hello, the fact I hold a conversation with you is the exact opposite of what the Sanctuary tells me to do. So, buddy, I really don't abide by all their rules."

He let out a breath as he ran a hand through his hair. "I know. I shouldn't have suggested that. Your acceptance of me is proof you don't."

She folded her arms and looked at him smugly.

"It doesn't change how sadly misinformed you are about my kind. Yes, some of us are pure evil. So much so that even your great Nathaniel would piss his pants in their presence, but we all didn't fall for the same reasons, and not all of us made the same choices. That's where your Sanctuary is blind. And once they succeed in exterminating all of us, they will move on to your kind. You damn well know that is true."

The words knocked the smile right off her face, even

227

though she secretly believed the last part to be a hundred percent true, but that was neither here nor there. "I don't even know why I'm having this conversation with you."

"Because you know there is more to life than being a Nephilim." His words were full of passion and belief. "That you deserve to be more than the Sanctuary's killing machine, because eventually the Sanctuary will turn on you. When that happens, what do you have? Nothing, because your whole life has been this one thing!"

"What?" Startled, she took a step back. Something she rarely ever did. "Why am I even listening to you? What you're saying makes no sense to me. You're the enemy, Julian. Of course you would see it as me not having a life or whatever."

He stared at her for a moment. "Of course you would see it that way. I don't see you as Nephilim, and you don't see me as a Fallen." As he argued, the blue of his eyes deepened. "I see you as Lily. I see you for who you are, even though you don't."

"How do I see myself, Mr. I Know Fucking Everything?"

"You don't see yourself at all. Not as Lily. You see yourself only as a Nephilim. What is your creed? To hunt down the Fallen, kill the minions, and protect your fellow Nephilim at all costs? Where is Lily in that?"

Whoa. Her face scrunched up. "What the hell is this? I know what and who I am."

He looked doubtful. "Then tell me!"

His demand set off a chain reaction of events. Unable to face the harsh reality, she did the one thing she never did. "You know what, forget this." Lily spun around and ran.

Well, tried to run was a better way of putting it. She made it to the ledge and was about to leap when Julian snagged her around the waist and hauled her to the ground. Part of her recognized what Julian was saying was correct, but the other part refused to acknowledge it.

He set her down, and she immediately made a bad decision in a string of bad decisions. She half pushed, half swung at him. He stepped to the side, and her momentum sent her stumbling past him. He tried to catch her once again, but she twisted and they both crashed to the dust-covered rooftop.

Pissed off and very aware of his hard body pressing down on hers, Lily immediately began pushing at him. "Get off me!"

Julian easily pinned her hands down beside her head. "I've followed you for eight years, Lily. I know you better than you know yourself. I have watched you make decision after decision. Besides the apartment, I have never seen you do one thing for yourself. Your entire being centers on the Sanctuary and your duty, while other Nephilim have a life outside their obligations. Where is your life?"

She shook her head frantically. *Tell him that you do make decisions outside your duty*! She couldn't form the words. Besides him and the apartment, she hadn't done a single thing for herself. He knew this after watching her for so long.

"Do you know what the Fallen call the Nephilim? We call your kind cannon fodder, and you were cannon fodder for the Sanctuary the night you went after Baal. You did so for the Sanctuary, and where were they when you lay there broken and near death? Did you make such a foolishly brave decision as Lily or as a Nephilim?"

"Stop this." She didn't want to hear it.

"Damn it, Lily, you are more than just a Nephilim. You are Lily." His grip around her wrists loosened. "You will be fearless in battle, but the idea of wanting something for yourself terrifies you. What we have? It's the first time you've allowed yourself to do what you've wanted simply because you wanted it. That terrifies you. I can see it every time you are around me. You fight what you want, and you're scared the whole time. You're afraid this makes you a bad Nephilim. Not a bad person, but a bad Nephilim."

His words didn't just startle her into submission; they shocked her to the core. The truth had never been so potent, so shattering. Her hands unclenched as her chest rose and fell raggedly.

The edges of his hair brushed her cheeks as he leaned in. "For eight years I've waited for you to realize that. I've waited for you to see yourself for who you really are. You're Lily Marks, a beautiful, extremely clever woman whose capacity for compassion sets you apart from the Nephilim. It's not your fighting skills or how good of a warrior you are. It's the fact you look at me and see a man rather than a Fallen.

"Underneath all the duty and obligation is Lily. And do you know what you do to me?" he continued passionately. "Of all the people, Nephilim and humans alike, you've been the only one who has ever made me wish I was a man and not what I am. You did that—Lily, not the Nephilim."

She stared at him, wide-eyed and silent. What he said . . . well, it was probably the nicest thing anyone had ever said about her. How he saw her was simply amazing, because all the people she knew, including herself, only saw her as a hunter. But what Julian saw terrified her, just as her feelings for him—and how badly she wanted him—terrified her.

He rested his forehead against hers. "Oh, Lily, don't you see? There's nothing wrong with wanting love, the house, and even the damn picket fence. Desires and passions do not make you a bad person."

Oh damn, she was really close to crying. She turned her head, squeezing her eyes shut. He pushed back the curtain of reddish-brown hair that fell across her face, gently turning her to him. She opened her eyes, damp with unshed tears. If she knew better, had some experience in these sorts of things, she would have thought the way he looked at her meant something powerful and real.

His fingers trailed down her cheek. "Lily?"

"I really hate you right now, you know that?" she murmured.

"No you don't. That's the whole problem. You don't hate me at all."

She exhaled unsteadily. No, she didn't hate him. But she kind of wished she did. It would make things a hell of a lot easier. But Julian understood her in a way Luke and Nathaniel never could. The invisible barriers slowly cracked.

He kissed her so deeply that she thought her soul would burst into flames. He laid claim to her soul, just as he had already done to her heart.

CHAPTER NINETEEN

Two weeks after Julian had basically handed her the truth, and his words still brought a smile to her lips. The kind of smile that didn't fade even as she stared down at the minion she had just vanquished. Stepping away, she gazed out into the night sky.

Damn, she was tired.

Between monitoring Michael's training and hunting at night, she was only getting four hours of sleep tops. Granted, she would get at least five and half hours of sleep if she'd stop sneaking off to spend time with Julian.

The soft breeze kicked up, stirring a few tendrils of hair around her face. She gave a little half smile. She'd gladly give up an hour or two of sleep before she was due back at the Sanctuary if it meant going to sleep well sated.

Julian was rather adept when it came to ways of entertaining her. He used his lips or his fingers, and she was never uninterested. They hadn't done it yet, although they came close a few times. Just last night she begged him to take her. She hadn't cared that they were on the rooftop of the Hilton. Right there, out in the open. She had wanted him that badly, and he had known it.

Julian had still refused her. Damn him.

Although Lily was reluctant to admit it, it wasn't just his touch she looked forward to all day. Things had changed since that night they had fought and Julian had forced her to confront her feelings. She no longer thought of him as a Fallen—if she ever really did. As dangerous as that was.

They even exchanged phone numbers. When Julian had ordered her to enter his cell number and the numbers for all three clubs he owned into her phone, she had found it hilarious. He had looked at her strangely, and she'd tried to explain why she thought it was funny they were now just at the exchanging-phone-numbers stage. He didn't get it, and she had given up on trying to explain.

Her smile spread.

The voice in the back of her head picked up, whispering, *Remember Anna. This is what happened to Anna.*

Swatting the voice to the side, she stepped to the ledge, and a shiver danced over her skin. Turning around, she was surprised as a giant of a man landed in the middle of the roof.

Gabe sauntered toward her, a cocky little grin on his lips. "Hey, babe, long time no see."

Lily almost stepped back, but stopped before she toppled over the ledge. Other than passing each other at the Sanctuary, she hadn't seen Gabe since the night in the laundry room. Heat tinged her cheeks. "Hey," she said lamely.

He stopped in front of her. "Haven't had any bad shifts recently. I'm kind of disappointed."

Now the tips of her ears burned. "Yeah, well, things have been . . . good."

His smile spread as he studied her. Gabe was good-looking—very much so. Any girl, Nephilim or not, would be throwing off their panties for him, but Lily didn't feel the slightest urge to do so.

"Well, you know where to find me." He hopped up on the ledge beside her. "Even if you're having a good shift." Then he bent, kissed her under her ear, and jumped.

She stood there, face flaming. "Sweet baby Jesus." Spinning around, she waited a few minutes, then took off for the spot she'd been meeting Julian.

Five minutes later, she landed on the balls of her feet atop the Hilton Hotel, a little grin playing over her lips.

"You took long enough."

She crouched, perched on the ledge. "I had to work, unlike some."

"I don't think work is what kept you."

Lily frowned. "What do you mean . . . oh God, don't tell me you heard Gabe and me? I didn't feel you."

He walked up to her. "The Nephilim wants to sleep with you."

She busted out laughing. "Gabe? Gabe wants to sleep with a lot of people."

"But you've—"

"Are you jealous?" She laughed again.

"Never," he said, though not in an entirely convincing way.

Lily leaned forward, clasping his smooth cheeks in her hands. Bringing his lips to hers, she kissed him softly. "You have nothing to be jealous of."

"Of course not." Julian scowled. "Anyway, I do work."

Not believing it for one second, she took a moment to appreciate the sensual tilt to his lips, the overtly male swagger, and how the shirt hugged his upper body. God, she could drink him up all in one gulp. "Convincing the young socialites of DC to do naughty things isn't work."

Julian looked offended. It wasn't believable by any means. "I would never do such a thing."

"Really?" she snickered.

"Well, there was this nun I convinced to leave the church to pursue a career in pole dancing." He flashed a wicked grin. "That was fun."

"Seriously, Julian, what do you do all day?"

He rested his hands on her bent knees. "I don't think you want to know."

They were back to the one topic Julian wouldn't budge on. No matter how many times and how many ways she asked him, he refused to tell her what he did, as if doing so would be handing over his trade secrets. Lily was still curious, not thwarted. "Try me."

He looked down at her, arching one eyebrow. "I slept till noon, if you must know."

She curled her lip. "Lucky."

He grinned. "Then I observed a young man who was following this little girl far too closely."

Ugh. She didn't like where this was going. "Um, what do you mean?"

Julian slid his hands over her hips. "What do you think I mean? I believe his name was Larry. Anyway, Larry likes little girls."

"You didn't . . . I mean, you didn't put that in him did you?" She was afraid of his answer. It wouldn't be unheard of. The Fallen made humans do things they normally wouldn't conceive of doing. It was a way they sought to cure their boredom.

He made a face at her. "Give me some credit, Lily. No. I could sense his . . . tastes. So I watched as he followed her to this alley where she waits for the bus to take her to her grandmother's. I simply suggested the urge to leave."

"To the girl or the man?" she asked.

"The man," he said, lifting her off the ledge and placing her on her feet.

She eyed him. "Where did he go?"

Julian shrugged nonchalantly. "Oh, out in front of one of those big trucks that pick up garbage," he explained blandly. "I figured that was fitting."

She winced. "I don't really know how to feel about that."

He took her hand, guiding her across the rooftop, and led her into the shadows, far away from prying eyes. "You did say you probably wouldn't want to know. After that, I simply people-watched."

People-watching after urging a man to walk in front of truck? How utterly . . . what? How could she really sum that up? She glanced over at him. He was watching her curiously, waiting for her reaction. She sighed. "Okay, I probably shouldn't have asked."

Julian chuckled. "Do you want me to tell you I told you so?"

"Well, it could have been worse." She decided tentatively. "At least it was a wannabe pedophile."

"Oh no, he was a pedophile. He just hadn't been caught yet."

She swallowed, sickened by how some people could be so evil all on their own. "Okay, well, I can't say I am totally displeased with what you did."

"Aren't you bloodthirsty?"

She grinned. "It kind of comes with the job. What about the little girl?"

"She made it to her grandmother's house safe and sound." Julian reached down, catching a piece of hair in his fingers. He twirled it around his index finger. "What did you do today, my Lily?"

She untangled her hair from his finger. "Training and more training," she told him. He reached for the hair again, but she slapped his hand away. "I've never had to train someone before. It's a cross between extraordinary boredom and complete lack of patience." She paused, adding thoughtfully, "On my part, that is."

"You impatient?" he teased. His hand closed around her much smaller one, bringing it to his lips. He kissed her palm. The touch sent shivers all the way to her toes. "So how is he coming along training-wise?"

She shrugged, deciding a truthful answer couldn't hurt. "He picks up things remarkably fast."

"And you are still impatient?" he asked. "You're very hard to please."

She observed the hand wrapped around hers. Pressing against him, she gazed up into his striking blue eyes. "Not really. Not when it comes to you."

"Oh really?" he murmured. Julian slipped his arm around her waist, pulling her up to the tips of her toes. He brushed his lips over hers once, then twice. Lily immediately softened against him. "I'm thinking that perhaps you wish to put that to the test?"

"Perhaps," she agreed. No longer exhausted, she wrapped her arms around his neck. "Maybe we should try that out?"

Julian's lips curved into an indulgent smile. "Insatiable." He lifted her up like she weighed nothing, holding her at eye level.

His strength always gave her pause. She was strong, but he was supercharged. It reminded her of how fragile she truly was compared to him. The girl in her loved it—that girl was foolish and easily wooed. The Nephilim side of her was uneasy, knowing that power could end her life in an instant. It was like being split in two when she was with him.

He placed his lips against hers, and those thoughts simply vanished. It didn't matter how many times Julian kissed her; she could never quite prepare herself for the onslaught of feelings. It was like every nerve in her body fired at once, overwhelming her senses and leaving her breathless.

"Lily. Step back."

She froze against Julian, her eyes snapping open. So lost in him, she hadn't sensed another Nephilim.

Oh . . . oh crap, this was going to be bad.

"Step back now."

She would've done so because of the sheer malice in the voice, but Julian's arm tightened around her, making it nearly impossible for her to move. He slowly lifted his head to look over her shoulder. What she saw in Julian's face filled her with dread. From the tight line of his mouth to the dangerously narrowed eyes, Lily recognized how hazardous this situation was about to get.

"Julian," she whispered. "Put me down."

He inclined his head toward her. "Who is this Nephilim that you would allow to order you so?"

"The Nephilim that will kill you," answered Micah coldly.

Her heart jumped. "Julian, please put me down."

He stared at her for a moment before he released her. "Of course," he murmured.

She straightened her halter top with quick motions before facing Micah. Her cheeks burned and her heart beat so fast nausea rolled through her. How was she going to explain this?

Micah stood several feet in front of them, his legs spread wide and a wicked blade ready in his fist.

"Micah," she began awkwardly. "I'm not sure . . ."

"Shut up, Lily," Micah ordered.

"Excuse me?" she sputtered as Julian stiffened beside her.

Micah's eyes danced over her before returning to the seething Fallen behind her. "I've followed you."

She wasn't sure she heard him correctly. "What?"

"I followed you," he said again, louder. "I've been following you, but the last couple of nights I lost you. Now I see why you run off so quickly."

Rage swamped her as she stared at him. "Who in the hell do you think you are to be following me?"

He sneered. "Who in the hell do you think you are? I'm not the one screwing the enemy. Come on, Lily, I used to respect you." Micah clenched his fists. "You have given yourself to him like some street whore— worse than any minion."

Before she could utter a word, Julian had the Nephilim by his throat, dangling him over the edge of the hotel. Below was a dark alley. The drop wouldn't kill Micah, but it would do massive damage.

"Julian!" Lily screamed, rushing after them. "Stop it!"

"What did you say to her?" Julian demanded in a low, deadly voice.

"You heard what I said, you damn freak!" Micah raised his arm, intent on stabbing him.

Julian caught Micah's arm and twisted until the blade slipped out of his hand. Micah yelped as the dagger fell into the darkness. "I think you need to apologize right now."

Micah gripped Julian's forearm. "Over my dead body."

Julian's smile was cold. "That can be easily arranged." He moved Micah farther away from the safety of the ledge.

She grabbed Julian's arm, but he didn't budge an inch. "Knock it off. Both of you need to stop!"

Neither of them listened. Julian thrust Micah out farther while the Nephilim struggled against him. The situation was quickly spiraling out of control, and Lily didn't doubt that if Micah called her a name one more time Julian would indeed drop him.

She pulled on Julian's arm again, desperate. When that didn't work, she slugged him in the stomach. "Julian, listen to me. Let him go. Now," she begged. "Let go of him for me. Please."

Julian peered down at her. "For you?"

"Yes!" She forced a smile. "Put him back down—on the ground, gently." She felt the need to clarify her request.

He stepped away so that Micah no longer hung over the edge. Lily nodded reassuringly, praying Micah would remain quiet. The last thing she needed was him to say something antagonizing. But then Julian tossed Micah to the roof. "He still needs to apologize," he grumbled.

She nearly laughed with relief. Julian would destroy the Nephilim if push came to shove. She glanced at Micah.

Julian exhaled heavily, seeming to collect himself. "He should apologize."

She kept a wary eye on him just in case he had a change of heart. "Why were you following me?"

Micah straightened his shirt. "Someone is feeding info to the Fallen. My guess is the one who is sleeping with them."

She immediately threw her arm up, blocking Julian. It didn't stop his response. "Keep it up, you little shit. I will fucking break you."

"I'd like to see you try!"

"Are you accusing me of betraying the Sanctuary?" The irony of the situation didn't pass her, not even in her anger. She suspected Micah, and he suspected her. It would be comical if she didn't feel like letting Julian drop him off the building.

Micah gave her a dismissive look. "Honestly? You act all offended, but you don't deny what you are doing. The circle knows, Lily. The circle suspects you."

It was like being smacked in the face. Granted, she knew her relationship with Julian didn't shine a favorable light upon her, but for them to think she would actually betray them? She wanted to kick them all in the face.

"What your circle suspects is what they are led to believe," Julian sneered.

Lily frowned at the cryptic sentence, but out of the corner of her eye, she saw Micah's left hand slip behind him. He was fast—they were trained that way. If she hadn't been Nephilim, she wouldn't have even caught the darting movement.

Without thinking twice, she pushed Julian back and

spun into a roundhouse kick. Julian stumbled backward, stunned by her unexpected move. Her kick connected with the fleshy part of Micah's arm, and the dagger clanged against the roof.

Micah exploded into a sea of curses, lunging for the blade. Lily's knee connected with the broad side of his face, sending him flying. The kick would have snapped the neck of a man, but for a Nephilim it only stunned him.

Time seemed to stop as she stared down at Micah, breathing heavy. Lifting her head, she turned to Julian. What she had done hung between them.

"Go, Julian," she gritted out.

Julian had a hand over his heart. "You defended me?"

There wasn't time to discuss the ramifications of her actions. She could sense another Nephilim. She darted between Julian and Micah. "Go now. Another is coming." In other words, what she pulled with Micah she may not be able to get away with again.

Micah slowly climbed to his feet, rubbing his jaw. Lily grabbed the blade, casting one last look over at Julian. "Please go," she whispered urgently.

He hesitated. "Lily, I . . ." He stopped as she pleaded with her eyes. He gave a curt nod, and then he was gone.

Blood trickled from Micah's split lip. "You really shouldn't have done that."

The soft thud of boots landing on the rooftop drew Lily's attention. Not sure how to explain any of this, she kept her eyes on Micah.

Luke came to a halt beside her, surveying the damage. "What happened?"

Micah wobbled a bit on his feet. The kick had been powerful. She hadn't restrained herself at all. "She's betrayed us."

She hadn't betrayed them. She only . . . what? Bared arms against one of her kind. Did that technically mean she had betrayed them? Maybe not in the way Micah would insist, but she had turned against him in favor of Julian. She'd fought a Nephilim to protect a Fallen.

Luke's eyes narrowed. "What in the hell is he talking about, Lily?"

She glanced away from Micah, clenching the blade in her hand. Up until this moment, she never had to question her actions. Not even when she accepted that she wanted more, wanted Julian. She was still a Nephilim, born and trained to fight the Fallen and their minions. The line between their kind was clearly drawn ages ago, and she'd always operated on the principal that the Fallen must be stopped no matter what. She'd been able to convince herself that her relationship with Julian didn't affect her duty. She was still Lily, but with one single act against her brethren she had changed everything.

She dropped the blade. The sound was thunderous and final. "Micah has been following me. Apparently he suspects I'm working with the Fallen."

"What?" Luke frowned at him. "He's been following you because Nathaniel asked him to."

She sucked in a sharp breath. "Why?"

"Because of Baal," answered Micah. "But that has nothing to do with what happened tonight. Luke, it's her. She's been feeding info to the Fallen."

Laughing, Luke clapped him on the shoulders. "You're a good hunter, but you're dumb as a bag of fucking rocks if you really think that's true. Lily is loyal."

His unwavering faith in her bruised her worse than Micah's accusation. "He found me with Julian."

Luke stiffened. The amused grin slowly slipped away. "What?" was all he asked, and in that one word was a world of meaning.

"What do you think?" hissed Micah.

"Shut up," Luke snarled. He stepped away from him. "What were you doing?"

She lowered her eyes. "We were talking."

"Didn't look like talking to me," said Micah. "I always lose her around this time, but tonight I kept up with her. They were all over each other." Revulsion laced his words.

"Lily. I knew you were . . . friendly with him," Luke whispered hoarsely. "But not like that. Not after what happened . . ."

She tore her gaze from the lightly stained cement. "We kissed."

Luke stared at her, and the deep disappointment he wore nearly broke her heart. She shifted uncomfortably under his gaze. It was like standing in front of Nathaniel and being lectured, but far worse.

"That's not all." Micah shoved past Luke. He

glared down at her. "I went after Julian, and she attacked me!"

He was right, and Lily was wrong on so many different levels, but she felt her temper rise nonetheless. "You tried to stab him in the back!"

"Is that true, Lily?" Luke demanded.

"Yeah, I kicked him in his arrogant face."

"Do you even realize how serious this is?" Luke grabbed her arm, shaking her. "This isn't a joke! What you've done is reprehensible. Attacking another Nephilim in defense of a Fallen? Charges could be brought against you, Lily!"

She tried to pull away, but his hold was bruising. If she had thought of that for a second before she attacked Micah, she wouldn't be in the situation she was in. "I understand. It doesn't change what I did."

Luke shook her again before dropping her arm. "Micah, leave now," he ordered. "Do not breathe a word of this."

"Are you serious? You'll protect her now?"

He whirled on the other Nephilim. "I will take care of this. Do not question that." He turned back to Lily. "You can trust this will be addressed."

Micah looked like he wanted to stay, or at least get in a good swing at Lily, but Luke had the authority. Lily did, too. Most likely she didn't after tonight, but that was a moot point. With one last biting glance at Lily, Micah loped off the hotel.

The two remaining stood in silence. Lily wasn't sure what to say. She knew she messed up and let what she felt for Julian get in the way. All she felt was guilt and not regret. Two very separate things. She didn't regret stopping Micah but felt guilty because she had violated Luke's trust.

"Lily," he began softly. "What are you thinking?"

She closed her eyes. "I don't know."

"You don't? Do you have any idea how much trouble you are going to be in?" he asked. "And I know you won't ask me to not tell Nathaniel."

She wouldn't drag Luke down the path she had so willingly chosen.

"Has he coerced you somehow? Tricked you like what happened to Anna?"

Lily's head shot up. "No," she said firmly. "Julian has never made me do anything I didn't want to do."

Her words didn't help. He pulled back as if she'd slapped him. "After what happened to Anna?"

She snapped. "I'm not Anna! Damn it, I'm not her! And Julian's not—"

"Not what, Lily? A Fallen? Because that's what he is. Shit. I thought you knew better than this. I suspected there was more to it, more than what you were willing to admit to, but this?"

She ran a nervous hand over her hip. Maybe if she was honest with him, he would understand. Luke always listened to her in the past. She inhaled softly, meeting his gaze with her earnest one. "Julian isn't like the others. He hasn't fathered a Nephilim. He doesn't corrupt innocents like the others do. He is different."

Luke looked like he wanted to laugh. "That's what he's told you."

"I believe him. He's not bad. You have to see that. He's saved my life twice, and God knows how many times I don't know about."

"So he did nothing to Micah?" Luke raised his brows.

Deciding that lying would likely come back and bite her in the ass later, she told him what happened and how Micah's comments had provoked him. As she told the story, Luke grew angrier. "But he didn't hurt him, Luke. I did."

"Which makes it all the worse." Luke stopped and sighed heavily. "I don't think Nathaniel would take it as a breach of Contract, but you will be punished."

She swallowed. A breached Contract was basically going rogue. She would be thrown out of the Sanctuary, left to fend solely for herself. It had been far before her time when the last Nephilim had breached their Contract.

Some of the steam behind Luke's anger faded as he watched her. She felt terribly small now, lost and unsure. "I think its best that you come back to the Sanctuary immediately, admit fault, and stay as far away from Julian as possible."

Pressing her lips together, she ran a hand through her windblown hair. "I need some time."

Luke's brows shot up. "What?"

"Time," she repeated. "I need time away. I have to think about this."

"You shouldn't have to think about anything, Lily! You know this is wrong, and it's gotten out of hand."

A hundred different emotions bubbled up in her, spilling over. "I don't know if this is wrong!" she yelled. "I've never done anything to earn any distrust. I have always put the Sanctuary and my duty first!" She turned away, trying to rein in some sort of control. "My whole life has been dedicated to this, and I didn't ask for any of it."

Luke stepped behind her. "None of us did, but this is our life."

She stared out over the city—the night teeming with bright lights, streets filled with humans and minions. There were people out there living and dying. Some were even falling in love. Three things Lily couldn't do so easily, and, damn it, she wanted to be like them instead of what she was. She wanted the freedom to choose.

"This isn't you," he whispered.

She paused for a moment, then murmured, "Maybe it is." She smiled halfheartedly. "Thank you for running Micah off. I do owe him an apology, but if he follows me one more time . . ." She let the threat hang between them.

Luke leaned forward. "Don't do this, Lily."

He knew her so well. "Michael is doing very well." She cleared her throat against the sudden tightening. "If you could check in on him later for me, I'd appreciate it. Rafe has been wonderful."

"Lily," he protested. "Please. It will be worse if you don't come back with me. Please."

"I just need some time. I know that isn't what you want to hear, but I'll be back," she told him. "Ready to face whatever Nathaniel deems fit."

"Come on. We can go to him together. You know how Nate is. He's not going to be too hard on you." He forced a smile, but it didn't reach his eyes. "You have him wrapped around your finger after all."

She stepped up on the ledge and inhaled deeply. "Don't follow me, Luke."

"Lily!" He reached for her. "Don't! Think about this for a second."

Her decision was already made, her path chosen when she let Julian in. She launched herself off the rooftop, disappearing into the night sky.

CHAPTER TWENTY

Julian was waiting for her on the balcony of her apartment. She sensed him the moment the building came into view. Nerves made her fingers tremble as she fished out her keys and let herself in. The first thing a Nephilim should do after committing any wrongdoing would be to hightail her butt back to the Sanctuary and report immediately to Nathaniel. The worst thing she could do was turn her back and go into hiding.

It was too late now as she crossed her living room, unlocked the balcony door, and stepped aside. "Hey," she murmured.

Julian entered, his bright gaze settling on her. "Lily . . ."

"I know." She threw up a hand. "I shouldn't have stopped Micah, but I did." She met his gaze. "Can you give me a few minutes? Make yourself at home." She gestured at the couch. "I'll be right back."

She headed for the bedroom, quickly discarding her hunting clothes in favor of cotton shorts and a baby-doll tank from the large armoire.

Julian had moved to the couch, sitting motionless with his eyes closed. She approached him slowly, wondering what he made of all this. Was he happy she had defended him? Guilty? Or did he also think she made a mistake? Biting her lip, she sat beside him. He immediately turned to her, a soft smile on his face.

"I admit. I'm surprised."

"You're surprised that I stopped Micah?"

"Yes." He ran the tips of his fingers down her arm.

She forced a casual shrug. "Seemed like the right thing to do at the time."

"And now?" he asked.

"It still does." She laughed at his doubtful expression. "You stopped when I asked you to. Unlike Micah, you were walking away. You didn't deserve to be stabbed when you weren't attacking him."

He seemed to consider her reasoning. "But I did attack him."

"And you stopped," she reminded him softly.

"Only because you asked. If you hadn't been there, I wouldn't have." He leaned back against the cushion. "I would have killed him."

Her eyes widened, needing to hear it spoken out loud again. "But you didn't."

He glanced at the television. "How much trouble will you be in?"

She sighed. "A decent amount, I imagine. I mean, I don't think Nathaniel will kick me out or anything, but he's not going to be pleased."

"You're here." He frowned thoughtfully. "Doesn't that mean you will be in even more trouble since you didn't go to him?"

Odd how much he knew about the Sanctuary and

their rules. She eyed him curiously. The sandy-blond hair fell forward, curving against his jawline. He was at ease on her couch, even though his mere presence swallowed it whole. "More so when I don't show up in the morning, but it is what it is. I need time to think about . . . all of this."

He tipped his head to the side. "You're here because of me?"

This was not going to be a night where she could just lie through her teeth. Inhaling softly, she answered honestly. "Yes."

A wondrous smile appeared, and he leaned forward, capturing her lips in a deep kiss. She thought she would surely melt into the cushions if he continued to kiss her like that.

When he pulled back, she was breathing heavy and his eyes were like brilliant sapphires. "Will they come looking for you?" he asked.

"I don't think so. They tend to give me my space if I ask for it."

He peered up through sooty lashes then. "Thank you, Lily, for risking what you have to defend me."

Caught off guard by his thank-you, she laughed self-consciously. "You're really not like them."

"Neither are you."

Lily shifted, stretching her legs out in front of her. "I'm no different."

"Is it not an issue of black and white with the Nephilim?" he asked as he grabbed her wrists. He ran his thumbs over the silver cuffs she always wore, the daggers hidden inside expanded. "Is it not your duty to kill me?"

"What . . . are you doing?" She tried to pull her hands away, but he held on. He brought them to the vulnerable spot under his ribs—right where she had aimed for the first time but had missed by a fraction of an inch. The same spot Micah had gone for. Her eyes widened as he pressed the tip of the very deadly blade against his flesh.

He met her stare. "Why aren't you like the rest of the Nephilim?"

Why wasn't she? That was a good question. She could kill him right now. It was what she was supposed to do. What she had been raised for and what she had prevented earlier. Yet, sitting here beside him, she couldn't. She would never be able to. She knew just like she knew the sun would indeed rise in an hour or so.

He removed his thumbs and the blades retracted. "Nothing is simple, is it?"

Her gaze dropped to his hands that were sliding past her wrists. His touch, soothing and unnerving at the same time, consumed her. "No."

He pulled her into his lap. Her legs fell across his long ones, and her hands rested against his shoulders. "I think you have quite a bit of free time."

The lightning-hot fire in her veins was already simmering. "You?"

Julian cupped her cheek. "I have all the time for you, Lily."

Her heart did a weird little flip. She inched one leg over to rest beside his hip. "No nuns to corrupt?"

"No."

Her gaze settled on his curved lips. "No politicians to sway into a scandal?"

His hands dropped to her hips, cradling them. "No. You okay with allowing a minion to see another sunrise?"

She grinned. "Now, what kind of Nephilim would that make me?"

"My favorite kind," he answered.

"Is that so?" She giggled, feeling very unlike herself.

He brushed his lips over the curve of her chin. "We have all this time. What should we do?"

She could think of a dozen things, but only one she really wanted. She brought her hand down his flat stomach. Her grin became impish as she felt him harden under her heated core. She shifted so that the most intimate part of her pressed down on him.

Julian growled softly. One hand cupped the back of her neck, guiding her lips to his. His kiss was questioning at first, gentle in nature. Then it deepened, becoming more demanding. As his tongue gained entry and swept over hers, she felt it all over her body.

Soon his hands were everywhere, slipping under her shirt, caressing the hard peaks of her breasts, curving over her rear, and slipping under her shorts. Lily moaned into his mouth as one finger slipped inside her. She was already so hot and wet that it nearly sent her over the edge, but she wanted more. As his finger pumped in and out of her, she ran her hand under his shirt and over the smooth, hard skin. His breathing quickened, and when she ran her fingers over his lower belly his head fell back.

She wanted to feel him inside her, needed him to be. It was a wild desire, one born out of unbridled lust and another emotion she wasn't ready to delve too deeply into.

"Julian, I want you." She unsnapped the button on his jeans.

"You have me," he groaned.

That brought a delighted smile to her face as she wrapped her fingers around his wrist. "Not like that."

His finger stilled, his liquid gaze met hers and flared seductively. "You don't know what you are asking for," he said, voice husky and thick with need.

With a sense of will she didn't know she had, Lily pulled his hand away. "I know you want to."

"More than you ever know, but . . ." He trailed off as she rubbed his hard length through the jeans. He swallowed. "Lily, it changes everything."

Of course it does. She would no longer be a virgin. Julian would indeed be her . . . first, and the knowledge thrilled her. "I know. I want this." She climbed off him and stood. "I want you."

He was on his feet in seconds, the jeans hanging low on his hips. "You have to be sure. There will be no going back."

Flushed, she curled her fingers around his. "I think we passed that part a while ago."

He stared at her, eyes keen and ablaze. Julian seemed to waver; an unknown battle warred within him. "I mean it, Lily, this cannot be undone."

She wasn't stupid. It wasn't like her virginity would grow back if she wished it. Snarky thoughts aside, she was touched by his concern for her. It was obvious he worried she would regret it. Sex was just sex, and that was what she wanted desperately.

With a soft smile, she tugged on his hand. "I'm sure."

He let out a ragged breath before swooping down and claiming her lips in a feverish kiss. There was so much passion and power in that kiss she wondered what she had gotten into, but then he pulled back and pinned her with a molten stare.

She panted. "Okay."

His smile was crooked. "Okay."

She had been the one to initiate this, but Julian quickly took over. He led her into the dimly lit bedroom. Her heart fluttered unsteadily, and her stomach knotted in anticipation.

The back of her knees brushed against the soft bedspread, and without saying a word, he removed the gray shirt he wore. The very air that was so laden with sexual tension seized in her lungs.

Julian was utterly magnificent. From the hard expanse of his golden chest down to the ripped stomach that begged to be touched. The unbuttoned jeans slipped farther down his hips, exposing a fine dusting of golden hair. No mortal man could be built such a way. He was heavenly, a product of perfection.

She silently lifted her arms when he hooked his hands under the hem of her halter. He quickly disposed of the material, and she could feel his heated gaze drift down her bare skin. She responded immediately. Her nipples hardened and her stomach hollowed.

Next came her shorts, and then she was completely nude. All of her—the fine scars that riddled her body and the marks that had been left behind were visible. She couldn't hide as he took her in.

Her hand fluttered over a thin scar that sliced from the edge of her ribs to her belly button. Baal had given that to her, along with the mark on her thigh. Julian pulled that hand to his lips. He first kissed the top of her hand, then the inside. Then he brought the palm of her hand against his chest, above where his heart rested. The simple and sweet gesture brought a rush of tears to her eyes. She swallowed, unable to say anything.

"You're so beautiful," Julian murmured against her lips. He wrapped one arm around her waist, lifting her against him. His kiss ignited the fire in her. "Perfect for me. You would never know how much you are."

She stared as he stepped back, stripping off his jeans. Absolutely marvelous, and big . . . very big. An awfully naive part of her doubted that this would work. It was one thing having her hand or mouth wrapped around him, and totally something else to consider that going in her.

But then he lowered himself, pushing her back against the bed, trailing his lips over her legs and stomach. He settled over her breasts, where he suckled and nipped. He took his time, slowly moving over her, licking every inch of her skin. It was like he sought to memorize every part of her body. Or claim it. Whatever it was, Lily didn't care. She'd let him do this for eternity.

Her body arched against him, aching and tense. He drew every breath from her, every moan and whimper. Her fingers clawed at his chest and arms. He lifted, halting her progress. Capturing her hands, he pinned them beside her head.

Desire, rife and powerful, spread through her. She had never felt this way before, and when he nudged her thighs apart, she nearly cried out. She felt him against her, hot and hard. So very close to where she yearned for him to be.

Julian brought his lips back to hers, releasing her hands and moving one of his to rest over her wet cleft. He supported himself with his arm, continuing to delve into her mouth while gently working one finger in and then two. Soon he had her bucking against his hand and his member.

He worked her toward the edge, her breathing erratic. Her hands clenched his arms, and the sounds she was making should've embarrassed her. But she didn't care. She wanted more.

He lifted his head, staring down at her. There was something quite frightening and a bit intoxicating in his wild gaze. It mirrored what she felt inside but couldn't vocalize. She felt all over the place, full of anticipation and near crazed with need.

He slowly withdrew his fingers, eliciting a sharp whimper from her. As his gaze fixed on her heavily hooded eyes, he guided his erection to rest against her sex. She thought she'd come apart at the first wicked touch, but she had been wrong. It was when he slowly inched his way in that her body came alive.

Julian reached out, laying a hand against her cheek. His thumb drifted down to her full bottom lip. "Do you trust me?" he asked softly.

She wrapped her arm around the one he used for support. "Yes."

He bent his head to hers. "This may hurt. I'll make it quick."

She wasn't quite sure what he meant by making it quick, but she was really beyond coherent thought. With one last caress over her cheek, his hand dropped to her hip once more, and he thrust deep inside.

Sharp, stinging pain shot through her. She froze at the incredible pressure of fullness.

"Relax," he whispered, his eyes glowing like sapphire jewels. "It will get better. I promise you."

She bit down on her lip, nodding. She wasn't sure how this was going to get better. It felt like he was going to rip her in two.

He didn't move. Even as his arm trembled around hers, he remained still, buried deep inside her. Eventually the stinging faded to a dull ache, and the fullness began to feel somewhat . . . good. Tentatively, Lily moved, and the sharp throbbing she felt wasn't from pain.

"Oh," she whispered. She tried it again.

"Oh indeed," Julian groaned.

The fire the simple movement evoked in her propelled her further. She rocked her hips against him, and Julian's hands clenched into a fist. "I think you're getting the hang of this," he grated.

She tipped her hips once more, and Julian's restraint broke. He began to thrust himself deeper into her body. Lily had never felt so full before and so powerless over her own body. And yet, it was wildly erotic.

Appearing as if he was no longer content with her tentative moves, he cradled her hips, thrusting into her over and over again, increasing in intensity until it became a feverish pace that nearly tore her apart with pleasure. She lifted her legs, wrapping them around his hips, bringing him deeper.

Her head spun as the bliss built inside her. Somehow in this moment, she felt bonded with him. It was more than just sex, more than two bodies enjoying each other. She couldn't explain it, but she knew this was more. It was meant to be and always had been.

Julian moved faster, grinding against her as her hot, wet slickness enveloped him. His touch was everywhere, as was hers. He let go of her hips, cupping her breast. His mouth dipped to one taut nipple, and he sucked it. The piercing draw from her breast and the relentless pounding was too much.

Kicking her head back, she screamed as she shuddered around him. It was an incredible moment in her life. Finally unleashed from the chains she wore in mindless abandon, she was free. And it felt so damn good. The spasms racked her body in tight, sensual waves, throwing her so high, she never wanted to come down.

Julian's head tipped back, and his arms tightened around her. He roared his release, burying his head in the crook of her neck. One last spasm sent her body jerking against his, and then her arms fell to her sides. Her head swam as she lay beneath him, wanting him to remain inside her forever.

Minutes passed, and then he nipped at her soft flesh, chuckling when she whimpered. He lifted himself onto his forearms. She felt him jerk inside her once again, and she shivered. "I knew it would be like this," he said.

She arched a brow lazily. "Did you?"

"Yes." He brushed a light kiss across her lips. "Are you okay? Do you hurt?"

She glanced down at where their bodies still joined together. She was sore but still in one piece. After that, she expected she would have to put herself back together. "I'm okay."

Julian placed another kiss against her cheek. "Stay here. I'm going to get something."

When he slowly withdrew, she felt the delicious pull. She bit down, closing her eyes. Too sated to really care what he was up to, Lily let herself drift off into the warm afterglow. She heard him rummaging around in her bathroom and then water gushing from a faucet.

He returned to her, a damp washcloth in his hand.

She frowned as he sat next to her and reached between her legs. Lily flushed. "You don't have to do that. I can—"

Julian focused on her eyes. "No." Then he began to gently wipe away all traces of her virginity.

She wasn't sure how to feel about him tending to her in such a way. This was more intimate than what they had just shared, and it left her feeling out of sorts. Once he was done, he stood and disposed of the washcloth in the basket by the closet.

Lily sat up and winced. *Okay, a little sorer than I originally thought.*

"Are you okay? I shouldn't have let go of myself like that. I could've hurt you."

Her eyes widened, but it wasn't his words or the ache that caused her reaction. That first night when he had come to her apartment, she had never laid eyes upon his back. In fact, he had always kept his back from her, and now she saw why. How she had never noticed this escaped her.

The taut skin over each of his shoulder blades bared the angry marks of where wings had been. The skin once torn open and stitched back together. The flesh was puckered and painful-looking. Each vicious cut was at least six inches long and two inches thick.

Julian stiffened. "Does it bother you?"

"No. I just . . . didn't know." It wasn't like she saw the Fallen in a state of undress that often. Typically, she killed them or ran tail. "Does it hurt?" she asked, feeling foolish for doing so.

He shook his head. "Not for many years."

"Oh." Lily had this strange urge to touch the skin. To come so close to what made the Fallen who they were. "Will it ever heal?"

"I will bear the mark of my fall for eternity."

That was a long time to be reminded of his disgrace. Then again, he fell, and she doubted that was the worst of his punishment. As wrong as it was, she felt sorry for him. What it must have been like to make one mistake and lose everything he had known or cherished. It had been his choice, but had he realized the consequences and how vast they would be?

Gazing up at him, she realized she had never really considered the Fallen's pain before, their loss. If she was cast out of the Sanctuary for one mistake, wouldn't she turn bitter? Would the loneliness their kind faced over the centuries be enough to turn them into the creations she hunted?

"I'm sorry."

Julian's eyes widened. "You'd apologize for my fall?"

Not sure if she had made a mistake by uttering those words, she shrugged. He had been relatively evasive when it came to the reason why he fell, but it seemed unfair that lust had brought him down to Earth.

What a traitorous line of thought, she realized.

He stared a moment, then smiled. "You're a strange Nephilim."

She almost laughed. "You're a strange Fallen."

"That I may be, but you have nothing to apologize

for. Not for me. Besides, not a part of me regrets my choice any longer. It is what it is." He lay on his side, supporting his head with one hand, watching her curiously, completely at ease in his nudity. He reached out and guided her down beside him. Once he had her tucked against him, he continued. "Leave with me."

"What?"

"Leave with me," he repeated. "We could go far away from here."

Lily stared at him for a moment and then laughed. It was a combination of disbelief and surprise. "You aren't serious."

"I'm not?" His fingers slipped over her rib cage. "We could go anywhere in the world. There are places far enough away that even your duty to the Sanctuary cannot reach you, Lily."

He was being serious. Oh, damn. She pushed up so she was eye level with him. "Julian."

"You won't have to worry about getting in trouble," he pointed out rather casually. As if what he was suggesting was no big deal. "You wouldn't have to answer to anyone. You could be free."

His words held a certain appeal. It was more than the idea of no longer being tied to the Sanctuary, but the fact he wanted her to leave with him. The notion did silly things to her heart and clouded her thoughts.

There were days when she wanted nothing more than to disappear. The overworked and underappreciated syndrome, but she never seriously considered leaving. She had to remind herself it wasn't an option as he trailed those agile fingers over the tips of her breasts. Her mouth watered. "I can't, Julian."

His fingers slipped to the other breast that was now aching and heavy. "You can do whatever you want."

She licked her lips. "I can do what I want now."

Julian raised a doubtful brow. "That isn't true. You're chained to your duty." His finger curled around her hardened nipple as he spoke. "Do you think your Nathaniel will allow this to continue?"

Lily bristled. "Nathaniel has no control over me like that."

"He doesn't?" Julian chuckled softly, his smile tender. "He controls everything. He holds your Contract. Does that not mean you must obey his every decree?"

"Yes, but . . ." She trailed off. There was no pretty way of looking at this. Julian was right.

"There are no buts, darling," he whispered as his gaze fixed on her rosy peaks.

"You don't understand," she argued. "As nice as what you offer sounds, it's not possible."

He shifted against her. "We will see."

She glanced down to where his body brushed hers. He was hard, and all thoughts of forcing him to understand it could never be an option were thrown out the window. "Julian?"

He paused, grinning devilishly at her. Then he pressed her back down as he placed himself over her body. "I believe I could do this all day."

One gentle thrust set her on fire. She reached down and cupped his rear. "I think I agree."

And Julian did, over and over till they collapsed into each other's arms. He didn't mention her leaving again, and Lily was grateful. They were able to create a little cocoon in her room, where the world outside didn't exist. In his arms, she could forget about her duty and what she would face when she returned to the Sanctuary. It didn't matter that it was only temporary.

CHAPTER TWENTY-ONE

She woke to find the sheets completely removed from her and Julian's lips latched onto her breast, drawing her nipple deep into the warm recesses of his mouth. Dazed, her hand fluttered to his head. A ball of lava formed in her belly. "What . . . what are you doing?"

He lifted his head, smiling down at her. "I was beginning to think you'd never wake up. It's late in the afternoon."

They hadn't fallen asleep until the sun started to rise, and her muscles ached in a delicious way. When he hadn't been doing crazy things to her body, they had nestled together, talking until they both passed out.

Sleep still fogged her brain as her lids fluttered open. There was a wicked glint to his azure eyes and a mischievous tilt to his sensual lips. He picked up her right hand, bringing it to his lips and sucking her finger into his mouth. She felt the pull all the way to her core.

"What are you doing?" she asked, breathless.

"I want you."

"You have me," she said, using the same words he had told her while on the couch.

"Do I?" He sat up, swinging his legs off the bed and standing in one fluid motion. "Prove it to me."

Her heart thundered as she rose unsteadily. Things seemed to blur around the edges as her eyes locked with his. He gripped her shoulders, bringing her to her knees on the bed so that she was kneeling in front of him. The unspoken demand was clear, and her skin tingled.

She reached out, wrapping her hand around his cock without breaking eye contact. Moving her hand from his base to the head, she felt him swell in her palm.

"I woke up earlier, and all I could think about was you." He brushed his knuckles across her cheek. "I can't stop thinking about you— about this. It consumes my thoughts."

She shuddered as his hand dropped to her breast, tweaking her nipple. Dipping forward, she darted her tongue out and circled his engorged head as she watched an array of emotions flicker across his striking features.

He groaned, staring at her with such intensity she felt like a goddess. She stroked his rim, laving the ridge with her tongue and then back to his head, lapping at the moisture beading there. "You like this?"

"Yeah . . . I like . . . a lot."

Her tongue followed the length of his throbbing member. He reared against her as if she had done something rather drastic. "Oh, you like that more?"

His lips parted, and he nodded. She did it again, and this time her lips followed the path. His hand left her breast, balling in her hair, opening and closing mindlessly. She kind of liked him like this, completely vulnerable to her. It was usually the other way around.

Before long, he was cradling her head as she worked him with her lips and tongue. His groans sparked her own lust, boiling her from the inside. But then he reached between them, grasping her free hand and lowering it to her own sex.

Pulling back, she recoiled from what he was silently urging her to do. "I . . . I can't."

He lowered his chin, his heated gaze piercing hers. "You can."

Her cheeks flamed with embarrassment even though her sex was throbbing, excited by the idea of pleasuring herself while she pleasured him. "Julian . . ."

Shifting slightly, he guided her hand down until she cupped herself. Then, as she watched him, his finger pushed hers inside. She moaned from the wicked act, her skin flushing for a whole different reason.

He guided her hand until she was doing it herself, then cupped the back of her head and urged her to pick up where she had stopped. Taking him in her mouth once more, she sucked harder as she thrust against her hand.

Julian's eyes grew luminous. "Oh God," he groaned, picking up rhythm, forcing her to take his full length as she slipped another finger into her wet folds.

Suddenly, he pulled away from her mouth and wrapped his own hand around the base of his member. "I want to watch you finish yourself," he ordered roughly.

The erotic act of pleasuring herself while he watched made her dizzy. She wanted to refuse, but it seemed like her moral compass had fallen to the wayside. Unable to say no, she eased down onto her back and moved her fingers in and out. This wasn't the first time she had touched herself, but with him watching it was so much more potent. Her toes curled as she came close to the edge.

He kneed her thighs apart and knelt between her legs, slowly stroking himself as his eyes followed her fingers in and out, covered in her arousal. "Harder," he whispered.

And she did. Pumping her fingers, she arched her hips up to meet her own thrusts. Her head tipped back, and her soft moans filled the bedroom as she watched him through glazed-over eyes. Her hips came clear off the bed as she grinded against her fingers. Her heart was thundering deep in her chest and stomach. The need for him to be against her consumed her in a way that left her panting with want.

His scorching gaze followed her arousal as it ran down her thigh. Never breaking eye contact, he bent at the waist and lowered his mouth to her thigh. Using his tongue, he lapped up the slick moisture. The act toppled her right over the edge. She came, writhing shamelessly.

He climbed over her, his attention feral and possessive. Slipping an arm under her waist, he flipped her onto her belly. Her fingers dug into the sheets as Julian rained kisses down her spine, over her hips and her plump cheeks. Then he drew her to her knees, using his thigh to push her legs farther apart.

She was primed, ready, her sex filling with anticipation. This . . . this was what she'd needed, what she desired so badly. For him to take her, to fill her. His tip probed her moist entrance, teasing her until she squirmed.

"Tell me," he said, holding her still as he ran the edge of his cock over her swollen lips. "Tell me you want this."

She threw her head back. "Yes! Yes!"

He thrust into her, gripping her hips with bruising force. He pulled her back against him as he plunged into her savagely. He pressed his lips to her damp temple, cupping her sex in his hand as he continued to pump his hips. "This is mine," he told her, voice thick. "It always will be."

She broke apart, shattering into a thousand tiny pieces as her release crashed through her and milked his cock with such force that he growled. She cried out his name over and over again as he drove into her. Julian's arms tightened around her. One more deep thrust and he came, shouting her name. Panting and slick with sweat, he brought her down to the bed.

Minutes, maybe hours, passed before either of them could form a coherent thought, let alone a whole sentence. He tugged her across his chest, running his hand through her hair idly. They lay together, tangled in each other's arms, while Julian made her laugh with his twisted take on current affairs and she fascinated him with tales of her training and first battle.

Her cell phone beeped from the bedside table. She

didn't remember dropping it there when she returned to her apartment. Reluctantly, she wiggled out of his embrace and snatched her cell. Flipping it open, she quickly scrolled to her texts while Julian dropped a line of delicious kisses down her spine.

"I could nibble right here," he murmured, catching the flesh just above her hip between his teeth. "Or here . . ."

She glanced over her shoulder at him, grinning. "You're insufferable."

He chuckled against the small of her back. "You like my kind of suffering."

That she did, but she opened Luke's text: U need to go to Nate NOW. Her heart sank, and, just like that, the cocoon around them unraveled. Reality crashed over her. She was in trouble, big trouble.

Julian stilled behind her. "What is it?"

Snapping her phone shut, she twisted around. Concern—for her—dampened the heat in his eyes. She cupped his cheek, leaned in, and kissed him. When she pulled back, she forced a smile. "Nothing, but I have to get ready and go."

His gaze dropped to the phone in her hand. "It's the Sanctuary?"

She nodded. "I need to go to Nathaniel. If I don't, there's a good chance he'll come here."

A different kind of heat flared in his eyes. "Let him."

She kissed him again. "It'll be okay. Nathaniel has been like a father to me. He'll be pissed, but he'll get over it." She hoped that was the case.

He pulled her against him, holding her tightly to his chest. He rested his chin atop her head. "I don't want you to go back there."

"Julian . . ."

"Because I can't follow you there," he said. No Fallen or minion could enter the Sanctuary, as the ground was blessed. "If something were to happen, I can't help."

Warmth spread through her chest as she wiggled free, catching his chin in her hand. She forced him to look at her. "Nothing is going to happen to me there. I'll be okay. You have nothing to worry about."

He didn't let go at first, but then he did release his hold . . . and followed her into the shower. And when they stood under the hot spray of water, he stared down at her with such tenderness in his gaze that she felt those tears again building behind her eyes. Then he lifted her, pressing her back against the tiled wall, entering her slowly. For a little while, as he brought her to the edge and back, she let herself forget what was waiting for her outside her apartment.

A few hours later, Lily walked through the front lobby of the Sanctuary. When Sandy didn't respond to her greeting, she felt the flush of anger and embarrassment all the way to the tips of her ears. It was obvious Micah had not kept quiet. She was going to kick Micah again. She could see it, and it filled her with a vicious amount of happiness.

That pleasure was short-lived.

The moment she stepped inside Nathaniel's office, a coldness settled over her skin and seeped into her bones. This was going to suck in more ways than she could count.

Nathaniel came out of one of the smaller rooms, dressed in full evening attire. Lily stared, wide-eyed. She couldn't help it. He was a handsome man—okay, more than just handsome. He was one of the best-looking men around, and in all his current finery he would even give Julian a run for his money.

The only thing misplaced was the black tie that hung around his neck undone. Lily had a sinking suspicion that she had held him up. Nathaniel attended a lot of the "important" dinners in the city, keeping an eye on politicians. Most likely Senator Sharpe and his cronies.

And she had royally screwed that up judging by the displeasure on his face.

"Do you have any idea what I was pulled out of?" he asked, but before she could answer, he continued. "I was at a dinner—a fund-raiser hosted by Senator Sharpe. The same one we know is tied to Asmodeus. I was there to see if I could gain any insight on what he was doing. However, that didn't work out, now did it?"

"I'm so—"

"Don't apologize," he cut her off.

She fidgeted by the door, trying to smile. It came across as a grimace. "I guess Luke told you?"

Nathaniel didn't respond as he walked past her, slamming the door shut. She jumped a good three inches off the ground.

"I should explain—I mean, I can explain." He stopped in front of her. All six foot six inches of him glowered down at her. She swallowed heavily. "Nathaniel, I—"

"There is nothing you could possibly ever say that would explain to me why you attacked one of your own in favor of a Fallen. Absolutely nothing, Lily." He didn't mince words. "Do you even know how disappointed I am right now?"

Oh, she could take a guess. It probably ranked somewhere near epic level. She stared down at the floor. The weight of his disapproval and anger pounded on her. "Yes."

"No. I don't believe you do know." He prowled a small circle around her. "I never thought I would hear myself say this, but here I am. I don't believe anything you're about to tell me."

She couldn't really remember when she had seen him this mad. She had pulled some pretty wild stunts as a teenager, but even then he looked at her fondly. Now, when Lily had the courage to sneak a peek at him, his stare was as cold as glaciers.

"I'm sorry."

"Sorry?" he repeated as he grabbed her chin, forcing her to meet his eyes. "You attacked Micah. Nearly broke his damn jaw. And all you can say is 'I'm sorry'?"

"He kind of deserved it?" she joked weakly.

His grip tightened. "Are you fucking serious?"

Her eyes went wide. There was a chance that joking had been a very bad idea. "I know I have a lot to explain and I will. Give me a chance."

He stared at her for a hard moment before releasing her. He threw his hand up at her to talk.

"Julian had walked away from Micah," said Lily, even though his eyes narrowed warningly. "Micah tried to attack him, and I couldn't let him." Need a good reason, one that does not involve attraction. "Not after all the times Julian has come to my aid. I couldn't let him be taken down like that."

His brows shot straight up, and then he laughed. "You think to lie to me? You're beyond infatuated with Julian! Enough to risk everything you have worked for!"

"I am not infatuated with him," she denied, and God, it sounded lame.

"Damn it, Lily. I don't need this right now." He went to his desk. "I don't need you becoming the next big problem."

Her skin prickled. She closed her eyes, wetting her lips nervously. "What do you want me to say?"

"You can't say what I want you to say," he responded quietly. "You and I both know the truth, and half of the circle already suspects the worst. All eyes are on you."

Yeah, she figured that out when Micah accused her, but to hear Nathaniel say it was like getting kicked in the gut. She stepped forward. "You don't think it's me?" she whispered.

He looked down at her. "I think you have gotten yourself into something very . . . complicated."

She plopped down in one of the chairs in front of his

desk. "Nathaniel, I would never betray the Sanctuary. I don't want people thinking that."

He shook his head. "You should've thought of that. Before. Now the damage is done. Your reputation is scarred, and I hope whatever it is you think you have with Julian was worth what you have done."

She frowned at him. "Julian has nothing to do with this."

Nathaniel came back around the desk, sitting in the chair opposite her. "Do you even have a clue what you've done? Not only to yourself, but to the entire Sanctuary? The circle suspects you, Lily. They won't be searching for the real culprit."

"Then I will," she answered. "Luke and . . . we will."

He watched her carefully. "I think Luke is even more disappointed than I am."

"Luke will get over it." She ran her hand over the mark on her thigh. "I mean, I will talk to Luke."

"Julian is Fallen, Lily. Did you happen to forget about Anna? Do you really think Luke, of all people, is going to 'get over it'?"

Her fingers stilled. "Julian is different."

"I'm sure Anna thought Crosio was different, too."

She gaped at him. No one had spoken the name of the Fallen that had killed Anna. Crosio had only lived a few hours after Anna's death was discovered. In a rage, Luke had destroyed him on his own.

"You forget once they lose their grace it's in their nature to manipulate and deceive. Especially to get what they want, and they will stop at nothing to achieve it. You cannot trust Julian. Never forget that."

An ugly thing in her reared its head. All of them treated her as if her instincts were that of a naïve child who wanted to believe the best in everything. They forgot Lily had witnessed firsthand how devious the Fallen could be. A roaring heat blossomed in her, intense and consuming.

Nathaniel closed his eyes, sighing. "I see it's already too late."

Her hands clenched. "Too late for what?"

"You already trust him."

She thought about saying no, but mentally said screw it. Nathaniel was already mad. "Yes."

The tips of his slender fingers tapped along his chin as he studied her. "How far has your relationship progressed?"

Her entire face puckered up. There was no way in holy hell she was going to talk about this with him. She'd rather face a roomful of deadheads on crack than discuss her sexual activities.

"I don't like this topic any more than you do," he offered.

"Then don't ask."

He leaned forward. "If you've progressed to a sexual relationship with him, then I need to know. You've already proven a liability out there with what you did to Micah. If he attacks a Nephilim, I need to know you will be able to fight him."

"How would me having sex with Julian prevent me

from fighting him?" she demanded, cheeks burning. "That's the most ridiculous thing."

"Do you know nothing of the Fallen, Lily? Have you forgotten everything I've taught you?" He stood, running his hands through his hair. "If you've had sex with him, then you've bonded with him. You'd never be able to fight him. He'll always—always know where you are. I don't even know if hallowed ground could stop him if he wants to come here for you." He turned, facing her. "Do you have any idea how much jeopardy that puts the Sanctuary in?"

Shit. How could she have forgotten that? But Julian was different. He would never use what happened between them as a way to get inside the Sanctuary. And he didn't seem to know that he could follow her here. But his warning, before he caved to her pleas, came back to her.

Color rose in her cheeks. "Julian is different. He's my friend—that's all. But if he were to hurt one of us, I would be able to fight him."

"Micah—"

"Unprovoked and without due cause," she retorted angrily. "He tried to sneak up on Julian. Micah's lucky I stopped his idiotic attack, because I doubt he would have successfully rendered Julian helpless or walked away from the attack."

"Lily, this situation may spiral out of control. Once the circle . . ."

"Why does it have to spiral out of control?" she demanded. "You're acting like I've done something horrendous. All I did was kick Micah, and you know what? I'd do it again."

He arched a brow. "That's nice, Lily. That's why I must forbid you from leaving the Sanctuary without my permission." He held up his hand the moment she opened her mouth. "You will not disappear for an entire day and expect Luke to cover for you. Each night I expect you back in the Sanctuary."

She flew out of her seat. "You have to be kidding. You can't do that!"

He stared back, eyes like hard stone. "Damn straight, I can! Do I need to remind you who is boss here?"

He was treating her like she was twelve! There was no way she could stand for this. She knew the circle would see what she did as a travesty of unheard proportions, but to limit her freedom like she was a prisoner was outrageous.

He turned away. "You may go to your chamber."

Her eyes narrowed. "You have no right to forbid me to leave here."

Nathaniel whirled, crossing the distance between them in one second. "I damn well can!"

"Nowhere in my Contract does it give you or any of them power like that. You're acting like . . . you're my father or something. You're just my boss, Nathaniel. You just hold my Contract. You can't stop me!"

"Stop you from what?" His arms tensed like he wanted to shake her, or worse. "Stop you from getting yourself killed or getting another Nephilim killed? Stop you from seeing Julian? Is that what this is all about? You will disobey me for him?"

Lily stood her ground. "Don't make me choose."

Nathaniel faltered, staring at her. Shock flickered in his eyes, and then a cold mask settled over his handsome face. "If you think there is a choice, then you're sadly mistaken. There is no choice, Lily. It's only your duty to the Sanctuary. Do what you will. You're correct. I cannot stop you."

She let out a ragged breath. *There is no choice. It's only your duty to the Sanctuary.* Those words burned through her. Without saying another word, she headed for the door. Nathaniel stopped her.

"If you ever go after another Nephilim again because of him, or put any of them in jeopardy due to your misguided faith, I will end this," he advised coolly. "And you will be punished, Lily. I will dissolve your Contract."

CHAPTER TWENTY-TWO

The sharp slice of Nathaniel's words haunted Lily long after she stormed out of the Sanctuary. She sucked in air sharply as she perched beside a stone gargoyle. Antsy and still energized by anger, she dropped to the ledge below and then to the alley. The first minion she came across she cut down without so much as a word. The second, she toyed with. The third minion had tried to run, but she had brought it down in cold malice.

She continued into the wee hours of the morning. Anger shifting into guilt, guilt back to fury, pity to self-righteousness, and finally by the last kill she decided that she might be bipolar.

No amount of flying from building to building assuaged the turmoil of emotions in her. At some point, she recognized the bulk of her anger was directed at herself. She had done wrong. No matter how much she saw the good in Julian, others would never see what she saw, and she shouldn't expect them to.

When Julian met up with her, it wasn't at their usual spot. She'd avoided the Hilton, unsure if she could face him right now. But he found her anyway, deep within Rock Creek Park.

He stalked toward her, head low. Strands of hair obscured most of his face, shielding his eyes.

Her insides tightened. Excitement and anxiety swirled. She raised an unsteady arm. "I . . . I can't do this right now."

"I told you I didn't want you going back there." He didn't even miss a beat.

How had he known how badly it went? She wasn't sure, but when he stopped in front of her, every muscle in her body locked up. Then she whirled, taking off. She couldn't deal with him right now or what he made her feel. Hell, she couldn't even deal with herself.

She didn't make it very far.

Julian snagged her from behind and flipped her around, pressing her until her back hit rough tree bark. Catching her wrists in one hand, he pinned them above her head. "Why do you run from me?" he growled. "I'm not the enemy."

If he wasn't the enemy, then who was? The Sanctuary? Her?

As he stared down at her, a look of fierce possessiveness shot across his face. She shuddered. And when he pulled her against him, she expected him to take her right there.

But he didn't.

Julian cradled her against him, wrapping one arm around her tightly and sinking his other deep into her hair. And she was desperate to be closer to him. She nuzzled against him, spreading her hands across his back. With him, she was just Lily—not tethered to the

Sanctuary or to anything—and she could only be that with Julian.

"I'm sorry," she whispered.

"Why are you apologizing?" He lowered his head, kissing where her neck met her shoulder. "You've done nothing wrong. Don't apologize for them. I can't—I won't leave you."

Lily squeezed her eyes shut. "I don't want you to."

He was silent for a very long time, holding her to him. "You think to keep us both?"

Tipping her head back, she met his stare. "I do."

A small smile pulled at his lips as he smoothed his hand over her head. "It won't be easy, Lily."

Nothing was easy, but that didn't mean she was going to just give up. She could deal with this. And she would. There was no other choice, unless she wanted to lose everything—including Julian.

Michael landed hard on his back for what seemed like the hundredth time in the last hour. However, he was a bit smarter this time. He immediately blocked Rafe's booted heel from connecting with his throat.

Remy chuckled from the other side of the mat. "He's catching on."

"Finally," muttered Rafe, removing the pressure.

He wanted to tell them where they could shove it, but he had tried that already. And it had not ended well. He'd probably be pissing blood for the next week. Climbing slowly to his feet, he stretched the kink out of his back. "One more time."

One more time—just one more time until Michael got it.

Rafe nodded, and pride shone in his eyes before he attacked. He moved with a series of fast jabs and leg swipes Michael was able to dodge and then kicks. The kicks were always what got him. No man should be able to kick that fast and hard.

"Slow it down. It's not about how fast you can move, but how well you can anticipate his next move."

Startled by the soft advice, Michael wasn't able to block the crescent kick Rafe delivered, and on the floor he went.

Lily hadn't spoken since she'd arrived this morning to watch him train. She came in, lifted her chin curtly at them, and then sat down on the mats. Every so often he had glanced over at her. She watched them intently, but he could never read her expression. The only thing he could tell was that she looked exhausted. Faint shadows blossomed under her green eyes, and there was a weary pull to her lips.

Remy bent down to her, several thick dreads obscuring whatever it was he whispered in her ear.

Michael picked himself up. "One more time," he gritted.

Lily pushed herself up from the mat. Her long hair was pulled up in a messy knot, and she wore loose-fitting sweats. Even rumpled and exhausted, he knew he shouldn't underestimate whatever she was up to.

Rafe turned to her. "Wanna give it a try?"

She nodded as he stepped aside. "You move too fast.

287

In hand-to-hand combat, simply moving faster than your opponent is only a benefit when you're the attacker." Her hand snaked out, slamming into his chest. He staggered back with a scowl. "However, defending yourself is simply anticipating the next move. He will tell you where he strikes next without words."

Michael rubbed his chest with the heel of his palm. "Was that necessary?"

She flashed a small grin. "Watch us." Lily turned to Rafe with a small nod. He launched into attack with the same amount of ferocity that he held when he went after him.

Michael crossed his arms over his chest. Instead of Lily ending up on her ass, she dodged his blows. The entire time she kept her eyes on Rafe. Within seconds she pushed forward, and to Rafe's irritation, she easily deflected each kick and jab he sent her way.

"Arm!" she called a split second before Rafe threw a punch. "Leg!" she yelled again. Over and over, she called out each method of attack right as Rafe delivered it. He moved faster, but she still managed to catch it a second before he did. "Watch his body! See how the area tenses before he uses it. The muscles will twitch or tremor." She blocked a fierce sidekick that would have hurt like holy hell.

His eyes narrowed on Rafe, eventually seeing what she pointed out. It was a fine tremor. No matter how Rafe tried to change it up, his body gave away his next move. After he picked that up and grew a bit more confident, his attention wandered over to Lily.

She was rather amazing to watch. Quick-footed and strong, she moved like a skilled dancer. She really got into it, too. Maybe a little too much. There was an air of violence to her. Part of her must thrive on it because eventually her lips curved into a delighted smile as Rafe grew more agitated with her ability to outperform him.

The midget ninja was enjoying herself.

A smile pulled at his lips as his hand slid under his shirt, over the crucifix she had brought to him.

Lily backed off, and Michael took her place with Rafe. After a few minutes, he was able to anticipate the moves. Not as quickly as she had, but he didn't end up on his back again. That was a hell of an improvement. Even Rafe seemed to think so. Instead of breaking for lunch with the usual routine of running the underground tunnels, he allowed Michael to go straight to the cafeteria. He felt like he'd moved up a grade.

Lily disappeared while they headed to lunch, but returned a few minutes later looking . . . off. Michael watched her curiously as she grabbed some food. The whole time she kept her head down as she surveyed the piles of lunch meat.

"What's up with her?" he asked around a mouthful of roast-beef sub.

Remy's gaze flickered to Rafe. "Nothing."

"Bullshit."

"If you think you're brave enough to broach that question with her, please let me know ahead of time," said Rafe. "I would like to be out of swinging range."

Michael snorted but didn't respond. Lily sat beside

him with a plate full of meat but no bread. She picked at the food listlessly, and no amount of effort Remy or Rafe made to draw her into conversation seemed to work.

He nudged her arm when Rafe and Remy left to dump their plates. "You okay?"

She glanced up, her expression unfathomable. "Yeppers."

"You don't seem so. Did something happen yesterday when you were gone?"

The cool exterior cracked a bit, but it wasn't anger that poked through. It was agitation. She looked at him for a moment, her eyes shuttered. "No, nothing happened yesterday."

His gaze dropped to the hand that rested next to her untouched plate. It trembled for a few seconds before it stilled. Lily seemed unaware of the movement. "Hey, if you need anyone to talk to?" he offered. "Though I don't know how much help I'd be. I'm bat-shit crazy since I've been here."

Lily laughed softly. She opened her mouth but caught a glimpse of the door and froze. He followed her gaze. Two Nephilim walked in. He recognized one of them as Micah, and he wasn't a fan of the cocky son of a bitch. He'd trained a few times with him, and the guy seemed to take great relish in any mistake Michael made.

He'd never seen the other Nephilim, but he seemed important. He walked with an air of authority. A swagger that begged someone to try to mess with him.

His long, black hair was tied back at the nape of his neck, and he had the same pale blue eyes all the male Nephilim seemed to share. He was taller than Micah and much broader.

The newcomer looked down expectantly at Lily as they passed, as if he thought she would say something. Micah, on the other hand, shoved his middle finger in her face and mouthed, "Whore."

Lily started to rise, but Michael was faster. Without thinking of the consequences—like getting his ass handed to him—he snapped the offensive finger backward. Micah let out a howl of pain that made Michael quite happy. "Try to act like a goddamn gentleman."

"Oh snap." Lily giggled.

The other Nephilim simply stared at him. "Well hello, rookie." He had a strange accent. Slavic or Russian—someplace where it was cold and Michael had no intent on ever visiting.

Once the shock wore off, Micah was clamoring to get to Michael. God must have been smiling down on him because Rafe and Remy appeared and restrained Micah.

"You broke my fucking finger!"

Michael's lips twisted. "Maybe you should learn how to speak to a lady?"

"A lady?" he sputtered. "Who in the hell are you talking about?"

He started forward again, but Lily stopped him. "Come on. It's not worth it."

Micah tried to shrug off the grip the other two had

on him. "Man, I'm going to break every bone in your body." He laughed. "You can count on it, you little prick."

"Dude, let it go." Remy pushed Micah back. "It's only your finger. It will heal in a few hours."

Lily shuffled Michael past them. "Adrian," she greeted the Nephilim who had entered with Micah.

"You and I will be talking soon," he replied.

She gave him a curt nod before turning back to Michael. "Come on, Superman. He packs some kryptonite in his punch."

Behind them, Micah shrugged off Remy and Rafe, still cursing up a storm. Michael snickered, feeling kind of badass. "You know, I didn't like the ass before. Never had a real reason, but now I do."

Lily didn't respond as she led him back to the training room. He had to walk fast to keep up with her. "You know, a thank-you would be nice," he said after a few moments.

She frowned at him. "I didn't ask you to do that. I would have taken care of him."

Okay, never mind then. "So what was his deal?" he asked once they entered the training room. They had some time to kill before Remy and Rafe returned.

Lily shrugged as she walked away. "He's an ass. You said it yourself."

He followed her. "Most men don't call a woman a whore for no reason."

Her expression soured. "Um, thanks."

"That's not what I meant." He stepped around the

dummies he practiced stabbing techniques on. "He's obviously got a problem with you."

She picked up a wicked-looking blade. "It's really none of your business." She shoved the blade at him, handle first. Thank God. "Get to ripping and tearing."

He flipped the blade in his hand. "So . . . what you got going on later?"

She stopped midstep. "What?"

"I'm asking what you're doing later. Hunting? Clubbing?" he asked. "Whatever it is you Nephilim do when I'm locked in my cell—oh, I mean bedroom."

Sighing, she gave him a dismissive wave. "Practice."

He made a face at her rigid back. "I'm trying to make chitchat." He sliced at the dummy. The synthetic skin was disturbingly lifelike. It split like butter.

"Please stop."

"It wouldn't hurt you to be nice," he chided.

"It wouldn't hurt you to shut up."

"Jesus!" He threw the blade into the dummy. It sank deep into the fake flesh, the handle vibrating from the impact. "I'm trying to have a freaking conversation with you! You know, a normal one people have every day. Hey, how are you and all that shit. Is that so hard?"

She raised one delicate brow.

He now felt like flipping her off, but that would make him a hypocrite. With a disgruntled groan, he turned away. "You know, since I've been here I haven't spoken to a single person outside. My cell doesn't work here. Can't get service anywhere I go in this damn place."

"It won't," she answered.

He twisted around. She stood with her arms crossed. "Yeah, I figured that out." He plucked the blade from the dummy. It made a gross sucking noise. He stabbed it again. "You know, I don't even know if I will ever be allowed to leave here."

"You will."

"And if I do, will I have any friends? Will I even be able to have friends? How can I when I'm this . . . Nephilim?"

"You don't need friends," she responded bluntly. "You have us. That's all you need." Her face pinched.

"Yeah, you guys are my friends? I don't think so." He took another jab at the poor dummy. "You go and have drinks with friends. You actually hold conversations with them."

"Did you have many friends?"

Michael stopped. Besides that being a very odd question to ask, he wasn't sure how to answer it. He considered Cole a friend. There were a few guys on the force he considered buddies. A few women who were a little more than friends, but none he would call to just hang out with.

"I had friends," he answered finally.

Lily shuffled closer. "I've never had a friend outside of the Sanctuary." She held her palm out. He handed her the blade. "Everyone I know lives here . . . or has." She twisted her wrist, showing him how to correctly hold the blade. "It will be hard for you to maintain your friendships."

Afraid of responding and having her shut down or insult him, he remained quiet as she handed the blade back to him. He held it correctly this time.

"The minions are a tricky bunch. If they spot you with a human, they'll use them against you. The humans we have here take a huge risk. I guess it's the money and intrigue that keeps them here." She shrugged. "Minions can't come here or anywhere near here. The tunnels that run under half of Federal Triangle have been blessed and consecrated. It helps protect the humans coming and going. Holy ground and all—the minions hate it."

He hadn't known that, but it made sense. It also made him want to laugh, because all he could think was how utterly stereotypical.

"Anyway, you have to be careful with your friends, or you'll probably see them die."

Michael's eyes widened. Nice. He made another swipe at the dummy. Holding the blade correctly seemed to make a more effective cut. Huh, go figure. "So you said I wouldn't be forced to stay here. When will I get to leave?"

"You'll begin hunting as soon as we think you're more of an asset than a liability. At first you will hunt in pairs or more. From there, you decide if you want to stay here or risk it on your own."

"You do that."

She shrugged. "You know . . . I've checked into your past."

His brows furrowed. "Why?"

"I'm nosy," she admitted. "I couldn't find anything remarkable about you."

"Well, thanks." He paused. "So you've been snooping?"

"Yes." She didn't look at all bothered by it.

"So what did you find out?"

"Your mom was a devout Christian who taught handicapped children. You went to church every Wednesday and Sunday. She taught Sunday school."

Michael stilled. There was nothing to say.

She continued blithely. "After her death, you were sent into foster care. Anyway, you excelled in sports. Played football and basketball—you were better at football. You dated the high school prom queen. May I add that is totally cliché?"

"Yeah," he said. It was a little unnerving to hear someone tick away his life.

"You went to college and obtained a degree in finance. Boring. Then you got your master's. Even more boring. Went off to work for some firm that paid you beaucoup bucks. Had some life-changing epiphany that made you decide to be a police officer."

"You know, that is really creepy."

Lily winked. "Did I miss anything? Oh, yes. You were busted for fighting when you were in college. Your drunk-off-his-ass friend decided to take on an entire bar. You got caught in the middle. Sucks being sober, doesn't it? By the way, Nephilim can't get drunk."

He blinked. "Well that explains that mystery."

She continued. "But there is this plant that is totally

the equivalent of ten tequila shots, but that is neither here nor there. You've never been engaged. You did come close to some pretty little blonde in college, but she totally slept with your roommate."

He dropped the blade. "How in the hell do you know this stuff?"

Lily flashed a smile. "I'm all knowing—omnificent."

He stared for a minute. "You mean omniscient."

"Whatever." Her grin remained.

He shook his head, picking up the blade. "Anything else you want to tell me about my life? Step up that creep factor a little more?"

She looked straight into his eyes, and as casually as if she'd been asking him to pass the salt, said, "Your mom didn't kill herself."

CHAPTER TWENTY-THREE

Everything seemed to stop, even Michael's heart. He stared at her, dumbfounded. "What did you say?"

"Your mom didn't kill herself," she repeated. "She had defensive wounds on her hands that indicate she put up a good fight."

He couldn't think. All his life he denied what everyone told him: that his mother had killed herself. He could never reconcile the memories of her with the body he had found on the bathroom floor. That hadn't been his mom.

It wasn't until he became a police officer and saw one suicide victim after another that he swallowed his pride. People did crazy things, and no one knew why. There weren't always answers, and sometimes people's problems ran so deep no one could ever see them. Now Lily stood there and told him she hadn't done it. She had been murdered.

He still couldn't think.

Blindly moving, he grabbed her arm. He ignored the warning that flashed in her eyes. "Who killed my mother?"

She glared at him. "I don't know."

"I don't believe you." His grip tightened. The

knowledge of his mother's true fate ignited a war of emotions: happiness, despair, sorrow, and fury. "You know everything else but not who killed her? Bullshit."

Lily jerked her arm, but he held on. "Why would I lie to you about that? I don't know. No one does. And I've looked into it, trust me."

He knew he was hurting her but couldn't get his hand to release her. His chest was squeezing. "Tell me who killed my mother, Lily."

Rafe and Remy entered just then. The two Nephilim slowed as they sensed the tension in the room. "Hey, what the hell is going on?" Rafe called out, his pace picking up.

Lily forced a smile. "Nothing," she said tightly. "I was just showing him a move." In a much lower voice, "Let go of me now, or I will break your face."

Michael's lips thinned, but he dropped her arm. If all those terrible emotions weren't rolling through him, he would have been ashamed at the angry red marks he had left on her arm. "This isn't over," he whispered.

She threw down the knife; the blade sank through the mat. She started toward the door and spotted Luke hovering there. "Thank you for sticking up for me earlier," she said as she breezed past.

"Hey, man, what was that about?" Remy asked as he plucked the knife out of the mat.

Michael stared at the door. Lily was gone. "What she said."

Remy arched a brow, but he didn't push it. Rafe launched into another round of training, but this time

Michael went at it with a fierceness he had never displayed before. His anger and frustration gave him an edge he didn't have earlier. It was the first time he knocked Rafe down, and Lily wasn't even there to see it. Nor would she ever know she was the cause of it.

"What is going on?" Luke demanded the moment he reached Lily's side.

She rubbed her arm absently. That was going to bruise. Why had she told Michael the truth like that? "What are you referencing?" she asked tiredly. "There are so many things."

"Don't be a smart-ass," he said as he cast a dark look at one of the Nephilim. "You know exactly what I am talking about. What the hell is going on?"

She sighed as she walked beside him. "You know what happened. You were there—for part of it at least."

"Is that where you were all day yesterday?"

She didn't answer. Instead, she walked past him.

"You were with him, weren't you?" His question exploded through the hallway like gunfire. Several Nephilim en route to the training room stopped. Some were openmouthed, while other's watched with morbid fascination. This wouldn't be the first argument they witnessed between Lily and Luke. Their spats were legendary.

"Jesus," she muttered, picking up her pace.

"What the fuck you looking at?" he yelled at a group of enthralled Nephilim. "Lily, what are you thinking?"

he asked, and this time his voice was, thankfully, much lower. "Damn it, Lily, slow down."

She came to a complete stop. "Is this better?"

He towered over her. "I'm supposed to bring you to Adrian, you little idiot. I would like to know exactly what happened before then."

"Yeah, he said he wanted to talk earlier," she responded blandly. She pushed the button for the elevator. "Are you going to tell me where we need to go?"

"The rooftop," he answered. "Lily, I don't think you understand how serious this is."

She was starting to get the hint. Really, she was. She was just so freaking annoyed that she couldn't muster up the concern. She waited with a sullen expression on her face.

"On top of everything else, Gabe returned this morning with his brother," he explained, darkness settling over his face as he pushed the button to close the elevator. "Two more Nephilim children were taken."

She rubbed her hands across her thighs. "Shit."

"Exactly. So you can understand why the circle is a bit pissed right now." He pushed the emergency stop button.

"Luke?" She turned to him, exasperated.

"Now you are going to tell me what you did to piss off Nate, and I mean besides the fact you attacked Micah over that Fallen."

"His name is Julian. He has a name. He doesn't answer to 'that Fallen' or whatever. It's Julian."

Luke stared at her. "Do you even hear yourself?" He

didn't wait for an answer, which was good because it was going to be a whopper of a smart-ass response. "He has a name? Well fucking la-di-da! That doesn't change that he's the enemy last time I checked."

Her irritation grew. "Luke, I know. I know you're concerned, but don't ask me anything about him. You won't like the answers . . . and it's really none of your business."

"Shit! Are you kidding me, Lily?" He placed his hands on her shoulders. "You are talking to me—Luke. I'm not the enemy here."

Pressing her lips together, she shifted from one foot to the other. A flash of guilt went through her. She didn't need to be such a jerk to Luke. He hadn't done anything. "I'm sorry. I know." She ran a hand over her head, smoothing down the fine strands of hair that escaped the bun. "Don't ask me about him. Okay? I understand you won't see him like I do, and I'm not ready to try to convince you any different."

Luke moistened his lips. "Okay. Forget . . . Julian, for now." His pale eyes flashed. "What happened between you and Nate? I've never seen him so angry. He about took off my head this morning when I stopped by the office."

"Sorry about that," she murmured. "He's a little pissed off at me."

"A little?" he asked with a harsh laugh. "After chewing me a new asshole for letting you run off, he then launched into a tirade about how we need to lock you up."

"Lock me up?" She bit down on the string of curses that weren't going to make anything better. "Nate needs to lock up Micah! He was admittedly following me. I caught him snooping around Nate's office. No one seems to care about that."

"Oh, Lily," he groaned. "He was following you to keep you safe and because he thinks you're the traitor."

"Likely excuse," she grumbled. "What about the office?"

"Who knows? Come on. Adrian is waiting on us." He pressed the emergency button but didn't say anything more. Not as the elevator started or as it went up a couple of floors. His silence didn't soothe her like she thought it would. It made her more worried.

"Luke?" she asked finally.

He studied her, his eyes dark and troubled as he folded his arms across his black shirt. He looked like someone who was leading a condemned man on his last walk.

She swallowed. "What's going on?"

"What do you think, Lily?"

She didn't know what to say to that, and there wasn't any time left to respond. The elevator came to a stop. Luke stepped forward, adjusting the fallen strap of her tank. Then he smoothed back her hair. His brotherly preparations really made her feel like she was taking her last walk.

As the elevator door opened, she tried to convince herself she would be able to clear things up. Hopefully she could come up with a couple of good reasons that explained her recent behavior, because right now she had none that she knew any of them would care about. At least none any of them would appreciate.

The bright summer sun beat down on her, and she shielded her eyes from the glare. Why had they picked the rooftop in the hot August sun? Did they plan on tossing her off the roof?

Her stomach fluttered nervously as she spotted Adrian. When he turned to face her, she couldn't gauge what he was thinking by his expression. He was as impassive as ever. Being almost as old as Nathaniel, Adrian was a mystery to her. All she really knew of him was that he was someone you didn't want to mess with. Then again, every Nephilim knew that.

Tall, with hair reaching his shoulders, Adrian reminded Lily of a warlord, one of those on the front of a trashy romance novel about to raid a village and whisk away the virgin princess. He was decked out in leather pants and a black, long-sleeved shirt. You'd think he'd be sweating bullets like Lily already was, but Adrian never seemed warm enough. Whatever cold and bleak country he had originated from had left him with piss in his blood forever.

Luke placed his hand on the small of her back, inching her forward. She hadn't realized she'd stopped walking. Adrian wasn't going to be like Luke or even Nate. There were no personal bonds between them that would save her ass or let her get away with snide, offhand comments. If he asked her a question, she was going to have to answer it.

Whether she liked it or not.

When she stepped closer, she realized Adrian wasn't alone, and Luke hadn't been entirely forthcoming with her. Across the rooftop and hidden in the shadows of the fearsome gargoyles stood Danyal and Nathaniel. As she neared Adrian, they converged on her all at once.

At that moment, she totally recognized the seriousness of the situation. And she wanted to run, and run very fast, but she wasn't a coward. Besides, a girl streaking across the midday sky would raise a lot of questions.

Damn it.

Adrian inclined his head at Luke before turning his frosty gaze upon Lily. "It has been a long time since we've talked. How have you been?"

She squinted up at him. "I doubt you are really interested in how I've been."

Somewhere behind her, she heard Nathaniel sigh, but her response brought a genuine smile to Adrian's well-formed lips. "I see you haven't changed a bit. Still the incorrigible little girl attached to Luke's hip with Nate wrapped around her little finger."

Nathaniel stiffened behind her. Danyal shifted uncomfortably. Adrian was painfully blunt, and he always seemed to need to be reminded Nathaniel was actually his boss and not the other way around.

Folding her arms over her chest, she refused to be intimated by him—by any of them, for that matter. "I see you're still an ass."

"Lily." Nathaniel sighed exasperatedly.

Adrian waved a dismissive hand. "Let's get to the point, shall we? We have a traitor among us. Someone has been working with the Fallen to expose the names and locations of the vulnerable Nephilim. That person has to have access to the Book and a strong enough connection to a Fallen to be able to move among them and not be harmed."

She didn't think the traitor—who she truly believed was Micah—needed to trust the Fallen at all. As long as he was giving them something they were interested in, then he would be safe. That is what she told them, and she was met with four cynical pairs of pale blue eyes. Whatever . . .

"The Fallen operate by no code," Danyal interjected. "It doesn't matter what is being done for them. They're as likely to kill you as they are to say hello. There has to be some level of a relationship there."

She glanced at Danyal. He must have been working when he was summoned to the Sanctuary since he was dressed in a suit minus the jacket. "I don't think all the Fallen operate the same."

Luke let out a long-suffering breath. "What she means is she doesn't think a relationship with the Fallen is necessary since the information being shared is literally priceless."

Danyal's gaze flickered over to Luke. "That's not what I'm getting at."

Unconsciously, she shifted closer to Luke. Damn, she was stuck. No one was in her corner except Luke, and they were outnumbered. She turned back to

Nathaniel and Adrian. "You all suspect me because of Julian." There; she'd said it. Now they could get on with their tribune and decide if they were going to kick her off the island or not.

Adrian's brows lifted, but he didn't show any other reaction. "You attacked a fellow Nephilim to protect a Fallen."

She figured at this point she needed to answer as quickly as possible, without much detail, or ask for a lawyer. Sadly, the Nephilim didn't get lawyers in their Contracts. That was something someone needed to suggest and pronto. "Yes."

"Why would you do something like that?" Adrian asked.

She had already explained it to Nathaniel, but it didn't appear he was going to speak up for her. His lack of communication, and the fact he wouldn't look at her, stung. She knew she had upset him, but she hadn't betrayed any of them.

And Nate knew her, right? She wanted to believe he did, but the conversation with Julian days before about no one really knowing who she was seemed painfully true. "Julian had walked away from him, and he tried to stab him in the back."

"So?"

"So?" she repeated dumbly, as if they should see what was wrong with that without having to spell it out. "Micah intentionally provoked him. Julian left it alone, but Micah went after him. He was unarmed and not attacking Micah."

"The Fallen are never unarmed," Nathaniel said, staring off into the sky with narrowed eyes. "Whether it is their strength, their intellect, or their manipulation. They are always armed."

"How far has your relationship with him progressed?" Adrian asked.

Her entire body went rigid. She did not blink, nor did she hesitate. "We are friends."

"Friends?" he repeated. "Lily, you know that's impossible."

"Obviously, it's not. I consider him a friend, like any normal person would."

Danyal stepped forward. The look on his face said he was trying to understand her, trying to figure out how she went from super-Nephilim Lily to the Lily who stood in front of him. "How can you get past what he is?"

"He's saved my life, multiple times, and he's never done anything to put me in jeopardy—or any of you, either. I trust him," she explained earnestly.

Danyal shook his head slowly. "And it's no more than that? Like with Anna? She had been manipulated into a serious relationship."

She didn't know if Anna had been manipulated or not. Luke knew more about those circumstances than anyone else did, and he wasn't talking about that. Ever. "I don't see how this has anything to do with Anna."

"And if we demanded you stop seeing him as a friend today, would you be able to do so?" Danyal asked.

She gaped. Hell, at this point she didn't care if their

concern was even valid. It was pure principal. How could any of them tell her who she could be friends with, who she could care about, or who she . . . ?

"Lily?"

She raised her chin. "No one has the right to tell any of us who we can befriend."

"He's a Fallen, Lily!" Danyal snapped, losing his customary cool facade. "There shouldn't be any question. There shouldn't be anything you have to think about."

Adrian tilted his head to the side, his gaze finding Nathaniel's. "Nate and I believe there is much more to this than a mere friendship. It would explain many things. Has the relationship become one of a sexual nature? Answer the question, Lily."

She looked at Nathaniel, feeling horribly exposed. He had asked her that question just yesterday, and she had told him exactly how she felt about answering. To hear that he had discussed her sexual activities with Adrian mortified her. Not as much as knowing she was going to have to answer them. She shuffled uncomfortably, near panicked. She was a grown woman, but this was her personal, intimate business, and these were her coworkers. Her friends. And Nathaniel was like her father. It was just . . . gross.

"Adrian, I don't think this is necessary." Luke stepped forward. His gaze found Nathaniel's. "Don't," he asked, pleading. He seemed to be the only one who understood how this was affecting her, and the only one who cared.

Nathaniel's lips formed a tight, hard line. "Lily, answer the question."

This was horrifying. She felt sick to her stomach, and it wasn't from the sun. She felt her face flush, and she was near tears. So angry she thought her skin would boil off her bones.

"Lily!" Nathaniel ordered, his patience snapping.

"Yes! Yes! Okay? Does that make you all happy?" she nearly shrieked.

Nathaniel's jaw clenched, but there wasn't a flicker of emotion on Adrian's face. He had already assumed their relationship had progressed to a sexual one. For whatever reason, he only waited to hear Lily admit to it.

She wanted to vomit, right there, on his leather boots. God, she would have happily done so if she had actually had more than a bite of her lunch. Instead, she swallowed down the taste of bile. "So while you guys bother yourselves over whether I'm having sex and with whom, the person out there who is actually betraying us is doing so without an ounce of attention on him!"

Danyal raised his head. "And who would that be?"

"Micah," she responded. "He was snooping around Nate's office, and he is a complete arrogant jerk!" The last part wasn't really a valid reason for suspicion, but she couldn't help but throw it out there.

"And what were you doing in Nathaniel's office?" Adrian asked casually. "I'm quite curious."

Her heart skipped a beat. Everything was surreal.

310

She was outside, but it felt like the walls were closing in on her. Both Luke and Nate had told her she was beginning to be suspected. Micah had confirmed it, but she hadn't really believed they truly thought it was her. Even during this meeting she thought they were upset with her about Julian, and not that they really thought she was helping the Fallen gain access to the Nephilim.

"I was looking for Nate to see if we could give Michael a break for the weekend, but he wasn't in his office. Micah was." She left out the part that she'd copied a couple of the personnel files. That would definitely not work in her favor.

"We don't suspect Micah," Adrian responded, and that was the end of that.

She turned back to Luke. The wild turmoil she was feeling must have been written all over her face, because Luke shook his head at her. Her hands curled into fists as a bead of sweat trickled between her breasts. She turned to Nathaniel, believing he was the one person besides Luke who would always have her back. "What's going on?" she whispered.

"There will be an investigation into your attack against Micah and whether you have had anything to do with the information that has been handed over to the Fallen," he answered. He at least had the cojones to maintain eye contact with her.

"An investigation?" she stammered. "What does that mean?"

Adrian stepped back, handing over control to

Nathaniel completely. This part, the one that was coming, was Nathaniel's duty. He handled the personnel issues: the write-ups, the punishments, the suspensions, and the all-feared breach of Contract.

However, none of this was making sense to her. Her head swung wildly from Nate to Luke. Then she saw it coming like a freight train that couldn't be stopped.

And it was about to run right over her.

"Your hunting duties have been suspended until further notice."

"What?" she exploded. People on the streets below had to have heard her it was that loud.

"Your access to the Sanctuary has been restricted to the aboveground levels and to level four only. You will have no other access. You will only be allowed to continue your training with Michael, but once your training is complete for the day, you will be required to leave the premises."

"Has the entire circle agreed on this?" Luke demanded, coming to life beside her. "This is the first I've heard of this."

Nathaniel's eyes turned cold. "I don't need the circle's agreement."

Her chest rose and fell with each heavy breath she took. "What if I didn't have a place to go? You'd throw me out on the street, Nathaniel?"

"If you didn't have a place to go, you would be secluded in one of the isolation cells. That is still an option," he warned icily.

Was she supposed to actually say "thank you" to

that? "So you don't trust me to hunt, but you trust me to train Michael? That makes no sense!"

Adrian, no longer able to remain silent, spoke up again. "Your indiscretion must not interrupt his training. He has done well under you and Rafe, and we cannot run the risk of undoing everything he has learned."

"In other words, you don't trust me to be out there hunting and running amok through the Sanctuary in case I take a peek at the Book, but you want to be able to keep your eyes on me at some point. Oh, and none of you want to be saddled with training someone."

"Lily!" Nathaniel's voice rose. "Your suspension begins immediately, and I strongly advise you cease any contact with the Fallen."

"Wait, I will take full responsibility for her," objected Luke. "If she hunts, then I hunt. That will also solve the problem of the Fallen. He doesn't come around when I am with her. He never has."

Nathaniel shook his head. "The decision is already made. The suspension stands as is."

"Do any of you understand what this will do to her reputation?" demanded Luke. "This won't stay secret for long. The other Nephilim will find out. There will be no stopping the damage."

"She should have thought about that before she slept with the Fallen, placing herself in such a bad light," Adrian shot back.

Lily started forward, coming close to swinging on him, but Nathaniel grabbed her arm. "Everyone has been sworn to silence. The knowledge that there is a traitor will not leave the circle, nor will the knowledge of why you have been suspended."

Danyal snorted. "There're so many reasons why you'd finally be suspended, Lily. They will assume it's any number of things. All anyone knows now is that you and Micah got into it."

"Shut up," she seethed, wanting to plant her fist in his face.

Nathaniel's grip tightened. "All of you leave now. This is over."

With Nathaniel's patience at an end, and her temper near explosive levels, the other Nephilim left with the exception of Luke. She turned to Nathaniel, her hurt clearly visible for him to see. "You said—"

"It doesn't matter," he cut her off, dropping her arm. "The moment Micah told Adrian what happened, there was nothing I could do to halt this meeting. The only reason you weren't suspended yesterday was because I had hoped this wouldn't blow up. Stop looking at me like I've kicked your puppy into oncoming traffic, Lily! For far too long, I have let my fondness for you get in the way, and your behavior has increasingly gotten out of hand."

"My behavior?" she demanded in a low voice. She was quite curious what he was referring to that was so bad.

He raised his hand, cutting off anything else she would have said. "Your suspension is more for your benefit than it is anyone else's."

314

She looked at him like he had grown fifteen heads. "How is this for my benefit?"

Nathaniel took a step forward, causing Luke to immediately move closer to her. "They don't trust you, Lily. What do you think will happen if you are out there hunting and get cornered or you have to call for help? Do you think they'll come to your aid?"

"Nate, come on." Luke's displeasure was rolling off him in waves.

"No, she needs to hear this. She needs to know how badly she has screwed up. She will be out there on her own, and you can't be with her every second."

Lily stared aghast, unwilling to believe that. "The others will help me."

Nathaniel barked harsh laughter. "The others will follow their lead. Lily, I cannot have you out there and be unprotected if something goes wrong. Not until this is cleared up."

She stepped back. His words felt like a slap in the face. She turned before they could see how strongly affected she was. "I assume you don't expect me to finish training Michael today?"

"No. You may leave. Get whatever you need from your room. I won't require anyone to go with you. Report back here Monday for training."

She nodded, not trusting herself to speak. She started to walk off, but Nathaniel stopped her.

"Lily, they wanted you locked up, but I couldn't allow that. I don't think it's you," he said, and for the first time his voice reflected the heaviness weighing on him. "At least, I don't think you know it is. I don't know if he has manipulated you, or you're under some sort of compulsion, but until we find out for sure, this is the only way."

Her eyes shut, and she drew in a deep breath. She didn't know what hurt her more. The fact he couldn't trust her, or that after all these years, he really didn't know her at all.

"Lily?" Luke called out to her.

She forced a smile and faced them. "It's okay. Be safe out there." She glanced at Nathaniel, her heart in her throat. "You, too," she added. And before she broke down in front of them, she turned and raced back into the building.

CHAPTER TWENTY-FOUR

Lily had hopped on the metro and rode it to the Gallery. She made it that far without breaking down or calling Julian, but once she stepped inside her apartment, she had dialed him. He had answered on the second ring. All she could ask was if he could come by her apartment. He hung up without responding, and she felt a chill race down her spine and the air behind her stirred.

Whirling, she found Julian standing before her. Startled, she clutched her throat. "I'll never get used to you doing that."

He pulled her against him and kissed her. "What's wrong?"

She bit down on her lip. Calling him was probably foolish, since he was the main reason she'd been suspended, but who else could she go to? "I've kind of had one of those days . . ."

His gaze fell upon her arm as he guided her to the couch. "Why is your arm bruised?" He grabbed her hand, holding up her arm.

"Long story," she murmured, "but not the problem, Julian."

He didn't seem to like her answer. "What's happened?"

She hoped she hadn't interrupted anything important.

God only knows what his day actually consisted of, but she told him everything that had gone on that day.

He listened quietly and didn't pass over any of the important stuff. When she got to the point of Nathaniel demanding that she answer whether or not they had slept together, his lips thinned to a tight line.

"I've been suspended from hunting and given restricted access to the Sanctuary. Apparently, I'm supposed to feel lucky I wasn't locked up in one of the cells, and that I am still allowed to train." She forced a laugh. "Lucky me."

His entire body stiffened. "Let me get this straight. They've suspended you because of your relationship with me, and they suspect you of betraying the Sanctuary?"

"Yes." She smoothed her hand down the cushion.

"Did they at least give you an option of not seeing me to avoid suspension?"

Odd question. "Kinda . . . they asked if I would, but my answer didn't guarantee that I wouldn't be suspended."

"Well . . . how did you answer?"

"Um, I said they couldn't tell me who I could see." She felt his gaze on her as she stared at her hands. "I lost my temper, and the way Nathaniel was yelling at me . . ." She trailed off as she felt his fingers curve around her lowered chin, turning her head toward his. "What?"

"I'm surprised you admitted it. That is the second time you have risked yourself for me."

She shrugged self-consciously. She wanted to tell him she thought he was worth it but couldn't work up the nerve to do so.

"You could have told them you wouldn't see me. That probably would have gotten you out of the suspension and back into their good graces, but you chose not to."

She stared into his bright eyes. "Yeah, I chose not to."

He seemed to think about something for a second but then kissed her softly. "You risked everything for me. I'm . . . honored."

She felt herself flush again as her eyes darted away from his. "It is what it is."

He tucked a strand of hair behind her ear. "So what do you do now?"

"I don't know. Find out who is betraying them, clear my name, and all that stuff."

"You're kidding, right?" he asked, a small smile playing over his lips. "We could leave. You know that. They've turned against you, Lily."

She winced at the reminder. "Julian, I have to find out who is betraying them, and not just to clear my name. Someone is betraying them, and they're not even looking anymore."

"So?" he demanded. "Let them dig their own graves. It should no longer be your concern."

"It is my concern."

"Why?" Julian stood, prowling the length of her living room like a caged animal. "Why would you even care, Lily? You can't tell me you aren't hurt by

Nathaniel or how quickly all of them turned on you."

She understood his anger, but it was for her benefit. "It does hurt, especially Nathaniel, but I can't turn my back on them because they have."

He knelt before her, capturing her hands. "Lily, my offer still stands. I could take you away from this. To islands so beautiful the hurt Nathaniel has given you would fade away as soon as you laid eyes upon them." He brought her hands to his lips. "Let me take you away."

Once again the offer was tempting, and even more so now than before. She shook her head again. "Julian, they are my friends—my family. Someone is betraying them, and it's only going to get worse. I have to help them."

He kissed her hands once more before he released them. "You're so pigheaded." He smiled at her sour look. "But my offer always stands. All you have to do is let me know."

"Okay."

"If you won't let me take you away, then you have to let me help you. Who are the likely suspects?"

She launched into a tirade about Micah, telling him about the stuff she'd read in his personnel file and how he was snooping around Nathaniel's office. Julian actually seemed to agree with her, especially after he realized Micah was the "little shit" from the other night.

"No one else seemed to find any of this suspicious?" he asked.

"Only Luke, but he's outnumbered." She pushed at her hair. Suddenly, something occurred to her, and she turned toward Julian. "Do you know who it is?"

He met her stare and didn't hesitate. "No."

"You wouldn't lie about this, would you?" she asked. "Because if you know, it would really help me out, and if you didn't tell me, I would be pissed." And she meant it, too.

"It's not like we hang around in large groups, gossiping about what the other is doing. I do pick up information from time to time, because some do frequent my bars quite regularly," he told her. "And even if I did, what help would it be? They wouldn't believe you if it came from me."

She sighed, disappointed. Figured it wouldn't be that easy. "I need to find out who Micah is working with."

Julian was silent for a moment but then smiled. "What we need to do is find some minions and make them talk."

She arched a brow. "You think I haven't already tried that?"

His smile spread. "But you haven't had me with you. I have . . . ways of making people talk."

No doubt. Picking up on what he was suggesting, she stood. "You want to go hunting with me?"

"Actually, I was suggesting I go find Micah and make him talk," he said. "Or I could just take care of him."

Her mouth dropped open. "No. No, Julian. You killing him, and I know that's what you plan, will not help me. And stop grinning like you'd enjoy it."

He didn't stop grinning. "I would."

Lily folded her arms.

"Okay. If that doesn't suit you, then I could go hunting with you."

The idea was insane. And a little bit laughable. A Fallen hunting minions to make them talk. She ran her hands down her face. If they were caught together by any of the Nephilim, she knew her Contract would be breached. "This is risky."

"It is." He turned away, staring out the window. "You know what I prefer, but if you're insistent upon discovering this traitor, you will not do so alone."

Mulling it over, she glanced at the wall clock. "I don't usually start hunting—"

"Until after nine, I know." He faced her. "The time frame works out perfectly."

"It does?"

He crossed the room, dipping his head to her neck. His lips brushed over her skin, causing her to shiver. "That gives us just enough time."

She placed her hands on his chest. "Weren't you doing something when I called?"

"I was at my club in Bethesda." He snaked an arm around her waist. "But they'll live without me."

Already, she felt her insides tightening, a pool of heat gathering in her core. Her body had absolutely no sense of priority. But the minions wouldn't come out until later tonight . . .

Then he caught her earlobe between his teeth and

tugged. Her breath came out in small gasps until he let go, his hands splayed across her lower back.

"I need to . . . I need to shower first. I'm sweaty." Somehow her brain still registered that she'd been training half the day.

"I can help you with that." He scooped her up, smiling when she laughed. Heading through her apartment, he stopped once to kiss her and then again to help her get out of her workout clothes. "It's probably a good thing you won't take me up on my offer."

"Why's that?" She tugged his shirt over his head, then moved on to his pants.

"Because I'd never get anything done." He stepped out of his pants, standing gloriously nude in her front of her. "All I'd want to do is worship your body all day."

She walked backward into the bathroom, stopping when she hit the sink. "I don't see anything wrong with that."

Leaning around her, he reached into the shower stall and turned on the water. Steam quickly filled the bathroom. When he straightened, he tucked his hair back. The look he gave her was curiously intimate.

"What?" she asked.

"You're beautiful."

She rolled her eyes. "Flattery will get you laid."

"I sure hope so." He dipped his head to her breast, drawing her nipple into his mouth, teasing it with his tongue and teeth. The way he devoured her breast and then the other drove her crazy. Tight coils sprang low in her belly as she watched him worship her body.

When they did move into the shower, Julian was more interested in tasting every part of her than he was with helping her wash. Not that she minded. Her legs were literally shaking when he knelt and peered up at her through thick lashes.

She placed her hand on his cheek. Her chest swelled with a powerful foreign emotion as her eyes locked with his. He lowered his mouth to her sex, making a long, deep swipe with his tongue. She didn't even have time to catch her breath before he did it again. His tongue swirled and stabbed, turning her insides to mush as she clasped the back of his head, greedily rocking against him. Then he sealed his mouth over her clit and sucked hard. There was nothing but white-hot pleasure as her orgasm rocked through her. Lily's knees buckled, and he caught her as he stood and entered her with one quick thrust.

Maybe this was wrong—everyone besides her believed so—but as her head lulled back and he took her the closest to Heaven she'd ever been, she decided this kind of wrong was so right for her.

Hunting with Julian was kind of weird.

This was the second night in a row they took to the streets, and she still hadn't gotten used to doing this with him. Like she said, it was weird.

Weird because it was like hunting with Luke, with the exception that she couldn't stop looking at Julian and remembering what it felt like to have his mouth on her, his fingers in her, the way he kissed her ... She cleared her throat, focusing on the humans crowding the street near the Verizon Center. Her cheeks felt hot.

But then she gazed at him again.

God, he was beautiful. She always thought he was, but she never really grasped just how beautiful he truly was. Out here, with the moonlight and the weak flicker of streetlamps, his cheekbones seemed more pronounced, his hair softer, and the indent above his upper lip more lickable.

All around them, people passed her over to stare at him. Male, female, the young and old stared at him. It was more than his looks, she quickly realized. He had this confident swagger that begged people to get out of his way.

She sighed, shaking out her shoulders. They'd been at this for four hours without a deadhead or minion in sight. Last night had been a bust, too. Other than the two deadheads and a minion who practically pissed himself the moment Julian touched him, they hadn't made any headway. The only thing she accomplished thus far was making herself horny. "Where in the hell are they?"

He tucked his hair back, eyes scanning the crowd as they rounded the avenue. "You do this every night? Walking around until you hear a deadhead?"

"Pretty much." She shoved her hands into her cargo pants, catching two girls in their early twenties checking out Julian and whispering. A grin played across her lips. "It's usually busier than this, especially on a Saturday night."

"I'll have to take your word for it." He smiled. "Hungry?"

"Always."

They stopped at a late-night eatery and hung out there for a little while. She made sure to pay attention to her Nephilim radar. Exchanging stories while they ate, she was amazed by how comfortable she was with him doing normal things—human things.

It was like a date—a weird, twisted date that would probably end with them killing something, but that was splitting hairs.

Afterward, when they headed back out into the musky night, she smelled rain in the air. Julian clasped her hand, and her heart exploded with ecstasy. How many times had she seen humans doing this, or Nephilim who hadn't accepted the Contract? Too many times for her to count, and never once had she thought it would be her doing something so mundanely beautiful.

Overcome by the normalcy of holding his hand, she tugged him off the sidewalk and inside a dark parking garage.

"What?" Surprise colored his words.

Standing on her tiptoes, she pressed into him while still holding his hand. She kissed him like she'd never kissed him before. Her lips bruised from the intensity, but Julian was all about it. He swept his free arm around her, growling against her parted lips.

"You have no idea what you've started," he warned

in a low voice. "I will take you right here, inches from the sidewalk."

She started to tell him that she was completely down with that, but then she heard the eerie whining of a soul . . . and felt the shiver that accompanied a minion. It was so close, so unmistakable, that it shocked her to immobility for a second. This was what they needed—a deadhead and the minion that had coaxed the soul into the human.

Score.

Julian's hand squeezed hers as he tipped his head back. "They're right up there, aren't they?"

"Yeah," she said. She wiggled out of his embrace, pulled her hand free, and released her blades. "Really odd timing."

"Yes."

She knew he was thinking the same thing. There were no such things as coincidences. Together, they started toward the ramp that led upstairs. Her eyes flickered over the shadows as they passed an unmanned security booth. She had a feeling she knew where the guard was.

The awareness increased, like an invisible finger trailing down her spine. She caught Julian's brilliant gaze and nodded.

He glided in front of her and then simply disappeared. Show off. She rolled her eyes and broke into a light-footed run. Rounding the sixth ramp, she vaulted over the cement wall and landed in a crouch.

And she found the guard.

He stood beside a Mercedes, staring down at his dark uniform. A funny smile twisted his lips as he tugged on the material. The first thing a deadhead did when it came to was check out its clothes. It cracked her up. She laughed.

The deadhead jerked in her direction. He tipped his head to the side. "Nephilim."

Straightening, she wiggled her fingers. "Hello. Nice night, huh? Mind telling me where your buddy is? I really don't feel like looking for him."

Actually, that was what Julian was doing. Popping in and out, tracking down the minion. It was still here; the tingling at the base of her neck told her so.

The security guard rushed her, and the adrenaline of the battle swept through her. Almost as good as sex, but not quite. She planted her booted foot in the deadhead's chest, knocking him back several feet and to the ground.

The deadhead sprang up, letting out an inhuman growl. Lightning streaked across the sky. Seconds later, thunder crashed and echoed through the garage. Summer storms—Lily loved them.

When he came at her again, she spun around and grabbed him by the shoulder, preparing to deliver a deathblow. Another shiver, much more acute and potent, exploded along her nerves.

Fallen.

Several things happened next. Over the deadhead's shoulder, the minion rushed down the lane. There was a flash of bright light, and then there was Julian, cutting

328

the minion off with a mean clothesline. The minion hit the ground with a grunt, momentarily stunned.

Julian whirled around. "Lily!"

She dipped and kicked, taking the legs out from underneath the deadhead just as the air stirred unnaturally around her. Her heart stuttered as she leaped to her feet, twisting around.

Not even a few feet in front of her was Baal. "Hello, darling. Miss me?"

CHAPTER TWENTY-FIVE

Shit. That was all Lily thought before rage took over, dampening the fear. "You son of a—"

Julian shot passed her, crashing into Baal first.

Baal hit the cement beam, laughing as Julian clasped him by the throat and lifted him off the ground. Unaffected by Baal's abilities, Julian got all kinds of hands on with him. "Is that how you greet your brethren?" Baal asked, grasping Julian's hands. "It's not very polite."

"You have no idea how long I've wanted to kill you." Julian slammed him back. "How badly I've wanted to hear you scream."

"Oh." Baal laughed. "Is it because your little Nephilim prefers my touch over yours? I bet she does. After all, my mark will stay with her long after you're gone."

Julian punched him in the nose. Dark blood spurted across Baal's seductive face. "I'm going to kill you. Slowly." Another punch. Then another that splattered more blood. "But before you take your last breath, you will get on your knees and beg Lily for her forgiveness. Do you understand me?"

She liked the sound of this.

The deadhead growled behind her. Pissed that she had to miss Julian beating the living tar out of Baal, she spun around to shove her blade into the deadhead's chest. But that wasn't what happened. The minion, back on his feet, slammed into her and knocked her aim off. Her blade dug into the deadhead's shoulder.

"Shit," she grunted, throwing the minion off as she aimed at the deadhead again. But the damn thing dodged her blow and bit her arm—fucking bit her arm! Yelping, she pulled back. Blood smeared her arm. "Jesus! You better not have rabies."

"He likes the way you taste," the minion taunted. "I know what I'd like to take a taste of, and it's not your blood."

Lily fell back, shaking off the pain. The minion and the deadhead circled her. Distracted by her scream, Julian had lost his grip on Baal, allowing the other Fallen to get a good punch in. Julian staggered back as the two grappled. Forcing herself to focus on her own fight was hard, but she did.

"Pretty little Nephilim," the minion cooed. Icy-blond hair fell over his eyes. "Wanna take a walk on the dark side?"

"Really?" she said. "That's the best you have?"

The minion sneered. "You're already whoring it out for the Fallen. Shouldn't take much for you to spread those—"

She shot forward, twisting to the side as she planted her foot right in his face. The minion's head snapped back. "There," she said. "My legs were spread. You like it?"

Howling, the minion's face contorted, mouth dropped wide and gaping as he launched at her. They needed to keep a minion alive to question, so when she dipped under him and shoved the blade into his stomach, she knew he'd be down for the count but not out.

The minion hit the floor, twitching and making tiny, squealing noises as the silver infected him. She whipped around, spotting the deadhead near the exit to a lower ramp. Taking off after him, she spared a quick glance over her shoulder.

Julian had Baal on his back, throwing punch after punch. From what she could see, barely any of Baal's face was recognizable. Maybe they wouldn't need the minion after all.

"Hey," she called out. "Where do you think you're going?"

The deadhead rounded the ramp. She picked up speed, springing over the cement riser. Hitting the dead-head on the back, they crashed into the pavement.

Quickly, Lily rolled the deadhead under her. Straddling his hips, she raised her blade. "You shouldn't bite and run off. It's rude."

The deadhead snapped at her again.

"What the hell is it with you and biting?" She brought down her hand, shoving the blade into his chest this time. "Man, I better not start foaming at the mouth."

Popping onto her feet, she hurried back to where the minion and the brawling fallen angels were. She wondered if she would have to get some kind of shot after tonight.

Julian currently had Baal in a headlock. Good for him. Blood ran like rivers down Baal's sneering face as he was thrust to his knees. Grabbing the minion by his hair, Lily forced him to sit up. Her eyes locked with Julian's for a moment, and he winked. Only his lip was split. Otherwise his face looked like it normally did: perfect.

"So, do we keep both of them?" she asked, bringing the sharp edge of her blade to the minion's throat. "They can be useful."

"That's up to you, sweetheart." Julian tightened his arm around Baal's neck. "But this one isn't leaving here."

"Lily," Baal grunted, "I have something to tell you."

Every cell in her body demanded that she run over there and kick him in the junk, but she ignored him. Looking down at her captive, she pressed the blade in. "Who is the Nephilim feeding names to the Fallen?"

"What?" the minion wheezed, clutching the wound in his stomach.

"You heard me. Don't make me ask you again." She dug her fingers into his hair, yanking his head back. "The second time won't be as nice."

"Lily, look at me," Baal commanded.

"Shut up," Julian said.

The minion made another pitiful rasping sound. "I'd

rather have . . . you cut off my head than go against him."

"Who? Go against who?" she demanded.

Baal laughed. "He's not going to tell you anything."

"Shut up," Lily said, turning back to the minion. "We can make this hard or harder. Cooperate with me and that's the difference between a painful death and a really painful death."

It took quite a bit of convincing, and by the time the minion had started to talk, his throat looked like hamburger meat, and she'd lost count of how many times Julian had hit Baal.

"Okay. Okay," the minion gasped. Little bubbles of blood frothed on his lips. Thank God he was starting to talk, because it was really grossing her out. "I don't know who the Nephilim is. Wait! Wait." He gasped, staring up at her with transparent eyes. "All I know is that he's arrogant. He's been . . . he's been meeting with other minions, passing the info along. He ends up killing half the minions after they deliver the information."

Lily's eyes met Julian's. Excitement bubbled in her. They were getting somewhere. "At least now we know it's a guy."

Julian arched a brow. "We knew that."

"Party pooper," she muttered, turning back to the minion. "What else do you know?"

"You stupid, fucking minion," Baal growled.

"I'm growing weary of your mouth." Julian sounded bored. "Keep it up, and I will rip out your tongue."

"But not before I beg for her forgiveness?" asked Baal. He spat out a mouthful of blood. "Right?"

"So this Nephilim has been killing half of his contacts?" When the minion didn't answer, she shook him. He was fading. The poison of the silver blade was doing its job slowly but surely. "Answer me!"

"Yes," he gasped. "He thinks he's . . . better than us, but the stupid shit doesn't realize he's turned." A raspy, guttural laugh rose up through the minion. "All I've heard is that it's a personal thing."

All of this sounded like it could be Micah, except the personal thing. Arrogance was Micah's middle name. "Details?"

The minion laughed again. "Don't know any, but . . . that pisshead over there probably knows, goddamn Fallen."

No honor among evil creatures of the damned. She almost laughed. "Who are the contacts running the information back to?"

There was pause, and the minion shuddered. "Asmodeus."

"Christ," Lily muttered. This was worse than she had originally thought.

"That's all I know," the minion said. "Now finish it."

She'd never really tortured a minion for information before. Julian had dealt with the last one. She sent him a questioning look. He nodded.

"All right then, good night." She slammed the blade through the minion's chest. There was a gasp, and then he was no more.

"How's the arm?" Julian asked.

She waved dismissively at the bite marks on her forearm. "I'll live."

"Why don't you come over here and let me kiss it?" Baal suggested with a leer.

Wiping her hands on her pants, she slowly approached the two creatures. Eagerness crept over Baal's face. His tongue darted out through his bloodied lips. Without stopping, she ignored Julian's curious gaze and kicked Baal between the legs.

"Damn it!" Baal roared, doubling over as far as Julian allowed.

Julian chuckled. "That's my girl."

Lily knelt in front of Baal, careful to stay out of his grasp. "I think next time I'll use my blade down there."

Baal laughed harshly. "Then how will we be able to consummate our relationship?"

Bile rose in her throat. "You're sick."

"And your skin feels like Heaven when I mark it."

She didn't have a chance to react. Julian spun Baal around and coldcocked him in the face. Julian's face contorted in rage as he pulled Baal up by his shirt and slammed him back down. This went on until she stepped forward, placing a hand on Julian.

"That's enough," she said quietly. "I know he can prove that it's Micah betraying us."

"He's not going to tell you anything. Baal is Asmodeus's little bitch now." He flipped Baal back around, clasping his arms behind his back. "Believe it or not, but he is loyal to Asmodeus. I am curious as to how that happened."

"Oh, you know how Asmodeus is. He asks for one goddamned favor and you're stuck with him. He got me about four years ago. Haven't quit him yet," Baal said, as if they were discussing the weather and he wasn't bleeding all over the place. "You'd know how that is, Julian. Huh?"

Julian stiffened.

Grinning, Baal looked up at Lily. "But I . . . have something even better to tell you."

"If you can't tell me who's been betraying the Sanctuary, then you have nothing I want to hear."

Baal laughed. "You're so naïve. It's sexy."

Her hands curled into fists. "Tell me who is betraying the Sanctuary. Is it Micah?"

"Micah?" Baal tried to stand, but Julian pressed on his back more. "I don't know who the fuck that is, and I don't care. And why do you care, little Lily pad? From what I hear, they've tossed you on your ass for shacking up with this one." He jerked his head back at Julian. "Screwing the enemy? How deliciously cliché. You're not the first, but you know that. That pretty blonde had spread her legs, too."

"Do not talk about Anna," she spat.

Another hoarse, wheezing laugh escaped him. "Tell me, was it worth being kicked out of the Sanctuary for him?"

Anger snapped along her skin. "I wasn't kicked out."

"Yet," Baal murmured, lifting his head again to pierce her with the same vibrant, blue eyes Julian

337

had. "Is his cock so good that it's worth losing everything?"

"That's it," Julian snarled as he brought Baal to his feet. He looked at Lily. "He's not going to tell you anything. You want to do the honors?"

Part of her wanted nothing more than to shove the blade deep into Baal's throat, but there would never be another chance to capture a Fallen. A tiny flame of hope ignited in her that she could get him to talk. And if she just had to deal with his insults, she could live with that.

"Give me a few more minutes," she said, drawing in a deep breath. "Do you know who the Nephilim is, Baal?"

His bloodied lips twisted into a smirk. "Yes. So do you."

Her eyes narrowed. "Then it's Micah?"

Baal sneered. "How about I make you a deal? I'll tell you who it is if you let me tell you a secret."

"Lily," Julian warned. His powerful muscles bunched around Baal's neck, surely choking him. "This isn't wise."

Maybe not, but she couldn't care less what his secret was. "I need something that links Micah to you all. Just his name won't work. I need evidence."

"Sure. I can do that for you," he said.

Hands clenching, she waited for him to continue.

"You have to come a little closer, darling." Pain and anger flickered across his face when Julian's arm tightened. "It's kind of hard to talk with . . . this asshole choking me."

"Don't come any closer," Julian warned, eyeing Baal. "He's up to something."

Lily took a cautious step forward anyway. "He's always up to something."

Baal sneered through the blood. "Do you know I've killed every dark-haired, green-eyed woman I've come across in the last eight years? Hundreds of them. And very slowly. They reminded me of you, sweetheart. And all of them—every last one of them—screamed for mercy. Just like you screamed." His eyes drifted shut, and he groaned low in his throat. "They begged, and I heard you begging each—"

Moving inhumanly fast, Julian spun Baal around and slammed him into the cement beam. "Shut up," Julian snarled. "Shut. The. Fuck. Up." Each word punctuated with a brutal jab to the face.

Lily felt sick as images of faceless and nameless women assaulted her. That was Baal's secret? She realized then he wouldn't give her any information on Micah. He wanted to taunt her with his cruelty and sickness.

"That's not all," Baal gasped. A mouthful of blood ran down his chin. "I fucked—"

His words were cut off by a wet, sickening crunching sound. All these years Lily dreamed of the moment when she'd be able to watch the life go out of Baal's eyes, but when it finally happened, she turned away. She felt hot and cold all at once. Nausea rose sharply.

Then there was silence, and all she could hear was the sound of her own ragged breathing. Seconds later, a flare of intense white light lit up the parking garage. Baal was no more. Her shoulders slumped as his words went on replay.

Strong arms surrounded her, turning her and holding her close. Lily tipped her head back. "Do . . . do you think he was telling the truth?"

Julian smoothed a hand down her cheek as he stared over her head. He didn't answer.

Lily sighed. "All those women—"

"It's not your fault," he said, looking at her. "None of what Baal did is your fault."

She knew it wasn't, but it didn't make it easier to swallow. "I guess I should've listened to you."

Julian laughed, but there wasn't any humor. "You're Lily. I really didn't expect you to listen to me, but I wish you had." He bent, brushing his lips over her forehead. "At least it wasn't a total waste. Baal is dead, and the information the minion provided may turn out valuable. And we now know it's Asmodeus pulling the strings. That's something."

"Damn it. I know Baal knew who it was."

"He would never tell you if he did. Many would rather face an eternity in Hell with Him instead of betraying Asmodeus." Julian kissed the top of her head as he clasped her hand, threading his fingers through hers. "It's late. Let's go."

She let him pull her away, but she couldn't help but look back. A black mark seared the cement beam that

Baal had been against, the only reminder of the fallen angel. Shuddering, she thought of those women, and how she would have been one of them if it hadn't been for Julian all those years ago.

CHAPTER TWENTY-SIX

Sunday should have consisted of more hunting and sleuthing, but instead it involved eating in bed and bad action movies.

And sex, lots of sex.

"I'll never let you out of this bed," Julian murmured. "I think I could keep you here forever."

She climbed on top of him. "Haven't you had enough?"

He grasped her hips, sliding her toward his erection. "I'll never have enough."

Really, she believed him. He had been insatiable. Not that she was complaining. It was nice to forget everything for a little while, especially after the night before. Hovering above him, she clasped his hands to the mattress. "I have to go back to the Sanctuary tomorrow."

"I can't believe you are going back to that place." He glowered at her.

"Julian." She sighed.

"I cannot fathom your devotion to a place and people who have so willingly turned their backs on you."

She wiggled a little, watching him squirm as he tried

to concentrate. "Not all of them have turned their backs on me, Julian." Luke had called her cell at least a dozen times since last night. "I know it's hard for you to understand, but it's not like being cast out of Heaven. I'm allowed back into the Sanctuary. And well, you're not allowed back into Heaven."

He gave her a droll look.

She snickered. "Anyway, you promised you wouldn't bring this up anymore."

He quirked a sandy-colored brow at her. "Some promises are hard to keep."

Lily grinned. "Well you need to work on that." She slid down him, her lips so very close to the part of him that was growing rapidly. "Tomorrow I have to go back. And tomorrow night we need to start looking for more minions."

He was watching her with eyes filled with anticipation. "Yeah, tomorrow . . . Nephilim stuff. Sure."

"Julian, I have never heard you so unintelligible. That sentence didn't even make sense."

"No?"

"No." Her pink tongue flicked over the throbbing head of his cock.

His lips parted. She did it again, and this time her lips followed the path. His hands balled into fists under hers. Peeking up through her lashes, she gazed at his enthralled face and wanted to bring him to the same pleasure he had so selfishly given her in the beginning.

Of course, Julian had other plans, and in one swift

movement, he sat her down on his throbbing member. She tipped her head back, reveling in how good it felt.

Somewhere during the weekend, Lily had decided that proving Julian wasn't evil became as important to her as finding out who was betraying them. When she shared this with him, he actually laughed and then wished her good luck.

But Lily was determined. There had to be a way for the other Nephilim to see him like she did, and she told him she would find a way. Instead of laughing at her this time, he kissed her softly. "Having you see me as you do is good enough for me, Lily."

Those words touched a part of her, one that was tender and vulnerable. Curling herself around him, she rested her head on his chest and smiled. Her phone rang once again, but like all the other times, she ignored it.

"Stop the limo!" the senator yelled for a second time as he adjusted his tuxedo. "Damn it, is a good driver too hard to come by these days?"

The man across from him smiled lazily. "Remold was a great driver, but I didn't like the way he looked at me, and you know my temper. It's not my strongest suit."

Senator Sharpe's gaze narrowed on the thing sprawled across the leather seat. God, he hated minions more than he hated the fallen angel that held him by the balls. Temperamental and unpredictable, the one who shared his limo tonight had snapped the neck of his driver last week. Sharpe still had no idea what had provoked Gareth to do such a thing, but he would never understand minions.

"How long will we have to be at this thing?" Gareth asked, clearly annoyed with the charity event being held at The Mayflower.

"You don't need to attend this," Sharpe responded thinly. Frankly, he wished Asmodeus hadn't sent one of his minions with him. It wasn't like he was going to do anything to jeopardize his plans. Sharpe didn't have a death wish. Not yet, at least.

Gareth sighed. "I hate these fund-raisers. It's Sunday night. There are better things I could be doing."

He didn't bother with a response. Flicking a piece of string off his tuxedo, he prepared himself to mingle with the city's elite power players attending the fund-raiser at the magnificent hotel. The senator only had a moment of warning before the door opened, and a dark form fell across the opening. Moving astonishingly fast, the shade darted into the limo, taking form beside the smiling minion. The door swung closed behind it.

His heart pounded painfully as the pressure settled over him. Spittle blew across the seat as he struggled to breathe. His face was shoved back into the cool leather when he tried to lift his head. "What is this about?" he gasped as his fingers dug into the seat.

Gareth chuckled idly. "Hello, Nephilim brother."

Senator Sharpe froze as the hand that held him tightened around his skull. It was the Nephilim, the one from the Sanctuary.

"How dare you even acknowledge me?" said the Nephilim, voice laced with revulsion.

Gareth snickered and then said, "Oh, how you think you're so much better than us. When you are just as wicked as me, Nephilim."

The tension in the limo heightened to near unbearable levels. The senator was afraid if Gareth continued to taunt the Nephilim, he would be the one who ended up with a snapped neck. The Nephilim shifted over him, and there was a crunching sound that made Sharpe's insides crawl.

Trying to remain calm in his precarious position, Sharpe managed to twist his head far enough so that he could breathe a bit more easily. "Do you bring names . . . for me to give?" he asked, his voice panicked and pitiful even to him. He hated the sound of it, detested how much power these things held over him. God, if he could go back in time he would have never slept with the secretary who started all of this. *I should have fired that bitch*!

"Why else would I be around your kind of scum?"

The senator knew better than to point out any of the Nephilim's current character flaws. He hoped Gareth would also refrain from doing so. He struggled to get the words out. "What do you want me to tell Asmodeus?"

"The cop is progressing through the training faster than initially expected. He has been offered the Contract by the Sanctuary."

"Contract?" he sputtered. He had no idea what the hell the Nephilim was talking about.

"Asmodeus will know what that is."

The hand that wasn't smashed under his chest curled into a fist. He felt helpless. It sickened him. "Is that all?"

He laughed. It was a much harsher sound than what Gareth made. It was twisted, cold and flat. "Tell him that two more Nephilim have been discovered in Montana. They are female. He should find that particularly interesting."

Something fell beside the senator's face. From what he could see, it looked like a file. "Is that all?" he gritted out again.

"For now," responded the Nephilim.

The pressure was suddenly gone, and the sweet smell of honeysuckle floated in through the open limo door. Senator Sharpe pushed himself up and immediately started fixing his rumpled tux. He glanced over at the surprisingly quiet Gareth. A scream lodged in his throat.

Pale dead eyes stared sightlessly up at the senator. The minion's head lay on the polished shoes of the senator, mouth open wide in a silent scream.

Horrified by the brutal violence, he stared at the minion's slumped body as his hand clutched against the sudden pain in his chest. "Jesus Christ."

Monday had consisted of training a very sour-faced Michael, who didn't like anything she had to say. She avoided being alone with him because she really didn't have the answers he needed.

She also spent time avoiding members of the circle, which hadn't proved too difficult since most of them were avoiding her like she had the black plague. She stuck to the training room and cafeteria, where the likelihood of confrontation was slim. The only ones who talked to her were Rafe and Remy. Either they didn't know all that had happened or they were good at pretending Lily was still the cat's meow. She tried to find Nathaniel to tell him about Baal and the info gained from the minion, but he was never in his office, and he didn't return any of the messages she'd left with Sandy.

Luke had cornered her the moment she stepped foot inside the Sanctuary, demanding to know why she couldn't have returned one phone call all weekend. She gave him a look that said he would rather not know, and now she was avoiding him, too.

Monday night, she and Julian scoured the entire city for more minions but came up empty-handed. Not a single corrupted Nephilim nor a human possessed moved around the streets. The night turned out to be a total bust when it came to making any progress with who was betraying them.

On the flip side, Julian had gone back to her apartment with her for a rousing round of lovemaking. That wasn't too shabby.

The rest of the week went like that. Michael grew more annoyed with each passing day, especially after he realized his personal time was really turning out to be more like indefinite leave. Annoyed wasn't the

UNCHAINED

greatest description. He finally did go ape-shit, and only after he was hauled off to Nathaniel's office—without Lily—did he calm down.

Lily continued to play hide-and-seek with the circle. Eventually, she stopped trying to avoid Luke and told him about Baal and Asmodeus. Thank God she had told him in the corner of the training room, because when he realized she had been hunting with Julian, he also went ape-shit on her.

"You've been hunting with him?" Luke demanded.

Her gaze darted to Rafe and Michael. "Luke, lower your voice. You heard me the first time. It doesn't matter. Baal is dead. And we know the Nephilim betraying the Sanctuary is an arrogant male and has been feeding info to Asmodeus."

"It doesn't matter?" His voice rose. "Are you insane?"

Michael missed his mark with the knife and faced them with a deep scowl.

"Now look what you did," she muttered.

"I don't care," he said, much lower. "Lily, when you are being suspected of working with the Fallen, the worst thing you could do is go hang out with them."

She exhaled slowly. "Did you even hear me? We know Micah is working with Asmodeus. All we need is evidence."

"Lily." Luke sighed. "Why are you so hell-bent on it being Micah?"

"Because it is him!" she hissed back.

"You little shithead, do you think Nathaniel hasn't been watching Micah? Do you think I haven't been?"

349

She huffed. "Whatever. Nathaniel doesn't think it's Micah. He thinks I'm being coerced."

Luke dragged his fingers through his messy brown hair. "You're wrong. He's followed Micah, and he hasn't found anything. Now he is looking at other possibilities."

Lily was so not ready to let go of the sense of betrayal that came with Nathaniel. "So who is he looking into?"

Luke turned to watch Michael. His silence was her answer. She swore. "What do you expect?" he asked quietly. He looked at her crossly then. "You're going to hate me, but I'm going to Nathaniel. This has to stop. And your ass needs to be locked up."

She whirled on him, hands balling into fists. "If you do that, so help me, you will never see my ass again."

He cocked his head to the side, not at all worried. "You're not fifteen anymore. You can't just run away."

She opened her mouth but couldn't come up with anything clever. Of course he wouldn't forget the night when she did try to run away after Nathaniel refused to allow her to accompany Luke on a hunt. It hadn't been one of her finer moments.

"I'm worried about you," he said quietly.

She scanned his face. He did look worried, like he hadn't slept in days. There were faint shadows under his eyes, and his irises were almost transparent. "Don't worry about me, Luke. I have things under control. Give me a couple more days, and I will have something that proves my innocence." Hopefully, she could figure out a way at the same time to prove to them Julian wasn't evil, too.

UNCHAINED

"I don't know."

"Please, Luke." She gripped his arm. "You know me. You know I will pull this off. I always do. Please, just give me a few more days?"

He stiffened. A muscle popped along his jaw. Terse, awkward silence stretched out between them. "You and Anna are a lot alike, you know that? Both of you had Nathaniel eating out of the palms of your hands. And neither of you could see what you were doing to the people who cared about you. Sometimes it's hard to tell you two apart."

Lily sucked in a sharp breath.

"You're going to end up just like her."

"Luke," she gasped.

He closed his eyes, seeming to gather himself. "You love him, don't you?"

She opened her mouth to deny it, but her denials died on her lips. Did she love Julian? She wanted to say no, that it was just about sex and companionship, but her heart fluttered.

Luke laughed, but it was without a trace of humor—of Luke. For a moment, well, she didn't recognize him at all as he stared like she was a virtual stranger to him. Unease knotted her insides. "Luke . . ."

Blinking, he finally placed his hand over hers. "Yeah, I know you usually pull something off. Whether I'm going to like the outcome or not is yet to be determined."

Relief shot through her. "I know you hate this, but please give me a couple more days. Please."

"I'm such a sucker," he grumbled. "Just don't disappoint me. Promise me you will stay away from Julian, and I won't go to Nate."

She glanced away, unable to lie looking him straight in the eyes. Even Lily had her limits. "I promise."

Sweat poured and his legs screamed out in protest, but Michael kept pushing. Hours ago, Rafe had left the training room. His parting order was for Michael to run a combination of suicide sprints and burpees until he could no longer move.

"Had enough?"

Michael lunged up from a push-up. He was surprised Lily was still here, considering she usually disappeared seconds after training ended. "No."

Lily watched as he sprinted the distance of the room to drop down into another burpee. "You look like you've had enough."

He flipped her off on his way past. Anger boiled under his skin as he sprinted the distance of the room, dropping down into another burpee.

Lily laughed, planting herself in front of him. "Stop—it's an order."

He slowed with his hands on his hips. He took a moment to walk off the burn. Only when he didn't think he'd start wheezing like a fool, he faced her. "You gonna tell me who killed my mother?"

"I've already told you I don't know. No one does."

"I don't believe you," he said. "You know everything but who killed her."

She sighed. "Hey, I was just checking on you. I didn't come here to argue. I'll see you later." She turned away.

He didn't want her to leave . . . not yet. Shoving down the anger, he ran the back of his hand over his forehead. "Sorry. I'm going stir-crazy. So how long have you been watching?"

She turned back to him, folding her arms over her chest. "Long enough to know you need more time."

His brows shot up. She doubted him, but at least she was staying. "I'm ready now."

"You think you're ready to take me on?" She cocked her head to the side. "If you can beat me, then maybe."

"I think I'll do fine," he offered without an ounce of doubt. He knew if he could prove to her he was ready, then he could get the hell out of this place. He nearly forgot what the outside world looked like.

Lily stared at him. Dark shadows blossomed under her eyes, dulling them. "I'm not going to go easy on you, buddy."

"I wouldn't expect you to." He cracked his neck. The Bugatchi jogging pants hung low on his hips as he straightened. "Let's do this."

Lily invited him forward with a saucy grin. She waited till he was only a foot away before she launched a brutal offensive. She was fast and light on her feet. He would feint in one direction to avoid a sharp thrust and end up with a sideways kick in his midsection. Before long, he wound up on his back, panting and swearing from a fierce spin kick.

"I didn't think you were ready," she announced, not even out of breath.

Expelling harshly, he jumped onto the balls of his feet. He was better than this. He'd been fighting not only Rafe, but two or three more Nephilim at a time. "I'm not out yet, darling."

"Darling?" she repeated. "I'm so not impressed."

He smirked, grabbing two of the half-circle blades off the floor.

"Oh, so you want to play hard?" Lily released the blades from her cuffs. "Getting a bit big for your britches?"

Michael didn't respond to that. Instead, he flew into a butterfly kick, bringing the blades down as he landed. Lily met him with a wild laugh. Blow after blow, they went after each other. Michael blocked a series of kicks and jabs that would have knocked a lesser man on his ass. He kept up with the moves easily, and even got a little cocky. "Come on, Lily, I've heard you can do better than this."

She sneered right before she turned on her heel gracefully, and with one powerful roundhouse kick, she knocked both of his legs out from underneath him. The blades flew from his hands on impact.

She stood above him, smirking. "Never let your guard down."

He coughed, rolling to his side and staring up at her smug face. "Never let your guard down?" Moving lightning fast, he went for her legs. He snagged the edge of her foot.

Unable to catch herself, she landed halfway across his lean body. But before he could react, she placed the sharp edge of the blade to the fragile skin of his throat. "Now what are you going to do?"

He glanced at the sharp blade and then back to her bright, laughing eyes. Lily was strong and incredibly fast, but he had damn near a hundred pounds on her and a foot or more in height. Using the grappling skills Rafe all but beat into him and the advantage of strength, he locked his legs around her hips and rolled. He peered at her. "What are you going to do?" he taunted.

She tried to kick out her legs, but the iron strength of his thighs pinned them to the floor. When she lifted her upper body to throw him off-balance, he quickly forced her back. "Well," she sputtered, "apparently you are very adept at grappling."

He grinned. "Now you want to tell me I'm not ready? When I took you out?"

"Well, shit." She smiled. "You just might be ready."

Staring at her, he laughed. "That's all I've wanted to hear."

She frowned. "Good. Now get off me."

He rolled off and sat cross-legged beside her. "I can't believe I actually got one up on you. I'm kind of impressed with myself."

Slowly, Lily sat up and looked at him. "Don't get too big of a head. It was only once."

"We could go again, but I feel bad about beating up on a chick." He grinned, but it quickly faded as another reality settled in. "Shit. You know what I just realized?"

"What?"

"Some of those deadheads and minions will be females." He shifted his weight from foot to foot. "Man, besides that deadhead in the stairwell that day, I've never hit a female in my life."

"Well," she said slowly. "Don't look at them as females, you know? And trust me, when the first one tries to rip out your intestines, you'll get over it pretty quickly."

"Hopefully they all try that then. I won't have such a complex."

Lily smiled. It seemed to Michael some of the tension had eased from her body. He watched her for a few seconds, wondering what it must've been like for her to grow up in this world. When he asked, he was surprised that she answered.

"It's hard to explain," she said. "The Sanctuary became my family, you know? And all of this—the fighting and the craziness—is second nature to me. Some days nothing shocks me."

"And others?"

She lifted her head, eyes large and somewhat distant. "Some days I wish I was you and no one had found me."

"I don't know. Living and not knowing what I was? All of this would've been easier. I could have avoided years of feeling like there was something more I should be doing." He laughed, shaking his head. "I know that sounds lame."

"No! No. It doesn't sound lame. Did you really feel that way?"

He nodded, relieved he was actually holding a normal conversation with someone. "I always felt like I was missing something, like a purpose."

"Wow," she murmured. "I had no idea."

He started to respond but was cut off by an alarming amount of yelling. Lily shot to her feet, then headed toward the door. Nearly ripping it from the hinges, she threw open the door.

Michael followed her into the hallway. The brightness of the corridor cast a harsh light on the scene before him. Farther down toward where the labs were, Lily had been brought to a standstill.

Part of him wished he hadn't followed her. He had seen a lot of bad things in his life, but . . . this was by far the worst thing he had ever seen.

Luke and Danyal supported a man slumped between them; his head fell forward and blood streamed from his messy blond hair. Michael couldn't even tell what the color of his shirt had once been. Soaked with blood, it had been ripped open, and strips of flesh hung from his bones.

They took a step, and the thing lifted his face, letting out a howl that turned Michael inside out. The Nephilim was utterly unrecognizable. Deep cuts ran from his scalp down to his chin, exposing tissue and muscle.

"Micah?" Lily gasped.

The receptionist from the lobby hovered behind them with a cell pressed to her ear. Her normally manicured exterior showed cracks as she ran a hand over her tightly crafted coif. "I don't give a flying shit who you are," she hissed into the phone. "Or what dinner I'm interrupting! If you don't get Dr. Winchester on the phone right now, it will be your job and your head!"

"What happened?" Lily asked.

"I don't know," Danyal answered, visibly shaken. "Luke found him."

Sandy flipped her phone shut. "The doctor is on his way. I'll get Nathaniel." She raced down the hallway.

Lily followed them into a room. "Luke?"

Luke guided the wounded man toward the bed. "Lily, you should leave."

She stood defiant. "What happened to him?"

"I have never seen anyone this bad before." Danyal grunted as he helped Luke lift the man onto the gurney. "I don't know if he's going to make it."

Micah moaned, prying one bloodstained eye open. "He . . . he did this to me."

Danyal moved to Micah's side. "Shush, don't talk. It's going to be all right. The doc is on his way. He's going to fix this."

"He did . . . this." Blood trickled from his mouth.

Lily leaned forward, but Luke grabbed her arm, swinging her away from the gurney.

She pulled out of his grasp. "Luke, what the hell happened out there?"

Luke cursed, rummaging through the cabinet until he found what he was looking for. He pulled out a box of needles and a bag of tranquilizer potent enough to take out a horse.

Danyal stripped off the remains of Micah's shirt, exposing what was left of him. Lily covered her mouth, stepping back into Michael. He steadied her, tried to be some comfort, but even he had to look away.

Luke jabbed the needle into Micah's arm as he whispered to him. Within seconds, the Nephilim drifted off into unconsciousness. Luke pushed away from the bed, closing his eyes briefly. When they reopened, his pale eyes found Lily.

Call it intuition or a terrible sense of foreboding, but Michael placed his hand at the small of Lily's back.

"What?" she asked, her voice barely a whisper.

"It was Julian who did this to him," Luke said, never once breaking eye contact with Lily.

Her face paled to the point that Michael feared she'd pass out. "No. He wouldn't . . . ." She turned to Danyal, who had retreated to a corner. "He didn't."

Danyal peered up through his fingers. "It is true."

"I saw him do it, Lily!" Luke said, holding her gaze. "You should have let Micah kill him when he had the chance. Now look what's happened to him. Your precious Julian did this. This is what you've risked everything for!"

"That's enough, Luke," Nathaniel ordered coolly as he entered the room.

"Enough?" He turned to him. "Will it be enough when we carry Danyal back here? When we carry Lily? Will it be enough then? He's a Fallen! This is what they do!"

Lily tore away from them, storming from the room, her eyes glinting with horror and anger. Michael started after her.

"Let her go, Michael." Nathaniel turned to the receptionist. "When will the doctor be here?"

She cleared her throat, her eyes fastened to Nathaniel. "Should only be a few minutes."

"Please make sure Lily is in her room. Lock her in if necessary." He faced Michael. "You should leave," Nathaniel ordered quietly. "You don't need to see this."

It was too late for wiping this memory from his head. Staring down at Micah sprawled lifelessly across the gurney, he now saw firsthand the violence between the Nephilim and the Fallen. Never had he seen such utter destruction or so much blood. It pooled on the floor beneath the bed in such great amounts that Micah shouldn't even be alive at this point.

"Are you sure it was Julian?" Nathaniel asked as he placed his hand over Micah's head. His intense stare met Luke. When the Nephilim nodded, he rose. "Where did this happen?"

"I don't know," Danyal answered.

Michael had forgotten about him. He looked over and saw the detective had his head in his bloodstained hands.

Before Nathaniel could respond, Sandy returned. "Nathaniel?"

He inclined his head sharply, not missing the dire tone in her voice. "Don't tell me."

She looked stricken and afraid. Stray hairs had come

undone, and her fingers twitched at her side. "I went to Lily's room," she said. Her nervous glance bounced off Nathaniel and Micah. "She's gone."

Luke went rigid.

Michael's stomach dropped. He turned to Nathaniel, praying his suspicion wasn't spot-on. "She wouldn't." He glanced down at Micah. "No, she wouldn't."

Nathaniel met his stare. "Lily would. She went after Julian."

CHAPTER TWENTY-SEVEN

Lily raced through the downpour, slipping over the rain-slicked roofs and down ledges. Nothing could erase the image of Micah's torn body.

Let me take care of Micah? No. No. No.

Had he done this for her? Oh God, she was going to be sick.

It didn't matter that she suspected Micah. He hadn't deserved that. No one deserved that.

She stumbled, then fell. Sliding down the slate roof of an old factory, she caught herself at the last moment. Lily hauled herself up, huddling against an awning as her world came crashing down.

Not Julian. He couldn't have done this. Ripped the Nephilim to bloody shreds, and for what? *You shared your suspicions with him. He had offered to take care of him. What did you expect him to do?* No! She had given him . . . everything. And her heart—oh God, she had fallen in love with him. Now she realized this? Now?

It couldn't be true, but it was. Luke had seen it, and he would never lie to her, no matter how badly he hated Julian.

Lily pressed her fist to her mouth, smothering a scream. She had defended him, intervened when Micah would have seriously injured if not killed him, and she . . . loved him. She saw Julian dangling Micah over the rooftop. Remembered his beautiful face twisting into a near hideous snarl as Micah tried to slip his dagger into his chest. What had she done? She had grabbed the dagger and tossed it aside.

She opened her eyes, staring at the dark sky as rain poured down her face.

Why aren't you like them?

Who says I'm not?

His snarling face was replaced by the one who touched her so tenderly. Held her in his arms, made love to her, and coaxed her slowly into his world . . . into loving him.

She launched herself off the awning, landing on the next building. Lightning crashed overhead, and thunder echoed off the steel around her. The storm was nothing compared to what she felt inside.

Within minutes she landed on the balcony of her apartment. She had left in such a rush, she hadn't grabbed her keys or anything. Thunder boomed overhead as Lily threw the small white chair through the reinforced glass door. It shattered into a dozen large shards. She unlocked the door, paying no attention to the piece of sharp glass that caught her hand and sliced it open. She didn't even flinch. In fact, she welcomed the hot sliver of pain that cut through the haze of a different kind of raw hurting.

Lily stepped into her apartment; the soaked shirt clung to her skin, and her hair curled around her face.

Each step she took left little puddles of water and blood behind. She left the balcony doors wide open.

In no time, the familiar awareness shifted through her. With her back to the door, she closed her eyes against the onslaught of sorrow and rage.

"Lily?"

Her shoulders stiffened at the deep sound of his voice.

"What's happened? I could . . . sense something is wrong. You're hurt."

She inhaled a ragged breath. With her heart imploding into useless mush, she faced him. His shirt clung to his stomach, following the supple ripple of flesh and hard muscle of his chest. Rain dripped from his thick eyelashes, and his eyes burned brightly.

Could something so beautiful be such a monster?

She saw Micah's battered body. Saw the way Luke looked at her. She remembered Nathaniel's warnings. *He is a Fallen. Never forget that.*

"Julian." The pain, the deep sense of regret for what she had to do was visible in that one word.

Julian noted the shards of glass. "Lily, what happened? Are you okay?"

"You know what happened." She held up her hand. "Don't come any closer."

Something flickered in his fathomless eyes. "Lily?"

She lowered her head. Her chest rose and fell with every painful breath, and her fingers curled. "How could you do that to him?"

"What are you talking about?"

"Don't lie to me!" she screamed. All the anger and pain bubbled over. She took a step toward him. "How could you do this? I trusted you!"

Julian raised his hand. "Lily—stop for a second. Tell me what you think I did."

"You ripped Micah to pieces!" She shuddered, and the daggers slipped from her cuffs. She watched as his gaze narrowed upon her hands, then returned to her face. "You tore the flesh off him! Did you do this for me? Because I suspected him?"

Julian didn't flinch. He met her wild stare with his own. "Don't do this, Lily."

There was no apology. No excuse—nothing. It felt like her heart had shattered all over again. "I have no choice. You left me no choice."

"I will not fight you."

Her eyes drifted shut briefly. She turned cold and numb. *Duty*, she told herself. *You have your duty, if not your heart or sanity.* "Then you will die."

She flew at him. He stumbled backward, caught off guard by the intensity behind each kick and blow she delivered. The edge of her blade etched across his chest. A bright red line blossomed and bled through his damp shirt.

But he did not attack. Julian blocked what he could, but Lily moved like a whirlwind. Her jabs were quick and precise. Another red line inked down his cheek.

"Fight me!" she screamed at him again.

"I will not hurt you." He blocked her swing.

"You already have!"

He flinched again, as if her words wounded him more than the edge of her blade. As Lily attacked, she thought of nothing but the blinding pain and shame she felt for trusting him, for loving him. Her thoughts were an irrational mess; her eyes brimmed with tears she refused to shed. And, my God, it had been Micah instead of her who ended up like Anna.

Julian knocked her arm away as her blade skated across his chest once more. "Stop this, Lily!"

She hit him with a double kick, slamming him into the wall. "I loved you!" she shrieked as she brought her right arm down on his chest.

Julian froze. Those bright eyes caught hers; his hands fell to his side. His beautiful face constricted. "Lily," he whispered.

She faltered. She couldn't catch her breath as she stared into those eyes. Lily saw him the first time he had saved her from Baal. Images of Julian carrying her back to the bedroom flashed before her. Kissing her, slipping inside her, and how he held her as if she were the most precious thing in the world. The way her heart swelled when she saw him, or the way her pulse quickened when he said her name so softly. She couldn't move.

Somehow she still loved him.

Her arm trembled. There were mountains of reasons why she should kill him, especially when he made no move to defend himself. It would be easy. It wouldn't be the first time she had killed a Fallen. That was all he was to her now—another Fallen that must be dealt with.

Oh God, she couldn't do it. Because deep inside her, some twisted part of her still loved him. A scream of frustration tore through her, and her arm dropped.

Julian pushed off the wall, capturing her slender wrists. "Lily, please stop this."

The worst thing was for him to touch her. It reminded her of too much. She tried to pull away. When that didn't work, she used a side kick, but Julian flipped her around. He grabbed both of her wrists in one hand, wrapping his other arm around her waist. "Damn it, stop this!"

Lily struggled fiercely, desperately needing to get away. Even now, her body responded to him, her heart ached for him. It made no sense, but she could feel the turmoil inside of him. The pain he felt.

She kicked out, and a plant crashed to the floor. Lily managed to get her feet against the wall, but Julian knocked down her legs with one powerful sweep of his arm. She yelped and swung her elbows into his sternum.

Julian groaned. "Lily, knock it off!"

She attempted to jab him in the stomach again, but he jumped out of the way and flipped her around so that her back was against the wall. He pulled her arms above her head. Pressing the full length of his body against her, he pinned her there. "Stop it!" he snarled inches from her face. "I don't know what the hell you think I did!"

He was crushing her, or at least that was how it felt to her. Maybe it was just a wild mix of emotions that were crushing her. "You know what you did!"

"I didn't lay a hand on your precious Nephilim!"

"Bullshit! He said—"

"The finger was pointed at me?" he asked as his grip tightened around her wrists. "Big surprise there. I'm a Fallen. It's reason enough for most of them."

Lily slipped one of her legs out from his, managing to kick off the wall. This seemed to only anger him. He put her back to the wall and held her there.

"I'm a lot of things, Lily. You know what I am," he said. "I have never hidden my nature from you. I'm single-minded—selfish to the core. I brutally protect what is mine." His eyes bore into her, flaring with anger and a need that made her go still. "I lost my grace eons ago. I'm a Fallen, but I did not touch that Nephilim. I'm not a liar."

Lily swallowed thickly. "Neither is Luke."

He shifted her wrists to one hand, grasping her chin. "Look at me, Lily. Listen to me," he ordered fiercely. "You said you loved me. How can you love someone you don't trust?"

"No! I didn't mean it."

"You lied? You can't fool me. You just haven't loved me as long as I've loved you."

"No. No!" She tipped her head back, letting out a strangled cry. Yesterday—days before—she would have melted at his feet if she had heard him say that. Now her heart crumbled. "What you did to Micah . . ."

"Forget about Micah." His hand slipped to the flare of her hip. "You question if I love you? Are my words not truthful? Hearing me say it is not enough for you?"

"No." Her hands curled, and the blades retracted harmlessly into her bracelets. "I don't want this—these lies. I don't love you." She was lying, desperately so, and quickly losing control of the situation, of herself. "You're just a Fallen. I was wrong. I saw you as a man and not what you are. I can't love what you are!"

Anger flared deep in his eyes. "You don't believe that. Not after all the passion we've shared."

She tilted her head away. Could he see through her so easily? Her heart stuttered in her chest as his hot breath caressed her cheeks, sending shivers through her.

"All I've ever wanted to do is protect you, ever since the first time I saw you fighting those minions and deadheads," he said. "It was probably after you stabbed me, but damn it, I'd never met anyone like you."

She squeezed her eyes shut. "Stop . . ."

"Before I knew it, I was following you when you weren't working. I watched you put the garden together outside. I followed you when you went to that club, hating that I knew you were with someone else and not me." He broke off, laughing harshly. "A fallen angel brought down by jealousy after hundreds and hundreds of years. You'd think I'd be above that, but I'm not. I wanted you day after day, night after night.

"Should I remind you of how much I love you?" His voice was husky, raw with emotion. "Do you need reminding of how much you love me?"

Everything was spiraling out of control. Anger and hurt, love and lust crashed down on her. Confused, she couldn't tell where his emotions began and hers ended.

"Don't doubt how I feel for you." He pressed his forehead against hers. "What I would do for you."

Lily shuddered as she twisted against the wall, desperately trying to escape the whirlwind of emotion building in her, but she was trapped.

"You question what's between us?" he asked, his voice sounding broken. "What I would do for you?"

Lily shook her head. "What you did . . ."

"I did nothing but love you."

To hear those words now shattered her, because it mirrored the strongest emotion inside her. She loved him. Cold reality slammed into her. She loved Julian.

"Lily . . ." he whispered, voice ragged.

Cold reality slammed into her. She pushed against his chest, stomach twisting dangerously. *I love a monster . . .* a monster who viciously gutted Micah. She pushed harder this time, and Julian finally released her.

"Please listen . . . to me."

"No." She swallowed against the sudden tightening in her throat. She felt sick, and her heart . . . God, it hurt something terrible. "I . . . I do love you, but I . . . can't do this."

"No, Lily, listen to me." He looked terrified, and she had never seen him this way. "I didn't do what you think I did."

She closed her eyes, wanting nothing more than to believe him, but Luke would never lie to her. "Please . . . please stop. It's in your nature . . . isn't it? We can't do this anymore. I brought this . . . on Micah. I brought this on myself."

He took a step forward, but she threw up her arm. "You've said you trust me, Lily. You've said you love me. Why can't you believe me? I haven't touched another Nephilim since I met you."

Lily met his eyes. Her heart demanded that she listen to him, to give him a chance, but her heart was foolish. "I can't. Luke would never lie to me."

The skin between his eyes puckered. "Is that who told you I hurt Micah?"

She nodded. "He saw you. And I trust him with my life."

Understanding flashed across his face. "You would believe whatever Luke would tell you. He has been by your side since the beginning, hasn't he?"

"Yes." It was all she needed to say.

He turned his face. "Then there is nothing I can say."

He was right. Lily loved him. God, she loved him more than anything. But what he did wasn't something she could tuck away and pretend never happened. And this . . . this was bound to happen. They could not exist in each other's worlds. She had hoped it would never be something like this that would tear them apart, but she had been stupid to rely on hope.

She took an unsteady breath. The wrenching in her chest increased. "You have to leave. Don't . . . follow me—don't look for me."

"Don't do this, Lily."

She turned away, her heart breaking. "Leave—please leave. We can't do this. I can't look at you and not see Micah. Just leave, Julian. Please, just go."

He inhaled unsteadily, his eyes drifting shut. Becoming as still as a marble statue, the sorrow that etched across his face was painfully striking, and resignation dulled his eyes.

He moved in a way she couldn't stop him. Capturing her chin with his fingers, he brought her lips to his. The kiss was deep and lasting—the intensity of it and the purity to it. It was no longer just a kiss but a heart-wrenching good-bye that nearly tore her apart.

When he pulled back, his touch lingered. "I love you."

With a rush of air he was gone, and it was like he had never been there.

Lily stood alone, her fingers trembling against her lips. She could still feel him. Not only on her lips but everywhere and inside of her. There was no shaking it, no denying it. In a daze she adjusted her clothing. She couldn't stay here, and she couldn't go back to the Sanctuary.

She stared blankly at the broken glass and destroyed pottery. The sickness and hurt threatened to consume her. She twisted, taking off through the balcony and into the night. Desperately running as if she could escape the events that led up to the moment her heart shattered into a million pieces.

CHAPTER TWENTY-EIGHT

There was no way they were making Michael stay at the Sanctuary while Nathaniel and Luke left to search for Lily. Only after threatening to leave on his own did Nathaniel finally agree. Since Michael couldn't be left alone, Luke was regulated to the more human method of travel to accommodate him.

Luke drove the Cayenne through the clustered streets, knuckles bleached as he gripped the steering wheel. He hadn't said a single word to Michael as he relentlessly dialed Lily's cell over and over again. Each time he didn't get an answer he grew more agitated. He pulled into a parking garage, not bothering to turn off the SUV before darting out the door and taking off. Out of habit, Michael grabbed the keys.

Michael raced up the stairs, gaining on Luke. Nathaniel had suspected she may have gone back to her apartment, or at least he had hoped so, and he had raced over the busy streets, beating them there.

Michael held on to the hope that she wouldn't have done what the others feared. She would know better than to go after something that had been capable of doing what was done to Micah, but Lily was wild. He had seen it in the way she fought. She was crazy enough to run after a fallen angel, and he suspected she was crazy enough to love one.

Wasn't that what all the odd looks were about whenever Julian was mentioned in the same sentence as Lily? Why everyone got so uptight and bothered about him falling for her?

Luke stopped outside Lily's apartment, rapping on the door with his knuckles. Seconds later, Nathaniel appeared, looking on edge. "She's not here. I've already checked all the rooms."

Michael quickly swept the room, noting the minimalistic design and clean white walls. There were little touches of Lily: a random shoe there, a piece of jewelry here, or bizarre paintings scattered along the living room wall. He stepped farther inside, seeing what had brought Luke to a standstill.

"These doors were reinforced. I helped her pick them out. A common burglar wouldn't have been able to do this," said Nathaniel as he stared at the shattered door.

Michael stepped around Luke, surveying the scene with an analytical eye. The officer in him immediately took over, noting several things at once. The glass had been broken from the outside. There was a plant and a stand shattered across the area rug. Several footprints were clearly visible in the dirt that spilled across the floor, some way too large to belong to Lily. There was also blood. It was mingled among the puddles of water and smeared across the wall.

Michael couldn't look at this as coolly as he should. He ran a hand through his hair, facing Nathaniel. The formidable man stared down at the floor, face drawn. "Damn it, Lily, what did you do?"

Luke inclined his head, dragging in a deep breath. "I'm going to kill him."

Nathaniel turned. "I should have . . . I should have done more. I let her get out of control, but he wouldn't have hurt her. I know this."

Luke's pale eyes snapped fire. "Are you serious? Do I need to remind you of what he did to Micah?"

Nathaniel stared at the splotch of blood far too high on the wall for Lily to reach. "You don't need to remind me, Luke." His eyes scanned the room. "Where Julian would have attacked any of us, he would not do so with Lily."

"Damn you!" Luke exploded, full of rage and exasperation. "She will end up just like Anna! Is that what it will take? Look at this! There was clearly a fight here. There is blood, part of her goddamned clothes is in my hand!"

Michael's eyes fell to the cloth Luke clenched. His stomach seized. "We need to find Lily. Now!"

Nathaniel faced both Nephilim. For the first time, Michael saw him exhibit some sort of emotion. Always calm and serene, Michael hadn't thought Nathaniel felt anything. He couldn't have been more wrong. Anger, waves and waves of it, radiated off him. A near unholy light filled his eyes, and he suddenly looked very dangerous.

"Call Danyal and every Nephilim available. Tear this city apart if you need to."

"This is on you, Nathaniel." Luke gritted out, backing away. "You could have stopped this at any time, but you didn't. This is on you. Just like what happened with Anna is on you!"

Nathaniel briefly closed his eyes. "This I know."

Rage—pure unbridled hatred—flickered over Luke's face a second before he charged Nathaniel. Instinct kicked in, propelling Michael to place himself between the two. "Stop this!" he ordered. "What the fuck is this going to solve? Who gives a fuck about who's to blame right now? This isn't important!"

Luke shoved himself away, his hands clenched at his side. There was a moment when Michael thought Luke wouldn't back down. The hatred that rolled off him was too potent to walk away from, but somehow he pulled it in. "This is over," said Luke, tone eerily final.

"Luke . . ." Nathaniel stared at him, his eyes widening slightly. "No . . ."

He shook his head before turning, then disappeared out the balcony doors. Michael followed his movements, stunned. "What does he mean? What is he talking about?"

"We need to go back to the Sanctuary." Nathaniel was already walking toward the door.

"What? We need to find Lily!"

Nathaniel turned on him. "We will, but first we need to go back to the Sanctuary. This isn't up for discussion, Michael. I don't expect you to understand, but I need you to listen to me and do exactly as I tell you."

There was something in his tone that gave Michael pause. "What's . . . going on?"

"Do you have the keys to the Porsche?" asked Nathaniel, walking out the door.

"Yes." Michael followed him. He was missing something huge. He knew it.

Nathaniel nodded. "I need you to get us back to the Sanctuary as quickly as possible."

Together they raced down the stairs and, once inside the Cayenne, Nathaniel pulled out his cell. Like Luke had done before, he tried reaching Lily—to no avail.

Michael gripped the steering wheel. "What is going on?"

Nathaniel held up his finger while he pressed another number on the phone. "Adrian, meet me back at the Sanctuary. We have a . . . problem." He hung up the phone, his hand clenching the slim model. "Michael, when we get back to the Sanctuary, I need you to check Lily's room. She may have gone back there."

He switched lanes, narrowly avoiding a taxi as he sped through the streets. "Are you going to tell me what's going on?"

"It's about Anna," said Nathaniel as if it made perfect sense. "It's always been about Anna."

Once they arrived at the Sanctuary, Nathaniel left him with orders to check Lily's room, before disappearing with Adrian, and strict orders to not leave the building.

Michael had never been more frustrated in his life. Lily was out there somewhere, possibly hurt or worse, and he was expected to just chill. When he entered Lily's room, he quickly discovered why no one had been able to reach her. Her cell phone lay next to her keys, the message light blinking rapidly. Sighing, he grabbed the phone and slipped it into the pocket of his pants.

There was no fucking way he was going to stand around. Whenever he closed his eyes, he saw Micah, and then Lily replaced Micah. Bloodied and beaten, lying dead somewhere out in the city. *Screw this*.

Nathaniel's orders be damned.

His mind made up, he left Lily's room. His first stop was the weapons' room. He quickly grabbed two vicious blades and leg straps and hooked them to his thighs. As he straightened, he noticed a large rack mounted to the wall. Various keys hung there, labeled with what they belonged to. He approached the rack, brows raised as he read some of the labels. It was like a bike enthusiast's wet dream—Michael's wet dream. They had everything: Hondas, Harleys, Indians, and various crotch rockets, but it was the Hayabusa GSX that caught his eye.

"Holy shit," he murmured.

It was one of the fastest bikes, accelerating to unimaginable speeds. The bike was made for all the adrenaline junkies in the world.

He didn't think twice about grabbing those keys before heading to the parking garage in the back where they kept the fleet of vehicles. It had to be the only logical place where the bikes were kept.

He was right. On the bottom level, behind a steel cage, were several dozen bikes under lock and key. Staring at the key for a moment, he then grabbed one of the knives. It cut through the mesh wire like nothing, and he could only imagine what it did to flesh as he kicked open the gate. The platinum motorcycle was like a beacon. There was a moment of appreciation as he approached the bike, knowing he would probably never have the luxury of riding this thing again.

This was probably going to get him kicked out of the Sanctuary.

"Hey."

Spinning around, he saw Luke. Immediately, Michael thought the worst—and maybe the best. "Did you find Lily?"

"No." He grabbed a helmet off the rack. "But I think I know where she would go. You game?"

"Let's do this." Michael straddled the bike, pausing before he slid the helmet on. "Lead the way."

"Trust me," Luke said. "We'll find her."

Lily couldn't breathe as she barreled through the crowded sidewalk. Where in the hell were all these people coming from? They seemed to be closing in on her, and though the sun had already set, the air was thick with heat and humidity.

Picking up her pace, she balled her hands into fists, ignoring the looks of people she bumped into or cut off. It didn't matter that she suspected Micah. He hadn't deserved that. No one deserved that.

Not Julian. Her mind rebelled at the idea. He couldn't have done this. Ripped the Nephilim to bloody shreds, and for what? But she had shared with him her suspicions. And he even offered to take care of him. God, there was a good chance she was going to vomit on someone.

She turned the corner, narrowly avoiding a couple holding hands. Her heart clenched so tightly she stumbled.

Micah would most likely die, and she . . . she was in love with a killer, a monster.

She was searching for a distraction—trouble really. Anything to ease the twisting her heart did every so many minutes, but like the days before, there were no minions or deadheads to be found. It had been hours since she left her apartment, and . . . it was really starting to piss her off.

Anger . . . Yes, anger was better than the swamping grief that waited. Her step faltered, and she stopped on the footbridge. The Anacostia River rushed below, dark and uninviting. She wanted to sit down—right there—and sob. She wanted to scream, wanted to crawl into a hole somewhere.

And . . . damn it, she wanted Julian. Wanted to find him, beat the living shit out of him for doing this to her, and she wanted . . . to pretend what he did never happened.

Lily pushed away from the ledge, grinding her teeth. She started forward, breathing slowly. She was a hunter before Julian, and she would be a damn fine hunter after him.

"Damn it!" she hissed. "Can I not find one more thing to kill?"

A teenage street thug came around the corner, but seeing the deadly look on her face, he backed away. She would have laughed, but then she probably would have cried. It was really turning out to be a terrible night.

At least you aren't sliced and diced like Micah, whispered that evil little voice that wouldn't shut the fuck up. Speaking of Micah, Lily realized they'd probably never know why he had betrayed them.

It had to be Micah. Maybe Julian did it out of some sick way of helping clear her name. However, that would be pretty useless considering the fact Micah wouldn't be confessing to anything or anyone anytime soon.

She knew it was crass to think of Micah like that, especially after what was done to him. And why was she in Anacostia? She hated this area—hated the crime, the hopelessness, and the fishy smell the river gave off every time a rainstorm came through.

And then she felt it—a minion.

Cracking her knuckles, she backed up a couple of feet. Empty, dilapidated row houses lined the street. Skeletons of their former glory, they were now inhabited by rats and the homeless.

But the minion wasn't there.

Lily almost grinned when she realized where it was—the old reform school they had brought Michael to. Taking off down the block, she hopped the fence

381

and headed around the building. The sensation grew, telling her she was on the right trail.

Entering through the busted-out window, she quietly crept through the abandoned classroom and hall. The doors at the end of the hall were open. Releasing her blades, she edged along the wall.

The balcony above the gymnasium was empty. Quickly, she scanned the upper level and then peered over the rusted railing. Empty.

"Come out, come out, wherever you are," she whispered, gazing up at the ceiling.

"I'm right here."

The voice sent shivers down Lily's spine. She recognized it, knew it to be a voice she should never hear again. She turned around, feeling her heart twist. "William?"

CHAPTER TWENTY-NINE

"Are you shitting me?" Michael peeled off the helmet, staring at the reform school. Jesus, he had hoped he'd never come back to this place. "She would go here?"

Luke tucked the helmet under his arm as he climbed off his bike, looking around with a frown. "We're gonna have to ditch the bikes, and there's a good chance we may never see them again."

Michael soured at that. "No . . . I like this bike. I want to keep it."

"We'll get you another one."

He sure hoped so. "Why would she come here?"

Luke pitched the helmet into a bush. "I just know Lily."

Michael looked over the fence. Ice flooded his veins. He had a bad feeling—a real bad feeling about this. He turned to Luke, but he'd already jumped the fence and stood on the other side, waiting.

"You're slowing me down," Luke said, then turned and strode off through the overgrown grass.

He flipped him off and followed. It took Michael a bit longer to make his way over the fence. He jogged to catch up to him. "So you think she went here to find Julian?"

They rounded the building and stopped in front of the same window Luke had pried the boards off over a month ago. Michael started to climb through first but stilled. The ice was spreading through his body, forming icicles in his stomach. A shiver ran up his spine. "I feel . . . something," he said.

"What do you feel?" Luke said from behind him.

Michael peered over the ledge of the window, pieces of wood and brick crumbling under his fingers. "I feel another . . . Nephilim, but . . ."

"But what?"

There was something else in that reform school—several things, or something really powerful. It reminded him of the feeling he got when he'd seen Baal, but much . . . much worse.

"You know what I don't get?" Luke said, his breath bouncing off the back of his neck. "How you've survived this long when you're really this stupid."

"Shit." Michael drew in a shallow breath and started to turn. The back of his skull exploded in pain, and then there was nothing.

Lily couldn't stop staring at William. He shouldn't be standing there. "You're supposed to be dead."

William glanced down at himself, smoothing a hand over his pressed polo and smiling in a smug way. "Nah."

Just the sight of him caught Lily off guard. His sudden reappearance was something she couldn't comprehend. Luke had killed . . . he had said so. It was only a moment she hesitated. That split second was enough time to give William the upper hand. She saw him move and raised her arm to block him, but it was too late. His fist connected with the side of her face. There was the sickening sound of bones crunching that seemed far away, and then fierce pain burst through her body as she staggered to her knees.

She lifted her head, spitting out a mouthful of blood. A rush of air served as a warning, but Lily couldn't move quickly enough. William's steel-toed boot connected, flipping her onto her back. She felt her cheek split open, then the warm cascade of blood that followed.

"Lily . . . Lily, I've always thought you would be smarter than this," taunted William. He reached down, grasping a handful of her hair. "You thought I was dead? Why?" He yanked her to her feet. "Ah, that's right. Luke told you so."

She swung the blade at his chest, but he caught it, snapping one of the daggers off her cuff. Shit. This wasn't going well.

William tossed the dagger over the railing. "Good old crazy-off-his-ass Luke." He swept her legs out from underneath her, sending her spilling to the dirty alley. "Do you know how truly fucked-up your BFF is?"

She couldn't afford to listen to him. Not when he had her on the ground. It was the first lesson every hunter was taught. Never let them get you on the ground. But his words were distracting her. She rolled onto her back, narrowly avoiding another boot to the face. Over the pounding of her heart, she heard the distinctive thump of something large being dropped.

"He killed that little Nephilim whore you call Anna. He's the one . . ." William jerked, his words cut off. He made a strangled sound, and they both stared down at his chest. A Sanctuary dagger pierced his heart clean through. Then William was gone, really dead this time.

Lily rolled to her side, staring up at Luke. It was hard to see through the blood pouring down her face, and her words came out slurred. "I thought you said . . . you killed William?"

He helped her to her feet. "I did say that."

She pulled away, nearly toppling over. She grasped the banister for support. "I don't . . . you . . . killed Anna?"

"I did kill Anna," he answered simply.

She stared at Luke, horrified. The walls tilted. "No, Luke, please no. You didn't. You know what . . . that means."

"It's okay now, Lily. Don't be afraid of me."

She staggered along the railing. A lump on the floor moaned. "Michael? Luke, what . . . what did you do?"

Luke grabbed her arm, spinning her away from Michael. "Don't worry about him. He's not going to be our problem. Not for much longer, anyway."

This had to be a nightmare. "I don't understand. Luke, you . . . loved Anna."

"I did love her, but she loved a Fallen!" he roared, his grip tightening on her arm. "I would have done anything for her, and she betrayed me!"

Lily pulled her arm free. The pain from the broken bones in her face was making her dizzy. She was having a hard time processing what he was saying. "Why didn't you come to me? Why didn't you tell me you needed help?"

Luke stared at her, confused. "I don't need help. I want to see the Sanctuary crumble upon itself. You were turning out just like Anna." He licked his lips, reaching for her again. "You went out and screwed a Fallen and messed everything up."

"Oh my God."

The sound of wood splintering somewhere on the ground floor turned into footfalls. It sounded like a herd of elephants running through the halls, and within seconds, the doors below busted open. Glancing over the banister, Lily felt her heart stutter.

Deadheads—deadheads way past their expiration date—rushed across the floor. Their bodies were twisted, hardened, and crusted over. The air then turned heavy, signaling the arrival of minions—lots of them.

"I made sure Micah was assigned to follow you. I knew eventually he would catch you with Julian, and with him being Micah, he would run straight to whoever would listen. Lily, you really should sit down. You look terrible." He pried her hands off the banister. "Don't worry about them down there. Did you know you can control deadheads?"

"Luke . . . what have you done?" she whispered.

"I wouldn't have done anything if it hadn't been for Nate's complete lack of control. If he had put his foot down once with Anna—just once—all of this could have been avoided." He wrapped an arm around her waist. "That son of a bitch did a number on your face. Shit. He wasn't supposed to touch you."

Lily's head fell forward. "You've . . . been working with the Fallen. It's been you . . ." Her stomach heaved. She thought back to the night they'd gone to Michael's apartment. "You . . . said someone . . . who hates the Sanctuary . . . hates Nathaniel."

He sighed, the same sound he made so many times when she would pester him about one thing or another. "It was Nathaniel's fault—the Sanctuary's fault. They made me kill Anna, Lily. If they had forbid her once, watched her just once, they would have seen what she was doing."

"No," she whimpered.

"Yes! I hate Nate for what he has made me do. This was the only way to really get him back. There was nothing else I could do but bring down the Sanctuary. It didn't take long to find a Fallen that was interested— really interested—especially in Michael."

Oh God . . . Oh God, it was him. Lily pushed against him, but he held on. "Luke . . . how could you?" Below the deadheads were turning their attention to the doors. Someone was coming. She forced her attention on Luke. "You . . . you hurt Micah, didn't you? My God, you did that?"

"Come on, lighten up. You don't even like Micah," Luke pointed out. "He was the perfect setup. I knew if I told you it was Julian, you would believe me. You knew Julian was capable of doing something like that. You just needed a push. Micah became that push, and it doesn't matter if he ever wakes up and tells the world that it was I who attacked him."

The image of Micah's battered and torn body flashed before her. How quickly she had believed Luke. She hadn't even given Julian the chance to tell her the truth. It had only been a few hours ago, but it felt like a lifetime.

Her heart shattered once more. Luke looked like he always did. He had that playful smile on his face, the mischievous twinkle in his eyes. It was like he was two people. And somewhere inside him was the Luke she couldn't let go of. "Luke, you have to explain . . . everything you have done. We can fix this. We can . . . make this better."

"There's nothing to fix."

"No. We've got . . . to get out of here and . . . find Nate and get . . . Michael help."

"You don't understand, Lily. We can't take Michael. Asmodeus wants him. And when Nathaniel comes, if he does, I will kill him."

She stared. "You're . . . crazy."

His face hardened. "Don't make me choose for you, Lily."

"Choose what?" she cried. The pain was clouding everything. It hurt to talk, to breathe.

"You're either with me on this or you're against me. I won't let you go back to the Sanctuary, back to Nate, and back to Julian. I will not allow you to do that to yourself." He jerked her forward.

Jennifer L. Armentrout

She staggered. "Luke, don't . . . do this. It's not you."

"Don't make me hurt you, Lily!" Fury contorted his face. "Don't make me do this to you, too!"

"I'm not," she whispered.

"Then you would be with me on this!" he screamed. "You would understand why the Sanctuary has to be destroyed. Killing Anna wasn't my fault. I wouldn't have hurt her if Nate had done his job. He let her leave that night, even after I told him what she was doing. I saw her, Lily. I saw her leaving the Fallen, and I knew what she had been doing." His grip tightened. "I lost it! I . . . stabbed her with our blade."

"I don't . . . I can't." She was crying. Tears mixed with blood, stinging the raw abrasions on her cheeks. "I'm not going to choose your side."

"Then you leave me no choice."

She watched as the Luke she had loved since she was five disappeared in front of her. In his place was someone she didn't recognize. His eyes turned flat and lifeless. The pale blue now seemed milky in the dim light. Had he turned? He had to have, from the moment he killed Anna. Luke had just hid it well.

"I'm sorry, Lily. I love you. I always will. I'm sorry you are making me do this."

Her eyes widened as he pulled out his blade. Her stomach dropped. She held up one hand. "Luke . . . what are you doing?"

He advanced on her. "I will make this quick. I did so for Anna. I will for you, too."

390

She stumbled back against the banister. Her gaze fell below. She could make the jump, but the deadheads would be on her in a second, and she was in no shape to fight them. There were too many. They would rip her to shreds in a heartbeat. She turned back to Luke. She didn't even release her blades. Much like with Julian, she would never be able to kill him.

And he knew it.

Luke sighed. "I taught you better than this, Lily. Never hesitate. Never let your feelings get involved."

He had, but it didn't matter. Several things happened at once. Luke lunged at her, and she threw her arm up to block him. He wasn't holding anything back. His blow shattered the bone in her forearm, sending her backward against the banister. It cracked but didn't give way.

Fierce pain blossomed all the way to her shoulder. She could sense others were nearby, but she doubted they'd reach her in time.

"I'm sorry," Luke said, and brought his blade home.

She stared at Luke's cloudy eyes. "No . . . I'm sorry."

Shock skated across his face, and his strike was off by an inch. But it was one of their daggers. Engraved with symbols and honed in holy water. It was deadly.

Lily screamed as the seven-inch blade cut through skin, muscle, and bone under her left breast. Luke held onto her as she turned to the side, her gaze falling to the floor below.

The door bulged, splintering apart. Several large chunks of metal mowed down a few deadheads that were too close. Standing in the doorway was Julian. In his rage, he stood like an avenging angel—beautiful, proud, and the deadliest thing to walk this Earth.

Just to see him again lessened her pain and fear. Even in his anger, his presence soothed her like no other could. He'd come for her, even after she'd blamed him. Lily tried to call out his name, but she couldn't form the words.

His gaze went up, settling on where she stood. He roared her name, pain and fury so potent that Luke pulled her back from the banister.

Luke yanked out the blade, and Lily shrieked. A fiery burn seized her chest. It was like Baal's touch but a hundred times worse.

Deadheads swarmed Julian from all corners. He was making short work of them, but they kept coming and coming. Lily could hear Julian howling her name.

Then the windows shattered, and Nathaniel and Adrian appeared. They, too, were swarmed by the deadheads and minions. The three of them were marvelous fighters, but they were far outnumbered. One deadhead would fall, and three would replace him. Then there were the minions to contend with. Trained just as the Nephilim were, they were just as deadly.

Luke held onto Lily, and he raised his blade once more. "This is your fault!" he screamed at Nathaniel. "You should have stopped her—stopped Anna!"

She saw Luke's blade out of the corner of her eyes, but she focused on Julian. He ripped through two more deadheads, and his eyes met hers. He wouldn't get to her in time, and it was already too late. The blade had done its damage, eating through her as it was designed to do.

Nathaniel and Julian yelled at the same time, but she only had Julian in her sights. He hadn't given up on her. Not once. Not even when she had given up on him. Luke brought the blade down to her neck, but the impact never came.

"I don't think so," said Michael, grabbing Luke's arm from behind and twisting the blade out of his hand.

Luke shoved her away as he whirled on Michael, another blade in hand. "How stupid are you, boy?"

Lily fell back against the banister. Her legs were strangely useless, and she slid to the floor. She peered down at herself, expecting to find flames shooting from her skin. Her white shirt was completely red, soaked with her blood. Through the haze of pain, Michael and Luke became blurs.

She was going to die.

Her heart sped up and then slowed. Twisting, she dropped her gaze to the floor below. Her eyesight faded in and out. Drawing in short and shallow breaths, she placed her hand against the wound and cried out.

And then Julian was beside her. She stared up at him, wishing she could somehow smooth away the devastation that marred his face. She tried to raise her hand, but her arm wouldn't respond.

"Lily, look at me," he ordered softly, slipping his arm around her waist, then pulling her onto his lap.

She screamed and shuddered. Julian winced. "It's going to be okay. Hold on, Lily. You need to hold on for me."

Her unfocused stare fell to him, her breathing shallow and erratic. "I'm . . . sorry . . . so . . ."

"No." Julian shook his head roughly. "It's okay. I know."

Lily could still hear Michael and Luke fighting, but their shapes were nearly identical. She couldn't imagine Michael winning this battle. Luke was far more advanced and had decades on him. She wanted to tell Julian to leave her, to go help Michael, but she couldn't talk. All she could do was moan as the fire spread through her insides.

Julian placed his hand over the wound. "I know what you want me to do. I'm not leaving you. They mean nothing to me, and you mean everything."

Fighting Luke was like fighting Rafe on crack. He deflected nearly every blow Michael sent his way, and Luke's fists connected with Michael's face more times than he could count. It was a savage attack, designed to do damage. Luke's booted foot hit him square in the chest, sending him tumbling backward.

"You think you can beat me?" Luke laughed. "Are you insane?"

Michael pushed up. He refused to look at Lily's crumpled body, knowing he couldn't afford the distraction. All he knew was that she was still alive from the heartbreaking sounds she was making.

"Apparently, you're the insane one," Michael taunted as he shook off the pain.

Luke took an angry swipe at him, nearly hitting him across the broad expanse of his chest. He was fast in his attack, cutting and jabbing until he backed Michael up against a wall. Through it all, Lily's words came back to him. Defending yourself is simply anticipating the next move. Find the muscle tremor. Watch where Luke looks . . . where he positions his body . . . He will tell you where he strikes next without words.

He had only seconds to slow it down, to pull it all into perspective. No time to think of Lily, no time to think of what could have made Luke do this. Seconds— he had only seconds.

Luke brought his fist down again, but this time Michael saw the move before he attacked. Launching himself off the wall, he blocked and jabbed. Luke spun, and his kick caught Michael in the jaw. Snapping back, he hit the ground.

"I'm not supposed to kill you," Luke said, his fingers spasming around the blade. "But goddamn it, you're making it awful hard to walk away."

"You're not?" Michael grunted. "Could've fooled me."

Luke smiled. "But then again, I'll be long gone before he gets here."

"He?" Michael struggled to his feet. Over Luke's shoulder, he caught a glimpse of Nathaniel vaulting over the banister. "Nathaniel?"

Whirling around, Luke's face was nothing but a mask of rage and accusation. "You! This is your fault! You could have controlled Anna! None of this would have happened if you had done your job!" He tore across the balcony at Nathaniel.

Michael staggered as Luke battled Nathaniel with violent ferocity. Nate could fall to Luke. If so, he would then try to finish what he had started—going after Lily. His eyes fell to Julian. The fallen angel cradled Lily to him, but she was reaching out toward them—toward Luke. Tears were streaming down her battered face. The pain in her eyes was more than just physical. She'd trusted Luke, loved him, and he had done that to her.

Something in Michael came to life. Burning through his veins like white lightning, snapping fire through every vein and cell. A rushing filled his ears. His legs moved without him realizing. A bright white light radiated from within, spreading over his chest and down his limbs. The blade burned in his grasp, felt heavy like a sword.

Luke turned around slowly, his eyes widening as he stared at him. "The Sword of Michael." He tipped his head, backing up. "It can't be. Abaddon . . ."

The light from Michael reached out, surrounding all of them. It was Nathaniel who ordered the blow, but it was Michael's blade that drove through tissue and muscle, piercing Luke's heart.

Luke looked down at his chest. Shock, and somewhere in the array of emotions that flickered across his face, there was relief. He seemed to gaze up—searching for something. As the light receded, Michael realized who he was looking for.

Falling to his knees, Luke dropped his blade and reached out, his arm extending toward Lily. The distance was too great, and Luke fell forward, unmoving and silent.

Michael stepped around Luke's body, his hands trembling as he reached Julian and Lily. His body felt ungodly hot, but the moment he got a close-up view of Lily, he wasn't thinking about himself anymore.

Nothing could've prepared him for how bad she looked. There was almost nowhere on her body that wasn't damaged. The bones in the left side of her face were shattered, as was her left arm. These things would heal, but it was the gaping wound that stole Michael's breath.

"Oh God," Michael whispered. "Can . . . anyone fix this?"

"I will die trying." Julian bent his head, brushing his lips over Lily's forehead. "I'm sorry, Lily. This will hurt, love." He placed his other hand over the side of Lily's face. The same light that had radiated from Michael now radiated from Julian's hands.

The first scream cut through Michael, but the second scream brought a cry of pain to Julian's lips.

Michael fell to his knees beside Lily, exhausted and dazed. He grasped her outstretched hand, holding it tightly in his. He looked up at the fallen angel. "Will she live?"

Julian winced at the shrill cry that racked her body.

Her leg came up, tense and bent at the knee as she writhed. "You need to go. You need to go now. The Fallen are coming for you. I'll be too weak to defend any of you."

Nathaniel stood behind Michael while Adrian came over the banister, looking like he wanted to fight some more.

Julian stared down at Lily. "Let go, Lily. Let it go," he ordered softly. "Let it go. Let me take away the pain."

Michael watched her eyes drift shut. The tension that coiled her body as tight as a bow snapped. Her hand went limp in his. "What did you do?"

Julian's cold stare met Michael's. "You need to leave now, or all of this would have been for naught."

Nathaniel placed his hand on Michael's shoulder. "We need to go. There are many coming. He's right." He looked at Julian as Adrian joined them. "But you're not taking Lily."

Julian gathered her close to him. His eyes turned to ice as he lifted them to meet Nathaniel's. "I fell from grace because I spared your life, but I will not spare your life for a second time. You try to stop me, and I will kill you as I was ordered to do the day you were born."

Nathaniel's eyes narrowed as he pulled himself upright, coming to his full height. "You hurt her, Julian, and I will kill you." He turned to Adrian. "Get Michael out of here now. I'll throw off the Fallen."

Adrian looked like he wanted nothing more than to go after Julian, but he grasped Michael by the shoulders, pulling him away. "Come on, we've got to hit the road."

Michael struggled against him, but before he could do anything, Julian turned with Lily in his arms and disappeared over the banister.

"What the hell was that back there?" Adrian asked as he propelled Michael out the doors. "The Sword of Michael?"

Michael gave a weary shake of his head. "I don't know."

CHAPTER THIRTY

The first thought Lily had upon waking was Luke. The sorrow and anguish that settled over her was the worst thing she had ever felt. A part of her went forever cold, forever gone with the end of her friend.

Tender flesh pulled as she turned slightly. Julian lay beside her, eyes closed and lips parted. Dark shadows bloomed under his eyes. All she remembered was his hands and bright light that seemed to sear the skin right off her bones. He'd healed her . . . again. But to reverse the damage the blade had done must have been exhausting. She hadn't known it could be possible.

Her body ached, and her face felt like it had been pummeled with a sledgehammer. There wasn't a part of her that didn't throb. She cautiously raised her arm, surprised to find the flesh bruised but manageable. He had healed the bones there as he had in her face. However, the emotional anguish was something even his angelic power couldn't heal.

Lily squeezed her eyes shut, though it hurt to do so. All she could think of was Luke. She should've seen what his love for Anna had done to him. This whole time she'd believed it was Micah, believed there was some grand purpose behind betraying the Sanctuary.

Instead, it had been a potent mixture of love and hate that had driven Luke to do all that he had. The moment he'd killed Anna, something in him had warped, turning everything good about him into something twisted. And all his hate had centered on Nathaniel and the Sanctuary.

Never would she understand how she hadn't seen this coming. Looking back, there'd been so many warnings. The things Luke had said to her about Anna, about her own relationship with Julian. Sorrow cut through her as sharply as any Sanctuary blade. She inhaled but the breath seemed to get stuck.

"Lily?" Julian rose onto one arm, his voice soft. "Are you in pain?"

She opened her eyes. Strands of sandy-colored hair fell over half of his face. "I'm okay," she said. "Are you? You look . . . off."

He ran a hand down the side of her face that wasn't currently chopped liver. "I'll be fine." His sapphire eyes searched hers intently. "Lily, I'm so sorry for what has happened. If I could take that pain from you, I would. I would take it all away."

She blinked back tears, telling herself Luke didn't deserve them. Not after everything he'd done. "It was . . . Luke."

Pain flickered over his face. "I know, love. I know how much he meant to you."

She closed her eyes again. "I should . . . have seen it."

"No." He came to his knees, leaning over her.

"There was nothing you could have done, Lily. It wasn't him anymore."

She grasped his arm, needing to feel something solid. "I want to hate him. What he did to Anna and to Micah." She paused, swallowing thickly. "He tried to bring down the Sanctuary, Julian. And he was like a brother to me. I loved him. I would've done anything for him."

"I know." He eased down beside her, finding her hand and threading his fingers through hers. He then brought her hand to his mouth, kissing her palm. "You can't forget him, love. Remember him for who he was to you for all those years. Keep those memories of who Luke was close to you. It's okay to hate him. And it's okay to not hate him."

Unshed tears filled her eyes as he placed her hand above his heart. "Julian, I'm sorry . . . I didn't give you a chance."

"You don't need to apologize to me, Lily. I understand." He pressed his lips against her temple and then inhaled slowly. "I thought I was going to lose you. I swear my heart stopped."

Their eyes locked as she squeezed his fingers. There was so much she wanted to say, but for the first time, she knew there would be time to say it all. And right now, as he smiled tenderly at her, she felt some of the aching in her soul ease.

"I love you," she whispered.

His eyes drifted shut, and when they reopened, they were intense and brilliant. "You have no idea how long I've waited to hear you say that and not run away from me afterward."

Lily did something she thought she'd never do again. She smiled, although it ached to do so. "Eight years, give or take an attempted stabbing?"

He laughed. "Sounds about right. I've never doubted your love, Lily. It has redeemed me in a way nothing else could."

"How so?" she asked.

"You've made me a better man," he said simply.

Her heart swelled in her chest, and there was a flutter deep in her stomach. Like Julian had said the night in Rock Creek Park, things weren't going to be easy for them. But as he lowered his head and brushed his lips across hers carefully, she knew he was worth it—they were worth it.

Michael eased himself down on the bed, unscrewing the lid to the balm that smelled of peppermint and a dozen mystery herbs. Whatever the hell it was, it worked on all his previous aches and bruises.

He didn't have much time to dwell on what had happened in the last twenty-four hours. Adrian had left him only a few minutes ago, and now Nathaniel stood at his door. He threw his shirt to the side, glancing up long enough to acknowledge the elder Nephilim's presence. "Have you heard from Lily?"

Nathaniel leaned against the door. "No."

He spread the balm over his bruised chest, wincing as it burned. "Will he . . . fix her?"

"I believe Julian will do anything to help her," replied Nathaniel. "I don't like what he is or what their relationship means, but I know Julian will take care of her."

Michael set the jar aside. "You seem to know Julian more than you've let on."

A corner of Nathaniel's mouth tipped up. "I was one of the first Nephilim ever born. Back when we were considered abominations and acted as such."

"You're a first-generation Nephilim?"

He nodded. "Someone has been doing their research. Julian was still an angel then. He was sent here along with the first wave of angels to eradicate the Nephilim children. I was a baby. Somehow Julian couldn't raise his hand against a defenseless child. His act of disobedience led to his fall." He ran a weary hand over his forehead. "It doesn't change what he is, but . . ."

Michael wasn't sure what to make of that, so he remained silent as Nathaniel pulled himself away from the door. "You haven't asked what you are, Michael."

"I'm trying not to think about that, what I felt when the light came from me. It didn't hurt . . . but it felt like lightning." He paused and considered, confusing himself. "It felt right."

"Your name was never in the Book because your father wasn't a fallen angel."

He stared at him for a moment. "What? Wait." It struck him then. "No shit."

"I suspected as much when your name never appeared. A first-generation Nephilim never does. And

404

then with the Fallen and the minions never finding you until the night in the alley, I knew you had to have been protected by a celestial shield." Nathaniel folded his arms. "All first-generation Nephilim are because of their powers."

His laugh came out short and harsh. "Celestial shield?"

Nathaniel nodded. "You can imagine what would happen if the Fallen were able to capture you. And it looks like Luke was working with Asmodeus. I'm not sure if Luke suspected what you were, but I know Asmodeus did. He sent Baal to retrieve you."

Michael's head was spinning. "What . . . what happened back there with the fire and the sword?"

"Your father is an angel—one that has not fallen. Contrary to what many believe and what is written, lying with a woman does not always result in an angel losing its grace. Sometimes the act is a calculated decision, as it was in your case. Like a business decision to tip the scales in one direction or another," Nathaniel explained. "You called upon the Sword of Michael— of divine justice—which means I now know who your father is, as does the Fallen."

The irony didn't pass him by. He stared at Nathaniel, wanting to laugh and punch something. "My father is the Archangel Michael?"

"Yes," he confirmed.

Now he couldn't even laugh at that. "This is . . . fucking insane." Michael took a deep breath. There were too many questions, but one needed answered more than anything else. "Do you know who killed my mother? Was it the Fallen?"

"I don't know. If it was, they would've suspected what you are and wouldn't have needed to go through humans or Luke to get to you." Nathaniel closed his eyes, and Michael could see the weight settling on his shoulders. "What Luke has done is inconceivable. The Sanctuary will suffer from his actions for years to come."

Michael didn't doubt that. All the young Nephilim Luke had sold out would eventually turn minion and corrupt more souls. And he wasn't stupid. Michael knew why Asmodeus was after him. The kind of power he felt, if only briefly, would tip the ongoing battle one way or another. There would be no going back to the life he had before Lily had coldcocked him in the alley in Anacostia.

Nathaniel left after that. It was much later before Michael even moved. Falling onto his back, he stared at the ceiling. It was a long time before he could set his mind at ease and find any sort of rest.

The shock of Luke's death had imposed a layer of silence throughout the halls of the Sanctuary. None of the Nephilim spoke, and not even the smallest child laughed. The sorrow and grief had saturated every nook and cranny within the organization.

Nathaniel had insisted the truth surrounding Luke's death and the events that had led up to it be kept secret. He believed that all of his years of duty and loyalty could not be forgotten, that his reputation alone had contributed to the success of the Sanctuary, and the truth could ultimately lead to its failure.

Torn between wanting to hate Luke and somehow forgive him, Lily had agreed. Only the circle and Michael knew that Luke had turned and the devastating deeds he had committed.

Strangely, once the shock wore off and the construed events of the battle started to drift through the halls, Julian's involvement hadn't been left out. Word quickly spread that a Fallen had fought side by side with the Nephilim, saving Lily's life. No one really knew what to think of that or what it meant. All they knew was that act signaled a great change was coming; for the better or worse was yet unseen.

Lily wasn't sure where any of this left Michael. Nathaniel insisted he needed additional training, and once Lily was up to par, she was to resume his lessons. The Sword of Michael bit was astonishing—and even a little frightening. The kind of power he had inside him could be catastrophic in the wrong hands. But no one was really talking about Michael and what he meant for the future of the Sanctuary. Nor was anyone speaking of Asmodeus and what he would try next to get his hands on Michael. Not yet. For today was a day of mourning.

The memorial service for Luke had been held three days after his death and two days after Lily's return to the Sanctuary. All the Nephilim and humans who worked at the Sanctuary attended the service. Luke had somehow touched them all. He had been that important.

And even though Lily couldn't figure out how to really come to grips with his betrayal, she knew his memory needed to serve a purpose.

Held deep within Rock Creek Park, the memorial service was assembled with the help of local law enforcement and government officials—those who were aware of what the Sanctuary truly was. The more heavily wooded section of the grounds had been blocked off to the public. Not even park rangers were allowed to go within seeing distance.

There the group of humans and half angels gathered together to remember Luke. Adrian stood behind Nathaniel, seemingly untouched by Luke's death. It was an act. Lily knew there would come a time when he would possibly accept it and maybe even forgive Luke. This was not the time. Micah had been unable to attend. The injuries Luke had inflicted on him would take months to heal, and she doubted he'd ever be the same.

Lily stood between Nathaniel and Michael, their tall and imposing figures dwarfing her slight form. They had not spoken during their trip to the site, and now they were slightly apart from the rest, but together.

The elderly priest led the prayer and issuance of remembrance. As he spoke about Luke's transcendence into Heaven due to his unwavering faith and loyalty, Lily shuddered. His soul—if his soul had still been present—would not have gotten past those pearly gates.

When the priest spoke of Luke's rewards in Heaven, she had enough. She quietly ducked out when the ceremonial pyres were lit. Other Nephilim and the human employees would now share stories about him. Memories meant to lift them up and carry on his name. There was no way she could remain there while this happened. No one would think her abrupt disappearance to be strange. They knew how close she and Luke had been. If anything, the eyes that followed her would be filled with pity.

As soon as she passed the line of parked cruisers that ensured the service wouldn't be interrupted, she felt Julian. He had come as far as he could. In the shadows of the oak trees, he joined her, wrapping her in his strong embrace and soothing the bundle of emotions in her heart.

He smiled down at her upturned face, smoothing his thumb around the fading bruise on her jaw. "I love you, Lily."

Nothing could prevent the smile from spreading across her face. Julian had saved her life three times now, but most importantly he loved her in a way that would eventually overshadow the dark spaces in her heart and soul. His love was more than that, though. It was something powerful, breaking the chains that tethered her to the Sanctuary and to her duty. With him, she wasn't just a Nephilim. She was Lily, just like he'd always seen her.

It had just taken her eight years to figure that out.

Feeling a little bit like her old self, she pressed against

409

him. "I think we can spare a few hours before we knock some minions' heads around, can't we?"

His eyes assumed a hooded quality. "What do you have in mind?"

With an impish sort of smile, she slipped her hand between them as she watched his face, loving how the hue of his eyes flared.

His arms tightened around her. "I think I got the idea."

Lily's laugh died when his lips captured hers. It would take more than a few hours before they would have enough of one another. It may even take an eternity for that to happen. And Lily was willing to find out.

ACKNOWLEDGEMENTS

Unchained was the second book I ever wrote, all the way back in 2008. To see it finally hit the world is an amazing experience. A big thank-you to Kevan Lyon, the agent of awesome, and to Karen Grove for tackling the project. Thank you to Stacey Morgan for not only reading the book, but for creating an epic editorial key and for loving Julian. Two of the first readers were Lesa Rodrigues and Carissa Thomas, and I have to thank you guys for not thinking what is this crap?

A huge thank-you to my husband, friends, and family for putting up with me during this journey. And a gigantic awkward hug to all the readers who made this book possible. You guys are amazing.